1961
SLIDING TOWARD ARMAGEDDON

1961
SLIDING TOWARD ARMAGEDDON

An Historical Novel

Donald J. Farinacci

NAVIGATOR BOOKS
SAN DIEGO, CALIFORNIA

1961, SLIDING TOWARD ARMAGEDDON

Copyright © 2012 by Donald J. Farinacci

Navigator Books

www.navigator-books.com

ISBN-13: 978-0-9852523-5-9

Printed in the United States of America

Dedicated to America's Veterans of the Cold War

1946 – 1991

"I'd strike the sun if it insulted me."
Captain Ahab, Moby Dick

"Berlin is the testicle of the West; when I want the West to scream, I squeeze on Berlin."
Nikita S. Khrushchev

"Then Mr. Chairman (Khrushchev) there will be war. It will be a cold winter."
John F. Kennedy

INTRODUCTION

'*1961, Sliding Toward Armageddon*' is an historical novel which tells a hitherto under-told story of danger and mystery, set against a backdrop of unparalleled geopolitical crisis.

That the book is a novel is immaterial to its verisimilitude. That which is fiction was designed to breathe life into historical fact. In place of a flat recitation of known dates and events, I have chosen to convey the truth through metaphor, dialogue and pathos. In other words, although the medium is fiction, the underlying story is not.

Truman Capote's masterpiece, '*In Cold Blood,*' transformed a literal narration of chronological facts into a work of art which read like a novel. Unlike Capote's masterwork, which is wholly nonfiction, '*1961*' is a novel, but I do believe it's possible to capture an historical epic through that medium. And there should be no doubt that the drama enacted on the world's stage from March 1, 1961 through November 30, 1962 was of epic proportions. There is probably no two-year period in history in which the world was in greater danger.

My conviction is that the novel is the medium best suited to portraying the tension, danger, fear, dread, hatred, envy, heroism, evil, and goodness of that singular era.

What I have attempted is a blend of historically accurate chronology of events occurring during the momentous year of 1961 with what I believe are credible human interactions and plot lines consistent with the historical narrative. Where inference and invention were employed, their purpose was to elucidate a larger truth buried within a framework of names, dates, and historically factual details.

This book does not reach beyond the year 1961 in its breadth. There were more than enough historically monumental events which occurred in that year—principally in Berlin, but also in Vienna, the Congo, Rhodesia and Cuba's Bay of Pigs—to deal with. Although the years 1961 and 1962 comprise an historical continuum, each year also had its own separate and highly significant story. The central story of 1961 was Berlin, while that of 1962 was the Cuban Missile Crisis. The roots of the Cuban Missile Crisis are found in both the Bay of Pigs debacle and the armed face-off between the U.S. and the Soviet Union over Berlin.

The story lines, interwoven with the plot of espionage, mystery and suspense, evoke the era. Inspiration for plot and characters were found in American classics in which invented story lines were locked in symbiosis with historical facts. Examples are James Fennimore Cooper's '*The Last of the Mohicans*,' E. L. Doctorow's '*The March*,' and Michael Shaara's '*The Killer Angels*.' Are Reitenhauser, Olney, and Penchak of my book, modern-day versions of Hawkeye, Chingochgook, and Uncas? If so, the parallels were purely subliminal.

Finally, it's a never-ending challenge to draw comparisons between both the crises and heroics of the Cold War and those of the hot wars in which America was engaged. Though comparisons are often-times odious, I do believe that there were distinct, major battlegrounds in the forty-five year long Cold War where—had we not prevailed—the U.S. would have lost the struggle against the Soviet Union. Among these, Berlin was first and foremost.

Berlin was more than simply a convenient venue for the world's two nuclear super-powers to flex their muscles. Beginning in early June of 1961 and continuing for at least the next six months, the divided city symbolized an island of freedom in a sea of totalitarianism.

The erection of the Berlin Wall and the crisis between super-powers which followed were major historical events. Those events formed a great adventure story, which I have tried to capture in these pages.

As you will discover, the voice of John F. Kennedy suffuses the story you are about to read. It is wholly integral to the narrative. A book about the events of 1961 would hardly be complete without the unique voice of that era.

Nevertheless, this is not another book about JFK. Instead, it's a story of misstep, misdeed, and blunder, ultimately redeemed by courage and wisdom.

— Donald J. Farinacci

CONTENTS

PART I — THE FIRST SEAL OF THE WHITE HORSE

CONQUEST

"When the lamb opened
the first seal, I heard the
first living creature say,
"Come and see! I
looked, and there
before me was a white
horse. Its rider
held a bow, and he
was given a crown, and
he rode out as a conqueror
bent on conquest.

Revelation 6

Part I, Chapter 1

Vanquish

Tehran, April 24, 1961

Dusk's first sentinels descended upon Tehran. A light snowfall accentuated the unseasonably cold April evening. Huddled in the front seat of a parked Citroen with arms crossed against their chests—trying to fight off the cold—were two American men in their early twenties.

With chattering teeth, the one in the driver's seat gazed intently at a seven-foot statue which faced in an easterly direction. The statue stood across a busy street from the ancient structure known as the Green Palace.

Plaintive distant wails of Moslem prayers pierced the twilit gloom. The man in the passenger's seat had his eyes pointed toward a magazine in his lap.

The driver noted his colleague's diverted attention from the corner of his right eye, and registered his mild protest. "C'mon, Osi, get your eyes off Miss February and back on the tall stone guy."

Indifferent to the rebuke, Osi gazed languidly in his partner's direction and replied in his typical monotone, pitched just north of a whisper. "Be cool, Dago. Mohammed has my full attention, but the young guy who publishes this magazine—Hugh Heffner—I can't believe the way he's swimming in money and dames. I mean, any real man would have to be a little bit jealous."

Intensifying his forward gaze, the other American grumbled, "Well, you shoulda been a skin magazine tycoon, instead of a spook, if that's what you wanted."

Osi opened his mouth to respond, but before he could do so, the driver grabbed him by his arm and spat out an urgent command. "Heads up! Look at the guy with the camera. He's now circled the statue twice and just started his third go-round."

"You mean the towel-head?" asked Osi. (He was a veritable fountain of racial and ethnic stereotypes.)

1

"Yeah," replied CIA special agent, Mario Tonelli. He raised binoculars to his eyes, and pressed forward against the steering wheel. "Look, he's doing something on the far side of the statue."

Osi Mattatussu, also CIA, raised his own binoculars, and began to share his colleague's excitement. "I see him, but I can't tell what he's up to."

For the past eight hours, the two CIA operatives had been staking out the statue of Mohammed the Prophet across the street from the Sadabad Palace Complex. They were following a tip from U.S. Army Intelligence in Munich that a Soviet operative would be making a major drop at the statue some time on April the 24th.

"Whatever he was doing," Mario said, "he seems to be finished now."

In apparent confirmation of the agent's words, the unidentified man ambled away from the statue, and vanished into the deepening gloom of the falling night.

Mario turned to face Osi. "We'll wait five minutes, to make sure he's gone. But then we have to move in before KGB beats us to the punch."

"Funny you should bring that up," Osi said, "because there's a black limo about fifty meters straight ahead, creeping toward us. I'm guessing that it ain't the Ayatollah out for an evening drive."

"Okay," said Mario. "Change in plans. We move in now. As soon as we get there, you assume a firing position while I try to find the package."

Both men immediately exited the car and raced in the direction of the granite Mohammed. They wore dark gray business suits with wing-tipped black shoes, but the soles had been specially constructed with the rubber treads of a runner's track shoes underneath.

Mario Tonelli was about five-ten, with the blinding speed and elusiveness of a scat back, which in fact he had been, during his football days at South Central High in Philadelphia. Osi Mattatussu was an American Samoan—six foot-three and 220 pounds of pure muscle—a natural athlete, who yielded little to Mario in the speed department.

A special urgency drove their race to the statue. They were fully aware of how critical this mission was. Munich Station had told them just enough to impress its importance upon them. The word on the street in Berlin and Vienna was that a KGB mole, deeply embedded in NATO, had tipped off the Castro regime in Cuba of the planned invasion at the Bay of Pigs by a CIA-organized force of Cuban exiles.

As a result of the tipoff, the previous week's invasion attempt had ended in disaster. Castro's army had been waiting for the insurgents when they landed on the beach. The survivors had been captured and assembled in a sports stadium, where they were harangued by Cuban communist leader Fidel Castro for the better part of two days about the virtues of Communism.

Some of the invaders had simply jumped over to the communist cause, and were now happy Fidelists. Many others had been imprisoned.

For the new American president, John F. Kennedy, the failed Bay of Pigs invasion had been an unmitigated disaster. Though he bore up well in the aftermath, he clearly had been humiliated and weakened as a leader in the eyes of the world.

All of which came back around to this dead-drop in Tehran. If the tip from Army Intelligence was accurate, the package would contain information regarding a Soviet plan to capitalize on the serious damage sustained by the U.S. president. The information might even be powerful enough to deliver a fatal blow to Kennedy's prestige and effectiveness as an international figure.

Osi reached the statue of Mohammed only a fraction of a second after Mario. Fortunately, the drop site was on the side opposite the black limo.

Using the monument for cover, Osi swiftly crouched into a firing position as he pulled a Smith and Wesson Colt .45 from his shoulder holster.

Mario knelt behind Osi's bulk, searching for breaches in the square base of the seven foot figure—openings where a document could have been inserted.

The base was constructed of white bricks, with about an inch of concrete between each one. At first sight in the semi-darkness, Mario could see no flaws in the concrete. He pulled a small flashlight from his suit coat pocket and prepared to make a closer inspection.

The limousine braked to a halt about thirty meters away from the statue. Four silhouettes emerged from the vehicle, each headed in a different direction.

"Uh oh, Dag," said Osi, using his favorite nickname for Tonelli. "Hostile's on the move."

"How many?"

"Four."

"No sweat Samo," replied Tonelli, reciprocating with his own sobriquet for the big Samoan.

"Right," Osi said, "but it's getting dark. I need to pick them off before they can flank us."

Mario concentrated on the row of bricks with greater urgency. Even with the flashlight, he could detect no irregularities in the concrete.

"I'm going to have to go brick by brick," he said. "Buy me some time. Give them an ultimatum—'Surrender or face immediate annihilation.'"

With Mario and Osi, the tighter the position in which they found themselves, the more they resorted to sardonic humor. As if in response, a bullet fired by Hostile whizzed over Mario's head. Taking advantage of the muzzle flash of the fired weapon, Osi opened fire and brought the shooter to the ground with a bullet to the left knee.

Mario continued working on the twenty four bricks. Only a miniscule overhang was available for him to grip each one. But the son of a mason from blue-collar South Philly had the powerful stubby fingers of a laborer. He rapidly probed each block—seeking to pry it loose. There was no play in any of them. It was an arduous task.

Osi had bought them a few seconds by dropping the first shooter, but the reprieve proved to be very temporary. As Mario gripped and tried to loosen brick number 8, shots began piercing the air around them.

Osi stared and listened intently for cadences in the shooting which might tip off the enemy's location. Hostile had not yet flanked their position but the bad guys were definitely getting closer.

Mario had just discerned looseness in brick number 9 when a bullet hit the base of the statue about three feet away from Osi, sending fragments of brick and mortar flying in every direction.

One particularly sharp piece of concrete lodged itself in Osi's right calf. "Son of a Bitch!" yelped the big Samoan. "What's taking you so damned long? I thought your old man was a Dago brick layer!"

"Never mind my old man," Mario said. "Maybe you should try shooting in the general direction of the enemy every once in a while."

Another three shots rang out—one of them grazing Mario's shoulder. He clamped down on his body's instinctive desire to recoil from the source of the pain. He gritted his teeth and remained silent, his face a mask of rapt concentration.

Three more shots rang out in staggered cadence, similar to Morse Code. Dot-dot-dash.

From the muzzle flashes, Osi could see that their position had been flanked by Hostile. He either took immediate action, or he and Mario were dead men. At least two of the shooters were grouped together on the opposite side of a slight ground elevation, about fifty feet away. Osi had a little surprise for them...

He slipped a hand grenade from under his jacket, popped the pin, and released the thumb lever. After a quick two-count, he lobbed it toward the pair of prone hostiles, a perfect arc that dropped the grenade right on top of the enemy shooters just as the three-second primer reached the end of its burn.

The detonation split the night with shrapnel and fire, instantly dispatching the hostiles to oblivion.

Osi was reaching for a second grenade when he caught sight of the fourth hostile, running back in the direction of the limo.

There were no more shots, and soon the limousine sped away into the darkness.

Mario had no difficulty extracting brick number 9. The thin package behind it consisted of four envelopes, secured by a rubber band.

He shoved it under his jacket and signaled Osi that it was time to go. As they rushed back to the Citroen with their prize in hand, the two men barely noticed the pain from their wounds.

Munich, West Germany, April 20, 1961

Captain Edwin Barnstable, the newly designated operations officer of the 409th Special Investigations Detachment, bolted from the telex room and made a beeline for the CO's office. His pace was brisk, his manner officious, his mood purposeful—fitting him like a fine Brooks Brothers suit.

On the surface, Barnstable appeared not much different than any other Cold War military intelligence officer. He exuded a sense of urgency, but one which was held in a state of quiet suspension until he was ready to unleash it. His equable exterior disguised the raging anger within him. Beginning in the depths of his emotional core and rising to just below the surface of his psyche was a boiling mass of molten lava, waiting to explode outward in a volcanic fury.

Ed Barnstable was the apotheosis of a cold warrior. He could easily have sprung from the same gene pool as a Winston Churchill or a John Foster Dulles. Barnstable hated the international communist movement with a messianic-type fervor. He had been too young to serve in WWII, so his rage had not been diverted toward the Nazis or Imperial Japan. His hatred of the Soviets and their minions was undiluted and deeply impacted, with precious little release. He had recently been diagnosed with a duodenal ulcer.

During his formative college years at Duquesne University in the late 40's and early 50's, Barnstable's intuitive anti-Marxist convictions had been reinforced by the Bolsheviks' repeated international outrages: the Soviets' bloody coup in Czechoslovakia; the sealing off of West Berlin, only to have it rescued by the Berlin Airlift; Stalin's show trials; his murderous cruelty toward his own people and those in Soviet-captive nations; the descent of the 'Iron Curtain' over virtually all of Eastern Europe. And despite the international focus on China, the USSR had clearly fomented the Korean War, by backing and encouraging Kim il Sung, the Soviet puppet in North Korea.

So the earnest (if somewhat stiff-necked) Barnstable had enrolled in R.O.T.C. at Duquesne. And in May of 1952, he had rolled off the reserve officer assembly line as a newly-minted second lieutenant.

His next stop had been a troop ship headed for South Korea. But war had brought him no catharsis. Stationed at Panmunjom, near the 38th Parallel, Second Lieutenant Edwin Barnstable had been assigned as junior intelligence officer under Ridgway's "G-2," or top intelligence officer. There, Barnstable's unrevealed frustrations had mounted as he did liaison duty between the Army and the U.N. Armistice Negotiation Team.

For the next full year, Barnstable had witnessed the continued slaughter as the negotiators argued over how and whether to repatriate North Korean and Red Chinese POW's. He had suffered quietly in the pit of his soul, watching the death toll continue to spiral as bureaucrats wrangled over the wording of useless documents.

Then had come the 1953 Armistice, which left the warring parties at the 38th Parallel, dividing the North from the South, at pretty much the same place they had started at the beginning of the war. Three years of fighting, more than two million deaths, including well-over forty thousand Americans, and nothing tangible had changed. Barnstable came out of the conflict with a promotion, but that did nothing to assuage his anger.

First Lieutenant Edwin Barnstable's wrath for the communist aggressors fed his decision to make the Army his career, and his quiet post-war duty at Aberdeen Proving Grounds in Maryland provided him with the opportunity to marry and start a family. But the desire for revenge against the Soviets burned deep within him.

He was very careful to never allow his un-slaked thirst for vengeance to affect the way he treated his wife and children. He took none of it out on them—only on himself. His untapped rage grew incrementally, and it only increased after Stalin died.

Stalin's ultimate successor, Nikita Khrushchev, was a short, stumpy, blunt instrument of a man. He stirred the cauldron of East-West tensions by perpetrating one provocation after another. Each new outrage fanned the flames of Barnstable's ire.

In his crude peasant manner, Khrushchev crowed when the Soviet Union launched Sputnik, the first unmanned space craft, into orbit around the earth.

The arms race began in earnest under Truman and Marshall, with Resolution NSC-68. Eisenhower and Dulles continued the escalation. Not one to be outdone (or at least out-talked), Khrushchev dramatically increased the number of Russian tanks, planes, troops, submarines and nuclear weapons through the 1950's. He blustered frequently about the soon-to-arrive 'Armageddon.'

In 1956, when Khrushchev bragged that "We will bury you," Barnstable spat contemptuously on the ground, but said nothing. Then, the pudgy Russian troll proclaimed that, "Berlin is the testicle of the West. When I want the West to scream, I squeeze on Berlin."

This crude half-witticism was the last straw for Barnstable. He immediately submitted his papers for transfer to the 44th Military Intelligence Group, in West Germany.

On March 29, 1959, the newly promoted Captain Ed Barnstable had boarded a plane at McGuire Air Force Base for Frankfurt, West Germany.

Now, on April 19, 1961, he was the operations officer of the Munich Station of the 44th M.I. Group.

Munich was a tinder-box of heated espionage activities, both ours and theirs. At the center of it all, Ed Barnstable was as pissed-off as he had ever been.

The commanding officer of the 44th M.I. was Major Fred Reitenhauser, a sly and subtle iceberg of a man, who kept seven-eights of himself concealed beneath the surface. As Reitenhauser's second-in-command at Munich station, Barnstable knew of the major's secret mole—code name "Carlton"—planted deep within the Soviet defense system.

According to Carlton, the KGB had their own mole buried somewhere in NATO. It was this KGB mole who had warned Castro of the impending CIA-sponsored invasion of Cuba.

The failed invasion had given both President Kennedy and the CIA a black eye, but Carlton had warned Reitenhauser not to fixate on Cuba. It was vital to see the larger picture. The betrayal at the Bay of Pigs was only the opening salvo in Khrushchev's latest offensive against the United States.

Under the code name 'Invictus,' the Soviet strategy would be implemented in stages throughout the remainder of 1961. A little more than a week earlier, on April 12th, the Soviet cosmonaut, Yuri Gagarin, had become the first man in outer space. Whether or not it was a planned part of Invictus, Gagarin's feat had been an enormous propaganda coup for

Nikita Khrushchev. The Russian leader was busy exploiting it to build even greater support in the Presidium of the Supreme Soviet for Operation Invictus.

Barnstable's smoldering rage was stoked to even greater heat by the Bay of Pigs disaster and the Soviet Union's latest victory in the space race. But his repressed rage was now mingled with excitement. Carlton had come through with reliable intelligence about the planned KGB dead-drop in Tehran. In turn, Reitenhauser had shared the hot tip with "Q," his CIA counterpart in Munich.

The CIA had managed to intercept the contents of the dead-drop. Within an hour, a courier would deliver a package of potentially world-altering magnitude.

Barnstable arrived at the CO's outer office in a state of excitement he hadn't felt since the day he'd received orders for Korea.

The operations officer (internally referred to as "Ops") was greeted in the outer office by the CO's secretary and special assistant, Gerda, a twenty-something West German national with a U.S. Top Secret security clearance. Given Major Reitenhauser's penchant for excellence, it was not surprising that Gerda embodied a harmonious blend of physical attractiveness, brains, and character.

"Good morning, Gerda."

"And to you too, sir."

"I need to see the major ASAP."

Gerda picked up the receiver, and dialed the CO's extension number. "Sir, Captain Barnstable is here to see you. He says it's urgent."

"Show him right in, Gerda."

Barnstable could hardly contain his excitement as he walked through the door. He found the commanding officer of the 409th Special Investigations Detachment with his feet up on his desk, reading the autobiography of Whittaker Chambers, the confessed former Russian spy who had become an anti-communist zealot. Chambers had exposed Alger Hiss as a Russian undercover agent, and had been instrumental in sending the former State Department official to prison for perjury.

Reitenhauser knew how concerned his operations officer was about Invictus, but it was not the CO's way to rise to the level of his subordinates' anxieties.

"A nasty business, this Chambers-Hiss affair," Reitenhauser said. "We like to think of the enemy among us as dirty lowlifes, hiding in dark alleys. What Chambers tells us is that a traitor can look, talk, and act pretty much the same as ourselves. In fact, we may have dined, played golf, or enjoyed a game of gin rummy with a Soviet spy—thinking he was a true-blue

American, while all the while he was betraying our secrets. I've asked Doug Booker to read everything he can get his hands on about the Hiss case. Some of it might be helpful in developing a profile for 'Groundhog.'[1]"

Major Reitenhauser closed the biography, using a finger to mark his page. "But Greta said it was urgent, so I'm guessing that you didn't come here to talk about Chambers. What have you got for me, Ed?"

"A telex just came in from the CIA station in Bonn," Barnstable said. "Their operatives in Tehran retrieved the drop, and they're personally bringing it here. They're expected to arrive by car within the hour."

The CO felt a little surge of adrenalin rush on hearing this news, but his excitement did not register on his placid exterior. With his feet still resting on his desk, he nodded slowly. "I heard through the grapevine that the two CIA men had a bit of a dustup with Hostile in Tehran. From what I hear, it turned into a pretty bloody mess. I don't know how good the CIA team is, but they must be fairly on the ball, because they took out a crack KGB field unit all by themselves."

Reitenhauser raised a languid eyebrow. "We should assume that Groundhog knows the couriers are coming, and that Hostile is tailing them. They'll probably try to intercept the delivery before it gets into our hands. Let's put Brand and Toomey near the front entrance to the motor pool ramp in their usual positions, with sniper rifles, just in case. And I want you and O'Malley to draw weapons, meet the CIA men in the motor pool, and accompany them up."

Barnstable very nearly sprang to attention. "Yes sir!"

With the exception of the motor pool and supply sergeants, all personnel of the 409th Special Investigations Detachment wore civilian clothes, and there was no saluting. Outside of the unit's offices, they used only first names. Even the name of the unit was a thin cover, suggesting a high-level CID[2] investigative function. In fact, Munich Station's sole mission was to conduct covert operations, to gather intelligence by the use of clandestine means. The official name for this activity was "Area Intelligence."

At breakfast that morning, Reitenhauser (who was simply Fred to friends and acquaintances) had read in the *International Herald Tribune* that despite what *Pravda* called the U.S.'s "blatant imperialism toward Communist Cuba," Premier Khrushchev "would not act rashly, as the Americans had." The article announced that the summit meeting between

---

[1] The U.S. nickname for the Soviet mole.

[2] U.S. Army Criminal Investigation Division.

Kennedy and Khrushchev, scheduled for the first week in June, would not be cancelled. It would be held in Vienna, as planned.

Fred's interior warning system had immediately given him an alert signal. The statements in *Pravda* were the usual transparent propaganda but, Fred had no doubt that the summit would be the next step in Operation Invictus.

Carlton had warned as much, and when had Carlton's predictions ever been wrong? His ability to see major Cold War occurrences before they happened was uncanny. From his office in East Berlin, the mole had somehow seen what no one in Washington, Tokyo, or Seoul had foreseen: the imminent North Korean invasion of the South, in June of 1950.

Carlton had also predicted that if MacArthur pursued the North Korean Army to the Yalu River at its northern border with Manchuria, the Red Chinese Army would intervene in the War.

Fred had tried to pass on this advance information to MacArthur's G-2[3] in Tokyo, only to be coldly rebuffed. The intelligence had been ignored, and the U.S. military had suffered what could only be described as a military disaster.

Gerda's elegant voice interrupted Fred's reverie. Her simple declaration over the telephone intercom was clearly enunciated, albeit in a softly tempered German accent. "Sir, the visitors have arrived, and Ops has gone down to meet them."

Mario Tonelli and Osi Mattatussu had reached the 409th without mishap, and they had detected no tail along the way.

Under normal circumstances, Major Reitenhauser would have simply directed the duty officer at the front desk to take delivery of the package and issue the couriers a receipt. But in deference to what the two CIA men had gone through to retrieve the item, Fred had Barnstable escort them into his office, where the four of them enjoyed coffee along with some friendly banter.

Fred was highly impressed with the two young CIA agents, and he would have enjoyed spending more time with them. But the package now sat tantalizingly on the CO's desk, beckoning his attention.

Mario and Osi sensed the major's eagerness to open the package. They were understandably curious about the contents, but they had no "need to know," so they politely excused themselves and took their leave.

When the CIA agents were gone, Fred punched the button on his desk intercom. "Gerda, please see if you can round up Booker and O'Malley

---

[3] Officer in charge of Intelligence.

and ask them to come in." His voice remained casual, but his eyes were fixed on the small package with the intensity of an x-ray.

O'Malley was Chief Warrant Officer Third Class Ted O'Malley, the deputy operations officer of the unit, who did double-duty as security officer. Booker was Case Officer-Analyst Douglas Booker, a civilian employed by the Army at grade GS-9.

Within five minutes, two male Caucasians entered the CO's office. The resemblance ended there. O'Malley stood six feet one inches tall with a lean and wiry build. He sported a pair of well-pressed gray slacks, polished loafers, blue blazer, crisp white Oxford and blue-striped regimental tie. His red hair was neatly sculpted into a flat top and he stood before the major with ramrod straight bearing, and a twinkle in his eyes.

Booker, by contrast, was about five feet ten inches tall with alert gray eyes that seemed to be disconnected from their sockets. They roamed and darted at will, quickly and haphazardly registering every detail within the periphery of their range. His gray plaid suit was not merely rumpled. Its deep-set mass of overlapping wrinkles suggested that the garment had gone through the washing machine with its occupant still inside.

Booker's dishevelment radiated downward to a wide tie depicting a pastoral hunting scene, embellished by a blotch of some unidentified compound (possibly, but not definitely from some source of food). His thick tortoise-shell glasses were misshapen from several years of use and sat against his face, at an angle. Blond hair hung down over his collar, not because of any deliberate style or fashion, but because Booker had a phobia about barbers. He too was thin, but with posture that had degenerated into a permanent slouch. His shoes were scuffed Cordovans, with broken and retied laces.

Yet, despite his sartorial chaos, Booker did not emanate weakness or nerdiness. Shining through his outer disarray was a certain suppleness of spirit and intellect, a taught and dangerous readiness to strike if provoked, in the manner of a tensely-coiled panther.

Making a quick visual assessment of the two new arrivals, Fred signaled them to be seated. Although Booker's moods and mindset were often difficult to divine, the CO's quick read of the mercurial analyst was positive. Booker had known the package was on the way, and his body language signaled a high level of alertness and excitement. O'Malley was basically a paragon of consistency, a rock. And to the major, he seemed the same as always. Fred felt instant relief. He badly needed these two men at the top of their game. As good as Barnstable was operationally, analysis was not his forte.

Fred distributed rubber gloves to each of those present, and all of them spent a few seconds maneuvering the gloves into place. Fred removed the rubber band from the package of four letter-sized envelopes, and passed them around for a quick inspection by each of the other three men.

The envelopes were made of a high-quality white bond paper, each with a visible watermark. They were feather-light, denoting very little, if anything, inside. The glue on the envelopes was unused, so that one could separate most of the flap from the container portion. The pointed tip of each flap, was fastened to the envelope by a seal composed of red wax, similar to the wax sigils usually associated with royal edicts, ecclesiastical decrees, and estate documents.

"Hmmm," murmured Doug Booker. "Obviously, the wax seal has some symbolic significance, since it clearly has no utilitarian purpose."

Next, Fred directed that each man hold one envelope, proceed to break the wax seal and remove its contents. A few seconds later each of the four held a 3 x 5 piece of white notepaper in his hands with writing on one side only. Fred asked them to hold up the notes so the others could see them all, and he did likewise.

A heading appeared at the top of each note. The one on Fred's note said "THE THIRD SEAL". Looking up, he asked the others to read the headings on their notes aloud. O'Malley's said "THE SECOND SEAL." Booker had the "FOURTH," and Barnstable, the "FIRST."

"Let's start with you Ed. Read your entire note."

"Yes, sir," replied Barnstable who read aloud with a tremor of excitement penetrating the calm veneer of his deep voice:

"THE FIRST SEAL
Come and see! I looked,
And there was a white horse.
Its rider held a
Bow, and he was given
A crown, and he rode
Out as a conqueror bent
On conquest.
Revelation 6."

Booker, whose eyes had wandered away from his colleagues and were now fixed on a crack in the ceiling, was the first to comment. His voice carried an air of clinical detachment, as if he were studying the molecular structure of a fruit fly under a microscope. "Odd how a legion of atheists have borrowed from the New Testament as the source of their symbolic speech. You would think they could have found something suitable in Marx, or Engels... or even Hegel."

The CO eyed Booker. "What do you mean, Doug?"

"The Book of Revelation," Booker said. "The Apocalypse. When we opened the envelopes, we were metaphorically breaking the first four of the seven sacred seals of the Lamb of God, Jesus Christ. Or so we are told by Saint John the Evangelist, the reputed author of Revelation. Each of us holds in his hands a note expressing one of the first four parts of the author's apocalyptic vision. The harbingers of the Last Judgment. The End of Days, symbolized by the Four Horsemen of the Apocalypse!"

Shifting his gaze to the Harvard class ring on the middle finger of his left hand, Booker, shook his head very slowly from right to left. "Powerful imagery... *Very* powerful."

"The Soviets are mocking us," he continued. "They're using the mythology of one of organized Christianity's most sacred creeds to announce a major offensive against the West."

"What makes you so sure of that Doug?" asked Fred Reitenhauser. He was careful to keep his tone conversational, rather than challenging.

"It's the confluence of imagery and history," Booker said. "The overwhelming majority of historians and biblical scholars believe that the first horseman symbolizes *conquest*. The second horseman symbolizes *war*. The third represents *famine*, and the fourth is *death*. Khrushchev has latched on to the most powerful allegory he could come up with, and I don't think he would deliberately associate such heavily-weighted symbols with a minor initiative. This is definitely something *big*, and I can only think of one thing large enough to fit the bill."

Booker regarded the broken wax seals on the four envelopes. "I'm sure of it," he said. "Khrushchev is signaling his intentions, to all the Soviet Republics—their Warsaw Pact allies, and the USSR's client states in Africa, Asia and Latin America—that he is about to start World War III against the NATO Alliance. It won't necessarily be a shooting war, mind you. But it will be a world war, just the same. Remember Lenin and Trotsky's prophetic vision about an international communist hegemony over the world? The Soviets are pushing that dream forward. They're trying to fulfill the ultimate destiny of Communism, at least as they see it."

Ted O'Malley held up a hand. "Whoa! Just a second there, Doug. Aren't you getting a bit carried away? All we've got are four envelopes containing biblical quotations. We don't know who wrote them, who they were intended for, or what they were intended to accomplish. You know that I respect your intuition, and your analytical skills, but we've got no evidence at all to support your interpretation. And you've got to admit, from bible verses to global war—even a non-shooting war—amounts to one hell of a leap."

Booker raised neither his voice, nor his eyes. "We have the Soviet's aims and triumphs of the last five years as corroborating evidence. Sputnik. The USSR's incredible arms build-up. The sheer size of the Warsaw Pact armies, and their dangerous proximity to Western Europe. And now, the Soviets have made the first manned space-flight."

O'Malley started to say something, but Booker wasn't finished yet. "Truman and Eisenhower relied on George Kennan's doctrine of 'containment,' and it worked, at least for a while. The Soviets have been frozen in place for the last dozen years, and now they are itching to break through NATO's invisible barrier. Khrushchev threw down the gauntlet to Kennedy earlier this year before Kennedy even took office. That's why the new president ordered his speech writers to insert some tough talk into his Inaugural Address."

"How did he throw down the gauntlet?" asked a skeptical O'Malley.

Booker rummaged through the junk in his various suit coat pockets for a minute or so before extracting a badly crumpled news article from somewhere deep in the chaos. He unfolded it and tried to press out the wrinkles. It was a page 18 article from the January 8, 1961 issue of the *New York Times*.

He read the lead paragraph... "In a major state speech yesterday in Bucharest, Soviet Premier Nikita Khrushchev outlined what he referred to as 'the new areas of peaceful competition between the two superpowers,' which he listed as 'national liberation wars' and 'centers of revolutionary struggle against imperialism' all over Asia, Africa and Latin America."

Booker leaned back in his chair. "That was Khrushchev's version of the Confederates' firing on Fort Sumter. You can be sure he'll escalate things going forward. Kennedy's prestige and credibility were badly wounded by the Bay of Pigs fiasco, and the Soviets smell blood. Just watch how Khrushchev moves in for the kill at the summit conference in Vienna, this coming June. That will be stage one of Invictus."

O'Malley, knowing that he could neither prove nor disprove future events, leaned back in his chair. He could see that Booker's prognostications were striking a receptive chord with the CO, so he was content to wait, and let unfolding events dispel some of the analyst's more extreme predictions.

But O'Malley's quiet resignation was disturbed by the sudden buzzing of the CO's intercom. An urgent telex message had come in from Group in Frankfurt. Three pro-American Congolese diplomats had been assassinated in Brussels, Belgium just after emerging from a limousine to attend a Belgian forum on the future of the Congo. Four men wearing masks, Che Guevara[4]-style fatigues and black berets had reportedly appeared from nowhere, and gunned down the diplomats with Kalashnikov assault rifles.

The 'International Red Guard,' a particularly virulent and extreme group of pro-communist militants, had already claimed credit for the assassinations. Minutes later, the official Soviet newspaper, *Izvestia*, had hit the stands on Moscow's streets, proclaiming the official view of the Presidium of the Supreme Soviet, that the shootings—though regrettable—represented a "justified out-pouring of rage by freedom-loving people everywhere" over the January 17, 1961 execution of the pro-communist leader of the new Congo, Patrice Lumumba.

Izvestia went on to state that "the reprehensible murder of Lumumba had occurred as a result of a conspiracy hatched by Secretary General of the United Nations, Dag Hammarskjöld, with the complicity and active participation of the Belgian government and the CIA."

Even as First Sergeant Peter Toomey was entering Major Reitenhauser's office with the message in hand, the telex machine was buzzing with a second message of even more dire import.

Washington, D.C., April 25, 1961, The White House.

Two Secret Service agents carrying walkie-talkies tried to block Ted Sorensen's entrance to the Oval Office.

The president, who had ordered that the door be kept partly open, heard the ruckus outside and shouted in its direction. "Hurry up and get in here, Ted! What took you so long? Couldn't you find a 'pahking' space?"

The Secret Service men immediately made way for the man to enter.

Sorenson, who hailed from Minnesota, was now just as used to the president's ribbing as he was to his broad Boston "A's." And since Ted

---

[4] The famous Argentine insurrectionist who was second-in-command to Fidel Castro in the Cuban revolution.

Sorenson probably spent more time with Kennedy than the First Lady did, neither man bothered with formalities upon meeting.

"So Ted, these 'bahsteds' calling themselves ... ah... 'Red Gahdes' shot the three Congolese envoys in Brussels, and ... ah... that son of a bitch Khrushchev had *Izvestia* practically call it an act of justice."

Before Sorenson could verbalize the shock which was already spreading across his face, the phone on the president's desk rang and the president's secretary, Evelyn Lincoln, informed him that Secretary of State, Dean Rusk, was on the other end and that it was urgent.

"Ah, good morning, Dean."

"Good morning, Mr. President."

"So what's going on, Mr. Secretary?"

"I am sorry to say I have some more bad news from Europe, sir. A car carrying four men, including one American, was fired upon about an hour ago at the Brandenburg Gate. We have reason to believe that the shooters were East German agents. Two of the car's passengers are dead and the American, who was driving, was wounded."

"What's the condition of the American?"

"Well, I don't know for sure but I just got off the phone with Willie Brandt,[5] and he says the American has been taken to a hospital in West Berlin. From what I understand, he's expected to survive."

"What do we know about the American and the other three in the car?"

"I didn't wait for NATO headquarters to get the answer to that one," Secretary Rusk said. "I called Tugwell Saylor, Commanding General of the 44th Military Intelligence Group in Frankfurt. Tug and I go way back to the early days of the Korean War. The American is one of his. The man's name is Warren Olney, and he's a high-level case officer assigned to Tug's Munich M.I. Station. The three others are East Germans, believed to be Olney's covert agents. The surviving East German is now in the hands of our military counterintelligence detachment in West Berlin."

"All right Dean," the president said. "Keep me posted."

The president hung up the phone and quickly briefed Sorensen on what Rusk had said, and on the rest of what he knew about the assassination of the three Congolese diplomats. When he was finished, he looked his young aide directly in the eyes. "Give me your gut reaction Ted. No hems, haws, or on the other hands."

Those who were unschooled in the nature of the symbiotic relationship between Kennedy and Sorenson might be curious as to why the president of the United States would want the unvarnished reaction of a thirty year

---

[5] Mayor of West Berlin.

old lawyer, political aide and speech writer before that of anyone else. But, those in the know would not have been at all surprised.

In many ways, Ted Sorenson was the president's alter ego—almost a second side of his nature: the intellectual and idealistic side. The president's brother, Bobby, leaned more toward action. Sorenson, by contrast, was contemplative in nature. He was aligned with the cognitive part of the president's mind. He was the lens through which Kennedy focused his ideas and rhetoric.

Some Washington insiders tried to oversimplify the relationship between Kennedy and Sorenson, by suggesting that the young aide was the actual *source* of the president's ideas and rhetoric. Although the notion appealed to Kennedy's detractors, it was false. Together, Kennedy and Sorenson formed a partnership of the mind, one which had produced a bestselling work of non-fiction, '*Profiles in Courage*,' as well as many celebrated policy papers and speeches, including Kennedy's historic Inaugural Address.

Sorenson scratched absently at his left earlobe. "My gut reaction, Mr. President, is that these incidents were coordinated. Each was aimed at one of the battlegrounds where the USSR intends to challenge the US. It's not an accident that the events involved Africa, where Khrushchev wants to establish Soviet dominance through so-called 'wars of liberation,' and in Germany, where he's making a determined effort to seal off the East from the West."

"I agree," said Kennedy. "We played right into their hands with the whole Cuba mess, and they're going to capitalize on our mistake."

He tapped the burnished surface of his desk with one forefinger. "The next big battle will be in Vienna."

Sorenson nodded. "I think you're right, sir. Vienna."

Munich, April 25, 1961

The next big battle for the 409th Special Investigations Detachment was taking place at that moment. Around the time the Secretary of State was briefing the president on the Brandenburg Gate shooting, Major Reitenhauser was reading aloud to his chief subordinates a telex message from Group, describing the same incident.

The small team was now assembled in a conference room. They had been joined by Chief of the Ops Support Section, Arthur LeBron, a GS-11 civilian and case-officer; by First Sergeant Peter Toomey, and by German Section Chief, GS-10, Mitchell Blake.

Although the others were seated, Fred Reitenhauser read the communiqué while standing, and he did not sit down when finished. Instead, he gazed skyward for a few seconds before firing off his first question to Barnstable and Blake jointly. "Who else besides the three of us knew about Olney's mission?"

Barnstable, Blake's superior when it came to matters of unit operations, answered for both of them. "Group's operations officer, Colonel Dabrowski, and whomever he told. As you know sir, 'Operation Excavate' is a joint 409th-Group project."

"Did CIA know?"

"Not to the best of our knowledge, sir," replied Blake.

"Ed, is that right?" asked the CO.

"Yes sir."

"Alright, then what conclusion do we draw?"

This time, Booker took it upon himself to answer the CO. "Sir, I think we can conclude that someone at Group, or possibly CIA, went rogue on us and clued Hostile in on the details of Olney's mission."

This time, there was no argument from O'Malley. He simply nodded. "I agree."

Fred held up the telex. "According to this, Warren[6] was wounded, and is under treatment at Adenauer City Hospital in West Berlin. Does he have any protection?"

"Only of the marginal sort," Barnstable said. "His hospital room is being covered by two West Berlin plainclothesmen, assigned by the mayor's offices."

"Not exactly a match for the KGB," said the CO. He nodded toward the assembled men. "Alright, that's it for now, gentlemen. You can return to your offices. I want some time to think about this."

The six men rose and filed out without comment.

Giving the men enough time to settle back into their offices, the CO buzzed LeBron. "Get back here, Art. Now!"

---

[6] Chief Warrant Officer Warren Olney, Deputy Section Chief of the 409th's German Section.

Part I, Chapter 2

Protect and Defend

West Berlin, April 26, 1961—0100 hours

Four men dressed in green doctor's scrubs rode a freight elevator in silence from the basement of Adenauer City Hospital to the fourth floor. One of them wore a stethoscope around his neck. Another carried a clipboard. The other two carried nothing.

They exited the elevator one at a time, at five-second intervals, and headed for room 418. The four blew past the nurses' station, drawing only a bored glance from a single nurse behind the reception desk.

Room 418 was located around the corner from the nurse's station, about half-way down the corridor, well out of sight for the nurse on duty. As the men entered that corridor, one at a time, they drew weapons. With two of them on each side, they edged along the walls toward Room 418.

Osi Mattatussu took the point, wearing scrubs at least two sizes too small for his bulk. He saw immediately that the guards who were supposed to be stationed in front of Olney's room were missing. Reaching a point roughly fifteen feet from the door, Osi stood witness as two dangerous looking men in orderly's whites dragged Warren Olney out of the room and into the corridor.

Osi quickly looked down at his clip board with feigned attention. His first reaction was one of relief that his team might be able to accomplish the mission without firing their weapons, that is if his three comrades— Mario Tonelli, Lugash Magyaar, and Etan Gaborski—were in the right position. The latter two were known to Osi only as Lou and Ed.

A third hostile operative, carrying a Beretta close to his side followed the abductors out of the room. The group turned away from Osi and headed toward an exit clearly marked "Ausfahrt."

The armed man fell in behind them, walking slowly backward to protect their rear.

Osi had planned to take the two abductors down with blows to the throat, and then (hopefully) grab Olney before he hit the ground. The armed rear guard forced him to instantly discard this strategy, and come up with a new one.

A quick thinker, it took him about a tenth of a second to formulate a Plan-B. Before he had a chance to communicate his intentions to the rest of his team, the decision was snatched out of his hands.

The air rang out with the sound of a gunshot, and Hostile's rear guard collapsed to the floor with a bullet between the eyes. The shot had come from Magyaar's Walther PPK, but there was no time for Osi to express his displeasure at the operative's undisciplined behavior.

Osi's reflexes kicked into high gear. He leapt forward toward the remaining pair of hostiles, not at all surprised to find Mario Tonelli at his elbow. The stunned abductors had no time to react. Osi and Mario were upon them in a flash, using their best manual combat techniques to take down the enemy operatives.

Gaborski grabbed Olney, and held him upright while Magyaar provided cover with his still-smoking PPK.

The hospital staff responded quickly, security guards, nurses, and orderlies converging on the scene of the mayhem less than a minute after the shot was fired. They found three dead civilians in the corridor, and two dead West German policemen in Room 418.

The patient had vanished.

Munich, April 26, 1961-0630 hours

Fred puffed on his pipe as he read the after-action report. He had recently traded his customary cherry-blend tobacco in favor of a licorice flavor, and was savoring its distinctive taste.

Happily, Olney was now safe in a hospital bed installed in a West Berlin safe-house. He was there attended to by private-duty nurses and U.S. military doctors from Group's pool of thoroughly-vetted medical professionals. The identity of the participants in the pool were known only to General Tugwell Saylor, and his operations officer, Colonel Edwin Dabrowski. Not only had the pool of nurses and physicians originally passed the most rigorous security check, but were also subject to ongoing investigation by the U.S. Army's 502nd Security Regiment, with its plainclothes sleuths, to make sure none of them had been compromised.

This time Olney's guards were Tonelli and Mattatussu, a vast improvement.

Fred allowed himself the faintest sigh of satisfaction over how the operation had gone. The use of the two CIA special ops men had been an obvious choice. Of course, Q would enter this one in the debit column of his mind, and decide that Reitenhauser now owed him one. Fred figured that was a small enough price to pay for the brilliance of Tonelli and Mattatussu.

The really inspired idea, however, had come from Art LeBron. Tapping his Agent number 14332 for some of the latter's best operational talent had paid real dividends. God-willing, the two spooks known as Lou and Ed could be of use in the future. But this thought only led Fred to the disquieting sense that he would probably need them and a lot more in the *very* near future.

When it came to the feints and counter-feints of war, Fred's instincts had never failed him. He knew as clearly as he knew the self-aggrandizing ways of Communist Russia that, as the Second Seal of the Apocalypse suggested, the Cold War of 1961 had begun. He had no idea when it would end, or even whether it would turn hot. For now, those were unanswerable questions.

Fred knew he had just dodged a bullet with the attempted abduction of Olney. No man could withstand the KGB's brand of torture indefinitely. Sooner or later, Olney would have broken and revealed some key info about the deep cover mole within the Soviet defense system.

The operative in question, code name 'Carlton,' was Reitenhauser's man from the ground up. He had been recruited by Reitenhauser, was controlled exclusively by him, and communicated with no one in the West except him.

While Olney did not know the true identity of Carlton, he *did* know the mole's cover name, the method by which he could be contacted, and the location of the dead-drop where he retrieved his messages. Munich Station changed-up the dead-drop site every week, but the information in Olney's head might be enough for a resourceful KGB to eventually identify Carlton. The viability of NATO's entire European intelligence system currently hinged on the continued anonymity of Carlton. Reitenhauser could take comfort from the fact that at least for the time being, Olney's secrets were secure.

At his East Berlin offices, Carlton, a high Soviet defense official, knew only that Olney had been wounded. He had been spared knowledge of the dramatic aftermath, and therefore, had been able to give his full attention to the mysterious Groundhog.

Part I, Chapter 3

Groundhog

Western intelligence knew almost nothing about the Eastern Bloc mole, upon whom the descriptive name Groundhog had been conferred by the mysterious Chief of the CIA's Munich Station, himself known only as "Q."

Knowledge of Groundhog's existence was restricted to CIA, U.S. Army Intelligence, and Britain's MI-6, because of information supplied by the commanding officer of the 409th Special Investigations Detachment in Munich, Major Frederick Reitenhauser.

Normally, the fact that a mere CO of a relatively small area intelligence unit was the source of such dramatic information would come as a surprise to most intelligence professionals. However, knowledgeable insiders within NATO's intelligence network were not in the least surprised. Fred Reitenhauser was not just *any* station chief. By 1961, his prowess in establishing a triangulated spy network, with himself sitting at the top in Munich, was a minor legend. From there one diagonal of the triangle reached eastward to Vienna, Austria and its super-spy, Army Intelligence Agent, Number 14332. The other diagonal of the triangle reached from Munich to East Berlin, the center of operations for the 409th's mole, known only as Carlton. The base of the triangle traversed a broad geographical area running from East Berlin through East Germany, Czechoslovakia and back to Vienna.

Reitenhauser had recruited Carlton and had become the mole's first and only case officer. Fred had also recruited Agent 14332, also know as Horst Berkenfeld, but had turned over control of 14332 to Art LeBron, with whom Berkenfeld enjoyed better chemistry.

Beyond purely existential knowledge, Western intelligence had become aware of only three additional facts concerning Groundhog. The most significant was that he enjoyed access to Western Bloc secrets somewhere at the highest levels of NATO's intelligence constellation. His dissimulation under a false identity had to be close to flawless in order to escape detection at such a high level. The second fact was that Groundhog had revealed to Soviet agents the CIA's plans to sponsor the invasion of Cuba, at the Bay of Pigs, by Cuban exiles living in the United States. The KGB with the Kremlin's blessing then tipped off Cuban dictator Fidel Castro and the rest is history. Only one person in the world had both the access and inclination to disclose Groundhog's disloyalty to American intelligence. That person was Carlton. He passed the info on to Fred Reitenhauser as soon as he acquired it, two days after the aborted invasion. The third known fact was that Groundhog had tipped off East German intelligence to the fact that Warren Olney would be extracting three of his agents—East German residents all—and bringing them 'in from the cold,' on April 25, 1961 at the Brandenburg Gate, as part of 'Operation Excavate.'

Carlton held the position of Minister for Defense Preparedness of the Western Soviet Republics. Yet, even from his high perch in the Soviet defense establishment, he knew only one additional thing about Groundhog. He had recently learned that Groundhog worked for Soviet military intelligence (GRU) and not the KGB. He had also learned that the agent's codename was 'Jurist II.'

Carlton had thus far kept this information to himself, considering its divulgence in the present climate to be far too dangerous.

Munich, May 2, 1961

For the past week Doug Booker had immersed himself in the saga of two accomplished Americans, Whittaker Chambers and Alger Hiss.

Whittaker Chambers, a native of Philadelphia, intellectual and writer, studied at Columbia University and eventually became a senior editor with *Time Magazine*. Alger Hiss, a native of Baltimore, attended John Hopkins University and Harvard Law School. During a short but illustrious career, Hiss became a clerk to Supreme Court Justice, Oliver Wendell Holmes, Jr., then became a prominent Boston attorney, a U.S. State Department official and Secretary General of the United Nations Charter Convention. He attended the Yalta Conference in 1945 as one of President Roosevelt's State Department advisors and eventually became president of the Carnegie Foundation for International Peace.

Chambers and Hiss came to know each other in the 1930's. They both were the products of dysfunctional families. Hiss's father committed suicide when he was a child leaving the family in dire financial straits and forcing them to live on in a type of shabby gentility. Chambers' father was bisexual, and left the family to live with his male lover.

Other than their tragic childhoods, Hiss, tall and elegant, and Chambers, short and plump, seemed to have little in common; that is except for one overarching fact of their existences: they were apparently both spies against the United States for Communist Russia during the 1930's, and perhaps into the 1940's as well.

In 1948, Chambers who claimed to have broken with the American Communist Party in the late 1930's, came forward voluntarily before the House Committee on Un-American Activities, admitted his past espionage activities for the Soviets and accused Hiss of having been a member of the same spy cell. Hiss was said to have personally handed over to Chambers and others classified State Department documents, which the latter gave to his Russian contacts.

Hiss vehemently denied the accusations and sued Chambers. Chambers went to the Justice Department, repeated the allegations and turned over his evidence. The U.S. Government prosecuted Hiss and secured a conviction for perjury. Chambers was the chief prosecution witness under a grant of immunity. Hiss was sent to federal prison for several years, disbarred as an attorney and disgraced as a public official. His brilliant career was in tatters and never repaired. He was finished as a public personage and as a lawyer before reaching the age of fifty.

Chambers wrote a book about the whole affair which not only detailed his and Hiss's spy activities but also offered his own rationale as to why he became a dedicated communist in the first place. It went on to explain, albeit self-servingly, his disillusionment, apostasy and conversion into a staunch anti-communist. He died in the early 1960's, still in his mid-fifties.

Booker had known the basics of the famous and controversial Chambers-Hiss drama of the late 1940's and early 1950's. But for days he had been spending virtually all his waking hours reading Chambers' autobiography, transcripts of the Un-American Activities Committee sessions dealing with the allegations against Hiss, the articles and speeches of Richard M. Nixon about the case, the trial transcripts and as many books and articles on the case as he could get his hands on.

The one fact which impressed Booker more than any other was the stark difference in the roles played by Chambers and Hiss. Though Chambers ate, slept and breathed revolutionary Marxism-Leninism and had become an influential member of the American Communist Party, Hiss's role in the Party was either non-existent or so obscure as to go un-noticed. Yet, as spies, their roles were reversed. Hiss was the high-level operative who marshaled sensitive and secret U.S. Government documents for his Russian contacts while Chambers was in reality little more than a delivery boy, a mule. The key was *access*. Hiss had it to an extraordinary degree, while Chambers had none.

There was little doubt in Booker's mind. If Groundhog was to be caught, they needed to look for a Hiss, not a Chambers. They could, as far as he was concerned, forget about looking among bureau chiefs, middle-managers and department heads at CIA, Military Intelligence, the FBI, the DIA[7] and the State Department. To catch the kind of traitor who learned about the detailed plans for the Bay of Pigs invasion, one would have to concentrate on the top of the pyramid: generals, agency heads, ambassadors, top diplomats, and high public officials of the United States; or those who worked directly under such highly-placed leaders.

Booker gazed distractedly at his expensive Swiss wristwatch, a gift from his rich parents on his graduation from Harvard. It was 0130 hours, a fact which meant nothing to Booker who had no appreciation of late or early in the conventional sense. With his feet up on the coffee table in the living room of his apartment, he grabbed a yellow legal pad off the table and began to write down a profile of Groundhog:

1. Male, early-30's to mid-50's.
2. Intellectual or pseudo intellectual.
3. Self-confident
4. Well-educated or highly competent.
5. Subtly magnetic personality.
6. Non-threatening.
7. Non-ostentatious.
8. Holds high-level job with extraordinary access.
9. Raised in dysfunctional family.

Booker paused momentarily and scratched his head before making a final un-numbered entry on the page:

Dangerous!

---

[7] Defense Intelligence Agency

Part I, Chapter 4

Invictus

Paris, June 2, 1961

The physician, dressed in an elegant Italian silk suit, monogrammed shirt with French cuffs, gold cuff links and silk patterned tie, carried an expensive doctor's bag made of alligator hide, as he hopped aboard the Orient Express—destination Stuttgart, Munich, Salzburg, and eventually Vienna.

Ten steps or so behind him was an athletic-looking young man wearing a suit right off the rack at Robert Hall's. A red cap carried the physician's single suitcase to his private compartment and helped him get settled in. The pursuer stood alertly in the aisle, his back to the row of locked compartments on the side opposite the doctor's compartment, and approximately five feet away.

The young man's name was Rufus Youngblood and he was a member of the United States Presidential Secret Service Unit. His mission, received from a senior grade supervisor at the White House, was twofold. He was to make sure the physician arrived in Vienna safely. And equally important, he was to make sure his doctor's bag also got there, free of theft, damage, or tampering.

The original itinerary called for the doctor to fly to Vienna in the same private jet in which he secretly flew from New York to Paris. But, the aborted attempt by two of Hostile's agents to grab the doctor's bag at the Paris airport's Passport Inspection Center, prompted a change of plans. For his trouble, the hostile who attempted to snatch the bag received a broken arm from the force of the blow administered by Youngblood to the elbow region. The other hostile agent promptly exited the area after first sustaining both a broken nose and a fierce blow to the solar plexus.

The physician was Dr. Max Jacobsen of New York, famous among Hollywood's stars for supplying them with pep pills, diet pills and pain pills. He was now popularly known as 'Dr. Feelgood.'

Since January 12, 1961, Jacobsen's Hollywood clientele, much to their annoyance, were rarely able to reach him in his offices. He now had a demanding patient who occupied the majority of his time and kept him on the road. Rufus Youngblood never referred to that patient by name, but only by the Secret Service's assigned title of 'POTUS,' an acronym for *President of the United States.*

Rufus now stood alertly near Jacobsen's train compartment. A porter had brought him a chair but he would not sit until he felt comfortable that there was no immediate threat. Though a regular member of the Vice Presidential protection team, he had received the present assignment due to his history of exceptional vigilance. He must not fail to squire Jacobsen and his doctor's bag to Vienna—to the building where a critical summit conference was about to start; but first to the suite of John F. Kennedy, the President of the United States.

John F. Kennedy suffered from a variety of ailments, including Addison's disease, intestinal disorders, and chronic back problems. His severe back pain had been treated over the last decade with corticosteroids, which by 1961 had caused his overall health to deteriorate. One of the more serious of his problems was an adrenal insufficiency. During the first six months of 1961 his health problems were particularly vexing: constant pain, prostate problems, sleeplessness and fatigue.

A team of White House physicians treated the underlying illnesses, such as his colitis and Addison's disease, but their efforts had been woefully inadequate in bringing his symptoms under control. He was now, on June 2, 1961, about to face-off with an implacable foe, Premier Nikita Khrushchev of the Soviet Union, in their first serious meeting. The stakes were enormous. The summit was analogous to a fight for the heavy weight championship of the World, the Rocky Marciano-Joe Lewis contest of international power politics. Each man needed to be at the top of his game. The ultimate fate of mankind might well depend upon it.

In the motorcade from the airport to the Vienna Palace of Justice, a robust and smiling Nikita Khrushchev waived confidently to the sparse and generally unenthusiastic crowds. His tepid welcome stood in stark contrast to the tumultuous greeting, usually reserved for royalty, which had been accorded to Kennedy by the throngs at the airport and lining the streets. But Khrushchev was undaunted by the mystique surrounding the handsome and charismatic American.

The Soviet premier was a formidable Chief of State, tough, shrewd, and resourceful. He had survived and triumphed through World War II at Stalingrad and in all of the mutually-destructive political wars of the Kremlin. He was rested, healthy, prepared and aggressive. When the bell rang, he would come charging out of his corner throwing his best lefts and rights at Kennedy and would try to take him down with a round-house punch.

Perception and psychology would figure greatly. The appearance of scoring points against each other would count just as much as the actual outcome of the decisions and agreements. Khrushchev was at the top of his game and ready for the challenge.

The Russian atheist liked thinking of himself as the First Horseman of the Apocalypse, the conqueror, *Invictus*.

Kennedy, on the other hand, carried the burden of his psychological defeat at the Bay of Pigs. As far as his personal fitness was concerned, he was so crippled by back pain that he might not be able to enter the Summit conference room except on crutches. He had also had another of his frequent high fevers in Paris, his previous stop, and his colitis had forced him onto a liquid diet. His face was puffy and his complexion pallid, from a combination of his maladies and medicines. And worst of all, he and his team had lost contact with Jacobsen and his bag of tricks.

Vienna, June 2, 1961, The Royal Hapsburg Hotel Presidential Suite

President John F. Kennedy, 46 years old, lay face down on a rubbing table, draped only by a towel. He held an unlit cigar in his right hand. His long-time aide and Boston crony, Dave Powers, rhythmically massaged his lower back. A cup of unfinished New England clam chowder, now cold, sat on a tray table, amid numerous containers of pills and tubes of ointment. Top administrative aide, Kenneth O'Donnell, worked the phones, chain smoking Marlboros. Ted Sorensen paced the room reviewing and revising Kennedy's planned opening remarks for the Summit Conference. Press Secretary, Pierre Salinger, was desperately seeking to get the Administration's favorite reporter, Scotty Reston of the *New York Times*, and presidential chum and *Washington Post* editor, Ben Bradlee, on the phone—to plant a story on how strong and confident the president felt about the imminent show-down at the summit.

The story would go on to stress the president's optimistic intention to forcefully establish with the Soviet premier a 'framework for mutual cooperation in bringing about arms-control and a real solution to the problem of Berlin.'

Propping himself on his left elbow, Kennedy faced O'Donnell. "Kenny, you better stop calling all those damn nobodies, and get me Clint Baker on the phone now! And if you can't get him, get me Director Hoover. I want them up off their asses and looking for Jacobsen. I made it clear to the Secret Service, the Bureau, and the Agency that I needed him here when I got here. You would think those silly bastards with their vast resources could carry out one simple order. I'll bet that son of a bitch, Hoover, didn't even put out the word."

"I'll try, Mr. President," said O'Donnell calmly.

"And while you're at it, Kenny, tell Evelyn that under no circumstances is she to let Admiral Combs in here until after Jacobsen has arrived and then departed."

Before O'Donnell could respond, the door to the president's inner bedroom opened and the Attorney General, Robert F. Kennedy, briskly entered, accompanied by a fit-looking young man.

"Jack, this is Agent Rufus Youngblood," announced Bobby Kennedy, without preliminaries. "He's got Jacobsen tucked away in a room down the hall."

Swinging his feet around and sitting upright on the table with the towel covering his lower regions, the president winced in pain as he addressed Youngblood,

"Ah, good job Agent. I know you ah... ran into some trouble in Paris but we can talk about that later. Right now please get Jacobsen and bring him in."

But, as Youngblood turned to leave, Bobby Kennedy gently grabbed his arm. "Jack, I think you should let Kenny and I talk to Jacobsen privately, to find out just what he has in that big syringe, before you let him inject it into your back again."

"Now wearing a grim and determined expression, the president responded to his younger brother. "Bobby, only Max Jacobsen's potion is going to give me what I need to get up and walk into that conference on my own, without crutches. And I'll be damned if the President of the United States is going to confront Khrushchev and all those other bastards looking like a fucking invalid. I don't care if all he has in his syringe is horse piss. It's the only thing that works."

"A subdued silence hung over the room. The issue had been settled. Youngblood went and got Jacobsen.

Part I, Chapter 5

Suspects

Bavaria, June 2, 1961

Q took smug satisfaction in the impressive array of powerful men enjoying drinks and female companionship aboard "Invincible," as it cruised down the Isar toward Munich. The guests on board included both bachelors and married men. The roughly equal number of female passengers were all in their twenties or early 30's and none of them were either wives or girlfriends of the male passengers.

Music was provided by a jazz quartet which offered a judicious mix of soft jazz renditions and dance ensembles. The booze flowed freely, the buffet was exquisite and the laughter floated above the deck and once there, rose to gently evaporate in the first dramatic hues of the early summer sunset.

Not a single other CIA station chief anywhere in the world had the cachet to assemble such a powerful group of movers and shakers, Q boasted to himself from his perch on the upper deck. He did not care much for socializing. Small talk annoyed him. His mysterious, withdrawn and non-engaging personality kept people at a distance anyway. He much preferred to sit imperiously above the assemblage and quietly observe their interactions, foibles and follies. There he mentally recorded each and every movement. He missed nothing and he remembered everything.

Q's guests weren't supposed to know his true identity. Their invitation from him came from Foster Wright, president of the U.S.-Western Europe Trade Council, a thin cover organization which didn't actually exist. Most of the invitees just played along.

Below him on deck enjoying the libations and female attentions were a group composed mostly of diplomats and NATO officials. Of course, some of his own underlings mingled with the group as well. Well forward on the starboard side of the craft, Remington Pierce, a CIA agent in Bonn, who employed the cover of cultural attaché at the American Embassy, was

31

introducing a particularly stunning young brunette to Llewellyn Chase, the special presidential envoy to NATO Command at Brussels. Further aft, the United States Deputy Ambassador to France, Charles Wilson Peck, was touching champagne glasses with a fetching red head. Leaning against the stanchion near the stern and engaged in earnest conversation were Colonel Edwin Dabrowski and Clyde Montgomery.

Dabrowski was the Operations officer of the 44th Military Intelligence Group. Montgomery was the top MI-6 official in Western Europe, and heir-apparent to the post of Chief of British Intelligence.

Q's annual cruise gave the attendees an opportunity to mix serious business with serious pleasure. Q chuckled to himself as Chase, casting a furtive look in his direction, apparently rejected the feminine assignation for the time being and politely excused himself. Q sat back in contentment.

Everything was going pretty much as planned. But, there had been one major surprise which had started his mental juices flowing. Standing directly below him was the intriguing Malachy O'Doherty, who owned no particular title or position but was as powerful as anyone else on deck. Mal O'Doherty, a long-time Kennedy family retainer, was a classmate and close friend of the president at Choate and Harvard. Since then no one with the possible exception of brother, Robert Kennedy, had enjoyed a closer relationship with Jack Kennedy.

O'Doherty's function with the president was ill-defined and amorphous. He clearly was charged with carrying out only the most sensitive of assignments, but apparently no one other than Mal and Jack himself knew what those assignments were. Rumors persisted of a slight chill in their relationship, caused by the fact that O'Doherty had been squeezed out of the White House inner circle by Bobby Kennedy, Kenny O'Donnell, and Larry O'Brien, the president's political brain trust.

Q was always bored by such unconfirmed rumors, but he now found himself greatly intrigued by a new puzzle. What was Mal O'Doherty doing floating down the Isar and out of contact with the president, at a time when the latter was engaged in one of the most critical confrontations of his political life?

Q was happy to have this new mystery to solve. It was what he lived for. As the CIA station chief sipped his sloe gin fizz, he reflected on how life was generally good. Power and intrigue were what made everything worthwhile as far as he was concerned, and his world contained plenty of both. But, a single strain of dissonance still marred his life and made it less than perfect. It was that god-damned Reitenhauser. For eight years, the exceptionally tough and talented MI officer had been his chief competitor.

Fred Reitenhauser was no match for Q when it came to sheer political power and access. But Reitenhauser had something special, an equalizer, which no other top spy master in Western Europe had: a mole buried deep in the Soviet firmament with unparalleled access to category '1A' intelligence. The highly disciplined Q quickly suppressed the wave of envy which swept over him. The mole might be totally anonymous *now*, but how much longer would that anonymity last in the face of the steady ascendancy of the Groundhog?

Munich, June 3, 1961

Fred Reitenhauser was disturbed but not surprised by Carlton's latest message just retrieved by an Ops Support man from a downtown Munich dead-drop. It was written in code but its translation could not have been more stark.

> "Soviets plan sabotage of Vienna Summit. Will seek to disable American president. Groundhog will lead the charge. His GRU cover name is Jurist II. Q may have info which will uncover his identity."

The CO read the message again. What did Carlton mean by *sabotage*? Was he referring to *physical* sabotage? An explosion, or some kind of actual attack? Or was he using the word figuratively?

And in what sense would Hostile try to *disable* President Kennedy? Again, would it be physical? Or something psychological, strategic, or even political?

Carlton's communications were always precise, so this ambiguity was unexpected. Perhaps he was simply repeating someone else's message verbatim, and he had no further information to offer. If so, who had written the message? Carlton must believe that the message was highly credible and important, or else he wouldn't have put Groundhog's official cover name in writing. Then again, Carlton had never lacked for balls.

The reference to Q in the message caused Fred to pick up the telex that had come through earlier in the day from Group's Counterintelligence Division, containing the guest list for Q's annual floating bordello.

Ever since Booker had completed his likely profile of Groundhog, Reitenhauser had become suspicious of just about every highly placed diplomat, military man, politico, bureaucrat and official in any way connected to the State Department, the Defense Department, NATO or the U.N.

He gazed at the list of names with great interest. The VIPs were listed on the first page and included:

```
----------------------------------

1. Charles Wilson Peck, Deputy U.S.
Ambassador to France

2. Llewellyn Chase, Special Presidential
Envoy to NATO

3. Clyde Montgomery, Chief of Britain's
MI-6 for Continental Europe

4. Remington Pierce, Cultural attache at
the U.S. Embassy in Bonn

5. Colonel Edwin Dabrowski, Group's
Operations Officer

6. Jurgen Kirtgaard, Under Secretary
General of the United Nations for
Collective Security

7. John Paul Byrne, a chief assistant to
McGeorge Bundy, National Security
Advisor; and perhaps most interestingly

8. Malachy O'Doherty, confidant, spy,
fixer and jack-of-all-trades for John F.
Kennedy, the President of the United
States.

----------------------------------
```

Then of course, there was Q himself, who might be the most suspicious of all.

Fred Reitenhauser had survived combat in France, Belgium, and Germany during WWII; the Korean War and the Cold War for seventeen years, by leaving nothing to chance. As soon as he had broken the seals of the four horsemen envelopes, he had dispatched Art LeBron to Austria to conduct a series of meetings with Agent 14332, to plan the protection of the president and his agenda at the upcoming Summit.

Vienna was firmly within Munich Station's jurisdiction, and the 409th's job was made easier by the deep and sophisticated network of covert operatives under 14332's control. By the time the formal sessions got underway on June 3, 1961, Agent 14332 had penetrated every facet of the proceedings. His sub-agents were in place as concierges, bellhops, desk clerks, waiters, elevator operators, cooks, door men, and hotel security officials. They were also stenographers, registrars, technicians, maintenance men, physicians, nurses and wine stewards.

The United States president and his entourage had absolutely no idea of the scope and depth of the protection Reitenhauser had arranged. If Hostile had any thoughts of poisoning the president's food or beverages, planting bombs or attempting an assassination, they were fooling themselves. The Secret Service guards assigned to the president and his party could have spent the three days sightseeing, and the president would have been no less safe.

Politics, policy and public perception, however, were an entirely different matter. Reitenhauser was convinced that Khrushchev and his minions (probably aided significantly by Jurist II) were seeking to lay an intricate trap for Kennedy, with the aim of embarrassing him, disrupting his presentations of U.S. positions, intimidating him by an uninterrupted verbal assault and holding him up to ridicule in the eyes of the world. As to what other tricks the Soviets might have up their sleeves, Reitenhauser could only speculate.

At 1400 hours, O'Malley, LeBron, and Booker arrived for a meeting at the major's office. Quick greetings were exchanged, and Fred got right to the point.

Handing each of the men a photostatic copy of Q's guest list, the CO explained to O'Malley and LeBron that Booker had developed a possible profile for Groundhog. He then read aloud the ten profile traits. He next asked each man to check off on the first page of Q's guest list, the name of each individual who might fit Booker's profile.

All three men checked off the following names: Peck, Chase, and Kirtgaard.

LeBron and Booker added Pierce as well. O'Malley added Byrne.

The CO dismissed his subordinates after collecting their lists.

O'Malley was off to Munich Airport with German desk chief, Mitchell Blake, for their flight to Vienna, where they would serve as the CO's eyes and ears on the ground

When his subordinates were gone, Reitenhauser sat at his desk for several minutes, puffing on his pipe and thinking.

He then wrote down his own selections of those whose character, personality traits, and backgrounds were in alignment with the profile that Booker had developed for Groundhog.

His own list contained six names:

MONTGOMERY
CHASE
BYRNE
PIERCE
O'DOHERTY
Q

Chase was the only person who appeared on all four lists. That was interesting, but nothing more than that at this early stage.

As Fred was first turning the notion over in his mind, Art LeBron ducked into his office long enough to drop off a sealed envelope. Inside was another guest list, compliments of 14332. It contained the names and titles of the invitees to the Soviet state dinner for the chief attendees of the Summit Conference.

The guest list from the state dinner had six names in common with Q's guest list:

Clyde Montgomery
Llewellyn Chase
John Paul Byrne
Remington Pierce
Malachy O'Doherty
Foster Wright (i.e. "Q")

There was Chase's name again. Coincidence? Maybe. Or, maybe not. It was time for a little more digging.

The next morning at 0730 hours Fred and Gerda hopped aboard a cable car headed for the old city of Munich where they would enjoy a sumptuous Bavarian breakfast at the home of Gerda's parents, Dieter and Gertrude Höltzmuller. Fred just had time to purchase a copy of *Suddendeutsche Zeitung*, less than a minute before the cable car took off. Sitting back on one of the comfortable plastic seats he began reading the Summit coverage which consumed the first six pages of the newspaper. Stunned by the sheer pomposity of the dramatic coverage and half-page photos, Fred almost missed the two inch by four inch news item buried at the bottom of page 8.

New York Physician Likely to Recover.

Renowned American physician, Max Jacobsen, and a dinner companion, Rufus Youngblood, were reported by treating physicians at Vienna City Hospital, as likely to recover after suffering severe food poisoning yesterday at the Royal Hapsburg Hotel.

Fred was fully aware of the important roles that were to be played by Jacobsen and Youngblood in Vienna. This was bad news. He suspected that rather than Hostile's having penetrated 14332's protective ring, it got to these two key players because their anonymity had kept them outside the ring in the first place. The implementers of Invictus had disabled and taken out of commission two key persons in the president's circle of protection.

The cable car slowed as it approached the ancient stone gate at Karlsplatz, symbolic entrance to the Old City. As Fred and Gerda hopped off, the CO's thoughts were elsewhere.

He spoke to himself below the threshold of audibility. "Horst (i.e. 14332) and his people are all well and good, but I need my own man in this fight. We've been getting our ass kicked and it's time to go on the offensive."

Part I, Chapter 6

A Knight's Quest

Twenty-five year old Staff Sergeant Kázimir Penchak was not so much a victim of oppression as its product. Man's cruel and unrepentant subjugation of other human beings had actually molded and animated his nature. As an infant, his developmental environment was marked by fear, sorrow and loneliness instead of the more common warmth, protectiveness and parental nurturing.

As a pre-teen in 1948, Káz experienced a passage to adulthood and gained the perspective of a survivor before even entering Junior High School.

Now, in 1961, his body was in its mid-twenties but his soul was of the ages. He was the Neanderthal who either slew the great predator, or was torn apart by its teeth and claws. He was the Roman centurion who either killed the Visigoth, or died on the stranger's blade, a thousand miles from home. He was the Ukrainian slave laborer, who either escaped his Nazi captors or died from exhaustion under the weight of their rocks. A sense of danger was fused with the marrow of his bones, and privation was etched on his heart.

But Káz Penchak had sublimated all of that, and now as he raced his Saab down the Autobahn from Würzburg to Munich, his thoughts were fixed only on the fact that the CO needed him for a mission. He wished Reitenhauser had told him more than just that he was "going on the road, so pack a bag." But the unpredictability of covert intelligence was one of the things that got his juices flowing. He loved its spontaneity.

"I better get gas," Káz said to himself, "and I'm not paying these Autobahn prices."

He exited the Autobahn near the town of Dachau, about two miles north of Munich, and headed down a suburban road toward one of his favorite service stations. Without the slightest warning the mere name, 'Dachau,' triggered a powerful word association process in his subconscious. Instantly and involuntarily his mind was immersed in his

Czechoslovakian parents' most commonly-told story of his childhood, how they were all forced to flee the Sudetenland for America in 1938, when he was only a year old.

His parents had been political activists who had opposed the annexation by Hitler of the Sudetenland, and its severance from the rest of Czechoslovakia. Betrayed by ethnic German neighbors, the Penchaks had to either flee, or face a Nazi firing squad. His mother had never fully recovered from the grief and trauma of having to abandon their home, her parents, brothers and sisters, and everything else that had forged their anchor in life. Káz's mother had died in 1955 at the age of 46.

In 1948, Kázimir, age 11, spent several months at the home of his paternal grandparents in the Sudetenland, which had been liberated from German rule upon the collapse of the Third Reich in 1945. Both his grandfather, Tomás Penchak, and uncles, Milan and Vaclav, were ardent followers of Jan Masaryk, the Czech foreign minister and leading progressive politician. Masaryk had been a member of the multi-party National Front Government.

February of 1948 heralded the infamous *Czech Coup*. The Soviet-backed Czech Communist Party took over the government. Jan Masaryk was found dead in the courtyard below his office window. The official cause of death was suicide but there was strong evidence to suggest that he was pushed to his death by a Russian intelligence officer. At roughly the same time, Tomás Penchak was found hanging from one of the beams in his garage. Káz was devastated and clung to his grandmother for support.

Next in the rapid-fire sequence of events was the murder of Augustin Schramm, an official of the Czech Secret Communist Police, widely believed to be behind the death of Masaryk. As retaliation by the communists, Milan Penchak was shot to death the next day. To avoid a similar fate, Vaclav Penchak fled Czechoslovakia a few days later in disguise with Kázimir in tow, posing as his eleven year old son. They traveled with forged documents prepared by the anti-communist Czech underground. It was 1949 before they arrived safely at Newark Airport.

Káz's cousin Milan Choc, a young philosophy student in Prague, had been arrested in the summer of 1948 for the murder of Schramm. Milan, who was Káz's favorite relative, had been tortured and executed.

As Káz pulled his Saab into the service station, the flood of unwanted memories produced a sharp pain in his chest, as if he had just been stabbed in the heart with an ice-pick. He reflexively took one hand off the steering wheel and clutched his chest as he brought the car to a halt. When the pain subsided, he moved his hand to below his left armpit where he felt the reassuring presence of his Colt .45 revolver in its holster, under his windbreaker.

As Káz often did, he spoke to his weapon, "With the help of God, old friend, we will shoot many KGB and Red Guard agents, in their foreheads, eyes and balls."

He then made the sign of the cross.

The jump from the CIA-owned Cessna was effortless and Káz floated majestically from an azure-blue sky to earth. He landed in a large clearing in the Austrian National Forest about twenty miles from Vienna. Hiding his parachute and jump suit, he talked himself through his mental check list: *knapsack with change of clothes and shaving gear, Swiss Army Knife, masking tape, 48 inches of rope, full canteen, first-aid kit, map and compass.*

Then he mentally checked off the items on his person: *false passport and international driver's license showing him to be Richard Havel, an American tourist; money; pistol; silencer; stiletto and spare .38 revolver, in ankle holster.*

He pulled on a pair of black-framed eyeglasses which were part of his cover. He wore a golf jacket, khaki pants with decorative belt, blue plaid button-down shirt, and tan bucks. A camera around his neck completed his ensemble. In one pocket of his jacket were his passport and license. In the other was a typed list with six names on it and nothing else. Those names, listed from top to bottom, were:

> Clyde Montgomery
> John Paul Byrne
> Remington Pierce
> Malachy O'Doherty
> Foster Wright (alias Q)
> Llewellyn Chase

Káz reviewed the list one final time, removed his lighter from his jacket pocket, lit fire to the paper. He dropped the burned remnants on the ground, and then watched until he was certain that the document had been completely consumed.

Then, he gazed at his compass and set out on a northeasterly course. In about two hours he would reach the town of Brünst, where he would catch a bus for Vienna.

PART II — THE SECOND SEAL OF THE RED HORSE

WAR

"When the lamb opened
the second seal, I heard
the second living creature
say, 'Come and see!' Then another
horse came out, a fiery red
one. It's rider was given power
to take peace from the earth
and to make men slay each other.
To him was given a large sword."

Revelation 6

Part II, Chapter 1

Ill Winds

Vienna, 3 June 1961, 0800 hours

Káz mingled with the gaggle of onlookers and media people. The early attendees at the Summit Conference would soon begin arriving at the Austrian Palace of Justice. Káz was six foot three, which usually eliminated any problem for him in finding a position from which he could see his target. As usual, he now had an unobstructed view of the stone steps in front of the neo-classical edifice, which would house the momentous proceedings. The formal meetings were to begin at 1130 hours.

Within minutes a black limousine turned right off of Ringstrasse and into the long half-moon driveway which widened in front of the imposing building. From Káz's advantageous position in a small parking lot for officials only, perhaps fifteen feet from the entrance, he saw the curbside rear door of the vehicle open and Soviet Minister of Foreign Affairs, Andrei Gromyko, emerge. He was immediately followed by Deputy Soviet Premier, Anastas Mikoyan, and then a third man whom Káz did not immediately recognize. Yet something about the man... his presence, bearing, posture—Káz couldn't really say what—was familiar. He quickly snapped four pictures in succession, each from a slightly different angle, of the three men, now conversing at the entrance with a group of official-looking greeters.

Káz closed his eyes and tried to visualize the pictures shown to him over and over by the CO of the men on the list of six. At first they were all out of focus in his memory, but gradually, one by one, they morphed into sharpened images. But Káz could not match any of them with the third man in front of him. But of course, he couldn't, thought Káz, as he shook away the cobwebs from his mind. All of those men are far too visible and prominent to be seen in public getting out of a vehicle with Gromyko.

Then from the recesses of memory it came to him, evoking a chilling flashback. This man was older, grayer, and sported a mustache. Otherwise the build, height, posture, and facial profile were the same. Káz had no doubt of the man's identity. Standing only fifteen feet away was the reviled 'Butcher of Prague,' the communist spy and torturer, Antonin Slezak. The man who had tortured and executed Káz's innocent cousin, Milan Choc, in 1948. The man against whom Káz had sworn vengeance.

The time for revenge had finally arrived. Káz turned away from the building entrance and pulled his .45 from its holster. Holding it at his side, he estimated the distance and angle to the target's heart. It was not a particularly difficult shot. Of course, Káz would probably be killed by the armed guards surrounding the Gromyko party. That would be preferable to capture.

The thought of dying did not give him pause. He had long ago reconciled himself to sacrificing his own life in order to exact retribution against the murderers who had killed his grandfather, uncle, and cousin. Slezak was number one on his list.

Káz gripped his weapon firmly and began raising it. In less than ten seconds he would dispatch the evil butcher to hell. Less than a minute after that, he too would leave this earth. He hoped to be reunited with his mother, and other martyred family members. The cold steel felt good in his right hand as he raised the gun higher, all the while checking to make sure his shot would be unobstructed. But he wasn't really worried. He could probably squeeze off a half-dozen rounds before he was brought down. In fact, he could probably shoot Gromyko too.

It was this latter thought which pulled Káz out of his trance. What was he *thinking*? If he shot anyone, he would destroy the mission, which was far more important than any personal quest for vengeance.

He stood for another handful of seconds, weighing the pleasure of shooting Slezak against the needs of the mission. At last, he let out a quiet breath, and slipped the pistol into his jacket pocket, zipping it closed.

Another day... There would be another day. Sooner or later, the butcher would wander into his sights again.

Suddenly, Slezak, after saying his farewells to Gromyko, Mikoyan, and the greeters, got back into the rear seat of the limo. The limo pulled away and began to drive slowly in the direction of Ringstrasse, one of Vienna's major boulevards.

Káz quickly went from one official car to another in the small parking lot, looking for one with the driver's door unlocked. He hit pay dirt on the sixth try, when the door of a blue Audi yielded and opened easily. Káz jumped inside, crossed the wires under the dash board, achieved ignition and took off in pursuit of the limousine.

He didn't have to tail the limo for long. It stopped ten minutes later in front of the Royal Hapsburg Hotel. Slezak got out and entered through the main entrance. Káz parked the car on the street and followed him into the hotel. Slezak walked purposefully through the lobby to a small gift shop adjacent to the main bank of elevators. A second man emerged from an elevator a few seconds later, entered the shop and walked directly up to Slezak. The two shook hands as the second man inserted a small envelope into Slezak's right suit coat pocket. Simultaneously, Káz, who had adjusted the F-stop on his camera to allow for the darker lighting conditions, snapped a picture of the exchange. The two men quickly exited the gift shop and headed in different directions. As they emerged, Káz had a full frontal view of each man's face. He had no problems with recognition this time. The second man's face was well-known to him. It was that of Foster Wright, better known as "Q."

Vienna 3 June 1961, 0815 hours

After five minutes or so of greetings, small-talk, pouring coffee and putting fruit and pastries on their plates, the eight men took seats around the table in Conference Room A on the fourth floor of the Royal Hapsburg Hotel. Taking a seat at one end of the table was McGeorge Bundy, National Security Advisor to the President of the United States. At the opposite end sat Secretary of State, Dean Rusk. Seated on both sides in no particular order, were George Kennan, Special Advisor to the Secretary of State and author of the U.S.'s policy of 'Containment;' Llewellyn Chase, Presidential Envoy to NATO; Paul Nitze, Assistant Secretary of Defense for International Affairs; John Paul Byrne, IV, Deputy to the National Security Advisor; Walt Rostow, Member of the National Security Council; and personal advisor to the president, Malachy O'Doherty.

Though the term was not yet in vogue in 1961, the group had assembled for what in modern parlance would be called a "power breakfast."

Bundy was the unofficial chairman of the gathering and led off the discussion. "So, gentlemen, what do we hear?"

All eyes turned in the direction of John Paul Byrne. Although holding the title of Deputy National Security Advisor, no one doubted for an instant his true role, that of chief intelligence operative for their Group of Eight. Byrne didn't just *happen* to be a former CIA covert agent. Bundy had chosen him as his deputy for that very reason.

Suave, debonair, with an exquisite Patrician bearing, the native of Sharon, Connecticut was the most recent Byrne in a long line of Connecticut Yankees dating back to the mid-sixteen hundreds. His original New World ancestors were maritime merchants and ship builders. But there had been no generations of idle rich in the Byrne line of descendants. It seemed that each succeeding generation was more successful than the one before it, with no dilution of the gene pool, in no small measure because Byrne men married only the daughters of other aristocrats, with similar breeding and education.

The twentieth-century generation of Byrne descendants was rich beyond all imagining, with a fortune said to exceed that of the Kennedys of Massachusetts.

By World War I, the transition from manufacturing merchant vessels to building battleships, aircraft carriers and submarines was complete. The World War II build-up had made *J. P. Byrne & Company* a national institution.

John Paul Byrne IV had been sent to Exeter and Yale by parental choice. By his own choice, he sought and obtained a commission as an ensign in Navy Intelligence upon graduation from Yale with a major in calculus. After six years in the Navy, serving mostly in the Pacific, he left to join the CIA. There he stayed for eight years, with his last assignment at Langley being that of Liaison to the National Security Council during the entire second term of the Eisenhower Administration. Now at the age of thirty eight, his career had taken a giant step forward, right into a large corner office in the Executive Office Building.

Byrne spoke with perfect syntax and precise diction in economical, yet elegant, sentences. "Mr. Ambassador, your expressed hope that the president and Chairman Khrushchev would begin to create an environment of mutual trust here has gotten off to a bad start. Last night, Khrushchev met with the Politburo and announced his intention to bludgeon President Kennedy at every opportunity. He told them that the president was weakened by the Bay of Pigs disaster, and that he would take full advantage of that fact."

Leaning back in his chair, the scholarly George Kennan responded. "That was only *part* of what I told President Kennedy. I also told him to keep his expectations low."

"Just a second!" O'Doherty snapped. "Are you saying that we should aim for *failure*, rather than *success*?"

Taken aback by O'Doherty's bluntness, Kennan was momentarily speechless.

Sensing his old friend's discomfort, Paul Nitze spoke up. "Those of us who have been dealing with the Commies for fifteen years, know that it is not as simple as black versus white, or success versus failure."

Not eager to take on the tough and combative Nitze in an area where the latter had far superior knowledge, O'Doherty elected not to respond. At least for the time being.

Llewellyn Chase was the next to speak. "Khrushchev can say any kind of nonsense he wants. Words are no match for ICBMs, and his peasant crudeness is no defense to our Polaris submarines. Talk is cheap. We've all heard his bluster before. I try not to laugh."

Secretary of State Rusk nodded in agreement, while Walt Rostow's face wore an expression of shocked skepticism. He couldn't believe how glib and naïve Chase was. To dismiss Khrushchev as nothing more than a peasant was the height of folly. The German generals hadn't seen him that way when he had commanded the defense of the Ukraine during WWII. And he currently had a hundred divisions of infantry spread all along the Iron Curtain. That was no laughing matter. For the Secretary of State to nod in agreement was even more shocking.

Fortunately, Bundy interceded to set the record straight in his typical deadly serious, yet low-key, manner. "Khrushchev is *not* just talk. Before joining you this morning, I personally informed the president that our reconnaissance planes out of Hamburg have detected five crack infantry divisions—three Soviet, and two East German—on the march from Dresden to the East German border. They were accompanied by two hundred and fifty tanks."

Bundy then looked at each man to gauge his reaction to the news he had just reported.

The two experienced and savvy cold warriors, Nitze and Kennan, clearly tensed up, but showed no sign of surprise. Rusk's face registered surprise and alarm. Chase appeared to feign surprise. Byrne's face was impassive but his eyes burned with a new, hot intensity. O'Doherty appeared totally indifferent to the news, while the astute Rostow simply nodded knowingly.

Vienna 3 June 1961 0930 hours

In the gift shop, Káz purchased a souvenir Austrian National Ski Team cap and placed it on his head, further enhancing his aura as a young tourist. While at the cash register he spied John Paul Byrne emerge from an elevator and walk quickly to the news stand near the front entrance. After making a purchase, Byrne leaned against a post, where he began reading a newspaper, in what appeared to be rapt concentration.

Byrne stood out in a crowd and Káz was not the only one to notice the handsome American. Two striking blond women, dressed casually and carrying the look of young Scandinavians, had followed him with their eyes from the time he got off the elevator. They now had strategically situated themselves no more than ten feet from where he stood. The ever-alert Byrne appeared to pay them no notice and they soon walked away. Reputed to be one of Washington's most eligible bachelors, Byrne had never been publicly linked with any one particular woman.

Káz moved out into the lobby and sat fiddling with his camera but with one eye on the bank of four elevators. After a while he noticed from the overhead floor indicators that one elevator had remained stationary on the 4th floor for several minutes. Finally, it began moving and when it reached the ground floor a single occupant emerged: a short, nervous-looking, forty-something man, dressed in a shabby suit and carrying a well-worn briefcase.

One thing Káz knew was Eastern Europeans. He was instantly able to distinguish a Pole from a Czechoslovak, and a Bulgarian from an Albanian. This man was a Russian, probably a Georgian. He was fidgety and seemed distracted. He looked furtively around the lobby and moved toward the exit. Káz knew instinctively that he needed to follow him. Intuitively, he took the nervous little man for some sort of a courier on an important mission.

The fleet-footed Russian was already half a city block away before Káz reached the side-walk. "Shit, I can't let this guy get away."

But, Káz knew he couldn't run either, lest he attract attention and place his cover in jeopardy. Now a group of school children in front of him further impeded his progress. The emotional Czech-American swore in frustration under his breath, believing he was about to blow the most important assignment of his young life. The little Russian was lengthening the distance between them. "I'm losing him. Screw this!" Káz took off running at full speed in pursuit of his quarry.

Now Káz had attracted attention! Two tough-looking security types crossing the busy street in the direction of the Russian quickened their pace. Káz, the Russian and the two new participants were on a collision course. So intent was Káz on the pursuit of the courier that he had not even noticed the two newcomers to the drama.

By running full-out he was gaining on his fugitive and it would only be a matter of about ten seconds or so before he caught up to him. For a second he lost sight of the Russian as a car turned into the side-street in front of him. And when the car had passed, the little man was gone. In great distress, Káz reached the spot where he had last seen the Russian. Looking about he noticed the entrance to a narrow alley a few feet ahead. Drawing his .45, Káz placed his back against a store window and edged slowly toward the alley entrance. Once there he held his weapon vertically in a two-handed grip and quickly peeked into the alley, without exposing his body.

About fifteen feet inside the alley, one of the security types held the Russian firmly with one big hand over his mouth while the other injected him in the arm with a large hypodermic needle.

Káz was stunned and speechless as the man holding the Russian let him slip to the ground. "Hi Káz," said O'Malley. Blake just smiled and waved as he placed the hypodermic back in its case. "We'll take it from here," said O'Malley softly as he picked up the Russian's briefcase. "But if you hadn't started running, we probably wouldn't have noticed that you were chasing this guy. He'll be unconscious for about an hour so you can just go back to whatever your assignment is here. Good job Káz."

Llewellyn Chase strutted quickly toward the entrance to the presidential suite with his harried-looking aide, Henry Fuchs, about three steps behind. Fuchs was weighed down by the heavy salmon-colored files he carried under each arm. Two Secret Service men confronted Chase at the door but after an interlude of questioning, examining credentials and checking inside, Chase was permitted to enter. Fuchs had to wait out in the hall. Pushing his glasses back on the sweaty bridge of his nose, Fuchs managed to catch his breath after several seconds. He didn't dare put the heavy portfolios down, notwithstanding that he stood no more than five feet from the United States Secret Service.

In his first week at Georgetown School of Foreign Service, he was taught that if important files or documents are entrusted to your possession, you do not relinquish control over them unless it is a matter of life or death, and sometimes not even then. Fuchs leaned awkwardly against the wall, trying to get a better grip on the bulky files. Perhaps he had taken the admonition of his Georgetown instructor a bit too literally. But Fuchs was not paid by Uncle Sam to make decisions on his own. He was paid to take orders from his superiors and to carry them out without deviating from the training manual.

Chase was a supercilious and demanding boss who was grossly inconsiderate of his employees. His subordinates invariably bore the brunt of the displaced anger Chase felt toward someone else. His convenient whipping boy right now was Fuchs. Chase had been chewing him out since the second he walked out of the meeting with the '*Group of Eight*.' His verbal abuse of Fuchs was diffuse and essentially incoherent.

But interspersed with his rants against Fuchs were sporadic complaints about what was really bothering him. "The president told Bundy and Byrne about the Eastern bloc troops on the move without even bothering to fill me in. I'm his envoy to NATO, and he leaves me in the dark! Boy, that burns my ass! And that fucking Rostow, looking at me like I'm some kind of callow school boy who forgot to do his homework. That sanctimonious prick!"

Fuchs made no comments when Chase went into one of his frequent tirades. It wasn't his place. He was assumed to lack both the standing and background to have an opinion worth consideration.

Chase frequently boasted about his gilt-edge education at Wellsley, Princeton, and Oxford, where he had studied under a Rhodes scholarship. Chase had also come out of the State Department Honors Program.

Fuchs had none of those things going for him. His lusterless early education was at Trenton Vocational High School, followed by four years at Camden State.

Of course, Henry Fuchs was not completely without bragging rights. To the surprise of everyone who knew him, he had scored in the top 100th of one percent among college seniors in the national graduate record exams for 1948. This obscure but significant distinction had earned him an unlikely acceptance by the Georgetown School of Foreign Service.

Vienna June 3, 1961 0945 hours

To say that President Kennedy was distressed by McGeorge Bundy's report of Eastern bloc troop movements would be an understatement. In the sitting room of his suite he had assembled Bundy, Rostow, Nitze, Rusk, Kennan, Chase, Robert Kennedy and Byrne. One of the president's main strengths, however, was his composure, and the only sign of his consternation was in his eyes, which flashed with a combination of anger and confusion. And although he would never admit it to anyone other than Dave Powers and brother Bobbie, Max Jacobsen's illness and hospitalization was causing him even greater problems. Having missed his early morning shot from the New York doctor, Kennedy was practically crippled with pain. Yet, he somehow tried to keep it all together. When his back was injured during World War II as a Japanese torpedo hit his PT boat, Kennedy was able to tolerate the pain through a process of disassociation. It was a trick he had learned during his many boyhood illnesses. Through meditation he removed his mind from the locale of the pain. He was doing it now as he sat in a straight-back chair facing his advisors. The disassociation, however, provided only temporary relief and as he addressed the assembled group, one of the White House physicians was on his way up the elevator to give Kennedy a shot of Demerol.

"Good morning Gentlemen, I'll keep this brief. I have sent my special Counsel, Malachy O'Doherty, to the Soviet Conference headquarters with a message for Chairman Khrushchev. The message states that unless all Eastern bloc troop movements cease immediately, we will cancel the Summit.

"As some of you know, we received advance warning from U.S. Army Intelligence in Munich of a Russian plan to disable our efforts at these meetings. Unfortunately, their intelligence turned out to be right on the mark."

"Mac, I want you and your group to stay in session until you get further word from me. While you wait, you are to prepare a list of options in case we have to cancel the conference. And don't waste any time with lengthy debate. It's now 10:00 A.M. and we are due at the Palace of Justice at 11:30 for the kick-off of the proceedings. That will be all."

Rather than rising to his feet, the president remained seated while the others, with the exception of Attorney General Kennedy, filed out. The president did not want them to see him being lifted to his feet by Powers and O'Donnell, while he grimaced in pain.

Ted O'Malley and Mitch Blake sat in their hotel room listening to the recording retrieved from the Russian courier's briefcase.

"Do you believe this? That's McGeorge Bundy's voice, Mitch. And from the first names being used, it sounds like Rusk, Nitze, Kennan and other top guys were there too.

Blake, equally astounded, replied, "Chase is there also. I've heard him speak at enough NATO forums to recognize his voice."

Stopping the tape recorder for a minute, O'Malley examined the entries printed on the plastic container. "This recording was just made forty five minutes ago. How in hell were the Russians able to tape one of our high-level meetings with security being as tight as it is? Every room in use is being constantly swept for bugs."

"Yeah," said Blake, "but the security teams would not have checked the guys at the meeting. Any one of them could have carried a tape recorder in on his person or in a briefcase."

"You got it, Mitch. Apparently, there's a traitor in our midst and he's uncomfortably close to POTUS... Maybe Groundhog is actually one of the Group of Eight. We don't even have time to go through channels with this. We have to try to put this tape right in the president's hands, *now!*"

Vienna, June 3, 1961, 11:15 a.m.

Fate's negative momentum seemed to reverse itself in the hour after President Kennedy dismissed the Group of Eight. By 11:00 A.M., the Soviet and East German troops had halted their march toward the border. Word had been received that Max Jacobsen and Rufus Youngblood would be released from the hospital that evening. O'Malley had managed to talk his way through the various protective shields to hand Kennedy the tape recording personally, and the President of the United States was feeling considerably better after receiving a double-strength shot of Demerol in his lower back. Hopefully, that would hold him in good stead until Jacobsen could administer his magic elixir that night, or in the morning.

Kennedy still had many weighty things on his mind: the shooting of the Congolese diplomats, the violence at the Brandenburg gate, the warning about Soviet intentions, Khrushchev's stated intent to wage verbal warfare at the Summit, the apparent poisoning of Jacobsen and Youngblood and, most critically, the possible presence of a traitor within the Group of Eight. The FBI had already been contacted and interviews of some of the eight men and their staffs would begin that afternoon.

As far as Kennedy was concerned, the two aides, chosen to accompany him to the conference from the beginning, were above suspicion. Dressed in dark-somber business suits, the president, Secretary of State Dean Rusk, and Under-Secretary of Defense Paul Nitze, entered a black limousine accompanied by three Secret Service agents at 1100 hours.

Part II, Chapter 2

A Dangerous Gambit

Something about the austere yet masterful portraits of a line of Hapsburg monarchs foretold the perilous confrontation about to begin. Hanging on the gray walls of the Hall of Justice, the paintings were icons of the Austrian-Hungarian Empire, now banished from the earth by dint of war, greed, and prideful arrogance.

As the technicians made the final adjustments to the microphones on each side of the long conference table and the stenographers settled into their places behind their short-hand machines, Soviet Premier Nikita Khrushchev and his two top advisors, Andrei Gromyko, and Anastas Mikoyan, stood waiting behind their chairs. At 11:30 A.M., John F. Kennedy, accompanied by Dean Rusk and Paul Nitze[8], entered the hall and walked swiftly to the side of the conference table opposite the Russians.

President Kennedy and Chairman Khrushchev shook hands, exchanged brief pleasantries and sat down facing each other on opposite sides of the table. The American advisors in turn took seats opposite their Soviet counterparts. There was no audience. The six men plus two stenographers and two Russian-English translators were the sole occupants of the cavernous hall.

Khrushchev wore a rigid, smiling veneer over deep facial lines etched in ill-will.

Only a Da Vinci could have done justice to Kennedy's stiff smile—an alloy of apprehension, grim premonition and mistrust—further infused with physical pain.

The 67 year old Khrushchev spoke first. "I heard you were a young and promising man in politics."

---

[8] Nitze had been chosen by Kennedy because of his expertise in the arms talks.

"Well, Chairman Khrushchev, let's hope that this meeting shows its own promise for a better understanding of the problems confronting our two nations."

"Yes, I too wish the conversations to be useful," was Khrushchev's limp but seemingly harmless follow-up. "But the first time I met you, you were a bit too young for such weighty matters."

Kennedy was uncomfortable with the obvious attempts by Khrushchev to emphasize the age and experience gap between them, and attempted to neutralize the Russian's play of the age card. "I've aged considerably since then."

This led to Khrushchev's pointed rejoinder. "I would be happy to share my years with you—"

On the surface the exchanges seemed like harmless banter but Nitze, the seasoned high-stakes negotiator, did not like the tone that was being set.

Then Khrushchev, leaning his elbows on the table, and thrusting himself forward toward Kennedy, made it worse. "It's a shame that the young always want to look older and older people want to look younger."

Changing the subject, Kennedy ventured, "Mr. Chairman, I think we need to spend our time at this meeting trying to find "ways and means of not permitting situations where the two countries would be committed to actions involving their security or endangering peace."

Khrushchev's eyes lit up as he readied himself to pounce on Kennedy's mild words. He spoke in a near shout. "It is not our country's fault that we do not have peace. The United States wants agreements that are at the expense of other peoples."

Kennedy managed to stay composed as he winced at the Russian's stinging rebuke.

But Khrushchev was just getting warmed up. "Your Secretary of State under Eisenhower, John Foster Dulles, wanted to destroy communism. There will never be peace between our two nations until we accept each other's systems."

Kennedy was not about to let that one go by unchallenged. He stated his rebuttal in an even but firm tone. "It is not the United States that is unsettling the global balance of power or seeking to overturn existing spheres of control, but the Soviet Union. This is a matter of very serious concern to us."

These words either incensed Khrushchev, or he feigned anger in order to seize the opportunity to escalate his attack on Kennedy. With a reddening face he continued his harangue. "The Soviet Union has not aimed to impose its will on any country. But nevertheless, Communism will triumph because history is on our side."

In the face of the monumental lie that the Soviets had not sought to impose their will on any other country, Kennedy still stuck to a moderate tone, though he too was beginning to take on a reddish hue, possibly because of rising blood pressure.

"The challenge, Mr. Khrushchev, is to find means of averting conflict in areas where our two sides have clashing interests."

"True" said Khrushchev, "but if we face a clash of ideas, communism will win."

Rather than directly rebutting Khrushchev's boast of inevitable victory, Kennedy somewhat weakly tried to return to his original point. "A clash of ideas should not be allowed to produce a conflict of interests which can lead to a military confrontation."

But Khrushchev had no intention of yielding his combative stance. "Are you suggesting that any expansion of communist influence would be seen as a reason for Soviet-American conflict?"

Before Kennedy could respond, the Soviet premier answered his own question. "It is wrong to believe that the spread of communism will threaten world peace."

Khrushchev then embarked upon a long-winded discourse on communist ideology, all the while attacking capitalism as a corrupt and exploitative system.

Without showing it, Kennedy was becoming more and more chagrined by where things were headed. He needed to divert the discussion away from the Russian's philosophical diatribe without delay. Otherwise the intended bilateral discussions would irretrievably deteriorate into a circus, with Khrushchev as the lion tamer and Kennedy the subservient beast of the jungle.

He needed to steer the dialogue back to the ostensibly reciprocal concern of 'miscalculations,' and away from useless ideological posturing.

"Ah, Chairman Khrushchev, it will not matter whose system is better, if ah... a miscalculation by one or both of us leads to nuclear war."

Khrushchev was unmoved. "All this talk of 'miscalculation' is just an excuse for getting the USSR to sit like a school boy with his hands on his desk. It is nothing but a means of trying to intimidate the Soviet Union, to inhibit us from expressing our ideas for which the U.S. has no answer. If it is war that the United States wants, it would be best to do it now. Why wait until both sides have developed even nastier weapons?"

Kennedy had not yet reached a full realization of just how little anything he said of a substantive nature mattered. Up to that point he had been in denial as to the full breadth of Khrushchev's iron-willed determination to sabotage the conference and the credibility of the new American president. But to try one more time to illustrate his point, Kennedy then offered as an example of a dangerous miscalculation, the U.S.'s failure to anticipate Chinese intervention in the Korean War. Khrushchev was only too happy to agree that the U.S. had made a major misstep.

As the participants broke for lunch, the president could only look back on the events of the opening session as a huge disappointment, one in which his initiatives proved to be feeble in the face of his Soviet adversary's relentlessly hostile offensive. During the luncheon to follow with Soviet and American Officials, he hoped to at least shift the tone of the proceedings. Interestingly, however, with all the talk of miscalculations," Khrushchev did not appear to recognize that by the posture he had chosen for the Summit, he had already made a major miscalculation.

June 3, 1961 1:30 to 3:00 P.M.

Antonin Slezak boarded a Soviet government jet headed for East Berlin. There he would engage in a private meeting with East German President Walter Ulbricht. He had already committed to memory the contents of the sheet of paper handed to him by the American spymaster. It was now ashes in a waste basket in his Vienna hotel room.

Q pushed the seat back as far as it would go before take-off. He was the private jet's sole passenger and wore an expression of smug satisfaction as he lit a fine Cuban cigar and took his first luxuriant puff. His brief sojourn to Vienna had been successful beyond his expectations. He couldn't wait to get back to Munich and on to the bridge of his yacht where he could do some serious plotting in blessed solitude. As a master would to a servant, he beckoned the craft's only stewardess by silently moving only the fingers of his right hand in a "come-here" motion. After placing his order for a double Johnnie Walker Black Label on the rocks, Q sat back and sighed contentedly.

The substantial FBI detail which accompanied the president to Paris and Vienna had traveled in its own plane. The agent in charge of the detail was summoned to the hotel suite of Attorney General Robert Kennedy, briefed on the surreptitious recording and ordered to interview Chase, Byrne, their staff people and O'Doherty. Kennedy knew that his order as to O'Doherty was a gesture only since O'Doherty had silently disappeared from the hotel and from the city within a half-hour after the meeting of the Group of Eight broke up. He gave no such instructions to the FBI as to Rusk, Rostow, Bundy, Kennan or Nitze. All of them answered only to the President of the United States at either a cabinet or ambassadorial level. They took orders exclusively from POTUS.

The attorney general didn't bother informing the FBI Director, J. Edgar Hoover, back in Washington, of his orders to the FBI contingent in Vienna. If Hoover complained, Kennedy would simply tell him that the situation was a matter of national security and there was no time to go through traditional channels. Of course, Hoover would never accept such an explanation and the relationship between the AG[9] and the Director, already chilly at best, was headed toward glacial proportions.

The elegant John Paul Byrne was dressed in an expensive Hart Schaffner and Marx suit, fitted white dress shirt and silk bow tie, for his interview. When it was completed, the nonplussed Byrne took the elevator to the lobby, purchased a copy of *U.S. News* and *World Report*, lit a Benson and Hedges cigarette and sat calmly reading his magazine from cover to cover.

Llewellyn Chase emerged from his interview appearing apoplectic. His body language bespoke extreme indignation. He looked down the long corridor for a scapegoat to take it out on. Spying the convenient Henry Fuchs, Chase tore into him for his failure to perceive the presence of the FBI in the hotel and to warn Chase so that he could make his getaway. Fuchs absorbed the cruel dressing-down with an almost masochistic passivity.

---

[9] Attorney General

Káz Penchak had made his way to the 409th's safe house located on a narrow street of specialty shops and neat guest houses, snaking its way down toward the Danube. After establishing his bona fides with the house manager, he was led to a telex machine in a dimly-lit, closet-size room in the rear of the building. With practiced hands, Káz typed out and sent a message addressed to Major Frederick Reitenhauser, "for his eyes only:"

```
----------------------------------------

Report Eastern Bloc Operative Antonin
Slezak met with Foster Wright/Gift Shop
Royal Hapsburg 3 June at 1845 hours.

Wright passed single Sheet paper/white
to Slezak/surreptitious.

Karl Pembroke

K.P.

----------------------------------------
```

In his office at the 409th, the CO read Káz's message aloud to LeBron and Booker. He also briefed them on the report from O'Malley, advising that a tape recording had been surreptitiously made of that morning's meeting of the president's Group of Eight, and that O'Malley had turned the tape over to President Kennedy personally.

Gazing penetratingly at his two analyst-advisers, Reitenhauser spoke,

"Let's summarize what's happened since the Bay of Pigs incident. The Russians have signaled a plan of aggression, including sabotaging the Summit. Eastern Bloc Operations have staged violent incidents in Belgium and Berlin. Carlton has gone out on a limb by revealing Groundhog's cover name to us as 'Jurist II.' Q has hosted a cruise on the eve of the summit meeting for Western Bloc higher-ups, some of whom the next day showed up at the Summit. Minutes before a meeting of the Group of Eight, attended by three of those higher-ups, Q showed up in the lobby of the hotel where the meeting was to take place and passed a piece of paper to Slezak, a Warsaw Pact spy and provocateur. Simultaneously, Soviet and East German forces—in substantial numbers—move toward the West German border. Then, they suddenly reverse direction. And last but not least, someone sneaks in a tape recorder to the highly sensitive Group of Eight meeting, and records the entire thing. Ultimately, the tape winds up in the hands of a Russian courier. So, what do we have here? Any ideas?"

It was never the CO's method to insist on quick answers. He expected from his top people only carefully reasoned evaluations and conclusions. Knowing this, LeBron and Booker sat in silence for a few minutes with looks of intense concentration on their faces.

As was his wont, Booker spoke first. "I think we have to be careful to separate the essential from the tangential. I believe the shooting of Olney and his men had little to do with the Soviets' overall plan. It was too isolated to be part of the main offensive. My guess is that it was done in connection with some future event, which right now is impossible to predict. But I believe that the murder of the three African diplomats was done to signal to NATO and the West that the Soviets mean business. It was like adding an exclamation point to their four-part Apocalypse Manifesto."

"I suspect that the Soviet/East German troop movements were a show of force," he said. "Probably designed to frame the Summit meeting and to establish the tenor of the meetings as combative and confrontational, rather than conciliatory. As for Q's interaction with Slezak, Q could *himself* be Groundhog or Jurist II, but I seriously doubt it. It is more likely—if Q has gone off the reservation—that he's Jurist II's handler. That's more his style. But with someone as devious and opaque as Q, one never knows. We should just keep Káz's report to ourselves, and wait to see how Q's flirtation with Slezak—if that's what it is—play's out."

"The most useful thing we can do is to try to catch Jurist II. If he is high up in the NATO defense establishment, he will be a great help to the Eastern Bloc in the weeks to come."

"How do you propose we do that?" asked Reitenhauser.

LeBron responded before Booker had a chance to formulate his answer. "We're not a counterintelligence outfit. We have neither the time nor the resources for things like surveillance, mail-openings, break-ins, electronic spying and interrogation. Plus, if we tried to do those things we would wind up stepping on the toes of C.I.[10] and risk turning the whole operation into a Keystone cops routine. But, we do have two resources that maybe no other area intelligence operation in the western world can match. We have Agent 14332 and we have Carlton. It's time to unleash them and make the identification of Jurist II their top priority."

---

[10] Counterintelligence

"All right gentlemen," said a pensive Fred Reitenhauser as he stared at his desktop. Raising his head and smiling inscrutably at LeBron and Booker, he added, "I suppose I have a lot of thinking to do. Whatever we do, we have to run it solely out of our shop, without the knowledge of Group Command. I can't expose either 14332 or Carlton to anyone outside this station. We'll convene again in twenty four hours."

Vienna, June 3, 1961, 3:00 P.M.

Tensions between the two world leaders abated somewhat at lunch. The presence of aides and press-relations people helped create a more lighthearted and convivial atmosphere.

Kennedy's droll wit was also on display. "What are those two medals on your jacket, Mr. Chairman?"

"I am proud to say that they are Lenin Peace Prizes."

"Well, I hope you get to keep them."

For once, even Khrushchev laughed. But during lunch, Khrushchev affected a bipolar personality, switching rapidly from pleasant to pugnacious. It all seemed calculated to leave the impression of an erratically dangerous politician.

During a stroll through the magnificent gardens after lunch, Khrushchev was no longer the manic-depressive. The erratic, changeable Khrushchev was gone, replaced by the monomaniacal combatant.

From an upstairs window in the library of the Hall of Justice, Kenny O'Donnell and Dave Powers watched the two principals strolling through the gardens. Kennedy had mentioned to O'Donnell that he would work on establishing a better rapport with Khrushchev at lunch. From all outward appearances he had failed. The two men seemed to be engaged in a bitter argument. Khrushchev was actually circling around Kennedy as they walked, wearing a truculent expression and all the while shaking his finger at the American president.

As a worn-out Kennedy soaked in a hot bath at the end of the first day's session, Dave Powers commented that he had looked very calm in the garden while Khrushchev was verbally attacking him. The argument, as one would expect, was about Germany and Berlin.

"What did you expect me to do," responded the president, "take off one of my shoes and hit him over the head with it?"

At the afternoon session, Kennedy attempted to clarify what he meant by a miscalculation that could trigger a nuclear war. To provide an example, he admitted that he had made a miscalculation over Cuba.

But Khrushchev simply seized upon Kennedy's admission of a mistake as weakness. Pointing a stubby finger at Kennedy, Khrushchev handed down his indictment. "America shows no respect to peoples' holy wars. You see peoples' revolutions as communist plots."

Kennedy could have pointed out that less than a year after Castro's so-called 'holy war,' he had declared himself an avowed communist, established a totalitarian state in Cuba, and summarily executed many of those who had helped him ascend to power. Instead, Kennedy took a different tack. "Mr. Khrushchev, surely you must agree that war should be ruled out by both our nations. The current balance of military power between East and West means that both sides would be losers in the event of a nuclear conflict."

Khrushchev was unphased by the prospect of a nuclear war. Instead, he was exhilarated by Kennedy's apparent admission of nuclear parity between the two great powers.

The respective post session conversations between Kennedy and his staff and Khrushchev and his comrades were revealing.

To Walt Rostow Kennedy complained, "That son of a bitch, Khrushchev, he won't stop until we actually take a step that might lead to nuclear war... There's no way you can talk that fella into stopping. The U.S.'s only choice is to continue building its arsenal, and even consider a first strike if the Soviet Union continues its aggressive stance."

To other close associates Kennedy lamented, "I never met a man like this. I talked about how a nuclear exchange would kill seventy million people in ten minutes and he just looked at me as if to say, 'So what?' My impression was that he just didn't give a damn, if it came to that."

Khrushchev said to his close colleagues at Vienna about Kennedy, "He's very young. Not strong enough. Too intelligent, and too weak."

Khrushchev reaffirmed his plan not to negotiate with Kennedy. It would be much more productive and satisfying to discredit the American president instead.

Vienna, June 4, 1961, 7:00 A.M.

Paul Nitze and George Kennan were old friends and confidants. Over an early breakfast in the dining room of the Royal Hapsburg, they tried to make sense out of the previous day's stunning events.

Until the dignified Viennese waiter poured their first cups of aromatic coffee, they sat in meditative silence. The scholarly Kennan was the first to pierce the quiet of the nearly vacant though regally appointed room.

"In my days at the U.S. Embassy in Moscow, most of the rooms were bugged by the KGB."

Nitze looked up from his cup of coffee. "Of course George, but we weren't being bugged by one of our own people."

"Indeed," was Kennan's laconic reply.

The more loquacious Nitze was as bright as Kennan when it came to the intricacies of international power diplomacy, though he lacked the broad and unique macro vision Kennan possessed for postulating doctrinal strategy. Nitze, however, was a practical and bare-knuckled negotiator. His tactics and strategy were more of the situational variety.

Together, the two close friends and colleagues perfectly complemented each other.

"That bastard, O'Doherty, sure made himself scarce after yesterday morning's meeting of the group."

"Yes," replied the droll Kennan, "perhaps he had to return to Washington to write a new fight song for the president."

Nitze chuckled appreciatively. Though used to his friend's wry humor, it never ceased to amuse him. But his smile quickly vanished as he got down to business.

"We have enough to worry about right now without trying to catch a traitor. We'll have to leave that to the FBI. But once we get back to D.C., I'm going to make a call to Fred Reitenhauser in Munich. He's one of the few spooks I trust completely. You remember in '58 when Khrushchev gave the U.S. six months to get out of Berlin?"

"How can I forget it? We had no sleep for two days."

"Well Allen Dulles[11] suggested I fly from Bonn down to Munich and meet with this guy, Reitenhauser, to get his take on the seriousness of Khrushchev's ultimatum. Reitenhauser just sat there calmly puffing on his pipe and without asking a single question, said 'I'll get back to you within twenty-four hours.' Twelve hours later, I got a telex at the embassy from Munich. All it said was, 'He's bluffing.' I called John[**] who was in on my

---

[11] Director of the CIA and brother of John Foster Dulles.
[**] Secretary of State, John Foster Dulles.

mission with his brother and gave him Reitenhauser's reply. John then told Khrushchev to shove his ultimatum, up his fat can."

"Yes," observed Kennan in a somber voice, "but six months later, John was dead, from what the doctors said was a fast-moving abdominal cancer. But, I take your point. I think you should talk to Fred. He's a good man and we need to establish a back-channel on this whole untidy spy situation."

Then sighing, and staring out the massive front window, Kennan ruefully remarked, "It almost always comes back to Berlin, doesn't it?"

"Always," affirmed Nitze. "And Berlin will dominate the rest of the Summit conference also. Khrushchev smells blood now. Expect a new ultimatum on Berlin today. And we cannot afford to give an inch."

Vienna, Hall of Justice 11:30 A.M.—Day 2

The principals and their aides had scarcely lowered themselves into their chairs when Khrushchev, without preliminaries, began speaking. "Our government is determined that there will be no discussion of limiting nuclear testing or nuclear disarmament until the German question is resolved. The United States and its client countries, France and Great Britain, have unjustly occupied German territory for fifteen years and have cruelly frustrated the legitimate aspirations of the East Germans to have dominion over their own land."

A startled Kennedy gathered himself quickly to interject a question. "Well, Mr. Khrushchev... If you describe the American, French, and British zones as an *occupation*, what word would you use to describe the Soviet Union's presence and control in East Germany during the same time span?"

Without skipping a beat or acknowledging the glaring inconsistency which Kennedy had just pointed out, Khrushchev ignored the question and continued his speech. "All of that will change now. The USSR will soon sign a treaty with East Germany, which will invalidate all the 1945 arrangements for the four zones of occupation. The U.S., Great Britain and France will no longer have access by road and air to Berlin through East Germany. Of course, if the United States were to also sign a separate peace treaty with East Germany, Berlin would remain a free city. But I must warn you that a refusal to sign will end all rights of Western Bloc access to Berlin."

Kennedy felt the anger boiling up inside of him. His acid-reflux condition forced him to bite back an elevation of acid into his throat. Fortunately he had been blessed with an innate coolness, perhaps a genetic legacy from the smooth-talking Boston politician, 'Honey Fitz' Fitzgerald, his maternal grandfather.

His reply to Khrushchev's astounding ultimatum was cogent and forceful. "Our rights in Germany will not be surrendered on any one nation's whim. We were not handed those rights. Our country's military fought for them on the battlefield. And your nation was one of the four signatories to the agreement which established the occupation zones. Are you now reneging on your word? Because if you *are*, how can we trust you to honor any agreements between our two nations?"

Before Khrushchev could respond, Kennedy continued. "Here we're not talking about Laos. This matter is of the greatest concern to the U.S. We are in Berlin not because of someone's sufferance. We fought our way there... If we were expelled from that area and if we accepted the loss of our rights, no one would have any confidence in U.S. commitments and pledges."

He leveled his gaze at the Soviet leader. "Do not threaten the existing balance of power in Europe," he said. "If you do, the United States *will* respond."

Khrushchev listened, but did nothing to reduce the tension. By turns he had escalated the rhetoric of the Summit meetings with the express intent of achieving an impasse. He was not about to back off at his moment of triumph, albeit his sense of victory was illusory, and—as events turned out—the product of a dangerous miscalculation.

The portly Georgian charged on. "No force in the world would prevent the USSR from signing a peace treaty."

So it went for the remainder of the conference. Khrushchev's sole concession in the face of Kennedy's surprisingly strong response was a pledge not to sign the treaty until December.

The year 1961 thus promised to be one of the most dangerous in human history. At one point in their exchanges, Khrushchev stated that if the U.S. interfered with its plans to exclude travel rights of the Western powers to East Germany and Berlin, there would be war.

The wily Russian attempted to place the onus on the United States. "It is up to the U.S. to decide whether there will be war or peace."

The climactic flash point of the Summit had been reached.

Kennedy responded somberly, "Then Mr. Chairman there will be war. It will be a cold winter."

Back in America, the press were still preoccupied with how First Lady, Jacqueline Kennedy, had stormed Paris and charmed the stuffiness out of French President Charles de Gaulle. The legend of Camelot was beginning to take hold.

The reality was that the gauntlet had been thrown down by both of the two super-powers. The march to nuclear Armageddon had begun. The time clock began to tick down to December, when Khrushchev would sign his treaty with East Germany and block off Berlin. Berlin and West Germany were a vital interest of the United States, which it would defend at all costs. The battle lines were clearly drawn. But the first round of Operation Invictus had clearly been won by the Soviets.

Part II, Chapter 3

Aftermath of an Ambush

June 5, 1961

John F. Kennedy arrived at the U.S. Embassy in Vienna at about 10:00 A.M. for his pre-arranged interview with James "Scottie" Reston of the *New York Times*. Reston could not have missed the fact that the president was bone-weary, with blood-shot eyes, puffy cheeks and a pasty complexion. The vigor for which he was so famous was totally missing. Though it would have been an exaggeration to describe Kennedy as despondent, he was clearly down in the dumps.

Reston intended to confine himself to the policy issues of the Summit Conference in the early stages of the interview, and eventually get around to its more personal aspects. But upon arriving, the president walked directly to a couch, sat down heavily and pulled his hat down over his eyes.

"Pretty rough?" asked Reston.

"Roughest thing in my life," replied Kennedy, breathing a deep sigh. "Khrushchev just beat the hell out of me."

Kennedy seemed to Reston like a defeated man, and the reporter remained silent while the president attempted to pull himself together.

Finally, Kennedy sat up straight and spoke in the manner of one answering a question, though none had been asked. "I need to answer two questions. Number one, why did Khrushchev behave as he did? And number two, how am I to respond?"

Kennedy then answered his own questions. "He behaved as he did because he believes that the Bay of Pigs showed I was a weakling. He had no respect for me before the conference even started, and even less after the first day. As to the second question, the answer is that I now have to show in the clearest way possible that I cannot be pushed around. The security of the world depends upon it."

The president's voice took on a hard edge. "I will *not* play Chamberlain to his Hitler."

Later in the day, Kennedy sat alone stewing in his state room on Air Force One on the flight to London, where he would meet with British Prime Minister Harold McMillan.

Finally, he called Kenneth O'Donnell in and vented his anger, partially at Khrushchev for his nastiness and disrespect, but mostly at himself for his weak showing in the face of the Soviet leader's belligerence.

As Ted Sorensen was Kennedy's intellectual alter ego, O'Donnell was his political conscience and sounding board for matters related to Kennedy's performance. Nowhere was O'Donnell's function for the president more in evidence than during the Cuban Missile Crisis which would occur over a year later in October of 1962.

"Kenny, Khrushchev is a son of a bitch" but right now I'm even madder at myself. For the second time in the last three months, I have acted stupidly."

"Don't be that hard on yourself Jack. You've been hit between the eyes twice, early in your presidency."

"Yeah, well so was Lincoln and he knew how to respond. What I've accomplished is to increase rather than lessen the chances of war. You would think that no one in his right mind would fight a war that would kill millions of people over access rights to Berlin or because the Germans wanted to reunify their country. But, nations have blundered into wars for reasons even more trivial than that. Just look at World War I. We have to do better Kenny. Everything is riding on it.

Washington, D.C., June 10, 1961

Ted Sorensen entered the confines of the White House swimming pool located in the sub-basement. The leather soles of his new Florsheim wing-tips squeaked on the wet floor, and in his haste, he kicked water up onto his socks and the cuffs of his trousers. Sorensen carried a single-page telegram in his right hand: the source of his sense of urgency. At the deep end of the pool behind the diving board sat the President of the United States on a cushioned pool-side chair. He was dressed in bathing trunks, shower togs and a navy blue t-shirt emblazoned with the presidential seal over the right chest portion of the shirt.

As Sorensen had come through the door he had caught a fleeting glimpse of a shapely young woman in a tight terry-cloth robe being escorted out a far entrance by two Secret Service men. From long experience, he knew better than to ask any questions.

He now walked quickly, though unsteadily, on the wet floor in the direction of the president, distractedly pushing the heavy black frames of his thick glasses back from the tip and onto the bridge of his nose as he walked. The omnipresent Secret Service were there but out-of-sight and Kennedy was otherwise alone.

As Sorensen approached, the president raised his eyes from the copy of the *New York Times* sitting on his lap.

"Ah, slow down there Ted. It would be very undignified to fall on your Harvard Law ass."

As usual, Sorensen ignored the presidential ribbing.

"I hope you are going to take those expensive wing-tips off before you dive in the pool. Oh yes, I almost forgot, you can't swim."

Sorensen was not about to let this jibe go unanswered. "I *can* swim, Mr. President. I just don't care for it, and I have no time anyway."

"Ah, I see," said Kennedy, "so what have you got for me Ted?"

Without offering any explanation, Sorensen handed the telegram to the president. It was from John I. McCloy, the presidential envoy to the armament talks among the NATO powers, currently in progress in Brussels. Kennedy read the short telegram quickly:

```
FROM REUTERS, 11 JUNE 61.


KHRUSHCHEV TELLS IZVESTIA HE HAS DECIDED
TO CANCEL ALL DISARMAMENT TALKS. STOP

STATED INTENTION TO CONCLUDE AT EARLIEST
PEACE TREATY WITH EAST GERMANY. STOP

UNFETTERED ACCESS TO BERLIN WILL
TERMINATE BY END OF JULY. STOP.


MCCLOY
```

Kennedy looked up from the telegram and directly at Sorensen. The Irish twinkle in his eyes always present when he teased his young aide was gone. His expression had changed to one of grim resolve. "Okay, Ted, this is what we've been waiting for: an overt and very public act of hostility. Only this time we don't sit still like a row of ducks in a damn shooting gallery."

The words had poured out of the president's mouth in a clipped cadence of controlled anger, like shots fired in rhythmic succession.

Kennedy picked up the receiver off the phone on the small table next to his chair. A White House operator was instantly on the other end. "Get Paul Nitze on the phone," the president said. "He's at his vacation home in Maine."

Kennedy tapped his knuckles on the table during the twenty seconds or so it took for Nitze to come on the line.

"Yes, Mr. President."

"Paul, check all Reuters, UPI and AP press releases for today and then catch the earliest plane you can for D.C. I want to see you at the White House before 6:00 P.M."

The Pentagon, Washington, D.C. June 11, 1961

Assistant Secretary of Defense Paul Nitze retrieved a European exchange telephone number from his office rolodex and dialed it. An overseas operator interceded in the call and a few minutes later the phone rang in Munich, Federal Republic of Germany. Gerda answered the phone and immediately transferred the call to the CO of the 409th Special Investigations Detachment, Fred Reitenhauser. The major was expecting the call and responded immediately.

"Reitenhauser."

"Fred, how have you been?"

"Quite well, Paul. And you?"

"Oh, the president and Secretary MacNamara keep me running non-stop, but you know me. I wouldn't want it any other way."

"You and I share that trait, Paul."

"How about your man who was wounded over near the Brandenburg Gate? How is he faring?"

"He's recovering well and I hope to have him operational again within a few weeks."

"Listen Fred, you know why I'm calling. We've exchanged enough messages by courier to make you aware of how critical it is to the president to achieve our mutual goal.

"Say no more Paul. I had enough eyes and ears on the ground in Vienna to know what kind of a turn things took. In fact, I started my own excavation project right after the Bay of Pigs, so some of the ground work has already been completed. But, as I feared, our initial evaluations have made it clear that I need to do some special research on my own."

"That's exactly what I wanted to hear Fred. I'll pass that on to the president. Be careful, Fred, and good luck!"

"Thanks old friend. I'll need it."

After hanging up, Nitze made one quick call to arrange to meet Ken O'Donnell for a drink at the Capitol Lounge in a half hour. Nitze then hopped up from his chair, grabbed his suit coat, dashed out of his office without telling anyone where he was going and took the elevator to the VIP section of the Pentagon Parking Garage. He felt the excitement welling up inside him as he drove his Buick Regal on the George Washington Parkway. He crossed the Potomac into the relatively small area of the City comprised by monuments, a long mall and imposing government buildings, which together formed the nerve center of the international political power grid. Nitze was breathless by the time he entered the splendid interior of the Capitol Lounge on K Street with its deep, rich oak, mahogany and dark walnut surfaces, shined to a luster fit for kings and Washington A-listers.

Nitze was shown to a private room by the doorman, a room set aside for the president's top White House aides only: Ken O'Donnell, Larry O'Brien, Dave Powers, Pierre Salinger, Ted Sorensen, McGeorge Bundy, and Robert Kennedy.

O'Donnell sat alone at the room's small bar, and greeted Nitze warmly as he entered.

Nitze wasted no time on pleasantries as he briefed O'Donnell. "It's a go! Munich will use Carlton to dig out the Groundhog, and then go on the offensive."

Munich, 12 June 1961, 0755 hours

Fred hadn't slept well the night before and poured himself his second cup of black coffee while he waited for Barnstable and O'Malley to show up for their scheduled 0800 meeting. LeBron, Blake and Booker had been excluded. Making contact with Carlton and arranging a meet under safe conditions fell under the rubric of operations. For that he didn't need Booker's analytical brain and LeBron's special talent for espionage schemes. What he needed right now were efficient detail men who could both plan and execute a zero defects encounter. It had to go off like clockwork, with no hitches. They needed to be especially careful in preventing Q from getting wind of the meeting. Fred believed his Ops and Deputy Ops were well equal to the task. But what if something did go wrong? Although the danger of CIA's Munich Station discovering the planned meeting with Carlton was remote, if they did learn of it, that could spell disaster, should Q's interaction with the Commie sociopath, Slezak, be as toxic as it appeared.

The meeting lasted over three hours. Reitenhauser was a perfectionist who left nothing to chance. They went over the logistics of Fred and Carlton's planned face-to-face again and again, until all three men could recite them by rote, down to the smallest detail, the finest minutiae. Given the vital importance of the planned meeting, the decision was made to have Agent 14332, a master of disguise, meet with both men on separate occasions to assay what type of disguise would be most effective for each of them, given their appearances and demeanors.

Agent 14332, who Fred simply called Horst, ultimately transformed Fred into a professor of the humanities at Heidelberg University, Herr Albert Funk, replete with neatly trimmed beard, pince-nez, tweed jacket, starched white shirt, polka-dot bow tie and a cane.

Carlton on the other hand would be disguised as Paul Montpásse, a beret-wearing French artist, dressed in baggy pants and painter's smock. Under his right arm he would be carrying a portfolio of his sketches. Instead of a beard, his facial hair would consist of a thick black mustache. The location chosen for the meeting was Paris. The two men would meet in an out of the way dimly-lit bistro in Montmartre near the Artist's Corner, on the right bank of the Seine. The two men knew each other well so no exchange of bona fides would be necessary.

The CO's intense session with Barnstable and O'Malley finally broke up at about 1130 hours. Reitenhauser ate a sandwich at his desk as he carefully reviewed in his organized mind the agenda for the momentous meeting with Carlton. He made no notes and referred to no papers or documents of any kind. When he was finally satisfied with the meticulously structured agenda, Fred gazed at his watch and saw to his great surprise that it was now 1800. He had been sitting at his desk working for ten straight hours.

Reitenhauser was a bachelor with no one waiting for him back at his apartment, located in a small cul-de-sac in a distant region of Perlacher Forest, the U.S. Army housing area. Hungry and tired from his grueling day, he decided to stop at Oscar's, a tavern near the Kaserne[12] where the 409th's offices were located. Oscar, an Ameriphile, had made himself a small fortune since 1946, catering to the wants and needs of the U.S. Military occupiers. The balmy June temperatures had brought out a larger than usual crowd at Oscar's, but Major Fred Reitenhauser never had any difficulty getting a table. As soon as Oscar saw him come through the door, he hurriedly moved to greet his frequent guest and then whisked him toward a favorite table. The innkeepers and restaurateurs of South Munich all knew who Fred Reitenhauser was, and had no desire to leave him disappointed.

The somewhat weary company commander removed his suit coat, loosened his navy-blue tie and ordered a liter stein of Augustinerbrau beer, one of Munich's finest. Two or three sips were enough to start melting away his fatigue. While he waited for his order of bratwurst and oven-brown potatoes, Fred continued savoring the rich, strong beverage until a mellowness caressed his senses. Without any intent to do so, he gradually floated down a trail of reminiscence to a different time and place sixteen years earlier.

Berlin, May 1945

The four zones of occupied Berlin—American, British, French, and Russian—made for some strange bedfellows. Newly-minted Second Lieutenant Fred Reitenhauser was not sure why he instinctively liked his Russian counterpart, Field Lieutenant Uri Putyagin, who had been educated in England and spoke English fluently. They were teamed together in the search for evidence of war crimes at the ruins and rubble of what had been the Nazi political archives and the Reich-Defense Library.

Their relationship in the beginning was based upon a shared revulsion for the Nazi atrocities of WWII. But it soon became obvious to both of them that they were kindred spirits. It was almost as if the two men shared the same DNA, so perfect was the chemistry between them.

---

[12] Similar to a military compound.

When Fred saved Uri's life outside of the Allemagne Café in Berlin, after Uri was badly wounded by a German laborer whose sisters had been raped by invading Russian troops, their friendship was cemented. The two soldiers' superb work in Berlin led to their being named as investigators and evidence-prep men at the Nuremberg war crimes trial of 1945-46. Uri and Fred worked as a team and helped U.S. lead prosecutor, Robert H. Jackson, secure convictions against 21 of the 22 high Nazi officials on trial.

Then Fred went to Army Intelligence School and Uri back to Moscow to begin a promising political career. But Uri bridled under the repressive Bolshevik regime of the Soviet Union.

Fred and Uri did not meet again until a holiday trip by Uri to Vienna brought the two old friends together in a Vienna coffee shop in 1953. At that time, Fred was an officer with United States Army Intelligence in Munich and Uri had become the Minister of Defense-Preparedness for the Western Soviet Republics. Over coffee and Viennese pastry Fred had recruited Uri to spy for the United States. Though, truth be known, Uri had been seeking the job.

Uri had been planted as a mole, deep within the Soviet defense network, and the rest was history. Now, eight years later, the two men would meet again in France; but these days, Uri was known to Western Intelligence solely as Carlton. Only one other person in the world, Fred Reitenhauser, knew both his real and cover identities.

Fred was abruptly derailed from his tour down memory lane when Art LeBron materialized, seemingly from nowhere, to stand next to Fred's table.

"Art, what brings you here during dinner time? Oscar's chef isn't exactly in the same culinary league with Gina."

"As a matter of fact, Fred, dinner is warming on the stove right now and I intend to be home in ten minutes. But first I wanted to give you this," said LeBron, as he handed a sealed business-size envelope to the CO. "One of my boys retrieved it from a drop[13] at about 1700 hours. I drove to your apartment first but it was dark, so I figured you'd be here."

"Listen, thanks a million Arthur. I don't know why, but my intuition tells me this is important. Now get the hell out of here. Go home and have dinner with your wife. I don't want her mad at me."

Barely moving his head, Fred's eyes wandered about the crowded room. He then looked at the envelope. Nothing was written on it. Sealed, blank envelopes showed up in the dead-drops of the 409th three or four

---

[13] i.e. dead-drop.

times a year. When that happened, standard operating procedure was to deliver the envelope to the CO, or in his absence, to the Ops.[14] Despite the temptation to open the envelope, Fred decided he would wait till he got home. There he could open it under secure conditions. He put the envelope on his lap under his napkin as the waiter placed his dinner in front of him. Fred ordered a second stein of beer, only this time switched to the milder Lowenbrau.

Finished with his barely adequate meal by 1930 hours, Reitenhauser paid and left without any further chit-chat with Oscar. He was anxious to get home to open the envelope, now tucked into his inside suit coat pocket.

Munich had some hilly areas on both sides of the Isar River with gentle slopes easing their way down to the riverbanks. Near the Kaserne in which the 409th's offices were located—officially called The General Maxwell Taylor Complex—a secondary road going South past Oscar's, past the U.S. housing area and eventually in the direction of Garmisch-Partenkirchen, wound along a botanical garden and through a series of sharp curves. A low stone wall separated the road from the garden, which was situated at the bottom of a hill, perhaps a hundred feet below the wall.

Oscar's had been so crowded that Fred was forced to park his two-seater Ferrari in a small auto and bicycle parking area, extending up against a portion of the wall, recessed approximately seventy five feet in from the road.

Upon leaving, Fred walked up the winding road toward the indented parking area situated about a hundred yards from Oscar's. He leaned close to the wall to avoid vehicles negotiating the curves. The road was unlighted except for the headlights of the north and south-bound traffic.

Fred Reitenhauser had spent six weeks after parachuting into Normandy on D-Day, with the 82nd Airborne, leading combat patrols day and night across the farms and into the thick hedgerows and woods—encountering stiff German resistance all the way. Heavy firefights, Panzer attacks and ambushes by snipers were just part of his daily routine. Every moment was a battle for survival, as vast numbers of American, British and Canadian troops pushed forward toward a break-out from the Normandy peninsula. To stay alive, Fred had trained his eyes to instantly pick up any glint or shine, which might reveal the metal of a German weapon—a gun, knife or bayonet.

Now as he climbed up the road toward the parking area, Fred saw the unmistakable glint of a gun barrel up ahead. Pure survival instinct catapulted him over the wall only a slim fraction of a second before the

---

[14] Operations Officer.

muzzle flash of a Luger pierced the darkness. The shot, followed by three others in quick sequence, produced only the muffled noises of a silencer.

Fred landed on his side and rolled down the steep hill toward the garden for about seventy five feet until a tree stump brought him to a halt, sending a sharp pain through his left shoulder. He was instantly on his feet and when upright held a semi-automatic Beretta pistol in his right hand, yanked from an ankle holster. Fred dropped behind the stump and pointed his weapon up the hill. Two more muzzle flashes appeared at the top and bullets whistled through the foliage on either side of him. Fred fired several quick shots toward the origin of the muzzle flashes. Most of them hit the wall, sending bits of stone flying in all directions. Then, all was quiet.

Fred remained kneeling behind the tree stump, his weapon pointed up the hill toward the wall, his eyes peeled for even the slightest movement and his ears on full alert for any sound which might signal they were moving in on him. He saw and heard nothing. After fifteen minutes of silence and stillness, he rose slowly and headed by a circuitous, twisting route back up the hill. Still nothing.

When he reached the wall, he peered over it to the left and right allowing only his head to rise above the top. He saw and heard only the north and south-bound traffic. Using his right arm for leverage, Fred vaulted over the wall in one quick graceful motion. He silently thanked God for his combat training, even as pain shot through his left shoulder.

Fred moved quickly in a crouch along the wall until he reached the parking area. His Ferrari was close to the road, and he saw no signs of anyone else in the enclave. Of course, the danger of ambush from the other side of the wall was a real one. But Fred had no intention of hanging around.

Firing two quick shots in the air he dashed low to the ground back to his two-seater, quickly unlocked it, and hopped into the driver's seat. He took off with his wheels kicking up gravel and dirt in all directions, squealing tires leaving rubber streaks on the asphalt surface of the road.

A few minutes later, Fred stopped his car in front of the M.P. station, just inside the main entrance to Perlacher Forst, the U.S. military housing area. He entered the station, flashed his credentials to the desk sergeant, and asked for armed protection. The officer in charge was called and a two-man patrol jeep was assigned to escort Fred to his apartment. A second jeep arrived at the apartment building about ten minutes later. The M.P.s set up surveillance in front of and behind the building for the rest of the night. The word had been out for a couple of years now that Major

Frederick Reitenhauser was 'critical personnel,' entitled to protection on demand.

Once inside the bathroom of his apartment, Fred stripped off his dirt and moss-encrusted suit, shirt and tie and tossed them into the hamper. He then gingerly removed his undershirt and examined his shoulder. He gently touched and probed the huge purple bruise on the meat of his upper left arm just below his shoulder. It looked ugly but he didn't think anything was torn or broken. He would know more after getting it checked out in the morning.

Reitenhauser's greatest desire at the moment was to hop into a hot shower, but that would have to wait. First he opened the envelope which he had placed on the bathroom counter. Inside was a piece of 3x5 note paper bearing an inscription in black ink:

> We shall exterminate the evil icon.
> We shall execute its human instrument of treachery.
> We shall tear the disloyal traitor asunder-limb from limb, and leave his entrails on the ground.

Charming imagery. It sounded like the Red Guard.

Reitenhauser read the three-sentence note five times, then took a long, hot shower.

Wrapped in a large bath towel he read the note several more times. Given the events of the evening, he couldn't help but wonder if *he* was the 'human instrument of treachery,' and perhaps Uri the 'disloyal traitor.'

Part II, Chapter 4

Montmártre

"Monsieur Montpásse. It is I, Albert Funk," announced Reitenhauser as he approached the tiny table situated in a corner of "Toulouse," a café long on charm and authenticity but short on cleanliness, light and space. "Oui, Herr Funk," Uri responded, "I am so pleased to make your acquaintance. Please sit down; and do call me Paul."

"I will if you call me Albert," replied Fred with a genuinely happy smile and warm glow in his eyes. Of course, the purpose of this meeting was to discuss serious business but Fred could not hide his real pleasure at reuniting with his dear friend after so many years. Uri felt the same and shook Fred's hand with feeling.

Uri and Fred had many important matters to discuss, but before they began addressing them, they engaged in small talk, as each of them eyed and studied the other occupants. It was one p.m. and the establishment had just opened; so there were only a few other patrons. One of them was a fastidious looking gentleman dressed in cream-colored slacks, expensive Italian loafers and an open-neck shirt with burgundy cravat. Sitting next to him on the floor was a handsome French sheep dog. At another table were two women of a certain age wearing expensive jewelry and enjoying what appeared to be a mainly liquid lunch. There were two somewhat wilted and untouched salads on the table for cover, but they weren't fooling anybody. There was a young couple at a window table holding hands and rapturously gazing into each others' eyes. Finally, there was a fiftyish-looking man studying sheet music. Fred and Uri already knew he was the house piano player, Francois Le Brec, because a five by seven glossy of him was affixed to the outside wall next to the entrance.

Shifting his gaze toward the small stage on the opposite side of the room next to a bar, Uri spoke without in any way lowering his voice. "They say Edith Piaf performs here several times a year and will begin an engagement on Friday night."

Neither the proprietor behind the bar, the waiter taking another order for frozen daiquiris from the two women or any of the other customers so much as glanced their way or registered the slightest surprise at hearing Uri's heavily-accented English. To the contrary, no one even seemed to notice or pay Uri and Fred the least attention. But then this was Montmártre, a sophisticated and worldly corner of a great cosmopolitan city, the main reason it had been chosen for the meeting.

Toulouse had been well vetted by the Group security people and was rated A-1 for privacy. The acoustics were such that eavesdropping from another table was virtually impossible so long as one spoke at a normal conversational level. Fred felt comfortable enough to lead things off.

"Paul, as you know, my country's competitors have become very aggressive. Our new CEO in the U.S. made some early mistakes and his enemies are putting an extraordinary effort into making him pay for his transgressions."

Fred had not the slightest reservation about using code words, even though he would just be making it up as he went along. He held the utmost confidence that Uri would catch every meaning, no matter how cryptic. He always had before.

Before continuing, Fred signaled the waiter and ordered a fine Châteauneuf-du-pape and a liver paté. A loaf of freshly-baked French bread was already on the table.

After the wine and paté arrived and Uri poured a glass for each of them, Fred continued. "NK has been engaged in a non-stop verbal offensive—interspersed with violence—since the day Patrice Lumumba was executed in the Congo, a few days before JFK's inauguration."

"Well," observed Uri, "Lumumba was a special favorite of NK. He had serious hopes that the African would establish a communist regime in the Congo; and in doing so, become the symbolic leader of the Soviet-sponsored wars of liberation. They hoped to overthrow all Western-affiliated governments on the continent, and to replace them with Marxist regimes. When his hand-picked man went down, NK lost considerable standing in the eyes of powerful members of the Presidium. A big part of the Berlin thing is NK's effort to win back lost prestige. Berlin is strategic and political. Africa is personal. He blames the fall of Lumumba on Dag Hámmarskjöld and the United Nations, who he believes plotted to get rid of Lumumba."

"And," added Fred, after savoring a sip of red wine, "we know that NK has always hated the U.N. Especially since Korea. He sees it as nothing more than a tool of the United States."

"True, and when JFK stumbled badly with the Bay of Pigs invasion, NK was handed a great gift. But, what we must focus on is that none of this is situational. It is part of a two-year plan for 1961 and 1962, hatched by NK, Gromyko, Mikoyan and one or two others, right after Kennedy defeated Nixon in the 1960 presidential election. In secret politburo memos they call it the 'two-year war,' although its official name is 'Invictus.' Now the offensive has reached its most dangerous stage thus far. As we sit here a formal ultimatum is on its way to the U.S. State Department, that it either sign an agreement to remove its troops from West Berlin and cancel the four zones of occupation, or the USSR will sign a separate peace treaty with East Germany by December 31st, and cut off access to Berlin to all NATO nations."

Shaking his head, Fred added, "And in case you didn't get the word, JFK told NK at Vienna that if *that* happened, it would mean war. During one of their lunch-time strolls in the garden at the Palace of Justice, JFK pointed out that the Soviet Union had lost twenty million people in World War II but with modern nuclear weapons and delivery systems, they could lose that many people in just the first hour of a nuclear war."

"And what was NK's response?" asked Uri.

"Incredibly, he said, 'It's a good thing we have so many people.'"

"Yes, that sounds like NK to me. But, I wouldn't take the remark that seriously, Albert. I think it was mostly posturing."

"Well, that may be, Paul. But anyone who would even make a statement like that, especially to the head of State of the strongest nuclear power in the world, seems more than a little deranged to me. Anyway, let me tell you about a few other troubling things. You know about the assassination of the Congolese diplomats and the attack on my man and his people at the Brandenburg, so I don't need to spend any time on that."

"But, then there was the Summit meeting itself. Despite the tightest security I have ever arranged, Hostile managed to poison one of JFK's doctors and a Secret Service Agent at one of the official dinners. They are alright now but one can only speculate as to how the incident may have affected JFK's performance.

"Yes," said Uri, "I heard about it. Most unfortunate; but KGB always plays rough."

"There were also a couple of other things that I doubt you heard about. Someone recorded a meeting of one of the CEO's top internal security groups, called the Group of Eight. Fortunately, before it could be turned over to the Soviets, my people intercepted it and delivered it to the CEO personally."

"So, Albert, you think it's possible that Jurist II may be a hair's width away from the CEO?"

"Not likely anymore. The group has been disbanded and the FBI is investigating. But who knows how that is going to turn out."

On hearing this news, Uri sat back momentarily and took a sip of wine as he absorbed the implications of a possible traitor within the U.S. president's inner circle.

Putting his glass down and leaning forward, Uri lowered his voice an octave or so, "Albert, can you provide me with the names of the individuals in the CEO's Group of Eight?"

"Yes, but not now. We'll wait until we walk back to our hotels. But there's more. The same morning, in the same hotel, my man observed a brief meeting and an exchange of an item between Q and Antonin Slezak, followed by a quick exit from the hotel by both of them."

"Do you know what the item was?"

"No. We got a picture of Q handing something to Slezak, but we can't make out what it is in the photo."

Uri nodded, and Fred continued. "Since the Vienna conference, things have continued to escalate. The Soviets pulled out of the nuclear disarmament talks as you know and their rhetoric has become more hostile and bellicose each day. Then last week we retrieved this note from one of our boxes."

Fred handed the note to Uri on the wall-side of the table, which was shielded from the vision of all other occupants of the room. As Uri read the note he chuckled softly. "I wonder which one of us is 'the human instrument of treachery' and which of us the 'disloyal traitor.' Sometimes I think my countrymen are intoxicated by the exuberance of their own hyperbole."

Both men broke out into laughter at Uri's trenchant humor, a spontaneous reaction which somehow made the apparent death warrant a little less ominous, at least for the moment.

After a few minutes, their amusement subsided and Fred turned serious again.

"The same night I received the note, an attempt was made on my life as I walked from a restaurant to a parking area on an unlit Munich road. I managed to return fire and the assailant took off." Although Fred spoke these words in his usual matter of fact tone, they seemed charged with an electric current.

Uri appeared to be propelled backwards by their force. A combination of shock and concern flickered across his face, followed by an expression of agitation. "How could they have figured out so quickly that you are one of the main point men for the U.S.'s counter-offensive?"

Uri then offered the answer to his own question. "It *had* to be Jurist II. And he must be in a high enough position to access the most sensitive communications in the upper reaches of NATO's defense and security system. The rumors I have been hearing lately of a KGB 'hit list' may be well-founded."

Uri's voice became softer, and more urgent. "We need to identify Jurist II! This should be the top priority of Western intelligence. Not only are our lives at risk, but the continued anonymity of Jurist II is an ongoing danger to the life of President Kennedy."

Now it was Fred's turn to absorb ominous new information. An involuntary shudder at the thought of a hit list coursed through his body. He adjusted the pince nez on his nose and reached into a vest pocket for his pipe, already filled with his favorite licorice-blend tobacco. As Fred lit his pipe and puffed on it contemplatively, the expression on his face seemed to communicate only a determination to move forward with the business at hand. His finely honed instincts and intellect told him this meeting was probably of great importance to the fate of the world.

Fred and Uri sat in silence for a minute or so, deep in their own thoughts, before Fred spoke again. "Paul, I do have one new piece of information to share with you, which I hope might be of some help. I have mentioned to you in certain of my communications, a brilliant though eccentric analyst working for us who I call *Searchlight*."

"Ah yes, I recall those references well."

"Well, I sent Searchlight recently on a little mission, back to Washington, D.C. where he met with FBI director, J. Edgar Hoover. The FBI had just broken a ring of Russian sleeper agents in place in four major U.S. cities. Pending a hearing in Federal District Court, three of the spies are being held in FBI detention cells. I requested permission for Searchlight to interview them and Hoover granted it. Two of the three refused to even talk to my man but the third, a 42 year old with a wife and four children back in Moscow, was nervous and frightened over the prospect of spending the rest of his life in a U.S. prison. Searchlight carefully capitalized on that fact by getting the agent, who we'll call, "Sparrow," to answer a few questions. It turns out that Sparrow was military intelligence and not KGB. As a young recruit twenty-one years ago, his first assignment was with Intelligence Operations Planning. Searchlight asked him mostly innocuous questions but managed to slip in the one question I considered to be the most important. It was, 'Have you ever heard of a Russian spy named Jurist?' Without any further prompting and in a burst of pride, Sparrow answered, 'Yes, my unit gave him that name back in the 1930's. 'Who did you give that name to?' asked Searchlight. 'To the American, Alger Hiss,' replied Sparrow."

With this, Uri's right hand shook from excitement, though he managed not to spill any wine on the checkered tablecloth.

"Then Searchlight asked him, 'Have you ever heard of Jurist II?' 'Yes,' said Sparrow. 'He's an American too. I never met him, but I know he works for us.' 'Where?' asked Searchlight. With his chest pushed out and a look of triumph on his face, Sparrow answered 'At NATO headquarters for General Norstad.'[15]"

This time Uri could not stop himself from spilling some of his wine, which he quickly dabbed up with his linen napkin.

Uri's stunned response to this news consisted of one word, "Incredible."

But the espionage pro quickly gathered himself and then asked Fred a question. "I assume you'll want me to use every effort to learn Jurist II's true identity?"

"Yes," Fred answered, almost regretfully. "It will be dangerous, but it must be done."

"Say no more, old friend. I will try my best. Being Minister of Defense Preparedness of the Western Republics gives me a certain access which many of my colleagues envy. But you are right. It will be dangerous and you must conduct your own parallel investigation, just in case something happens to me."

"It has already begun," responded Fred. "I have used some of Horst's people to penetrate NATO headquarters."

"Ah yes, Horst, our old chess-playing friend from Nuremberg. He doesn't look like much, but I know he is very effective."

"The fact that he doesn't look like much," commented Fred, "is one of the reasons he is so effective. But, Paul, I have one overriding concern which we have not really discussed. If Q has been turned, as his Vienna encounter with Slezak suggests, our operations, our lives and the entire Cold War are in great jeopardy. I have been so concerned that I have even considered reaching out to two of Q's boys who have done some wonderful work for us in Tehran and in rescuing one of our resources in West Berlin from Hostile."

"I advise you not to do that Albert. Just leave it alone."

"Just leave it alone?" exclaimed an incredulous Reitenhauser. "How can I just leave it alone?" Softening his tone, Fred smiled and looked his

---

[15] NATO Commanding General, Lauris Norstad

old friend in the eyes. He had never known Uri to give unwise advice. "Paul, there has to be something you're not telling me."

Uri sighed and took a deep swallow of wine; then quickly refilled his glass. He never wanted to withhold any important information from Fred but sometimes one was best advised to keep some secrets to himself, for reasons of self-preservation. He gazed at the ceiling, a sign, Fred recognized, that meant he was debating with himself as to how much he should reveal.

Finally, Uri broke his silence. Lowering his voice, he said simply, "Slezak has been turned. He's been a CIA spy for five years. Q recruited him in Budapest at the time of the Hungarian rebellion. We all know Slezak is an evil prick but the information he gave Q in '56 saved the lives of scores of freedom fighters. It is true that he's a double-agent, but his main loyalty is always to the biggest payer. CIA pays him three times what he gets from KGB."

Now, Fred was astounded. He knew all about how the game was played and that sometimes it was pretty sordid. But, Slezak? Anyone would be surprised. It was almost like saying David Ben Gurian was a spy for the Arab League. But, during their long relationship, Uri had never once been wrong about anything important.

Intelligence could be a dirty game. A mix of the deadly sins inherent in human nature with the imperatives of secrecy, deception and clandestine operations sometimes resulted in an unsavory brew. But, the stakes were enormous and Fred had learned long ago to just hold his nose and move on, which he now did.

"Paul, what do you make of the Hiss connection?"

"I wouldn't read too much into it, but I do believe Jurist II is an American. There are simply too many signs pointing in that direction to support any other conclusion. The quick leaking of info to Hostile, which only an insider would know. The bugging of the meeting of the Group of Eight. Your man's profile of Jurist II. The Jurist connection itself, and what the Russian sleeper agent told 'Searchlight.' But, let's be careful. An obsessive search for a Hiss facsimile could lead us irretrievably down the wrong path. As an example, Whittaker Chambers was nothing like Hiss. He was basically a sloppy under-achiever, from a dysfunctional family."

"I agree Paul, but now I want your gut reaction concerning four possible suspects."

"First, Llewellyn Chase?" Uri responded without hesitation.

"He has high-level NATO access; and his devotion to his country is questionable. He's basically a narcissist dedicated mainly to himself. So, yes. He has to be considered a suspect."

"How about John Paul Byrne?"

"On the surface, the indicators don't point to him. He doesn't seem to fit the mold of a traitor and spy. He's too wholesome. But, he enjoys tremendous operating room within the Western Alliance, extraordinary access to the corridors of NATO power and was ideally situated to secretly record the Group of Eight's meeting. Also, I have always sensed something paradoxical in his nature. I think he definitely has to be looked at."

"Remington Pierce?"

"I don't know enough about him to have an opinion, one way or the other."

"Malachy O'Doherty?"

"Ah, that is an intriguing question. As the president's unofficial emissary, fixer and enforcer, he gets in everywhere, and stays as long as he wants. And, he has no particular belief in anything other than expediency. He's the ultimate pragmatist. The only philosophy he has ever revealed is, whatever is good for JFK is, by definition, the good. But, things are different now. He's been frozen out of any meaningful role in the White House. So, who knows? I wouldn't rule him out as the mole."

Fred and Uri again fell silent as they both pondered the best way to move forward toward identifying and catching Jurist II.

"I know what you're thinking Albert," said Uri, as he stared at Fred with the intense concentration of a psychic. "I remember well the expression you are wearing right now, from our one-to-one skull sessions in Berlin and Nuremburg, when we were closing in on a Nazi criminal. You're thinking, 'enough of this guessing game. To catch Jurist II we have to set a trap.'"

Fred smiled. "I could never fool you, Paul. It's a good thing we're on the same side. And yes, that's *exactly* what I was thinking. We don't have enough time to catch him by conventional means. We need a ruse good enough to make him reveal himself. But, first we need to fix Jurist II's location. I'm pretty sure he operates out of NATO headquarters but that's too big a place. I am going to have to send Searchlight back to Washington to re-interview Sparrow and this time he will have to go there bearing goods—a plea deal provided Sparrow talks and what he has to say is reliable. If he won't tell us who Jurist is, then he has to at least tell us where he is."

"But how are you going to get a plea deal for a top Soviet spy? Hoover will never agree."

"I can get it, contingent upon the value of the info. My contact within the Kennedy Administration has made it clear that stopping Jurist II is priority number one for the president. A mere plea deal? Don't forget who the Attorney General of the United States is."

That got Uri's attention. He immediately sat up straight; and excitement shone in his eyes.

"I've got an idea. When Jurist II gave GRU advance warning on the Bay of Pigs, the logical thing would have been an isolated channel of communication from him to his case officer, to the Presidium and stopping there. But, a massive bureaucracy often works at cross-purposes with itself and some over-zealous pencil-pusher decided a long time ago, that when an intelligence report was of high security value, each of the four ministers of Defense Preparedness had a need to know about it. So a copy of the top secret report wound up on my desk. The problem was that by the time it got to me in East Berlin the invasion had already taken place."

Fred interrupted, "So in a nut shell what you're suggesting is we plant a seemingly sensitive document wherever Jurist II works and see if it eventually winds up on your desk?"

"Correct."

"But suppose all that winds up on your desk is a copy of the report in an envelope from some mid-level bureaucrat in the Kremlin?"

"Ay," said Uri, "there's the rub. The same fool who devised the procedure of giving the four ministers copies of the secret reports, also gave us the right to trace them to their source so that we would have the full context for evaluating them."

Fred tensed with excitement. "How long would that take?"

"About ten days."

Fred's penetrating stare was now reminiscent of the one Uri got when they made their final plans to move in on Herman Göring in 1945. His green eyes bore in like twin piercing lights in an interrogation room. "But how do you know that your ability to trace this information isn't just a trap to catch possible Western spies within the Soviet defense establishment, who show too much interest in intelligence sources?"

"Well, I'll just have to take my chances and have an air-tight cover story ready in case anyone asks why I want to know," replied Uri. "As you know, my father is very high up in the party, so my explanations for anything are rarely questioned. Fear of Siberia is a big disincentive to asking too many questions."

Fred was reasonably satisfied with that answer as he sat back in his chair and drained the remains in his wine glass. "Well old friend, I guess you and I have a lot of work to do. Let's get the check and get going. I'll brief you on the members of the Group of Eight on our walk back to your hotel. I'll also let you know who the high-level attendees were at Q's annual floating soiree and bordello."

Uri found the description amusing. The expression in his eyes was a strange mixture of mirth and worldly regret. "Albert, the business you and I have chosen as our main vocation in life preys upon the flaws and peccadillos of mankind to a greater extent than any other worthy endeavor. God help us."

Fred simply nodded as the waiter appeared with the check.

When the two friends exited the restaurant, Fred spoke softly. "No need to worry about our safety on the way back to the hotel. You won't catch even a glimpse of it, but we'll be well protected."

Part II, Chapter 5

To Catch a Mole

Washington, D.C., June 25, 1961, 0800 hours

Paul Nitze, John J. McCloy and George Kennan sat around a small conference table in an out-of-the-way nook of the Pentagon. McCloy had just returned from the aborted Geneva test ban talks the previous day. On June 14, McCloy's counterpart, the Soviet delegate to the talks, informed him that the Soviet Union no longer had any interest in limiting nuclear production and testing. On June 15, Khrushchev went on television and told his people that it was urgent to change the status of Berlin.

George Kennan held no official position in Washington and hadn't since 1951. But, as the highly respected author of the U.S.'s policy of containment against the Soviet Union, he had acquired for himself the status of one of the 'wise men' of American foreign policy, and by virtue thereof, was an ex officio member of most important defense policy groups. He was now serving his third consecutive term in that informal capacity. Truth be told, Kennan was much better at formulating theories and policies than implementing them.

More of a pragmatist than a theoretician, former Secretary of State Dean Acheson breathed life into Kennan's theory by constructing the NATO Alliance and the Truman Doctrine. Acheson now enjoyed similar "wise man" status in Washington and would play a prominent role in the Cuban Missile Crisis of 1962.

President Truman himself extended Kennan's policy of containment to the Pacific rim through United States intervention in Korea; and John Foster Dulles, President Eisenhower's Secretary of State, completed the circle by concluding the SEATO treaty for the defense of Southeast Asia.

Paul Nitze, though not an iconic figure in the Pantheon of eminent U.S. diplomats, was an almost indispensable cog in the day-to-day machinations of the Cold War. His combination of erudition, strategic skill, vast experience, and toughness were invaluable to the presidents he

88

served. And his close friend, George Kennan, was both his conscience and sounding board.

After adding a second lump of sugar and then cream to his coffee, Nitze stirred it slowly and deliberately for far longer than could possibly be necessary to achieve a judicious blend, all the while staring into its murkiness.

Bemused by his friend's peculiar habit, of which he was well familiar, Kennan softly put his question to Nitze, "Have you found something important in your coffee you would care to share with us, Paul?"

Despite McCloy's muffled laugh, Nitze ignored his colleague's wry humor and continued to stir until he was ready to articulate his thoughts.

Finally he looked up and spoke. "Our man in Munich has made progress. I'm not sure how he pulled it off but he has placed Jurist in the office of General Norstad's G-2 at NATO Command headquarters in Mons, Belgium. Nothing more is known about his identity, but Reitenhauser has cooked up a decent plan for inducing Jurist to reveal himself. I can't go into detail but a major aspect of it involves a leak to the Soviets. The president and Secretary McNamara have been briefed and they want the plan to achieve a purpose beyond just catching Jurist. They feel strongly that as long as we are leaking info to the Russians, we should send them a strong message as well. The president wants to send them a clear statement of what they can expect from the U.S. if they seal off access to Berlin. "And what would that be?" wondered McCloy. "I've provided the president, Bob McNamara and Dean Rusk with a set of options. The three of them are meeting with McGeorge Bundy later and I should know by tomorrow whether the proposals will get the green light."

The White House, June 25, 1961, 0900 Hours

The president and Ken O'Donnell breakfasted on soft-boiled eggs in the small room adjoining the oval office while Ted Sorensen confined himself to black coffee.

The president found that his quirky digestive system tolerated soft-boiled eggs better than just about any other food, and he was not about to risk triggering another flare-up of colitis on this particular day.

Between bites of toast, Kennedy spoke about the day's plans. "Bob McNamara, Dean and Mac Bundy will be here for lunch at one, but it may stretch out. Either of you two fellows ever read SIOP-62?"

Sorensen said he had. O'Donnell had never heard of it.

"Okay, Kenny. Reading it from cover to cover will be your homework assignment for tonight. I waited till you finished your breakfast to bring it up. I didn't want you to choke on your eggs. SI0P-62 is the official codification of United States policy in the event of any nuclear confrontation with the USSR. Even if that lunatic, Khrushchev, only drops a demonstration bomb on one of those floating icebergs in the Bering Straits we list as islands, SI0P-62 says that our response will be to launch our entire nuclear arsenal against them. S.A.C.'s[16] first move will be to obliterate the Soviet Union. Of course, the Soviets may launch enough of their missiles first to wipe us out as well. George Kennan considers SI0P-62 the brainchild of mad men. I agree with him. The fate of humanity cannot, by any rational measure, depend upon such a rigid and inflexible calculation."

"If I didn't know better," the president continued, "I would have thought SI0P-62 contained the plot line for some Cold War thriller like a novel I read the other night, 'Red Alert,' by a fellow named Peter George. But I *do* know better. It's one thing to *talk* about a device which will trigger the nuclear annihilation of the world in a work of fiction. It's quite another thing when official U.S. policy begins discussing the very same thing. I need to know which silly bastards came up with this thing, so that I can fire them. I wonder if that S.O.B., Curtis LeMay, played any part in it."

The president sighed. "Well, regardless of who drafted it, SI0P-62 is no longer U.S. policy. I'm revoking it, as of right now. Kenny, get a letter prepared to State, Defense, and the Joint Chiefs for my signature. At our meeting this afternoon, we'll have to come up with a new policy, especially for an East-West confrontation involving Berlin. Ted, reach out to Paul Nitze. I have had him working on a set of protocols, and want to talk to him before the meeting. And I want you to join us in the meeting, Ted, but after lunch."

Brussels, Belgium, NATO Headquarters, 0930 Hours, June 28, 1961

"Congratulations, Lieutenant D'Cello," boomed the six foot four, 235 pound Captain Jack Lurch, as he stood and reached across his desk to pump the hand of the second lieutenant who had just reported to him. It's not every soldier who is considered to have the right stuff for NATO."

"Thank you sir, I'll do my best."

"I know you will, son. I would expect nothing less from a son of the Keystone State. I myself was born and raised near Philadelphia, in Bucks County, right on the Delaware. Played linebacker for Penn State. But that's another story. Today we'll be launching *you* on an assignment that many men would trade their eye teeth for. Staff officer with the G-2's Office of Investigations at Command Headquarters. A jeep will pull up front in five minutes, to shoot you right over to Mons. Do us proud, Vincent."

The second lieutenant rose, smiled and departed. As he walked down the corridor of the vast modern-Europe-style building, he couldn't help but wonder if that guy was for real. He sounded more like a cheerleader than a linebacker. And what kind of a name was Captain Jack Lurch? Wasn't there a comic book character by that name?

But so far things were going okay. It wasn't an easy transition for CIA Special Agent Mario Tonelli, with his blue-collar roots, to slide into the role and bearing of an officer. But Lurch (if that was really his name), had made his first real test easy by doing all the talking. The second real test for 'Second Lieutenant Vincent D'Cello' would come after he reported for duty to the G-2 at Command headquarters.

But as the U.S. Army staff car rolled effortlessly through the enchanting Belgium country-side, Mario could only really think about how fortunate he was to have landed such a plum assignment at the age of only 24. He had Reitenhauser to thank. The guy was really impressive. Somehow he had convinced Q to let Mario go out on an assignment of dubious promise and uncertain duration, which was risky as hell to boot.

First impressions were important and he would have to be at his best when he was introduced around at the G-2 section. Both the G-2, Lieutenant General Stephen Ames, and the Chief of the Office of Investigations, Lieutenant Colonel Barton (Bart) Spaniel had been clued-in on his assignment and cover; but it was up to Mario to avoid suspicion by everyone else, that he was other than what he said he was. This meant he needed to be super-alert and careful in his interactions with other personnel. Mario had been fully briefed by Reitenhauser and his man, Barnstable. He knew how thin the air was at the height at which he would be operating and how big the stakes were. Neither his side nor Hostile fooled around at this level.

One false move and he could easily wind up floating face-down in the river.

Munich, 28 June, 1961, 1400 Hours

"Gerda, please ask Ed to come in and then hold all my calls."

Minutes later the closely-cropped, groomed and spit-polished Barnstable stood stiffly at the door to Reitenhauser's office.

"Ed, come in and close the door behind you. Take a seat and relax."

Barnstable sat but looked anything but relaxed. In his freshly pressed solid gray suit and flawlessly erect posture, the operations officer looked the image of a new FBI agent reporting to his section chief on his first day on the job.

"Ed, Mario has reported in at Mons and Bart Spaniel introduced him around. He said Mario's performance was impeccable. He may hail from the streets of South Philly, but according to Bart, he looked, talked and acted like he just marched off the Plains of West Point."

Barnstable allowed himself an almost imperceptible sigh; and Fred noticed a slight slackening in the muscles of his neck.

"That's good news, sir."

"Ed, you can call me Fred when it's just the two of us."

Reitenhauser had been trying for some time to achieve a more relaxed Barnstable. The ever-present tensions of the work were bad enough. If an officer on the front lines of espionage could not somehow find a calm zone for himself within his every day duties, he would eventually burn out. In his fifteen years on the job, Fred had seen many promising intelligence officers burn out. Some with disastrous results... Alcoholism, suicide, mental breakdowns and even acts of treason. He recognized the early signs well and for that reason had made Barnstable one of his important projects. The challenge was to transmute the man's raw energy, efficiency, and devotion to duty into an effective and composed operational asset.

Reitenhauser's efforts would prove to have limited success. He did temporarily mold Barnstable into an effective operative—that is until 1968 on the eve of the Czech revolution when Barnstable would come crashing to earth. It was during what Fred would later call 'The Allemagne

Deception' phase of the 409th Special Investigations Detachment, that it all unraveled for Barnstable.

But that was seven years in the future. Right then, in 1961, Fred needed Barnstable badly and was determined to mold him into an improved professional.

"Ed, even though it was directed to my eyes only, I think it is important that there be two of us here who have a copy of the document which Mario will plant in the NATO G-2 section. But you must safeguard it under 'Inform-classified 1-A' and tell no one of its existence.

"Understood, Fred."

"Okay, here it is."

Fred handed a copy of a two page Department of Defense cablegram to Barnstable who read it slowly and carefully.

```
THE PENTAGON
WASHINGTON, D.C.

                    TOP SECRET

Dated: June 26, 1961

                         Classification: "Top Secret,
                              Inform-Classified 1-A"

To:
    Gen. Lauris Norstad
    Commanding General, NATO, "eyes only"

From:
    Robert F. McNamara,          McGeorge Bundy,
    Secretary of Defense of      Chairman of the National
    The United States of         Security Council of The
    America                      United States of America

Dear General Norstad:

By order of President John F. Kennedy, Commander-in-Chief of
United States Armed Forces, effective immediately and
henceforth, the following shall be official United States
policy as concerns the matters of East Germany and Berlin:

In the event that any hostile nation shall isolate and deny
access to the City of Berlin or to any United States
citizen, including U.S. military personnel, the following
```

four steps shall be executed, in the order in which they
appear below.

1. You are to probe with a platoon of troops in an attempt
to move through and past the blockade;

2. If that fails, stand down temporarily while our civilian
authority implements non-combatant activity, including but
not limited to an economic embargo;

3. If that fails, invade and bomb East Germany, upon the
President's orders and in particular East Berlin, with
conventional weapons.

4. Should that fail to lift all barricades and restore an
open and unimpeded Berlin, launch such nuclear weapons, in
conjunction with the Joint Chiefs of Staff of the United
States, as are required to achieve the objective.

The foregoing Step No. "4" shall be broken down into three
sub-steps which shall be executed in the following order:

Sub-Step A: Launch a demonstration bomb, but only upon
              orders received directly from the President of
              the United States;

Sub-Step B: Launch what will be officially referred to
              hereafter as "a small nuclear strike," but only
              upon orders received directly from the
              President of the United States;

Sub-Step C: Launch a "general nuclear strike," but only
              upon orders received directly from the
              President of the United States.

Respectfully yours,   Respectfully yours,
Robert F. McNamara   McGeorge Bundy

cc: Dean Rusk, Secretary of State

Barnstable looked up after reading the letter twice, astounded by what he had just read.

"Is this really U.S. policy or is it just a ploy to catch Jurist II and at the same time signal the Soviets to back off on Berlin?"

"It's real, Ed. I got the word straight from the mouth of Paul Nitze. As Assistant Secretary of Defense for International Affairs, he drafted the policy statement for Secretary McNamara and the president; and they approved it. But the whole thing was Paul's brain child. He devised it and sold it to the big boys. When Paul first presented our ideas on going after Jurist II, President Kennedy was adamant that there would be no bogus missives floating around concerning U.S. nuclear policy. Unless they were absolutely genuine, they weren't going out. And Paul has total credibility. Not too many people are aware of it, but he was also the author of NSC-68 for President Truman containing the original strategy for the vast build-up of U.S. arms, to counter the threat of Soviet armaments."

Barnstable was so impressed by the enormity of the situation in which he was immersed that he imagined he felt a slight flutter in his heart. "Major," he said, reverting to military formality, "what are your orders concerning 'special handling' of this project?"

"None. You, Ted O'Malley, and I have already worked out the plan of action, down to the most minute detail. Just stick to the program, work closely with Ted and I, and be alert to blips on the radar screen at Mario's end. Whatever you do, don't try to go it alone on this. And Ed, keep up a good daily exercise regimen and spend some relaxing time with your family. I don't care how big the operation is, we cannot let it consume us. It's critical to maintain an even strain."

But Barnstable had tuned out his CO after the latter responded to his question with the word 'none.'

Barnstable was already preparing a long and complex check list in his mind of potential pitfalls, contingencies and response options.

Mons, Belgium, July 1, 1961

Second Lieutenant Vincent D'Cello had been placed in charge of internal security for the Office of Investigations. The job of security officer was tedious, demanding and full of potential traps for the unwary. That was why a shave-tail Second Looey was put in charge. All throughout the armed forces, Second lieutenants (or ensigns) were considered expendable.

Classified investigations were no exception. That way, in the event of a security breach, the senior officers would have a convenient scapegoat: an officer on the lowest rung of the ladder, with no real cachet or clout. The annals of military history list untold numbers of second lieutenants as the authors of some of the worst SNAFUs. Many of them were just scapegoats.

In the intelligence game, however, things are seldom what they appear to be. No matter how big a mistake Lt. D'Cello might make in his job as section security officer, he would do so with impunity and it would be quickly covered up. The only consequences D'Cello (Tonelli) would ever suffer would be as a result of occurrences in his under-cover role, and such consequences could have no limits.

To protect his cover, Mario went about his duties as security officer like a whirling dervish. He seemed to be everywhere at once: making random checks of classified waste bins, updating operations codes to avoid needless repetition, changing-up dead-drop locations, reviewing agent reports for sloppy under-cover practices, changing lock combinations for secure areas on a regular basis, tightening up personnel and visitor log-in and log-out procedures, and on and on. The job was unbelievably boring, but it was a perfect cover for Mario's real function. Within a few days he had come into contact with every employee of the Office of Investigations. They all seemed to him like honest and competent professionals. None of them appeared the least bit suspicious.

Mario's access was unlimited. He knew who was in, had been in and would be in the section offices, at all times. And no one, with the exception of the G-2 himself, General Ames, would dare deny him access to files or documents, no matter how sensitive, given his power to file complaints for security violations against them. Barnstable had designed this superb cover and by doing so had gained Mario's new-found respect.

Mario had been told nothing about the individuals on the list of "persons of interest" who might possibly be Jurist II or constitute a lead to a discovery of his identity. Reitenhauser considered it important that he start with a clean slate and no preconceived bias against anyone, in order to avoid a tainted investigation. By the end of his third full twelve-hour day on the job, Mario had found no clues whatsoever.

At about 2200 hours on July 1st, Lieutenant Colonel Spaniel invited Mario (also known as Vincent) to join him for a late dinner at a French restaurant near the Spanish House and The Belfry, a famous and picturesque historical site of Mons.

Mario and the lieutenant colonel could have no communications concerning his cover role, in the unit's offices. It was far too dangerous.

The restaurant, "Le Seur," was a frequent NATO haunt and the maître d' made sure Colonel Spaniel always received a secluded table in a distant corner.

After being seated and ordering cocktails, Spaniel spoke first. Both men wore conservative business suits and could have passed for NATO civilian employees.

"In here, I'm Bart and you're Vincent."

"Got it," said Mario.

"So how's it going so far?"

"The cover is really working well."

Any leads?

No, not yet. But, I am curious about a few things.

"Shoot."

"We seem to get a lot of V.I.P. visitors at G-2 who have nothing to do with intelligence."

"Oh you noticed that, did you? Who in particular were you referring to?"

Well for one, I keep seeing presidential envoy Llewellyn Chase and his staff members walking up and down the corridors and in the cafeteria. I also noticed that he and his people signed in on all three days that I've been here.

"Correct, and for an entire week before that. Chase claims they are doing an audit of our overall G-2 operations. But with politicians, who knows whether they're telling the truth. And, we have had to put up with Chase's little troll, Henry Fuchs, skulking around and sticking his nose in everything."

Mario had no comment.

"There was another big shot. I think his name is John Paul Burns. I try to read the American newspapers as often as I can, and I've seen his picture a lot."

"Right, it's 'John Paul Byrne'," corrected Spaniel. "He's actually here on a fact-finding tour for Bundy, the national security advisor, and has spent most of his time at General Norstad's headquarters. He apparently just stopped by our department to say hello to General Ames. Byrne is quite the politician. Any others you've noticed?"

"Well, there's another guy who carries himself like a V.I.P. but I don't know who he is. Kind of heavyset. He's been lurking around for two days now."

"Yeah, he's Kennedy's top snoop and fixer, Mal O'Doherty. No one has an inkling as to what he's doing here, and there's no point in asking him. You'll either get some bullshit story, or he'll ignore the question. He's an abrasive, anti-social prick, and the guy gives me the creeps."

Mario mulled that over while he took a sip of his gin and bitter lemon. It also gave him a second to notice the pure anger etched on Spaniel's face.

"It sounds to me, Bart, that you've had more than a couple of visits here from O'Doherty."

"You might say that. He's been here constantly since the Summit in Vienna ended, almost a month ago. General Ames even called Norstad and asked him if he knew why O'Doherty was here. Norstad said he didn't even know he was here. But he said he'd call Washington and try to find out. That was ten days ago and Norstad never called back."

"Can I get a picture of O'Doherty?," asked Mario.

"Sure, I'll give you one in the morning."

"I guess that brings us to the question, Bart, that I've most wanted to ask you. Do you have any suspicions, or, if not, information, that might be helpful to me?"

Spaniel was a fiftyish career cop with a twenty-year background in CID before being assigned to the G-2 section about eight years before. He greeted Mario's question with a detective's hard stare that lasted a few seconds, but then answered in a soft and amiable manner.

"The truth is Vincent, I've thought about it constantly since I was briefed on your mission a week ago. We have a hundred people here working for the G-2. As a cop, I would already have eliminated two-thirds of them as suspects. But, for the last eight years I've been both a cop and an intelligence officer. I have had to add a new perspective as an intel guy. I don't have to tell you that in covert intelligence, anything is possible. The frumpy secretary from the steno pool with the horned-rim glasses could be a top KGB agent. Things are seldom what they appear to be. But, to answer your question more directly, we need to pose another question first. In the real world, not some Ian Fleming fantasy world, who at G-2 could consistently get access to secret information that would be worth passing on to the enemy?"

Without waiting for Mario's response, Spaniel leaned toward him and answered his own question in an even softer voice. "I hate to burst your bubble but there are two people only: the G-2, General Stephen Ames; and his Deputy G-2, Colonel Charles Stansfield.[17] To me the chances are only one in a million that either of those West Point graduates, World War II heroes, and career intelligence officers could be traitors to their country.

---

[17] Seven years later, in 1968, Stansfield would distinguish himself during the Warsaw Pact invasion of Czechoslovakia, as head of the 44th Military Intelligence Group.

But even if they *were*, no matter how much power goes with your mission, you would *never* get close enough to them to establish anything."

"Okay," said Mario, "that goes for those who are with G-2. But what about the outsiders we've been discussing?"

"Neither Byrne, nor O'Doherty nor Chase would ever gain admission to the core circle of an espionage conspiracy. They are much too high-profile for that. And make no mistake about it, the kind of secrets which evidently have made their way to the Soviets would have required a conspiracy. No one man could have pulled it off."

Mario found himself unconvinced. But, the discussion had gone about as far as it could for their first meeting. As they finished their after-dinner coffee, however, Mario thought of one additional question he wanted to ask Spaniel.

"Bart, it's probably a minor thing but I thought the Captain to whom I reported at Brussels acted in a bizarre manner. His name was Jack Lurch. What do you know about him?"

"There's no such officer by that name with NATO," said Spaniel evenly.

Taken aback by both Spaniel's answer and the speed of his response, Mario could not hide his surprise.

"Are you sure?"

"Vincent, I am the head of the Office of Investigations of the G-2 section of NATO. It is my job to know about every officer and non-com in any way connected to NATO. And there is no such officer named Jack Lurch. Tomorrow when I check the full personnel roster of NATO, I'm confident I'll also find no such name period.

"Then how can you explain that I reported in to a guy named Captain Jack Lurch?"

"I can't."

Spaniel saw that Mario was both perplexed and disturbed by this news and needed to be mollified.

"I'll tell you what, as soon as I come on duty tomorrow morning, I'll check the duty roster for Brussels and also call the Adjutant there to find out who greeted you the other day. We'll get to the bottom of it."

"I appreciate that," said Mario. But as they walked out of Le Seur, Mario wondered why Spaniel had to wait until the morning. After all, it's not as if the Army ever closes.

Part II, Chapter 6

Blow-Back

The White House, June 27, 1961—8:30 A.M.

"Look at this shit, Pierre! This has got to stop!" shouted President John F. Kennedy as he slammed the morning's *Washington Post* down on his desk and then angrily slid it toward Press Secretary, Pierre Salinger.

"Do you see there what Dick Nixon had to say about me? That 'Never in American history has a man talked so big and acted so little.' And the *Time* and *Newsweek* stories were no better, suggesting that the Pentagon wants to face-down Khrushchev over Berlin and I'm somehow putting a leash on them. That's a lot of crap! But it's partly my fault. In working to combine strength and flexibility, we've kept too much private."

"Well, Mr. President, you've had good reasons for not going public yet."

"That's true, Pierre, but we need to develop the knack of getting out front with the story at the same time we control the flow of what goes out. Remember, if there's a news vacuum, the media and our enemies will fill it fast with their own narrative. And if we let them do that, we're sunk. We have to control the message, starting right now."

The president rubbed the back of his neck. "I want to go on television. Set up a press conference for tomorrow night."

The Whitehouse Briefing Room—June 28, 1961—8 P.M.

The atmosphere was electric as the young and charismatic John F. Kennedy strolled swiftly and unannounced to the podium, which bore the Presidential Seal. He unsmilingly gazed out at the hundred or so reporters and cameramen in the room. Instantly, a buzz rose up from the floor boards and grew louder by the second, like an approaching squadron of bumble bees. Flash bulbs lit up the auditorium and TV cameras jockeyed for position.

"I'll take your questions," announced the president in an even tone; and then crisply pointed to a Washington newsman about ten rows back from the stage.

"Yes, Mr. Brinkley."

David Brinkley, Co-Anchor of the NBC Evening News, cleared his throat. "Mr. President, on June 15th, Walter Ulbricht, East Germany's head of government, threatened to shut off access to Berlin, including the city's Tempelhof Airport. Chairman Khrushchev has recently made similar threats. Can you tell us how your administration intends to respond to these provocations?"

"I'm glad you asked that question," the president said. "Let me just say this... No one, least of all this administration, can fail to appreciate the gravity of these threats. They involve the peace and security of the Western world."

Brinkley nodded gravely in agreement.

"Yes, Sandy."

Sander Vannocur, network journalist, checked his notepad. "Mr. President, does that mean that we're prepared to meet Soviet challenges over Berlin with an armed response?"

"There are a good number of options under consideration," the president said. "But the important thing to remember is that, in this perilous age in which we live, it's not productive for a nation to issue threats and ultimatums concerning the vital interests of other countries."

This was a clear shot across the bow of the Soviet ship of state.

Shifting his gaze to a different part of the room, the president pointed to another Washington correspondent, CBS's Bob Trout.

"Mr. President, are you suggesting that the crisis over Berlin could lead to a nuclear confrontation between the Eastern Bloc and Western Bloc nations?"

"Your question highlights a matter of the utmost concern," the president said. "Earlier this month, the Soviet Union walked out of the long-standing Geneva talks on the bilateral reduction of nuclear weapons, and the cessation of nuclear testing. Let me say that our government was greatly disappointed by their action. And, its timing—in close proximity to its statements on Berlin—does not instill confidence in us that they are prepared to place the safety of millions of human beings above their own narrow interests."

The remainder of the forty-minute press conference continued in the same vein. Without saying it in so many words, Kennedy was clearly sending a message to Khrushchev that the U.S. would not knuckle under to the USSR on the Berlin question; and that the Soviet Premier's plan to cut off access to Berlin to the Soviet Union's other three occupying partners, the U.S., Great Britain and France, could lead to nuclear war.

After Pierre Salinger and White House political coordinator, Lawrence O'Brien, agreed that any further presidential responses would simply be redundant, or even dangerous, Salinger simply signaled to Kennedy who nodded to the assemblage, and abruptly exited the stage.

The president often employed his dry wit during press conferences, much to the delight of his audience and to the much larger audience in front of their T.V. sets. But not this night. He deemed this particular session to be burdened by grave matters of peace and war, and did not want his message to the world diluted.

He had finally fired back at Khrushchev who had been having his way with things for far too long. Now, it was just a matter of waiting to see how the pugnacious street fighter would react.

Part II, Chapter 7

Deceit is Skin-Deep

July 10, 1961, Near Garmisch-Partenkirchen, Bavaria

Q sat back in his lounge chair on the patio of his charming chalet overlooking the Eibsee, a lake surrounded by fir trees, deep in the Bavarian woods. It was a magnificent Sunday morning, sunny and mild, with a few benign clouds overhead. In the distance stood the majestic Zugspitze, the highest mountain in the Bavarian Alps. On the glass table top next to Q's chair were a half-empty mimosa and a pack of Benson and Hedges filter cigarettes. Dressed in a silk smoking jacket, Q inserted one of the cigarettes into his holder and flicked his gold lighter. A servant appeared only to bring Q a second cup of morning coffee, which went perfectly with the cigarette.

Despite the appearance of serenity, however, Q did not feel serene inside. He had not wanted to give Tonelli to Reitenhauser for the special assignment and had resisted for several days after receiving a call from Paul Nitze. It took a phone call from the Director himself at Langley to force him to capitulate. The entire incident was humiliating, and Q bristled under the weight of the power Reitenhauser had come to wield. The man had influence which far exceeded his position and title. It was galling.

But Reitenhauser had his mole, with the cover-name Carlton, as Q had recently learned. And that was the difference-maker.

Q was forced to go along for the time-being. As much as he chafed under the unsatisfactory arrangement, had he not cooperated he would have been completely frozen out of the effort to catch Jurist II.

Q finished his coffee and now turned his attention back to his mimosa. In the distance the regal Zugspitze seemed to be challenging him to wage a counter-offensive which would restore him to his rightful place as the most powerful spymaster in Europe. He was more than up to the challenge and knew exactly how he would go about it.

July 15, 1961—The Belgian Countryside

Paul truly cherished the perks of his job. His first-class seat on the super-train from Bonn to Brussels made the scenic countryside all the more enjoyable. Having finished his first single-malt scotch of the late afternoon, he signaled the waiter to bring him another. In so doing, his eyes came to rest on a stylishly dressed, stunningly attractive Eurasian woman who seemed to be traveling alone. Maybe he would figure a way to buy her a drink and then dinner and then, who knows? The enchanting possibilities were unlimited when one traveled, especially for a handsome, debonair, and unattached man such as himself.

His official name was P. Remington Pierce and he was the cultural attaché at the United States Embassy in Bonn, West Germany. He was perfectly suited for this job because it basically consisted of glad-handing VIPs, charming their wives, arranging tennis matches and golf-tournaments and meticulously crafting the guest lists for Embassy theater parties and banquets. Paul's appearance and social skills were perfect for the job and he did it well.

It was, to be sure however, all surface fakery. Paul made the effort for one reason only. The job was simply cover for his real one, that of a counter-intelligence agent for the CIA; and he had no desire to blow his cover.

From all outward appearances, Paul was a sophisticated, well-bred gentleman in his late thirties. At cocktail parties, amid sometimes inebriated chatter, he would casually drop references to his undergraduate days at Stanford and his pursuit of a masters degree in art history at the Sorbonne. All of that too was a fabrication. The closest Paul would have gotten to Stanford in his late teens was the delivery-boy's entrance. And the Sorbonne? Paul never even got to France until he was thirty and that was on an American Express weekend bus tour.

In fact, most everything about Paul was a fake: his job, educational background; even his name. His last name was Pierce all right but "Remington" was his own pure invention.

His real identity was that of Paul Pierce, a stevedore's son from the back streets of Oakland, where he attended the University of Hard Scrabble, majoring in survival with a minor in street brawling.

He enlisted in the Army during World War II and attended Ranger-training school at Fort Bragg, North Carolina, where his obvious talent for mayhem caused him to shine above the other trainees. He parachuted into Normandy on D-Day with the 101st Airborne and was quickly put to work as a saboteur, demolitions expert and assassin.

While stationed in London a couple of months later, Pierce caught the eye of William, "Wild Bill" Donovan, Director of the U.S.'s principal spy agency, the O.S.S. Donovan quickly pressed him into service as an operative and prepared him for covert operations across German lines to conduct demolition projects against Nazi fuel depots and munitions warehouses. When the O.S.S. folded after WWII, Pierce moved seamlessly into the CIA, its successor.

At the Agency, Director Allen Dulles decided that with his looks and personality, Pierce was meant for bigger things than crawling on his back under barbed wire with plastic explosives strapped to his chest.

Pierce was ordered to enroll in one of the Agency's finishing school programs, where he was taught grammar, diction, linguistics, social etiquette, art history and literature. Paul was an avid learner and the finished product which emerged bore all the surface trappings of a well-spoken, culturally-attuned and sophisticated foreign service professional.

As he savored his second single-malt scotch on the rocks, Paul Pierce, now referred to exclusively as Remington Pierce, reflected on how far he had come from the grimy streets of Oakland. It bothered him not in the least that his whole persona was a construct of lies and deception. And now the powerful CIA station chief in Munich, known only as Q, had tapped him for a clandestine assignment, the existence of which would be known only by the two of them. Although Q's nominal title was head of Munich Station, this was a mere technical detail on the CIA's organizational chart. By now being answerable exclusively to Q, Paul was working directly for the top CIA spymaster in all of Western Europe. This was a big career opportunity for Pierce and he was determined not to blow it. Ambition had so dominated Pierce's entire career as an undercover agent that his colleagues' nickname for him was 'Macbeth.'

The assignment bestowed on him by Q was for Paul, the challenge of a lifetime. Somehow he had to insinuate himself into the good graces of the G-2's Office of Investigation in Mons, gain the confidence of the undercover man in place, whom he knew only as 'Philly South,' and then track the foot prints already put down by South in pursuit of Jurist II.

Eventually he would have to preempt "South," identify Jurist II himself, or alternatively, take Jurist II out-permanently! With his vastly greater experience and savvy, he should have little difficulty out-maneuvering the twenty-four year old South. Then again, South was Reitenhauser's man. So, despite his youth, he must be something special.

Reitenhauser knew what he was doing and employed no light weights. But Paul was confident all would go well, Q would receive the credit for bringing Jurist II down and Remington Pierce would bask in his reflected glory.

July 18, 1961—Mons, Belgium

Pierce's new cover had real weight to it, as befitted Q's diabolical creativity. Gone was Paul's light-weight role as an effete cultural attaché, a glorified social director. In its place there appeared a robust full-bird colonel, Price Lovett, Pentagon Liaison to NATO Command.

Upon arriving at NATO Headquarters in Brussels, Paul threw his double-barreled clout around, to find out if there had been any major personnel changes at NATO within the past several weeks. When he learned that the Office of Investigations attached to G-2 in Mons had taken on a new, young security officer, Second Lieutenant Vincent D'Cello, Paul was pretty sure he had found Reitenhauser's man.

When Paul later walked into General Ames' office at Mons, he promptly produced a bogus letter on the letterhead of General Lyman Lemnitzer, Chairman of the Joint Chiefs of Staff, introducing Colonel Price Lovett to General Ames, and bearing the cleverly forged signature of the top general.

The letter directed General Ames to grant the colonel full access to NATO Command's facilities, to enable him to conduct a top secret fact-finding mission of the greatest sensitivity and importance to the Joint Chiefs.

Neither General Ames nor any other personnel at Mons were to hinder or impede Colonel Lovett in the conduct of his mission, the details of which were highly classified.

When General Ames called the Pentagon to check on the legitimacy of Lovett, the CIA—with the help of the Defense Intelligence Agency—intercepted the call and told Ames that General Lemnitzer was on extended leave, in Aruba where his wife was convalescing after surgery.

Under his cover of security officer, Mario Tonelli had made progress in isolating the channel through which highly sensitive documents flowed. Those documents having the highest sensitivity rating could be signed for and logged into the G-2 section by one or more of only three individuals, General Ames, Colonel Stansfield and himself, Lieutenant D'Cello. Such documents were always in a sealed packet which regulations mandated be opened and read only in the Secure Room.

The Secure Room was a 10 by 15 foot interior, no-window office, containing nothing but an empty desk, desk chair and safe. Its door had a combination lock and, officially, only the same three officers had the combination. The combination was changed once every week. All documents having the highest classification were stored within the safe, and were never to leave the room. The identity of the persons actually having the combination to the safe was a well-guarded secret—not even shared with Mario—except that as security officer, he had been provided with the combination, as it was considered essential to the performance of his duties.

Armed with the combinations to the Secure Room's door and its safe, Mario had waited until everyone but himself had left the offices before planting the Reitenhauser-authored letter to General Norstad in the safe at 2200 hours on his fifth night with the G-2 section.

Now, Mario and his control back at the 409th in Munich, Major Reitenhauser and Captain Barnstable, could only wait to see if information concerning the document made its way to Carlton in East Berlin. Mario did not believe, even for an instant, that he, General Ames and Colonel Stansfield were the only persons who could gain access to the room and safe. Fortunately, his cubicle was opposite the door to the Secure Room so that he could keep it under surveillance, most times. His instincts about broader access to the room were correct. But, once the alleged Colonel Price Lovett arrived on the scene and took up residence in the office next to Mario's, everything changed.

Lovett was an intrusive and disruptive Cretan who interfered constantly with Mario's performance of his job. He shadowed Mario, peppering him with inappropriate questions and unwanted suggestions. Any element of quiet unobtrusiveness Mario had gained for himself was quickly dissipated. He had the sense that if Lovett could have attached himself to Mario's hip he would have. Mario had no idea who Lovett really was and no clue as to the nature of his mission. All he knew was that his presence was insufferable. Lovett was invariably in the office before Mario in the morning and as soon as Mario arrived, would "drop by" his cubicle to "brainstorm" security issues. If Mario left the offices for any reason, Lovett usually contrived some excuse for leaving also. When Mario was near the front of the line to deposit his pay check at American Express, Lovett was often at the back of the line. On Saturday mornings when Mario dropped off one of his uniforms at the post cleaners, Lovett could often be seen nearby, walking into the Class-6 liquor store, exiting the PX or just chatting with other patrons in the parking lot. If Mario (Lt. D'Cello) and Lt. Col. Spaniel stopped for a drink at the officer's club at the end of a long day, Lovett was either already sitting at the bar or would soon show up there. And there was no way of knowing where he would turn up. Like an apparition, Lovett seemed to just materialize. Even when Mario was relieving himself, Lovett would often appear at the adjacent urinal. Mario wouldn't even risk using the enclosed stalls in the lavatory. He would take care of that business in the mornings and evenings back at the BOQ. Most disconcerting of all, Lovett probably spent even more time than Mario surveilling the "Secure Room" entrance.

July 24, 1961—Mons, Belgium

Mario had noticed three individuals in particular who seemed to go out of their way to slowly walk past the door to the "Secure Room" an inordinate number of times during the course of the previous week. He guessed that if any or all of them were to attempt an entry into the room, it would be in the middle of the night, when presumably the offices would be empty.

For several days Mario had been studying the blueprints and floor plans for the G-2's offices, trying to figure out a way he could surveil the inside of the Secure Room without being detected. He finally came up with a plan. At the rear of the supply room, which was so dimly lit that without a flashlight one would almost certainly trip over objects on the floor, Mario had noticed one night a door in the ten-foot high ceiling, with a rope attached. The blueprints for the offices showed a crawl space above the ceiling, which ran the entire length and width of the office suite. Mario decided to do some exploring that night. First he needed to equip himself for his adventure. He left the office at 2300 hours to return to his quarters. There he located an extra flashlight, his Swiss Army Knife, a tape measure and a roll of electrician's tape. Mario changed into dark-colored civvies— jeans and a sweat shirt—and replaced his "Class A low-cuts" with moccasins.

He made a pot of coffee, and sat on his bunk with a steaming mug of black java on the night table and the blueprints on his lap. Using the scale at the bottom of the blueprints he calculated the distance from the rear of the supply room to the Secure Room at 47 feet. He took a few last sips of coffee, stuffed the tape measure, knife, flashlight and blueprints in the pockets of his windbreaker and left his room. From an empty room in the BOQ[18], he grabbed a thin, narrow mattress and rolled it up. Placing the rolled-up mattress under his right arm and putting his Phillies baseball cap on his head, he left the BOQ and walked back to the offices. The guard at the door waved him through without the least hesitation. This came as no surprise, because Mario was his boss.

Once in the offices, he headed straight for the supply room, stopping only to reach down to his best friend, his fully chambered Luger sitting in its right-ankle holster.

In the supply room, Mario shined a flashlight on the ceiling door and pulled down on the rope. The door gave way and revealed on its upper side hinged, folding steps, which when pulled open extended down to the floor. Still carrying the mattress, he climbed the door-ladder and slid into the crawl space. Having memorized the configuration of the rooms from the blueprints, Mario crawled in the direction of the Secure Room after first pulling up the ceiling hatch and closing it behind him. With flashlight shining the way, and dragging the mattress, Mario crawled for about five minutes and stopped. Before starting his crawl, he had taped one end of the tape measure to the top of the ceiling door and unfolded the measure incrementally as he crawled along until it showed he had moved a distance of 47 feet.

Mario was obviously not the first person to come up with the idea of spying on the interior of the Secure Room, because two feet in front of him a perfectly rounded spy hole had been bored through the plywood floor of the crawl space and down through the ceiling tiles of the room below. The lights in the Secure Room were on and a cylindrical beam of light shone up through the hole and into the crawl space. Mario laid the mattress flat on the plywood, situated himself on top, turned off the flashlight and placed his right eye over the hole. In that position he had a perfect view of the desk and safe in the area below him.

It was now 2355 hours. Mario laid still on the mattress and waited. His mind inventoried the risks and benefits of his surveillance project. It could be days before someone showed up in the room below, if ever. He might have to return to his stakeout each night until his surveillance yielded results. His instincts, however, tugged in the opposite direction. They told him something was going to happen soon.

Should the hole in the ceiling be noticed from inside the room, a couple of shots fired into the ceiling from below could easily put an end to Mario Tonelli. But somehow Mario believed that any hostile intruders would be

---

[18] i.e. Bachelor Officers Quarters.

totally preoccupied with opening the safe, locating the documents of interest, examining them at the desk, perhaps taking pictures of the documents with a Minox camera and then getting the hell out of there. While spying on them through the ceiling hole, Mario would have to lie perfectly still. Even the slightest noise could give him away. And, since someone else had already been to his surveillance spot, the possibility that he could have company at some point was not totally remote. That thought prompted him to remove his Luger from its holster and place it on the mattress next to him.

Mario laid flat on his stomach for what seemed an eternity. Checking the iridescent face of his watch, he saw that it was now 0315 hours. His well-honed discipline had allowed him to lay perfectly still for over three hours. But his muscles ached from the rigidity of his position. Although the black coffee he had back in his quarters had kept him from falling asleep, it also had filled his bladder, creating a strong pressure to urinate. Well, he would just have to hold it. Mario was determined to maintain his watch until dawn.

Then fate upped the ante. A noise came from the direction of the ceiling door. To Mario it sounded like a knocking together of wooden objects followed by a scraping sound. Beads of sweat broke out on his forehead, streams flowed from his arm pits. The pressure on his bladder grew more acute. But any temptation to change his position so that he faced the source of the noises was quickly dispelled when he heard the creaking noise below of the opening of the door to the Secure Room. His body tensed. His right eye rested flush with the aperture. He fixed his line of vision on the door opening below, muscles taut from the enormous pressure he felt within.

The volume of the noise in the crawl space increased and seemed closer. Mario grabbed his revolver and gripped it tightly. A solitary figure entered the Secure Room and walked quickly to the safe. Mario recognized him immediately. The noise in the crawl space grew even louder and closer while the individual below spun the dial of the safe's combination lock. It took him only seconds to unlock the safe, pull down the handle and swing open the door.

It took every ounce of discipline stored in Mario's body to keep his eye peeled on the room below as the source of the crawl-space noise seemed to be almost upon him. Then as if in one coordinated motion, the figure below placed a paper on the desk and sat down on the desk chair while a rat the size of a Chihuahua scurried past Mario. The noise ceased in the crawl space, the man below snapped a Minox camera repeatedly and Mario's tense muscles slackened ever so slightly.

The figure below placed something in the safe, closed the door, and spun the dial of the lock. Due to his ideal vantage point and the excellent lighting conditions in the Secure Room, Mario had recognized the paper as the letter to General Norstad he had planted in the safe a couple of weeks before.

It was almost over, thought Mario, but then it wasn't. As the occupant of the Secure Room turned away from the safe and toward the door, it again creaked open. Mario lay immobile in a state of semi-shock as he witnessed the entry into the room of Colonel Price Lovett, dressed in olive-drab fatigues and combat boots, holding a Colt .45 revolver in his right hand. Lovett pointed the gun at the other occupant of the room and shouted, "Don't move!" The command was superfluous since the man was paralyzed by fear into a stationary position.

"Who are you?" demanded Lovett.

In a tremulous voice the man identified himself.

"Let me see your credentials!"

In response, the man removed his wallet from his rear pants pocket and produced what appeared to be a photo I.D. card.

Lovett examined the card carefully, lifting his gaze from the card to the man's face and then back to the card.

Handing the card back to its owner, Lovett swung his revolver in the direction of the door, and commanded,

"Alright, let's go."

The man walked out of the room at gunpoint. Lovett followed him and slammed the door shut behind him.

Although as Colonel Price Lovett, Paul Pierce had the raw power to arrest the individual he had tailed to the Secure Room, he had no legal basis for holding him. He simply ejected the man from the building and silently congratulated himself for having identified Jurist II. What a feather in his cap this would be. He didn't even bother tailing the man. All Paul Pierce cared about was waiting until a decent hour and then calling Q in Munich to report what he had learned. It was then up to Q to decide what would be done about Jurist II.

Paul couldn't care less. As soon as he spoke to Q, his job would be done.

It was now 0345 hours. Paul stood in front of the NATO command building wondering how he could kill some time until 0600, when he would call Q, wake him up and give him the dramatic news. He remembered there was an all-night bar behind City Hall on the other side of the main square, right near the Belfry. He didn't feel like having a drink but maybe he could get a cup of coffee. "If the bar-keep says no, I can threaten him with my .45," said Paul to himself laughingly. He laughed a second time, truly appreciating his little joke. Paul was pleased with himself and having a wonderful time. Maybe he would have a drink after all to celebrate.

An hour and a half later at 0515 hours, Pierce emerged from the bar and walked out onto the street. From there he gazed upward to the steeple of the three hundred foot high Belfry. The cup of coffee he had ordered had been followed in quick succession by four shooters of Bailey's Irish Cream, one after the other.

Paul had a pleasant buzz on as he stared admiringly at the baroque style architecture of the Belfry. It would still be another forty five minutes before he would call Q, so he started wandering slowly down the narrow Belgian street in the direction of the Belfry and in search of a pay phone.

Paul Pierce never felt the blow to his head delivered at 0525 hours as he stood in front of the Belfry with his eyes arched upward. In a semi-conscious haze, he did experience the sensation of being dragged upward by someone or something powerful. The morning air out on the circular platform of the Belfry at the base of its steeple revived Paul's senses for a second as he was dragged toward the edge. By the time he was pushed over the railing of the platform, he was conscious, though disabled by the concussion from the blow to the head. Two sets of powerful arms had propelled him over the railing, as if he were a cardboard cut-out.

Paul bellowed with anger as he plunged almost 300 feet to his death. He had wanted a bureau chief's job back at headquarters in Langley, or at least a station chief's position in Paris or Rome. But his all-consuming ambition had put an end to those dreams, and to him as well.

Paul's screams of protest as he fell were heard by no human ears. They were drowned out by the exquisite sound of the 49 bells in the Belfry's carillon, which sounded its death knell, as he hurtled through space.

Mario had roamed around the old city for more than an hour and a half in the darkness, hoping to catch sight of either Lovett or the intruder in the Secure Room. Of course, it was possible Lovett had taken the intruder into custody and that the M.P.'s at this moment were transporting him to the stockade. But, he had seen no sign of either man, and as Mario roamed about, outside the main entrance to City Hall he was confronted by a small iron statue of a monkey sitting on a perch with the words "Le singe du grand garde" inscribed below. The symbolism was perfect. It was almost as if Lovett had placed the statue there to emphasize that he had just made a monkey out of Mario.

Mario gazed up at the Bancloque with its lighted dial overlooking the Grand Place. It was 0510 hours and he again started searching. He wandered over to the Spanish House, walked past it and wound up in front of the Belfry just as the bells of the carillon began sending forth their divine sound. Mario was for a moment mesmerized as the glorious noise infused the early morning darkness with its majestic beauty. Then prompted by a hunch, Mario approached the door of the Belfry to see if it was unlocked. But as he reached for the iron door handle the doors swung open violently, smashing into him and knocking him down on the top step of the Belfry entrance, and then down the twelve stone steps to the sidewalk. Laying on the sidewalk with the wind knocked out of him, Mario caught a glimpse of two burly, black-clad figures hurrying down the steps toward him. One of them was affixing a silencer to a hand-gun while the other was already pointing a revolver in his direction. Mario grabbed desperately for his Luger, realizing the chances of his shooting both assailants before they took him out were between slim and none. But now there was a third figure who appeared from nowhere behind the two hostiles descending the steps. The third man towered above the other two. Reaching one of the hostiles he fired a muffled shot into the back of his brain. In another split second he grabbed the second assailant from behind, threw a gorilla-sized arm around his neck and broke it with one violent twist. With the bodies of the two dead hostiles strewn on the stone steps, Captain Jack Lurch carefully descended the remaining steps to the sidewalk where he helped a stunned Mario Tonelli to his feet.

Munich, July 25, 1961

"Our man is coming in. There was an incident at the Belfry and he barely escaped with his life. It's too risky to keep him out there any longer. In any event, he made an identification at Mons. It's too early to tell of course, but he may have found Jurist II. I have already started the wheels turning on the follow-up investigation. Hopefully, we'll have proof-positive soon. In the meantime, the suspect has disappeared."

Fred had gathered Barnstable, LeBron, O'Malley and Booker together in the large conference room to brief them on the dramatic news from Mons. Barnstable had never looked happier; O'Malley was clearly excited;

LeBron too seemed thrilled by the news and Booker appeared pensive, but also pleased.

"But here's the twist," continued Reitenhauser. "Our guy had a rival who was apparently also in pursuit of Jurist. Due to a set of bizarre circumstances which I won't waste time on now, Hostile caught up to the rival and afterwards bumped into our man, by pure coincidence. They went after our guy too but my 'muscle' on the scene eliminated them; but not before they had tossed the rival off the top of the Mons Belfry."

The net result of the evening's events was two dead hostiles and another dead spook who couldn't be identified after hitting the ground face first from a height of three hundred feet. He wore Army fatigues but carried no identification. I tried to find out who he was and who he was working for but both NATO Command and The Company (i.e. CIA) have clammed up and are in information lock-down. I can't even get General Ames or Colonel Stansfield on the phone. And Q is said to be on a week's cruise in the Mediterranean.

The Whitehouse: Oval Office, July 25, 1961

"What is it that is so important, Kenny, that it couldn't wait until I finished the edits to this speech?"

The President of the United States softened his mild rebuke of Kenneth O'Donnell by flashing his famous Boston-Irish smile. Then as he took an emphatic bite of toast, he tossed another question at O'Donnell before the latter could answer the first. "Had breakfast yet Kenny? I can have Cook bring up some eggs for you."

One of John F. Kennedy's ways was to kid around with and tease those he felt closest to and for whom he had the greatest affection. To Kennedy it was recreational sport, and a way of alleviating the tension which seemed to engulf him and his inner circle eighteen hours a day.

The favorite targets for presidential ribbing were Kenny O'Donnell, Ted Sorensen, Dave Powers, Pierre Salinger and to a lesser extent, Bobbie Kennedy. In more formal foreign policy sessions, U.N. Ambassador Adlai Stevenson, whom Kennedy liked and respected, was nonetheless a target for his jibes. Kennedy was also very fond of Secretary of Defense, Robert McNamara, but meetings with McNamara were usually of too serious a nature, to lend themselves to jocular teasing and ribbing.

Ignoring his boss's opening zinger, O'Donnell got right to the point. "No thanks, sir. Already had breakfast. What I have to tell you can't wait. Got a wake-up call from Paul Nitze. The story he told me didn't make a whole lot of sense, but the short of it was that hostile intelligence murdered one of our undercover agents in Mons, Belgium. Nitze thinks the victim was CIA, but can't be sure. And, strangely, Army Intelligence, who just happened to arrive on the scene, then killed the two hostile agents."

Suspecting there was more about the incident than he was willing to let on to O'Donnell, the president chewed on the news for a half-minute or so before responding. "What do we know about our agent other than he was probably CIA?"

"Nothing yet. He was pushed off the Belfry in Mons and his body was too smashed up for identification."

"Well, lets get Nitze on the phone. The whole thing could be simply operational; but Bobby got the scoop from one of his sub-rosa sources at the Soviet Embassy that the son of a bitch ambassador there, Menshikov, has been whispering in Khrushchev's ear that I don't amount to much, that I don't have much courage. Bobby just sloughed it off as a sycophant's telling his boss what he wanted to hear. But, some of our enemies over at the Pentagon got wind of it and leaked Menshikov's words to the press, probably to pressure me into taking bold military action. And, of course, Khrushchev is always trying to goad me into doing something stupid by rubbing my nose in the Bay of Pigs mess. Bumping off one of our agents could have been a further provocation by the bastard."

"All right Kenny. I know what I have to do. Tonight's speech to the nation has to be a lot more than for the ears of millions of Americans in front of their TV sets. First and foremost, it needs to be directed at both the Kremlin and the Pentagon. Find Ted Sorensen and get him in here. You go back to your office and try to set up a telephone conference for me with Bundy and Nitze for 11:00 A.M. Until then Ted and I will be hard at work on this speech.

July 25, 1961—The Aegean Sea—off the coast of Crete

Q was too livid to even emerge from his state room of the Aristotle Onassis-owned cruise ship, *Neptune III*. He would not go ashore to Crete with the other sightseers from his party on this woeful day.

The main target of his ire was T. Nelson Spratt, the blue-blood, Yale graduate and Skull and Bones member who had been Remington Pierce's case officer for the Mons operation. How could he have allowed Pierce to wander so far from the operational plan? Q's anger at Pierce was just as virulent, but was somewhat counter-balanced by the grim satisfaction he took from Pierce's death and the manner in which he died. Over and over since getting the news by telex from CIA Munich Station at 11:00 A.M., Q had nurtured and cultivated the thought that in the few seconds it took for Pierce to hit the ground from the top of the Belfry, he had realized how he had fucked-up and let Q down.

As for that Ivy League sissy, T. Nelson Spratt, the bloody fool could kiss his career goodbye. Q would start things in motion to drum him out of "The Company," even before Q landed back on the French Mediterranean Coast.

Then, there was the man for whom Q's enmity had risen to its all time high: Major Frederick J. Reitenhauser. Q swore a blood oath to himself that Reitenhauser had beaten him for the last time. It would take considerable time and thought for Q to come up with fitting retribution. But whatever retaliation he chose, it would have to be one which included the clear message to Reitenhauser that he had been defeated by the better man.

July 25, 1961 The Oval Office, 8:00 P.M.

Dr. Max Jacobsen sat in a West Wing room with various White House staffers. Unlike the others present, he barely heard the beginning sentences of the president's much ballyhooed speech to the nation, so transfixed was he on the President's physical appearance as shown on the TV screen pushed against a government-gray wall. The additional steroids he had given Kennedy to relieve some of his tensions appeared to have worked.

Incongruously, however, Kennedy appeared simultaneously relaxed and uncomfortable to Jacobsen's trained eye. But Jacobsen knew that as soon as Kennedy began to ease into the address he was now delivering to hundreds of millions of people around the world, the discomfort caused by the heat of the Klieg lights and the hot summer night would melt away. And so it did as powerful words delivered in soaring cadences began to caress the ears of the multitudes, urgently seeking reassurance from the world's most powerful leader that he would protect them from nuclear annihilation.

As to America's legal rights in Berlin, Kennedy left no room for doubt that he would keep his promise, to make good on our commitment to the two million free people of that city. Pointing to a map he declared that, "it would be a mistake" for the Soviet Union to view Berlin as a "tempting target" because of its location more than a hundred miles within Communist East Germany.

Ratcheting up the drama the president then unleashed his eloquence in a fury of passion. "It has become, as never before, the great testing place of Western courage and will. We cannot and we *will* not permit the communists to drive us out of Berlin, either gradually, or by force. We will at all times be ready to talk, if talk will help."

Pausing only to elevate his volume and shift the tempo of his delivery, Kennedy punched out a stern admonition, "But... we... must... also... be... ready... to... resist... with... force... if... force... is... used... upon us."

Then, adopting a manner reminiscent of Franklin D. Roosevelt's famous fireside chats, Kennedy eased off his bravado in order to provide an explanation to his global audience, as if they sat before him in a classroom with a seating for five hundred million. "The choice is not merely between resistance and retreat, between atomic holocaust and surrender. Our response to the Berlin crisis cannot be merely military in nature. We have a duty to mankind, to seek a peaceful solution, if such a thing is possible. We will extend the hand of understanding, and we hope that our adversaries will be wise enough to accept it. But they should not mistake our compassion for weakness. We want peace, but we will not bargain away freedom in order to purchase it. We will *not* concede our rights, or the rights of our fellow humans."

Finally, with a flourish of unfurled rhetoric, the president soberly but forcefully delivered his overarching pronouncement to friend and foe alike. "We seek peace, but we shall *not* surrender."

The speech was Churchillian in its effect, rallying a beleaguered western world to make a stand against communist aggression, and to defend the right of Berliners to self-determination.

Americans and Western Europeans strongly approved of the president's determination and firmness.

Polls conducted after Kennedy's break-out speech provided revelations to the Administration. Sixty percent of Americans believed the Berlin stand-off would lead to nuclear war. Fifty five percent believed that Moscow would not back down from their intention to block-off Berlin. Surprisingly, however, there was little support among the public for negotiating with the Soviets.

Vacationing in the Black Sea resort of Sochi, Khrushchev threw a temper tantrum when Gromyko informed him of the content of Kennedy's speech. Upon his return to Moscow, he called Kennedy's disarmament representative, John McCloy, into his Kremlin office and told him Kennedy's position on Berlin and accompanying military build-up were taken by the Soviet Union as a threat of war.

McCloy took the opportunity to reaffirm what had already been communicated to the Soviet Foreign office via diplomatic channels. No unilateral treaty could abrogate the three Western powers' responsibilities and rights in West Berlin, including the right of unobstructed access to the city.

Part II, Chapter 8

Metaphor Transformed

August 12, 1961, West Berlin at Brandenburgplatz

Warren Olney loved the City of Berlin, its elegance, sophistication, and grandeur. The fact that he had been shot near the Brandenburg Gate not more than three hundred feet from where he now sat failed to dampen his ardor for the magnificent cosmopolitan center of German history, architecture and culture, that was Berlin.

This particular balmy summer evening marked the first time he had ventured out in public since that day almost four months earlier when the Red Guard had turned his Opel Kadet into Swiss cheese on wheels. The militant Red militia, in perforating his car with a blizzard of lead, had hit all four occupants.

Like Olney, his East German agent, No. 18339, had survived and was once again operational. But, Olney's two favorites, the Einmesser brothers, Jürgen and Hans, had expired from their wounds before they could even be extracted from the wrecked automobile.

Olney shifted his weight on his chair at the open-air café where he had just enjoyed a supper of cold meats: liverwurst, beef and tongue, together with an excellent potato salad, washed down by a bottle of Liebfraumilch wine. But, his rapidly healing abdominal and lower back wounds still did not allow him to sit in one position for more than fifteen minutes without experiencing sharp twinges of pain.

After adjusting his position to a relatively comfortable one, Olney lifted his brandy snifter almost imperceptibly above the surface of the table and offered a silent toast to his two fallen comrades-in-arms, immediately followed by an oath of retribution against their murderers. By one of life's little twists of fate, a reflex action had somehow caused his body to turn sharply in the direction of the driver's side window upon his being shot. Looking straight at him from the front passenger seat of the enemy's car was one of his attackers. Olney would never forget that face and especially

119

the jagged scar traversing from cheek to cheek across the bridge of the assailant's nose. If it took the rest of his life, Olney would bring the scar-faced attacker to justice. Or, at least to his own version of justice.

Agent 18339 later told Olney that the scarred man was a pernicious sadist, known throughout the Red Guards as 'Hate-face Heidégger.'

Olney usually dined alone. His sullen and withdrawn demeanor didn't attract many dinner companions. He preferred it that way. Until the Army sent him to Munich he worked alone too—as a black ops agent-handler and infiltrator behind enemy lines—first in Korea and then Indo-China. There he had no friends. Now, however, he had his first and only friend, Mitchell Blake, his section chief at the 409th in Munich. Blake was a civilian, a GS-11 who headed up the German desk under the enigmatic Major Frederick Reitenhauser. Blake was everything Olney was not: gregarious, extroverted, worldly and popular with just about everyone. And he was socially connected as well, having married the debutante daughter of a high U.S. Embassy Official in Paris.

For some odd reason, Blake befriended Olney, welcomed him into his home; and together they polished off a bottle of Glen Livet in their private booth at Oscar's one or two nights a week. "Oscar's" was a favorite watering hole for Americans in, or employed by, the U.S. Military in Munich. There Blake would talk and Olney would listen. But, their relationship was more complicated than that. Olney had intuited a dark side to Blake submerged deep within the recesses of his character. Blake sensed that Olney knew of this recondite side of his nature but was comfortable with the fact that he could trust Olney not to go there. The irony and paradox of a friendship in which neither man ever probed beyond the other's surface suited each of them just fine.

Although Blake and Olney worked together in the office, each preferred to go solo on field assignments. Olney had been relieved and excited when Reitenhauser finally pulled him out of rehab and sent him on his current mission to Berlin. He found undercover investigations both physically and intellectually challenging, and this one should be more so than most.

Olney decided he would just sip his brandy in order to justify his stay at the café until shortly before 2300 hours, the time of his appointed meeting with Agent 18339 at a small, dimly-lit municipal park on Friedrichstrasse. The park was approximately two hundred meters from the Brandenburg Gate. The agent would be crossing over from East Berlin under a time-tested "government official" cover, complete with forged documents and disguise. Olney was also fortified for their meeting by his own cover, that of an agricultural technology consultant employed by the United Nations.

The purpose of their meeting: for 18339 to brief Olney on the results of his inquiries in East Berlin as to the whereabouts of Jurist II, rumored to have fled to East Germany following an alleged identification by U.S. military intelligence in Mons, Belgium.

The combination of letters and numbers in the message from 18339, retrieved from a dead-drop at Templehof Airport, told Olney that the agent had something of the greatest urgency to report concerning Jurist II's whereabouts.

The excitement of being back to work, complemented by the effect of the brandy, opened the locks to Olney's theretofore imprisoned sense of purpose. Previously contained streams of enthusiasm began flowing in powerful currents through the passageways of his mind. But the flow of positive energy never quite reached the level of euphoria. Something counterintuitive in the stimuli impinging upon Olney's senses obstructed the river to the delta of his soul.

At first the stimuli registered only subliminally. Then, small anomalies of sight, sound and smell pricked his consciousness like a needle.

An unusually strong smell of diesel fuel exhaust blanketed Brandenburgplatz. A steady rumbling of trucks on the move was a discordant noise, not usually associated with auto-oriented downtown Berlin. Red and yellow lights began flashing everywhere within Olney's sight-line, as his ears were assaulted by the raucous noise of power-drills on the streets and avenues in the vicinity of the East Berlin crossing. Horns began to blare, at first sporadically, but then with greater frequency—as if part of a build-up to a symphonic grand finale.

Olney paid his bill, left the café and began strolling about in an attempt to get a better sense of what was going on. He soon realized that the noises of the vehicles and pile-drivers were coming from the East Berlin side of the gate. Loud voices carrying the authority of command emanated from that side of the crossing. The squeal of brakes from vehicles brought to sudden stops added to the cacophonous noise. Drifting into his second language, German, Olney exclaimed to no one in particular, "Es gefällt mir nicht." ("I don't like it.") His most disturbing discovery was that traffic, which at 2245 hours usually flowed freely through the Brandenburg Gate, had ground nearly to a halt.

Olney would not risk drawing attention to himself by asking anyone what was going on. Instead, he walked directly to Kaiser Wilhelm Park, arriving at 2255 hours. He hoped whatever was causing the disturbances in the area would not prevent Agent 18339 from showing up on time for their meeting at 2300. But in view of the weird things that were happening, he was beset by doubts.

Olney sat alone on a park bench for the better part of two hours before reluctantly concluding that 18339 was not going to show up for a meeting, for the first time during their three year relationship. He got up and walked the short distance to the Brandenburg crossing. It was now 0100 hours on 13 August, an hour when the buzz and clamor of Berlin would normally have begun to subside. Not so this time. The sounds and lights instead appeared to be building toward a clamorous crescendo. Added to the noises of pile-drivers and rumbling trucks were the sounds and sparks of welder's tools, and the piercing screeches of power-hammers driving nails and bolts into metal. And human voices were everywhere, louder and by turns more insistent and urgent, anxiously driven by the desperation born of infinite tasks to be accomplished in a finite amount of time.

Orders were shouted, men hurled curses at other men and at the fates, for bringing them to this time and place in human history.

Rough men were screaming commands to hurry up. "Macht schnell!"

Older and injured men were pleading for help. "Konnen Sie mir behilflich sein?"

The multifarious shouts and laments, the roar of hundreds of trucks and bulldozers; the crash of steel upon rock; the admonishing police sirens; the undulating beams of search lights and the growling/barking attack dogs, ready to be unleashed at those who would gather the audacity to question or interfere with Satan's work-in-progress, all combined with the acrid smells of destruction to produce a sound and light spectacular from the nether regions of Hell.

At the Brandenburg Gate, Olney still could not make out amidst the frenetic activity what was going on. He decided to walk parallel to the border in a westerly direction from Friedrichstrasse to Wilhelmstrasse, a distance of three blocks. At Wilhelmstrasse he turned around and walked back in an easterly direction, crossed Friedrichstrasse, passed the Brandenburg Gate and kept going. Soon he crossed over Leipziger strasse and walked due east for another ten blocks. There he selected a moderately-priced hotel, checked in with only his briefcase and took the elevator to a sixth floor room. Once inside he went straight to the small lavatory, relieved himself, washed his hands and face and flopped into the one arm-chair in the room. Olney sat in total silence and stillness for twenty minutes. He was interrupted once by a knock on the door from Housekeeping, to which he replied, "Bitte, Lassen Sie mich in Ruhe!" ("Please, leave me alone!")

Finally, after his mind had drawn a clear picture for him of the roughly fifteen foot-high barrier of barbed wire either erected or in the process of being erected along the border between East Berlin and West Berlin, he spoke two words. "Ich verstehe." ("I understand.")

Olney picked up the phone on the small table next to him and dialed Fred Reitenhauser's private home number. Although it was 0230 hours, Reitenhauser was still awake in his den-rendered temporarily sleepless by the twin problems of Q and Jurist II.

"Hello."

"Sir, this is Warren. I'm in West Berlin near the border. The communists are in the process of sealing off East Berlin by building a fifteen foot barrier all along the border. Construction began at about midnight.

"Right now it's barbed wire, but from the looks of the concrete slabs being trucked into the area on the East Berlin side, my guess is they plan to replace the barbed wire with a concrete wall very soon."

"Thank you Warren. Get back here as soon as you can."

"Yes sir."

But Olney had one job to do before returning to Munich. Grabbing his briefcase and room key, he left the room without checking to see if the door locked automatically behind him.

He didn't expect to be back. He tightened his black knit tie as he rode down in the elevator. In front of the hotel, he hailed a cab and instructed the driver to take him to Von Trippenplatz, Agent 18339's alternative crossing point from East to West. Unlike Brandenburgplatz, Von Trippenplatz was in a seedy, low-rent area of the city. The majority of its occupants were muggers, pick-pockets, drug pushers, pimps, and prostitutes.

Before exiting the cab, Olney unfastened the strap of his shoulder holster to facilitate a quick draw of his Beretta should it become necessary.

About fifty meters east of Von Trippenplatz was a railway bridge over the street. The tunnel beneath the bridge was unlighted; but carved into the interior stone wall of the tunnel was an entrance to a set of lighted stairs leading up to the tracks. If 18339 was coming it would be through that doorway and into the dark tunnel where the meeting between Olney and his agent would be shrouded in darkness. But Olney saw that there would be no appearance by 18339. The winding and interlaced tapestry of barbed wire did not stop at the tracks' edge but continued across and beyond, as if to stretch to infinity.

Berliners would awaken that morning to the new reality that one could no longer walk, drive, or ride between the two sectors of their once great city. And no one could predict whether they ever would again be allowed to cross the border that divided their own city.

In what came to be known as the Berlin Wall, the metaphorical "Iron Curtain" took on a physical reality. Two days after the barbed wire barrier was erected, it was replaced by concrete barriers. A permanent wall soon replaced the barriers. The wall ran for twenty-seven miles, all along the border between East and West Berlin, at a uniform height of thirteen feet. Barbed wire was erected on top of the concrete wall.

The emigration of thousands of East Berliners to the West, a phenomenon which had been bleeding East Berlin of workers, intellectuals, engineers, scientists, architects, physicians, ad infinitum, had been choking the life out of East Berlin and East Germany while infusing vitality into West Berlin.

The situation had been appalling to the Soviets and had to be stopped. A favorite joke in the halls of the Kremlin was that so many East Germans were fleeing to the West that soon Walter Ulbricht would be the only one left. The Berlin Wall was the Eastern Bloc's desperate and crude response. To stanch the eviscerating 'brain-drain,' the communists had imprisoned their own people in East Berlin, severing their ties to family, friends and fellow countrymen.

Those who attempted to scale the wall would be shot by the border guards. It was cruel but effective. It was also legal under international law and treaties, because the wall was built entirely within the Soviet zone and did not interfere with the Western Bloc's access to West Berlin. Most observers, however, saw it as a preliminary step to the inevitable and more dangerous step of sealing off all of Berlin from the West.

The inexorable slide toward Armageddon continued.

Part II, Chapter 9

The Norstad Protocol

August 14, 1961, East Berlin

Uri Putyagin—cover name Carlton—held his copy of what U.S. Army Intelligence was now referring to as the 'Norstad Protocol,' something of an intentionally misleading characterization, since the bait letter was a directive *to* NATO commander Norstad and not *from* him.

True to Uri's prediction, a copy of the letter planted by Tonelli in the "Secure Room" had eventually made its way through the bureaucracy to his desk.

It was presidential envoy Llewellyn Chase whom Tonelli saw remove the bait letter from the 'Secure Room's' safe. Chase had not been seen or heard from since that night but the "Protocol" had been provided to the Kremlin. All indications were that Chase and Jurist II were one and the same. Uri had already reported what had transpired to Fred Reitenhauser.

Uri could see just from the copies of notices of an unusually high number of scheduled meetings within the defense network of the Supreme Soviet, that the Norstad Protocol had started a firestorm. Corroborative of that fact was a tiny article on page 19 of *Izvestia*, reporting that Foreign Minister Gromyko was cutting his official visit to the Congo short and that Deputy-Premier Mikoyan had shortened his vacation to return to Moscow.

August 15, 1961—Munich

O'Malley grabbed Barnstable's right hand and shook it energetically, while simultaneously slapping him on the back.

Barnstable wore a grin from ear to ear, suggestive of a jack-o-lantern.

"Kudos to the major and the captain, for flushing out Jurist II," enthused O'Malley. "Let's hear it for our men! Hip-Hip-Hooray!"

He was joined by LeBron in two additional refrains.

"May the feathers in your caps lead to decorations on your chests," continued O'Malley, "and someday soon to stars on your shoulders.

"Here-Here!" said LeBron.

Reitenhauser didn't particularly care for congratulatory effusions in war time, a state in which they were deeply engaged. Thus far, in the Cold War, they really hadn't won anything. Nevertheless, celebrations were good for morale once in a while. He smiled broadly, and did nothing to dampen the high spirits in the room.

One of Fred's great strengths as an intelligence man and as a CO was that he missed nothing of importance. As his three trusted aides exulted in the moment, Fred couldn't help but notice that while Doug Booker joined in the celebration, the smile on his face appeared to have been painted there, as if he were about to go onstage in the role of The Joker in a theatrical production of Batman.

Fred knew Booker's ways well. While the latter was saying and doing all the right things, what Fred saw in Booker was a man merely going through the motions. The stiffness of his gestures, the falseness of his smile, and the skepticism in his eyes spoke volumes.

August 18, 1961, The White House

"East Germany was hemorrhaging talent" said Nitze to the president and McGeorge Bundy. "They had to do something to stop the bleeding."

"I can see that, and Khrushchev may have created a public relations disaster for himself by doing what he did," opined Kennedy. "Let's just let him twist in the wind over this one. But what burns my ass is that we received no advance warning that the wall was going up. Frankly, Mac, I am somewhat shocked that with all his resources in Germany, Byrne wasn't able to pick-up some inkling of what was going on."

"He did," admitted Bundy, "but each time he voiced his concerns at NATO meetings, Llewellyn Chase would deflate Byrne's suspicions by declaring that 'his agents in East Berlin' had reported that Khrushchev and Ulbricht would ride out the crisis until December, when they would sign a separate treaty, sealing off Berlin from the West."

"Chase turned out to be a 'traitah'," added Kennedy. "Anything new on the search for him?"

Bundy shifted uncomfortably in his seat. "I just got off the phone with J. Edgar Hoover. Not a word. It's as if he just fell off the face of the earth."

PART III — THE THIRD SEAL OF THE BLACK HORSE

<u>FAMINE</u>

"When the lamb opened
the third seal, I heard the
third living creature say,
"Come and see!"
I looked, and there before me
a voice among the four living
creatures, saying, "A quart
of wheat for a day's wages
and three quarts of barley for
a day's wages, and do not
damage the oil and the wine!"

Revelation 6

Part III, Chapter 1

Katanga

Mario Tonelli and Káz Penchak had their eyes fixed on two good-looking and flirtatious Australian girls ('Sheilas') at the end of the bar. It was 'Damen Frei' Night at Oscar's, and women could drink for nothing provided they ordered only beer or wine. Oscar wasn't about to give away the profits he made on hard liquor. But "Damen Frei" Night was a huge draw. Young American, German, British, and Australian women—most of them employed by American Express and the University of Maryland Extension Campus—flocked into Oscar's in droves, which in turn brought young GIs in even greater numbers into the establishment. Oscar had one major unwritten rule: no uniforms. He had found that men in civilian clothes behaved better—were less likely to get into fights over whose company or battalion could "kick the other company's or battalion's ass."

While Tonelli and Penchak conferred over how and when to make their move on the Sheilas, two other young men—taller and tougher looking—asked the ladies to dance.

As the girls and their escorts brushed past, negotiating their way through the crowd to the smoky dance floor, one of them turned her head slightly toward Mario and offered her critique. "Hey mate, got tired of waitin' for you two blokes to make your bloody move."

Mario stared into his beer glass in embarrassment.

Káz pretended he hadn't heard.

After a minute or so of silence, Mario finally spoke.

"You know who those two big guys are, don't you?"

"What big guys?"

"The two that just beat us to the punch with the Aussies."

"Beats the shit out of me. I dunno. Interpol? Airborne Rangers?"

"Nope. Ever hear of the Green Berets?"

"Who're they? French guerillas?"

Mario laughed heartily before answering. "No, but you're on the right track. The Green Berets are a new outfit that Kennedy just formed. They're actually a special anti-guerilla unit, who go into any war where we have a stake in the outcome. They live off the land with the friendlies in the boondocks; build them shelters, teach the latest in sanitation methods, give them medicines, train their counter-insurgency militias, and fight alongside of them. Their official name is 'Special Forces,' but Kennedy gave them the nickname, 'Green Berets,' and it stuck. They are one rugged and first-rate outfit."

"How do you know those two are Green Berets?"

"By their size, build and swagger. And also because I've seen them before in uniform, up at Wyoming Kaserne."

Now it was Káz's turn to chuckle.

"Wait... What were you doing up at Wyoming Kaserne? We have no people up there. It's all infantry and armor."

"Correct for the most part, but not completely. I can't talk to you about it in here."

Later, in Mario's new forest green BMW, on their way back to their billets, he confided in Káz as much as he felt he could, which was probably more than he should have.

"Say, Káz, it's no secret around the unit who my real employer is, is it?

"Nope."

"So I bet you wonder what I've been doing hanging around the 409th with no real duties."

"The thought crossed my mind."

"The fact is buddy, I got myself caught in the middle of a shit storm. Something really fucked-up happened over at The Company. People who I reported to over there are in a world of hurt and I hear that heads may roll pretty soon. The word is they're not only in trouble with regional headquarters, but also back at Langley, and all the way up to the White House. Any way, none of that's my problem; but right now I'm trapped in Limbo. I can't go back to The Company and they have nothing for me to do here. But to answer your question from before; the major got permission from Special Forces for me to train along with the Green Berets up at Wyoming, Kaserne, which includes trips down to Bad Tölz, not too far from Garmisch, where I'm going to be attending Ranger Jump School. Since, I'm technically a civilian, Major Reitenhauser had to pull strings back at the Pentagon to get clearance for me to do this. Of course, I'm grateful, but man I want to go back to work. Nothing tugs my whistle quite like being out on assignment."

"Me too," said Káz quietly, but with an angry passion seeping through his voice.

Gerda always sensed when a new project was in the works. The buzz of adventure was everywhere, right alongside the ubiquitous used pipe cleaners, crumpled tobacco packages, and cigarette butts floating in stale cups of coffee in the conference rooms.

At 0800 sharp that morning, the major hadn't so much walked as stormed into his office, his usual cheerful "guten morgan Gerda" replaced by a crisp "Good Morning!" laden with the air of command.

"Gerda, Art LeBron, Ted O'Malley and Ed Barnstable are on their way in. Let's set up in the small conference room. I'm not to be disturbed unless it's a genuine emergency."

Then in a lighter tone and with a smile, Reitenhauser softened the mood, "Oh and Gerda, don't be alarmed by the map of the Congo on the table. Just because you studied Swahili in college doesn't mean I'm sending you on assignment to Katanga Province."

"I'm relieved, sir," replied Gerda with a hint of wry wit. Somewhat perplexed, she proceeded to make the conference room marginally presentable and to turn on the coffee maker.

Fred wasted no time. Lives were at stake. No sooner had his three top subordinates taken their seats at the conference table than he began his briefing. "Gentlemen, you all know about Invictus, and how it is a multi-pronged offensive. Of course, the biggest push by the Soviets and their Warsaw Pact allies is over Berlin. But their active support of communist insurgencies in Laos and Vietnam are escalating. And in Latin America they're fomenting so-called 'wars of liberation,' with the help of Cuba, in several different countries.

"However, the hottest front right now is in Africa. The first Democratic Republic of the Congo. Civil War has been raging there between Leopoldville and Katanga Province for the better part of a year now, since shortly after the Congo gained its independence from Belgium and Katanga Province seceded from the Republic. Tensions also exist between Leopoldville and Stanleyville."

"Khrushchev jumped into the fray in the summer of 1960 before the ink was even dry on the new nation's charter, backing the leftist politician, Patrice Lumumba, for Prime Minister. Even though the pro-Western Joseph Kasavuvu was elected president, Lumumba won as Prime Minister and immediately became the real power in central Africa."

"U.N. Secretary General Dag Hammarskjöld worked hard to try to end the secession by negotiation; and persuaded the Security Council to send in a U.N. peace keeping force to police the border between Katanga and the rest of the Congo. His main interest was in preventing invasions by one side or the other across the border, while negotiating a reunification. But Lumumba wasn't satisfied with that. Katanga was rich with minerals— copper, cobalt, radium, diamonds—and still heavily under the influence of Belgium through the presence there of its political advisors and mercenaries. Lumumba, like the Belgians and Katanga leader Tshombe, wanted to get his hands on the mineral mines in Katanga Province. Whoever controls the Congo's natural resources holds the real power."

"The Congo presents the paradox of a poor people possessing rich resources. It's a fertile country which has neglected agriculture in favor of mining in order to reap huge profits through exporting minerals, mainly for the benefit of a few politicians and entrepreneurs, while the general population lives in poverty."

"Lumumba began haranguing Hammarskjöld to use the U.N. troops to go into Katanga and force it back into the Republic. Hammarskjöld refused, maintaining that it was not a function of the United Nations to interfere in the internal disputes of individual countries. This enraged Lumumba. If the U.N. wouldn't help, the Soviet Union would. He turned to Khrushchev who was only too happy to oblige by sending in troops, arms, military advisors and money."

"The Civil War heated up. Flare-ups of fighting between Lumumba/Soviet forces on one side, and U.N. troops on the other threatened to engulf the entire region in a full-scale war. But, Hammarskjöld continued flying in and out of both Leopoldville and Elisabethville, the capital of Katanga in search of a solution."

"In September of last year Lumumba was ousted as Prime Minister in a coup d'état. He was replaced by leftist Antoine Gizenga but refused to accede. He and his faction continued vying for power."

"The facts of what happened next are a bit hazy, but somehow Lumumba wound up in Lubumbashi in January of this year. He was tortured and executed shortly after his arrival. Belgian officers under Katanga command were present at the execution. This blew the lid off Hammarskjöld's efforts to restore peace and establish unity. The country was awash in anti-colonial feeling and emotional turmoil over what they viewed as the political assassination of Lumumba."

"Khrushchev exploited the situation by making a speech in which he blamed Lumumba's death on Hammarskjöld's removal of U.N. troops and threatened to support a socialist take-over of the entire Congo with Russian troops and Congolese leftist forces."

"In Washington, Kennedy had barely learned the geography of the White House before he was faced with a Cold War confrontation over Africa. He was shocked by Khrushchev's inflammatory words and at first couldn't quite believe that Khrushchev would risk the possibility of a world war over what was essentially a local problem. But this was only January. I'm told that in the last seven months he, like us, has come to view the Congo crisis as another major Soviet front in Operation Invictus. Carlton tells me that there is even a move afoot within the highest echelons of the KGB to assassinate Hammarskjöld. Naturally, I have passed this information on to Washington."

"Anyway, after the uproar over Lumumba's death, Hammarskjöld was forced to take a tougher stance with Katanga. The big sticking point was the continuation of a strong Belgian presence in Katanga where Belgian paramilitary groups enforced the continued bleeding of the Congo's rich mineral resources, just as it had done when it was the ruler of the roost in the old Belgian Congo under King Leopold II."

"Hammarskjöld forced Katanga to the bargaining table under threat of U.N. military intervention and wrested an agreement from Tshombe that all Belgian advisors, military personnel and mercenaries would be evicted from Katanga immediately. This was a couple of months ago. As it turned out, and not surprisingly, Tshombe lied through his teeth. The Belgian military personnel left but not the advisors and mercenaries. The agreement was a mere ruse to allow the Katanga government and the Belgians to continue doing what they had been doing all along. Too many people were getting rich off the mines to make any real change. To make things worse, once the official Belgian military units left, a new opportunity opened up for Khrushchev. As we know, nature abhors a vacuum and the Soviets moved in surreptitiously to fill it. Carlton also told me that there are now legions of KGB and GRU in Lubumbashi and everywhere else in Katanga. CIA has also upped its presence there in response and American and Russian undercover agents are now tripping over each other's feet. The risk of an international incident is very high. And to exacerbate the situation, the U.N. Security Council has now sent U.N. troops into Katanga to hunt down and arrest the Belgian advisors and mercenaries. The name of the intervention is 'Operation Rumpunch,' which brings me to the reason for this meeting."

"Paul Nitze and George Kennan, formerly of the Group of Eight, have been asked by McGeorge Bundy to closely, though unofficially, monitor the escalating crisis in the Congo. Nitze has called me several times in the past few weeks. Obviously, he knows that we have a resource who can provide information like no one else. But that's not the only reason he has been calling me, and this is highly sensitive. Nitze tells me the National Security Council believes that our station is one of the few overseas area intelligence units that combines both unique information-gathering with total trustworthiness."

"What about CIA in West Germany?" interrupted O'Malley.

"Glad you asked that question," Fred said. "Q has come way down in the estimation of just about everyone. He is catching most of the blame for the Mons debacle, and deservedly so. Nitze tells me the president is furious over the loss of a major CIA operative, combined with the disappearance of Llewellyn Chase. The president wanted to fire Q on the spot, and haul him back to Washington for FBI interrogation. Bundy told him that was impossible, so long as Q was running one of our top double agents, a former Czech assassin who is also one of Khrushchev's top enforcers. While Q's guy doesn't have the kind of high-level access of a Carlton, he is still very important."

"So, Q stays in place, albeit in a greatly diminished role, and Nitze says we are expected to pick up most of the slack. He gave me permission to hold on to Tonelli, whom we got on loan from Q. Tonelli stays on the CIA payroll but, for the foreseeable future, he's on special assignment to us. Right now, he's getting some special forces training over at Wyoming Kaserne, and down at Bad Tölz. Kázimir Penchak will be joining him in the program tomorrow, though he doesn't know it yet."

"I am forming a new team composed of Tonelli and Penchak as the field operatives with you, Art, as case-officer. I'll tell you the reason in a minute."

"Gerda, give Mr. LeBron the dossiers on Tonelli and Penchak when he leaves," ordered the CO into the intercom.

"Yes, Major."

The finely tuned antennae of Fred Reitenhauser instantly caught vibrations from Barnstable, which he interpreted as a bit of insecurity mixed with jealousy. Seamlessly, he continued, "Naturally, all operational plans for the new team's mission in Africa, which we'll call 'Operation Juno,' will be worked out in conjunction with Ed Barnstable, and will be subject to his approval."

Barnstable's discomfort meter dropped back to a scale just above zero.

"Okay, let me tell you about Juno," Fred said. "But before I do that, I want to bring you current on something else. As I told you, the fall-out from the Mons incident was enormous. But, our unit performed admirably and General Tug Saylor at Group has asked me to assign an analyst/investigator to take charge of the follow-up. There are simply too many loose ends for anybody's comfort level. That job has gone to Doug Booker, which is why you haven't seen him around the offices for the last few days. And Warren Olney is going to be tied up as well for the foreseeable future trying to take care of his agents on the other side of the Berlin Wall."

"But, back to our latest mission. There are over fifty million people in the Congo. It is the second largest country in Africa and the eleventh largest in the world. Because of sub-par agriculture and poor allocation of resources, it has always had a hunger problem, but rarely has this grown into a crisis. Up until a couple of months ago, feeding the population was manageable, with the help of the United Nations World Food Bank—even in the midst of Civil War."

"Suddenly, something has really gone haywire. Even in the secessionist State of Katanga, hunger has become a huge problem. In the rest of the Congo, the hunger problem threatens to escalate into a famine."

"Why would that be?" asked LeBron.

"The immediate reason is simple," said the CO "The World Food Bank deliveries aren't getting to the people. Why they aren't and what can be done about it is what we have to find out. It's not as though there is anyone we can ask. The entire region is in chaos. It's hard to tell who's in power on any given day. Gizenga didn't even take over Lumumba's seat of government in Leopoldville. He set up his government in Stanleyville. Then you have the former French province of the Congo run from Brazzaville; and Katanga Province run out of Lubumbasi, by Moise Tshombe. And, none of them like the United States. Add to this the jockeying for position by pro-Gizenga forces, pro-Tshombe forces, Belgian paramilitary units hired by the mine owners, Soviet-backed guerillas, U.N. Forces, CIA and KGB. It's a unholy mess from which we are receiving very little reliable information."

"The clear danger of a country-wide famine has to be dealt with quickly. With millions in the Congo and neighboring countries living at bare subsistence level, a major famine would trigger a transcontinental war."

"Tug Saylor has been advised by the State Department that they strongly suspect the impending famine to be the product of political design. If any group vying for power or attempting to sell its ideology can blame opposing ideological groups for famine, that's a pretty powerful political card to play. One of the main questions to be answered is who has the most to gain by creating famine in the Congo?"

"Combined Special Forces and Military Intelligence is sending a thousand-man contingent into Katanga Province at the invitation of Moise Tshombe. It will be composed of two hundred and fifty Green Berets, five hundred airborne infantry and two hundred and fifty administration/food distribution specialists. Embedded in all three contingents, under cover of the particular unit's military occupational specialty, will be covert intelligence specialists."

"The overall mission is to investigate the reasons for the collapse of the U.N. food distribution effort and to establish and protect by armed force, if necessary, the food, clothing and medical care dispensaries, warehouses and camps throughout the Congo."

"Tonelli and Penchak will go in undercover, as Green Berets. The landing will be at Elisabethville Airport, but once on the ground, our guys will break away from the main force to carry out their own operational plan. Generall Saylor has arranged for them to be met by an interpreter and a guide. They're regular retainers of Group from Brazzaville."

August 25, 1961, Elisabethville Airport, State of Katanga

A scuffle had taken place between American soldiers and demonstrators in the Arrivals Terminal of Elisabethville Airport. All along the exit corridor and behind the wooden horses, specially set up to separate the U.S. Special Forces Company from other passengers, demonstrators held protest signs and loudly chanted, "Colonialist pigs go home."

When a few young demonstrators leaped over the barrier and attempted to spray the soldiers with red paint, a melee ensued, as the Green Berets wrestled the demonstrators to the ground. When the scuffling finally ended and the demonstrators had been subdued by airport police, the Green Beret Company was missing two soldiers.

Tonelli and Penchak had slipped away unnoticed. They weren't missed. They stuffed their green berets into their fatigues' pockets seconds after being met by two Congolese escorts, who hustled them out of the building through a private exit.

Once clear of the building the four men jumped into the back of a gray van, which sped away and out of the small airport.

"Welcome to the embattled Province of Katanga gentlemen. I am Claude, your interpreter, and my friend here is Pépe, our guide."

Handshakes were exchanged.

"How did you like the little diversion we arranged for you at the airport?"

"Very well done," said Tonelli. "But don't tell me you arranged the entire demonstration?"

"Oh, no, no, Monsieur. We bought only the spray paint and the provocateurs," said Claude, who laughed with genuine pleasure as his eyes danced with mischief.

Pépe merely smiled.

Part III, Chapter 2

Port Franqui

August 25, 1961, The White House, 7:30 A.M.

The president and his younger brother, the Attorney General of the United States, were having one of their frequent wide-ranging, early morning conversations on the State of the Union.

"Ah... Bobby, did you... ah... heah... what that S.O.B. Khrushchev... said... ah... to Ambassador Thompson at the... ah, Kremlin?"

"No, Jack. Not yet."

After sipping coffee from his one physician-allotted cup of the day, the president picked up a State Department briefing memo from his desk.

"It says heah that when the Ambassador was told by Khrushchev that Dag Hammarskjöld had connived to kill Lumumba, and that the U.N. was being used to oppress peoples and help colonialists retain colonies,' Thompson replied that it 'would be wise to keep the Cold War out of Africa.' That prompted Khrushchev to pointedly ask the Ambassador, 'how socialist states could then support a policy of assistance to those who betray their own people'?"

"That sounds like one more example of how Chairman Khrushchev would sooner see millions die of starvation and disease than live under a capitalistic system," replied Robert Kennedy grimly.

August, 27, 1961—Port Francqui, Republic of the Congo, 2200 hours

The four men were identically dressed in black corduroys, black windbreakers and ski masks. From behind an inverted life boat which sat on a low platform they peered at two cargo ships docked side by side. It was low tide on the narrow sea coast of Leopoldville Province, in the medieval city of Port Francqui.

After dismissing their driver just north of the airport, Pépe had taken over behind the wheel with Mario riding shotgun. Káz and Claude sat in the back of the van where the latter entertained the sometimes taciturn Káz Penchak with captivating stories of espionage, intrigue and black magic in darkest Africa. For Káz, Claude's tales made the hard, bumpy, 22 hour drive to Port Francqui seem much shorter.

Upon arrival, they had hidden the van in a cluster of trees near the shore, locked it with their duffel bags inside, quickly consumed a breakfast of K rations and instant coffee heated on a sterno stove and headed out to do some reconnaissance of the city's docks. They were there basically because of a tip from one of 14332's sub-agents that the docks of Port Francqui were among the most corrupt and spy-saturated of any on the western coast of Africa.

They broke up before venturing out into 2 two-man teams. Káz and Claude were one, Mario and Pépe the other. All four men carried Smith and Wesson .45 revolvers, removed from the Americans' duffle bags, and equipped with silencers. The revolvers fit snuggly into the ankle holsters also supplied by Mario and Káz.

It was during the day that Pépe and Káz came upon the two cargo ships moored at a northernmost location on the five mile waterfront. The name painted prominently on the starboard bow of the larger of the two ships was "The Great Swede."

Since the only great Swede that Káz had heard of was Dag Hammarskjöld, he wondered if this wasn't a supply ship under contract to the U.N. World Food Bank. As it turned out, he was correct in his assumption. His reaction to the words painted on the side of the other ship was more visceral and intuitive. A covert operative's raw instincts were often the difference between success and failure. Between life and death.

The words were, 'National Front for the Liberation of Angola.' Why was that title setting off alarms in Káz's memory bank?

Later that day the four men traded info and ideas. They unanimously agreed that it was no coincidence that a cargo ship docked in a Congo port city where U.N. food bank shipments were received daily, just happened to bear the name, The Great Swede.

Only Mario and Káz, however, professed to see a connection between a probable U.N. supply ship and neighboring Angola's liberation front. Mario reminded them that the CIA had reported to all western intelligence agencies that the Angolan liberation organization had been infiltrated heavily by KGB from its inception; and now was considered to be little more than a front for the USSR and its communist surrogates in Angola. Angola was another nation in ferment with a powerful liberation movement seeking to cast off the yoke of centuries-old Portuguese colonial domination. It was one of the Soviets' favorite targets for a "war of liberation."

Yet Claude and Pépe strongly resisted the notion of a connection between the two ships. Why was that?, wondered Mario.

But now at 2200 hours as the four men peered at the ships, all doubt of a connection between them was dispelled. Spotlights shining from vertical posts on both vessels clearly revealed a wide plank connecting their docks. Both sides of the plank bore a three or four foot vertical mesh of hemp, or perhaps nylon, which served to keep the flow of cartons moving from "The Great Swede" to the Angolan ship by conveyor belt, from falling off into the water.

At the end of the plank on the Angolan ship stood a man holding what appeared to be a clipboard. Káz lifted his binoculars to his eyes and stared intently at the figure on the Angolan vessel. Was he checking off the arriving boxes on some sort of a manifest? His movements certainly suggested that he was. The pungent mixed aroma of the coastal air—an elixir of sea life, oil, gasoline, dead shell fish, fresh paint and seaweed served as a powerful stimulant to Káz's senses. His mind raced to a newly-formed imperative. "We need to get onto that Angolan ship," he spoke aloud. Káz's razor-sharp sensory perceptions allowed him to feel the fear emanating from the two Africans in reaction to his pronouncement. But he also caught from the periphery of his right eye the quick affirmative nod of Mario's head.

"Let's move," spoke Mario who shot out of their position like a sprinter off his starting block. Káz was only a step or two behind him. Claude was well-back from the pacemakers and Pépe took up the rear. Fortunately, they had moved the van to a nearby alley behind a bait and tackle shop and it was only a couple of minutes later that Mario and Káz arrived at the vehicle. Because of his CIA-training, Mario had been named by LeBron as team leader of the four-man group. He pulled one of the two key rings for the van from his jacket pocket and quickly opened the rear doors.

Mario pulled from the floor of the van a bulky, rifle style contraption with a steel hook sticking out of the wide barrel, and a trail of tightly-wound rope attached to the shoulder-guard.

Káz grabbed a dozen M-80 artillery simulators, often called 'salutes.' He handed three each to Claude and Pépe, as they arrived at the van. Three more went to Mario. He kept the rest for himself.

Then Mario and Káz each grabbed a pair of tight-fitting cow-hide gloves from their duffel bags, and put them on. Káz quickly felt for the presence of his knife in its belt-holster and nodded to Mario that he was ready. Mario picked up the rope-gun and commanded a firm, "Move out!"

The four men double-timed it back to the docks. Without stopping they moved out onto the dock adjoining the starboard side of the Angolan vessel. The "Great Swede" stood next to a dock located port-side.

When they halted in response to Mario's hand signal, Káz turned and looked directly into the eyes of Claude and Pépe. The fright shining brightly in both their eyes reflected a deeply-impacted fear.

Mario noticed it also and modified his plans accordingly. "Only Káz and I will board. Claude, you will fire off artillery simulators to drown out any noise made by our hook when it flies over the railing of the starboard side and hits the deck. Pépe, draw your weapon, move twenty feet back toward the shore and stand guard. Hopefully, since Káz and I will board starboard-side, 'Mr. Clipboard' and any of his helpers won't hear us coming until it's too late. Since we have seen no one on the deck of the Great Swede, I'm assuming that the cartons are coming up the conveyor belt from a cargo hold below-deck."

"If that's the case, we stand a better chance of getting on and off the Angolan ship without being discovered. Our objective is to disable the Clipboard man and any of his buddies—but not kill them—steal the clipboard, haul ass back to starboard side and rappel down the side of the boat. Any questions?"

"No questions, Monsieur Mario," Claude said. "But obviously you were never a Navy man, or you wouldn't have called this magnificent ship a 'boat'."

Mario chuckled appreciatively at Claude's attempt to break the tension. Káz gave Claude a reassuring slap on his back. Pépe grinned.

A half-minute later Mario pulled the stiffly-resistant trigger of the air-fired rope gun. The hook was propelled into the air and over the side of the railing just as the M-80's, giant firecrackers, exploded in quick succession.

Claude had impeccably timed the lighting of the fuses so as to completely drown out the thud and clang of the hook as it landed on the deck. Mario pulled hard on the rope three times before he was satisfied that the hook had anchored itself securely on the deck. Without further comment he quickly shimmied up the rope which was now laying against the side of the ship, and pulled himself over the railing.

A minute or so later, he grabbed Káz by the shoulders and pulled him safely over the railing as well. They pulled up the rope and pushed it out of the way. With Mario in the lead, they moved out with weapons drawn, in assault mode—one man moving rapidly forward while the other protects his rear until the lead man reaches a position of cover. Then the second follows and passes him until he finds a cover position, and stops. The process is repeated continuously until they reach their destination—which in this case took them to the ship's stern, around the stern and then forward on the port side toward the plank and conveyor belt located roughly midway between bow and stern.

As he had dashed past Mario's hidden position, Káz could make out the silhouette of the clipboard man's broad back. Since the success of their attack depended upon surprise, Káz made the split-second decision to take no further cover but to continue his thrust forward to the point of contact. The clipboard man was facing away from him and busily occupied examining the cartons as they moved past him on the belt and then downward to a level below deck. Káz picked up speed and closed with breathtaking velocity upon his target. He fully trusted Mario to take care of any one else on the other side of the conveyor belt, hidden from view by the girth of the target's broad shoulders. Káz fell upon his mark like a spectral force—unseen, unheard and unexpected—as if suddenly propelled from the netherworld.

The clipboard man never even felt the blow from the butt of the .45 pistol to the back of his head, delivered with enough speed and force to knock him unconscious but not crush his skull. He fell forward like a sturdy oak and came crashing down on the conveyor belt, bringing its forward progress to a halt. But his removal as an obstruction to Káz's sight line merely exposed a shocking vision of doom—an unforeseen horror—the twin openings of a double-barrel shotgun pointed at Káz's face—the darkness inside the barrels beyond their apertures holding an intimation of death. Káz could do nothing to impede his fate. The downward motion of his lightening thrust to the big man's head had left Káz off-balance and holding his weapon as a useless bludgeon. He felt the spirits of his murdered uncle and cousin beckoning him to join them in the dark and deep refuge of the land of hereafter. The man with the shotgun hesitated for a second before squeezing the trigger—perhaps because he was a seaman and a guard, not a soldier, cop, or gangster.

His want of ruthlessness saved Káz's life and probably his own too, because had he shot Káz nothing would have protected him from Mario's wrath. Instead, two muffled shots from Mario's Smith and Wesson brought the unfired shotgun crashing to the deck. The first shot went cleanly through the man's shoulder and the second smashed into the stock of the gun. Then falling upon his wounded prey, Mario delivered a sharp chop to the side of the man's head bringing him to the deck. To keep him from yelling out, Mario stuffed a bandanna in the man's mouth and tied it tightly. He also fired an additional shot into the flesh of his calf to keep him on the deck; and delivered a non-lethal blow to the back of his head knocking him unconscious.

Mario had sprinter's speed but Káz was even faster. They tore back to the stern of the ship, making the turn forward with an economy of steps. Káz held the clipboard with its sheaf of papers tightly to his side as he made his turn, and both dashed toward the location of the grappling hook and rope. They hoped they hadn't alerted any other gun-wielding crewmen. They wanted to get down the rope and onto the dock with no further incident.

Káz went first-rappelling down the side of the ship in about a half-dozen bounces, as Mario let out rope gradually from above. The clipboard was stuffed in his pants under the buckle of Káz's belt. The soft, thick tread of his athletic shoes gave him the traction he needed to make each bounce cleanly and efficiently.

Claude was elated for an instant as Káz touched down on the dock but his joy quickly turned to alarm as he spied several armed men standing on deck, near the bow and shining flashlights along the deck and railing.

"Oh no! Kázimir, look. We have trouble."

Káz turned around to see the men at the ship's bow—one of them now pointing in the direction of Mario—no more than two hundred feet away from him.

For the first time since they left the airport, Pépe was moved to utter a complete sentence. "Mr. Mario must now come down, must quick now come off the ship!"

"It's too late. They will be on him before he gets even half-way down the side. There's only one chance. Do exactly what I say," ordered Káz. "We can see them but they can't see us. We have to make them think the ship is under attack. Line up your M-80's on the dock—now! Mario and I left ours here, so we have ten altogether. Leave about four feet between each one. Claude, light the fuses at five second intervals so that the explosions will be staggered. It should sound like an artillery barrage. As soon as you finish, join Pépe and I in firing your weapon. Pépe, pause a couple of seconds between each shot. Aim above the men on the ship. Don't try to shoot them. They are not our enemy. They're just merchant sailors doing what they're told. Mario should follow our lead and fire his weapon also. Okay, move it! Start lighting those fuses Claude. Pépe begin firing your .45."

Káz and Pépe began their barrage, taking turns firing their weapons. Mario did the same—creating a cross-fire effect. The sailors ducked for cover but no sooner had they done that than all hell broke loose. The M-80's began exploding at staggered intervals, interspersed by gunfire. The combination of the guns and the explosions, followed by streaming shafts of light, set the night ablaze with the sights and sounds of all-out attack.

The shattering effect was more than the seamen could withstand. They had no experience in combat and no desire to gain any. The noise was deafening, the bursts of spectacular light awe-inspiring. The sailors held firm for a while but before the explosions and gunfire ceased, they had scattered and retreated. Káz turned on his flashlight and signaled Mario that the coast was clear. The young special ops man rappelled quickly down the rope to safety.

"Step on it Pépe," said Mario, "I want to put distance between Port Francqui and us fast!" When Pépe looked confused, Mario realized he probably didn't understand American slang expressions. "Drive fast," he shouted. Pépe now obliged by depressing the accelerator to the floor. The clunky van hurtled forward in a spasm of clanging metal parts and vibrating steel. They were beyond the city limits on the main road out of town and pointed vaguely in the direction of Brazzaville. There they would all be evacuated by a French cabin cruiser and transported to Salerno, Italy, where they would meet up with LeBron and O'Malley.

After an hour of driving close to the van's maximum attainable speed of 75 m.p.h., Mario told Pépe to pull off the road into a rest area, where no other vehicles were parked. It was now 0300 hours and few cars or trucks were on the road.

On a crude picnic table of sorts amidst buzzing mosquitos, the four men ate a meal of K rations washed down by cans of warm soda pop. But coming down off the incredible adrenalin rush from their adventure, they suddenly realized how hungry they were. The meal might as well have been filet mignon and champagne. What topped it off were the four juicy pears which Pépe produced from the van's glove compartment; and the flask of rum Claude just happened to bring along for "emergencies."

As the four new friends passed the flask around and took deep swigs of the rich, smooth liquid, their facial expressions told the story of the varied emotions they were feeling: elation, relief, excitement, satisfaction and triumph.

Back in the van, Káz began studying the sheaf of papers in the clipboard. At the top of the first sheet was typed in capital letters: CARGO MANIFEST OF GREAT SWEDE.

Flipping through the pages, Káz saw the manifest was comprised of hundreds of cartons containing canned fruits and vegetables, boxes of rice and pasta, cans of stew, spaghetti, soup, and juice; boxes of dried milk and powdered eggs, and so on. Roughly two-thirds of the items had been checked off—apparently by the clipboard man.

"It looks to me that the entire cargo of the Great Swede was being transferred to the Angolan ship," said Káz handing the clipboard back to Mario. Mario's response was a laconic, "Wow."

28 August 1961, American safe house, Salerno, Italy

A chilling early morning fog rolled in off the Mediterranean and up the shore to the bluff on which the grey-shingled safe house stood. Inside six men sat around a circular coffee table.

"Now let me make sure I understand this," ventured O'Malley to the four recent returnees from the Congo. "You boarded an Angolan merchant ship, on a rope during the middle of the night, assaulted two seamen, including one armed with a shotgun, disabled the seamen, stole the ship's cargo manifest, were discovered by armed crewmen—but on the brink of Tonelli's capture or death, you simulated a Howitzer and small-arms attack on the ship—scattering the crew and allowing all of you to escape?" O'Malley then leaned back with an expression on his face combining skepticism and bemused astonishment. He and LeBron stared at the men, waiting for confirmation or correction of O'Malley's succinct summary of the long story they had just heard.

"Yeah, that's about right," replied Mario. His three team members said nothing, but Claude nodded affirmatively.

O'Malley & LeBron sat in stunned amazement for a minute or so— O'Malley betraying his reaction by the twinkle of amusement in his eyes and his smile of admiration. LeBron was simply flabbergasted by the scope and audacity of the initiative his team had successfully pulled off.

"Well... ah... then theah it is," deadpanned LeBron, his John F. Kennedy impression heavy with sardonic wit.

Turning completely serious, he gave the team its orders. "Mario, prepare your after-action report with as much detail as you can remember.

Káz, you edit it. All four of you read the final version, and sign your names to it. Then I want the four of you to decompress and rest here for 48 hours. Walk or jog on the beach. Catch some sun. Swim in the Mediterranean. And be ready at 0800 hours on 30 August for transport to Frankfurt, where you will make yourselves available for debriefing before you return to your duty stations."

Then more softly, LeBron said, "Fine job men. I think what you have accomplished may be of great significance. We're glad you made it back safely."

31 August 1961, Munich

Reitenhauser had a full complement of his leadership people available for briefing just before most of them broke for the Labor Day weekend. It was with reluctance he had given the order that no personnel were permitted to leave Munich during the three-day weekend. Several disappointed wives had already made reservations for the beautiful getaways in the Bavarian Alps, southwestern Austria and the Black Forest. What was bothering Fred's conscience was that he didn't even have any solid information to justify banning all travel out of the city. It was just another one of those irksome feelings which came over him now and again that something troublesome was going to happen soon.

As he sat at the head of the conference table, distractedly cleaning his pipe, Fred found his sense of guilt slowly draining away as he recalled that not once in the many times he had felt a sense of impending disaster, had he been wrong. He wasn't wrong when his instincts forewarned him of the Berlin Blockade of 1948, the North Korean invasion of 1950, the Chinese intervention in Korea (also in 1950), the Soviet suppression of the Hungarian Revolt of 1956, and the Bay of Pigs debacle of 1961.

If he had to frustrate the holiday weekend plans of his personnel and their family members, so be it—even if he had nothing more to go on than instinct. Confinement to Munich was a small enough price to pay for being ready for the worst.

Seated before Reitenhauser at the conference table were Barnstable, O'Malley, LeBron, Booker, plus Czech Desk Chief, GS-12 Victor Havel; German Desk Chief, Mitchell Blake; his deputy, Warren Olney; and finally, Peter Toomey, the first sergeant of the 409th.

Reitenhauser put down his pipe in the large ash tray before him and began. "Gentlemen, I am pleased to report that an operational team of this detachment has uncovered solid evidence of the diversion of a U.N.-sponsored ship's entire food-relief cargo, intended for the Republic of the Congo, to the top communist-front organization in Angola. The particular Angolan ship has been interdicted by two U.S. Navy destroyers, also flying the U.N. flag, and forced to return the purloined cargo to the U.N. food distribution agency in the province of Leopoldville."

"But, this was just the tip of the iceberg," Reitenhauser continued. "Based on the hard evidence returned by our team to Group headquarters in Frankfurt, many other leads at Congolese ports and air fields have been pursued. The results in just the last three days have clearly revealed a massive plot to steal U.N. World Food Bank relief shipments and divert them to the communist front in Angola. Irrefutable proof has also been obtained by Group's investigators in the last 24 hours of the Warsaw Pact nations' complicity in the conspiracy. A good deal, but not all, of the food has been recovered. It's now on its way to the hardest-hit regions of the provinces of Leopoldville, Brazzaville and Katanga."

"It would appear that our team and our entire unit has helped to avert a wide-spread famine in the Congo. I personally believe the famine conspiracy to have been another phase of the Eastern bloc's Operation Invictus."

"In addition to thwarting the famine component of Invictus, U.S. Army Intelligence, Europe, has saved as many as a hundred thousand lives— men, women and children who otherwise might have starved to death in the Congo. Dag Hammarskjöld has called General Saylor, to personally thank him for Group's efforts in solving the mystery of the food disappearances."

"The part we played was pivotal and I consider it to be a victory for our entire detachment. But I would like to single out for special recognition those who were the most hands-on in our operation. They are operational planners Barnstable and O'Malley; Case officer for the operation, LeBron; and field operatives, Tonelli and Penchak, who risked their lives to make their mission a resounding success."

"The roots of the conspiracy apparently ran deep. Interpol and local police organizations have already made many arrests among U.N. employees and officials; at shipping companies; at local docks and airports. Rumors are running wild. Some believe organized crime was involved."

"It will be a long time before it is all sorted out. But, the famine crisis was not really the main reason why I called you here today. Another crisis—potentially greater-has arisen."

PART IV — THE FOURTH SEAL OF THE PALE HORSE

DEATH

"When the lamb opened
the fourth seal, I heard the
fourth living creature say,
"Come and see!"
I looked, and there before me
was a pale horse! Its rider was
named Death, and Hades was
following close behind him.
They were given power over a
fourth of the earth to kill by
sword, famine and plague, and
by the beasts of the earth."

Revelation 6

Part IV, Chapter 1

The Beasts of the Earth

Mario and Káz got together a couple of times over the long Labor Day weekend. Since the CO had confined all personnel to the city limits of Munich, there wasn't a whole lot to do for two guys in their mid-twenties who enjoyed athletic activities above all others. But on Saturday night they sampled some of the Munich night-life with a couple of young nurses Mario had gotten to know during his brief stay in the Munich Military Hospital, for treatment of his injuries sustained bouncing down the stone steps of the Mons Belfry.

Ella Fitzgerald was appearing at the Museum Island in the Isar River and the foursome attended the concert. Major Reitenhauser just *happened* to have four extra tickets for Mario, Káz and their dates.

After thoroughly enjoying the once-in-a-lifetime experience of seeing Ella perform live in her one-woman show, they topped off the evening by hitting a couple of jazz clubs in Schwabing, the night club district of Munich.

The next day, Káz and Mario met early to do some kayaking and canoeing on the Isar. The late-summer temperatures were in the low seventies, the sun shone brightly and the conditions were perfect. As they sat on the beach afterward enjoying a lunch of wurst on brochen (roll) with sauerkraut and a couple of bottles of Augustinerbrau, Mario murmured contentedly, "Káz, God is in his heaven and all is right with the world."

Both men clearly understood Mario was referring to that idyllic moment only. Once they returned to duty on Tuesday, there would be abundant reminders that there was plenty wrong with the world.

The friendship between Mario and Káz was of recent vintage. They had never met until Mario was shifted from CIA, Munich, to the 409th. They clearly had bonded during their Congo adventure and Mario was curious as to what made Káz tick-what motivated him.

"If you don't mind my asking, what made you want to become a special ops man?"

"I don't mind, but I'm not sure I know the answer. I had a pretty weird childhood. It's like I had a double life. On the one hand it was a typical American upbringing in the suburbs with Jerry Lewis, Little League, and the Milton Berle show. But on the other hand, my family carried a heavy weight on their shoulders. My parents were immigrants and displaced persons from the Sudetenland, who were forced to flee their homeland to escape the Nazis. Instead of normal, happy, American folks, I had depressed, frightened and lonely parents, trying to raise us in an alien land. They had no support from family or friends because most of them were back in Czechoslovakia. My mother died young and my father, a wire lather by trade, had a nervous breakdown. For the last ten years he has been out of work on 100% disability—existing on tranquilizer pills and T.V. dinners. And when I went back to Czechoslovakia for a visit as a pre-teen, I got there just in time for the Soviet overthrow of the free Czech government and its replacement by the Communist Party."

"My grandfather, uncle and cousin, followers of the Social Democrat, Masaryk, were all murdered by the Reds. I myself became a fugitive for the next year and didn't make it back to New Jersey until I had been gone from the states for a year and a half."

"For my whole life I have had to live with the results of what the Nazis and the Reds did. Together they destroyed my family. Both my mother and grandmother died broken persons. My father lives as a broken man. As I was growing up, some of my teachers would say that the Nazis were worse than the Reds. Easy for *them* to say. Their homeland was never invaded and plundered."

"They talk about WWII and how the Soviet Union was our ally in defeating Germany. What they almost *never* tell you, is that Russia and Germany signed a non-aggression pact in 1939, which provided that after the war each of them would get half of Poland."

"It's true that the Nazis were murdering racists—genocidal monsters— but when it comes to pure evil, it's tough to make distinctions. Stalin murdered twenty-million of his own people. Millions more are imprisoned in Siberia and the more-southern gulags."

"Churchill coined the phrase 'The Iron Curtain,' and it was a good image. But I see it more as a prison wall than a curtain. The Soviets have managed to turn all of Eastern Europe into one huge penitentiary with Khrushchev as the warden. To the Soviets, the Hungarian Revolt wasn't a revolution—it was nothing more than a prison riot. And now the evil bastards have even walled off East Berlin and threaten to deny us access to our own protectorate—West Berlin."

Káz stopped himself, his emotions beginning to overcome him.

"Tell me, Káz," asked Mario, "is you're family religious?"

"Ah... We try to attend mass most Sundays. That's about it."

"Well, my grandmother went to mass daily and practically knew the New Testament by heart. I never fully bought into it but I still remember some of the parts she would read to me."

Mario paused while a look of fond recollection softened his features. "Are you familiar with the Book of Revelation?"

"Vaguely."

"Well, there is a part of it which uses the images of the 'four horsemen of the apocalypse.' The fourth horseman, who rides a pale horse, symbolizes death. As I recall, in the Fourth Seal, Hades follows close behind the rider named 'death.' According to the verse they were the 'beasts of the earth' who were 'given power over a fourth of the earth... to kill by sword, famine and plague.' As far as I'm concerned, if this was a prophecy, it was a damn good one."

After an interlude of pensive silence, Káz spoke again while staring at the river. The words came from some place of deep awakening within himself.

"Yes, and the Soviet Union now has power over a fourth of the earth. But instead of swords, they kill with guns, tanks and bombs."

"Yeah, Mario, the moment they snuffed out democracy in Czechoslovakia and again when they put down the Hungarian revolt— slaughtered so many freedom fighters... each time I knew that they were 'the beasts of the earth' my mother also used to tell me about."

"Do you see us as warriors against the beasts of the earth?" asked Mario.

"I can't speak for you, Mario. I don't really know you well enough yet. I'm not really sure who I am or what I am. An escapist from an unhappy upbringing? A soldier of the Cold War? An adventurer? A freedom-fighter? Or maybe just an instrument of vengeance."

Mario smiled broadly as he gave Káz a soft punch in his upper right arm. "Well buddy, whoever you are, I'm sure glad you're on our side."

Part IV, Chapter 2

The Bell Tolls

Dag Hammarskjöld was killed on 18 September 1961. He was en route to the Congo in an attempt to negotiate a cease-fire between U.N. troops and Katangese forces. His Douglas DC-6 airliner crashed over Northern Rhodesia. Fifteen others on board also perished. The man who Khrushchev had vilified more than any other throughout 1961 was dead. John F. Kennedy called him "the greatest statesman of our century."

He was 56 years old. Witnesses on the ground reported a flash in the sky before the crash. The bodies of Hammarskjöld's two body guards revealed multiple bullet wounds. Official inquiries into the crash were soon to follow.

September 18, 1961, The White House

The Oval Office was engulfed in noise. There were several conversations in progress at the same time. The chatter was rife with men stepping on each other's sentences and fragmentizing them through interruptions. Occasional bursts of emotion produced elevated voices.

Kenny O'Donnell and Bobby Kennedy paced as they talked and gestured. Dean Rusk spoke mainly into a phone. McGeorge Bundy studied the early accounts of the plane crash which had come in over the wire from the American Embassy in Rhodesia. Paul Nitze—angry and grouchy—was involved in a heated argument with George Kennan. Dean Acheson pontificated to no one in particular.

Only John F. Kennedy was silent—his chin resting on his fist while he listened and ruminated, with sadness in his eyes.

"Hammarskjöld refused to use U.N. troops to defeat Tshombe and give the Leftists control over the entire Congo," asserted Bobby Kennedy. "And that's why Khrushchev had him killed," added O'Donnell.

"No," demurred Nitze, "that's not why he had him killed. Khrushchev doesn't really want U.N. troops in his targeted regions at all. They just get in his way and impede his wars of liberation. The only reason he harangued Dag about using them against Katanga Province was because the troops were already there. K figured that as long as they were in place, he might as well try to use them for his own ends."

Picking up on that theme, Acheson launched his most didactic tutorial of the afternoon. "One must never underestimate the Soviet," he warned, quaintly and pretentiously using the singular tense. "It is wily and predatory. It adapts well to changing conditions-slyly and instinctively manipulating the changed circumstances to its advantage. The Soviet smells weakness and exploits it ruthlessly. It saw Hammarskjöld's reluctance to use U.N. troops to force Katanga back into the Congolese Union, not as high-minded statesmanship, but as a soft Achilles heal. Once the Soviet perceived Hammarskjöld to be an inveterate diplomat and negotiator rather than a shrewd and powerful player like Willie Brandt, it felt secure enough to attempt his elimination."

George Kennan's eyebrows raised in reaction to what the former Secretary of State had just pronounced. "Aren't we rushing to judgment here? We have no real evidence that Khrushchev is behind this."

As an extension of their argument, Nitze responded to Kennan's remark. "Right, and we have no positive proof that the hen sitting on top of the egg actually *laid* the egg. But we can draw a pretty strong inference that it did."

"Well put Paul," intoned Acheson.

But now Kennedy had heard enough. It was time to take control of this directionless discussion. "I agree with George. We cannot afford to rush to judgment. Already we have Harry Truman out there, practically accusing the Soviets of Dag's assassination. And maybe he's right. But next thing you know, Le May and some of those other characters at the Pentagon will want to start revving up the engines of the B-52's. Has anyone spoken to Adlai? I'd be interested in what's being said up at the U.N."

"Not yet," said Bobby Kennedy.

Without further comment, the president pushed a button on his desk. "Evelyn, try to get Ambassador Stevenson on the phone."

Within minutes, the president and Stevenson were having their first of what they knew would be many conversations on the Hammarskjöld crisis. Stevenson had one piece of information that had not yet made its way to the White House. Despite early reports to the contrary, there was one survivor from the crash, Sergeant Harold Julien, who reported that a series of explosions had preceded the crash. Stevenson said opinion was clearly divided at the U.N., with the British and American diplomats favoring the assassination theory, while the French and most African diplomats leaned toward the theory that the crash was simply an accident.

Kennedy listened patiently, but when Stevenson ventured the opinion that the Soviets would not have had anything to do with it because that would have undermined their position in the disarmament talks, Kennedy became exasperated. "Adlai, during this entire year, the Soviets have demonstrated no concern whatever for the disarmament talks. Instead, they have engaged in an escalating series of provocations, starting with accusing Hammarskjöld of being involved in the death of Lumumba, encouraging civil war in the Congo, accelerating military aid to Castro, giving us an ultimatum on Berlin, cancelling the nuclear arms talks, erecting the Berlin Wall and seeking to cause a famine in central Africa. Enough! In the light of their track record over the past eight months, why would we dismiss the possibility that they assassinated Hammarskjöld?"

After Stevenson reluctantly agreed that they could not dismiss the possibility, Kennedy issued his order. "Adlai, I want your best investigators on the ground in Rhodesia within 24 hours to monitor all inquiries; and report daily to you directly. You will then report to me promptly each time you hear from them. Wouldn't you, ah... say Adlai... that the ah... situation warrants it?

"Yes, Mr. President."

September 22, 1961—Munich, 2300 hours

Fred knew he should have gone home hours ago. He wasn't accomplishing anything sitting at his desk with a pen and a legal pad in front of him. His habit when pondering a cipher, and going through mental cartwheels in an attempt to solve the mystery, was to jot down names, places and key words that might be involved with the puzzle. As he started homing in on the solution he would circle words and draw lines and arrows between them, hoping to create a chart which showed how everything was connected.

After sitting at his desk for four straight hours of solitary and uninterrupted time, the only thing appearing on the page was the logo of the University of Nebraska Football Team. Fred had grown up in a small town outside of Lincoln and the Nebraska "Cornhuskers" were near and dear to his heart. He had drawn the stylized "N" contained within a square border eleven times already and was working on number twelve.

The basic facts which were troubling him were not that complicated; yet he kept pressing the replay button of his memory over and over: Mario Tonelli clearly saw Llewellyn Chase remove the Norstad Protocol from the safe in the Secure Room. Chase left the room carrying the letter. Remington Pierce followed him out. The next day Mario checked the safe and the letter had been removed. Since exiting the Secure Room, Llewellyn Chase has neither been heard from nor seen. Jack Lurch examined the bodies of Pierce and the two hostile agents who murdered him, within minutes after their deaths, and none of them had the Norstad letter—although there was a brief time period after Pierce hit the ground for someone to have removed the letter from his person. The next time the letter was seen was when Carlton received a copy of it in East Berlin.

Where did Chase go after leaving the Secure Room? With Pierce following him, he probably left the building. But did he meet with someone else that night, or encounter someone who overpowered him and took the letter? Or someone who was given the letter by Chase voluntarily? Or did he simply leave Mons and turn the letter over to the KGB himself? There were many other unanswered questions as well.

Fred picked up the four page telex message which had come in earlier that day from Group, relating what was known thus far about the death of Hammarskjöld, and read it for the fourth time—this time somewhat wearily and with waning attention.

Without remembering exactly what had caught his attention in the last paragraph of the report, Fred flipped directly to the fourth page and re-read the final paragraph...

Hammarskjöld's body was recovered. The
first members of the search and rescue
team, including a Norwegian U.N. officer,
Björn Egge, reported that the body was
found about fifty to one hundred feet
away from the wreckage, and that there
was a hole in his forehead. Crew members
from the decoy flight also arrived on
the scene and viewed the body. They,
however, did not report seeing a hole in
the Secretary General's forehead.
Cockpit recordings of conversations
among members of the decoy flight's crew
revealed that the pilot, a Swedish Air
Brigade major, Göran Hamerdahl,
reported receiving orders from an
individual he refers to as Björ Istöuh,
apparently his U.N. ground control, to
change his flight-plan and head towards
the flight path of Hammarskjöld's
airliner. The pilot is heard saying that
his ground control made it clear that
the order came from Colonel Björn Egge,
the ground commander of the entire
operation.

Fred started getting a familiar itch on the circular bald spot at the back of his head. He read the paragraph again. The itch was now accompanied by a compelling intuition—the same type that told him Uri Putyagin was about to take a bullet as they walked up the dark Berlin street in 1945. That same intuition had told him more recently that an attempt would be made on Hammarskjöld's life. This time it was telling him that the death of Hammarskjöld and the events in Mons were connected.

It was time to start putting something more on the legal pad than the Cornhusker's logo. Fred tore off the top sheet of his pad, crumpled it and tossed it into the waste basket with his best one-handed set shot. He drew a line down the middle of a fresh sheet of paper. At the top of the left column he printed "Rhodesia;" at the top of the right, "Belgium."

Then he began printing names down the columns leaving two lines between each entry and plenty of space to write more after each name.

When finished he held the list up and gazed at it.

```
RHODESIA                        BELGIUM
DAG HAMMARSKJÖLD                MARIO TONELLI
MOISHE TSHOMBE                  LT. GEN. STEPHEN AMES
NIKITA KHRUSHCHEV               LT. COL. BARTON SPANIEL
ANTOINE GIZENGA                 LLEWELLYN CHASE
BJÖRN EGGE                      MALACHY O'DOHERTY
GÖRAN HAMERDAHL                 JOHN PAUL BYRNE
BJÖR ISTÖUH                     JACK LURCH
PATRICE LUMUMBA                 REMINGTON PIERCE
```

After reading the list twice, Fred shook his head. Man, those Scandinavian names were impossible to pronounce.

Somewhat compulsively, he made a new list of those names only and printed next to each one his take on how the name would appear if spelled phonetically:

```
DAG HAMMARSKJÖLD         DAG HAMMERSHOLD
BJÖRN EGGE               YOORN EGG
GÖRAN HAMERDAHL          GOOREN HAMMERDOLL
BJÖR ISTÖUH              YOOR ISTOO
```

He pronounced each name aloud, according to the phonetic spellings he had assigned to them. As he sounded out the last name on the list, he felt a shock of revelation course through his body.

He began writing other variations of pronunciation beneath the bottom entry:

```
BJÖR ISTÖUH
YOOR ISTOO
YOORISTOO
JURIST TWO
```

When he was done, he stared at the last pair of words on the paper. Jurist Two.

Then, he wrote a final variation:

There he was again. Jurist II, in the middle of everything, as usual.

Fred shut off his desk lamp, locked his office, and left the building after mumbling a good night to the duty officer.

For Fred, the night of September 22, 1961 was a sleepless one.

$$\star\ \star\ \star\ \textbf{\Large(☭)}\ \star\ \star\ \star$$

September 23, 1961, 0830 hours

"Colonel Dabrowski speaking."

"Colonel, it's Fred Reitenhauser."

"Frederick, how the devil are you? It's good to hear from you."

"I'm fine Colonel, but I'm calling you about what may be a pressing matter."

"Okay, shoot; but first, can the colonel stuff—just call me Ed. You and I go back too far together, starting back in '48 when we flew into Tempelhof Airport in that two-seater piper cub, to give General Clay the details of the Berlin Airlift.

But we can reminisce later. What's on your mind Fred?"

Ed, are you familiar with the telex report Group sent to its stations about Hammarskjöld?

Familiar? I wrote it. At the 44th Military Intelligence Group, the Operations officer, is no figurehead. The only thing I didn't write was the Norwegian and Swedish names. I brought in my Scandinavian linguist, Kurt Svenson, to sit through the cockpit recording on my second listen. But, the quality of the recording was uneven. It would cut in and out. I heard the names but I'll be damned if I could understand them. They were barely audible. I didn't listen to it again after the second time but I got one of our tech people to work on the tape. He cleaned it up and enhanced the volume enough so Svenson was able to make out everything on about his fourth try. Then my new Deputy Ops, Mueller, made a transcript of the recording with Svenson's help."

"Ed, does Mueller know about our little hunting expedition in Belgium?"

"Absolutely not. Why do you ask?"

"It would be helpful if you could hang up and read the transcript again with Svenson standing by to give you the pronunciations of the Scandinavian names. Then if something occurs to you, you might want to call me back."

"All right Fred. I should have known a conversation with you would never be simple. Let me hang up and see what you're driving at."

Fred stretched, stuffed his pipe with "Omaha's Finest" licorice-blend tobacco and slowly sipped his coffee. The caffeine registered with his neurons and synapses. His mind raced but his body was as calm as always—a gift from God. He never lost his cool—even in the most dire circumstances—not even when he and his patrol were surrounded in a fire-fight in the hedgerows of Normandy; or when he had to carry the wounded Uri to safety in Berlin, in '45, on the street with no name. He could not possibly have seen then that the singular act of saving a young Russian combat officer's life would produce Carlton, one of the West's most important resources of the Cold War—a man whom he was sure would soon be called upon again to come to NATO's aid.

The consensus in the highest echelons of Western Intelligence was that Jurist II had been blown, and would not be heard from again. Of course, that was predicated upon Jurist II's being Llewellyn Chase. Fred was never a hundred percent sure that he was. Chase had never seemed quite right to Fred for the role—too narcissistic and in need of flattery. Yes, a spy could play a very prominent and visible role—but at his core he needed to crave secrecy and anonymity to be effective. Fred believed that, to the contrary, Chase's essence was his craving for attention and publicity.

Fred's analytical mind and razor-sharp instincts told him that Jurist II had re-emerged. He was now convinced that the pilot of the decoy flight over Rhodesia had said "Jurist Two," and *not* "Björ Istouh."

Fred didn't really need Ed Dabrowski to confirm that for him, but as the commanding officer of an area intelligence unit, he needed to exercise due diligence before drawing a firm conclusion upon which a plan of action would be based.

The phone rang on Gerda's desk. The young secretary and gal Friday attacked it and picked up the receiver. "Yes sir," she said crisply. "Major, it's Colonel Dabrowski. He says he needs to speak to you right away."

Fred put the phone to his ear. "Hello, Ed."

"Fred, I'm hopping on a plane with Mueller in a half hour and we're coming to see you. So stay put."

"I'll be here, Ed."

"Oh and get that odd-ball genius of yours—Butcher, or Bucher, or whatever his name is—"

"Doug Booker," said Fred helpfully.

"Whatever. Have him sit in on the meeting."

"You got it."

"Fred, I'd like for us to meet at 1300 hours if that's okay with you."

"That's fine, Colonel."

"See you then," said Dabrowski, as he hung up. Fred noticed he didn't say "just call me Ed" this time.

Reitenhauser sat back in his chair and scratched his head. As to the Booker thing, he hadn't seen that one coming. He wasn't comfortable exposing Booker to Dabrowski. Doug Booker had just plopped his sixty page report of his investigation of the Mons incident on the CO's desk at 1900 hours the previous evening, and Fred hadn't even opened it yet. He had wanted to read it thoroughly and debrief Booker before Doug talked to anyone. But he couldn't say no to Dabrowski who had really made his request for Booker a direct order. Not only did Dabrowski out-rank Fred but on Group's organizational chart, he was the officer Fred answered to in the chain of command.

It was now 1000 hours, and Fred had had little sleep and no breakfast. Doug's daunting sixty page report stared up at him. If it could talk it might have said, "Well that's what you get, dummy, for bringing your superior officer into the situation."

But there was no time for second-guessing. He still had three hours to read and absorb the report, and there was no way Booker was going to open up to Dabrowski without Fred's knowing everything that was in that report. He better get busy reading.

"Gerda, tell Doug Booker to report here at 1245 hours sharp, get the new PFC in Administration to fetch me an egg sandwich from the coffee shop and put on a fresh pot of coffee."

Part IV, Chapter 3

Groundhog Redux

---

23 September 1961, Munich, 1300 hours

"Major Reitenhauser, Mr. Booker, this is my deputy, Major Matt Mueller, who will be working with us on this Jurist matter. Dabrowski set a business-like tone for the meeting right off the bat and the exchange of greetings was a bit stiff and formal. That was fine with both Reitenhauser and Booker. Neither of them had much patience with false affability. Dabrowski and Mueller took seats on one side of the conference table with Fred and Doug on the other.

Dabrowski immediately grabbed the reins of the meeting. "Here's the deal. Fred has discovered something which moves the matter of Groundhog, who we now know as 'Jurist II,' back to the front burner. The son of a bitch may very well be still operational. And if Jurist and Chase are one and the same, and the dirty weasel has resurfaced, it couldn't have come at a worse time. The governments of the Western Bloc nations are reeling over the twin disasters of the Berlin Wall and the death of Hammarskjöld. If it gets out that Jurist may have had a hand in the U.N. Secretary's death, the pressure on the U.N. and the United States to retaliate against the Eastern Bloc will be enormous. With the futures of both Berlin and central Africa at stake, who knows what kind of an ugly escalation might be triggered."

He nodded in Reitenhauser's direction. "Fred, General Saylor and I gave you and your people a lot of leeway in your attempts to identify and catch the mole. And you took us further along the road than we had ever gone. You placed Jurist in or near the G-2's section at Mons, established a connection to Chase, and planted the Norstad Protocol in such a way that it surfaced on the other side. As a result we have tightened security tremendously at NATO, USAR Europe, and CIA. We were able to locate information pipelines to the East, and close them off. You also greatly narrowed the range of suspects. And, if it turns out that Chase *is* Jurist,

159

you've identified the mole himself. Then, you shut down the famine in the Congo before it took hold. You and your people are deserving of all the accolades now coming your way... Nevertheless, Tug... General Saylor that is... wants me to take over. It's our responsibility to be more hands-on at this heightened stage of the ever-building crisis."

Fred nodded without speaking.

"The purpose of this meeting," Dabrowski said, "is to debrief you and Doug, so that we know as much as you do. Anyone who knows me well is aware of the fact that my debriefing method is not 'you talk and I listen.' Rather, it's I *ask*, and you *answer*. So before I start the Q&A, do either of you gentlemen have any questions?"

Both Fred and Doug answered in the negative.

"Okay then." Dabrowski said. "I've already interviewed Mario, so I know the basic facts of what happened in Mons. I wanted to interview Q as well, but the CIA won't let anyone near him. We don't even know where he is, which means we can't account for his whereabouts on the night that Hammarskjöld's plane was shot down."

"Let's start with the most obvious, Llewellyn Chase."

As Dabrowski turned his attention to Booker, Mueller removed a note pad and pen from his suit coat pocket and placed them on the table.

"Doug, the FBI interviewed Chase's assistant, Henry Fuchs, back in D.C., and he told them that Chase was in Mons at the White House's request to do a general audit of the G-2's operations. Did you find out anything about that in your investigation?

Booker raised both eyebrows and smiled before answering. "Believing Chase was in Mons to audit the G-2's operations for the White House would be like believing that the fox was in the hen house to audit the daily disappearances of the chickens."

"So in other words, you think Chase is Jurist II?" asked Dabrowski.

"I didn't say that," replied Booker.

Mueller blanched in obvious shock over Booker's cheekiness, but Booker continued unabashed. "Chase is, or *was*, a totally self-serving individual, who was in Mons to advance his own personal agenda. Any audit he conducted would, therefore, be useless, or worse. But that doesn't mean he was a spy."

"Please elaborate," said Dabrowski.

"Well, first of all it was no coincidence that Chase, O'Doherty, and John Paul Byrne were in Mons during the same time frame. As you may have heard, a bug was planted in the conference room where the Group of Eight was meeting the morning of the opening day of the Vienna summit conference. A tape of the recording wound up in Hostile's possession but was retrieved and delivered directly to President Kennedy.

Byrne suspected Chase of having planted the bug. He told McGeorge Bundy of his suspicions. Bundy, who knew that Chase had gone to Mons, sent Byrne on a so-called "fact-finding tour" which just so happened to land him in Mons on the first leg of the tour. The real purpose of the tour was to try to find out what Chase was up to. I have no idea what, if anything, Byrne learned.

O'Doherty is answerable only to the president and gives no information or interviews to anyone—save, of course, to POTUS. But, I did some snooping around at NATO Command Headquarters and found the paperwork relating to the Secure Room. It shows that both Chase and O'Doherty made application to General Ames for the combination to the Secure Room. Both applications were granted. This was a serious breach of security because neither man had either a top secret clearance, or a need to know. Of course, I have no idea of what kind of political pressure was brought to bear on Ames. We can never forget that Chase held the position of presidential envoy and O'Doherty needs no official position to throw his weight around.

Telephone logs at Ames' headquarters show that Ames and Commanding General Norstad spoke on the phone no less than a half dozen times a day. I rather suspect that any White House political pressure on Ames was channeled through General Norstad."

"Well, let's get back to Chase's claim that he was conducting a general audit at the White House's request. Other than your own opinion, what proof do you have that he wasn't?" asked Dabrowski.

"Ah," said Booker, "that brings us back to the strange little toad named Henry Fuchs. Fuchs was such a subservient lackey that he always walked a few steps behind Chase, carrying Chase's files—two bulky Salmon-colored portfolios, one of which he carried under each arm. Fuchs never left those files unattended. But, Fuchs was unable to leave Mons before I arrived, what with the demands on him to be available for interviews from the many police agencies which swarmed into Mons to investigate Pierce's murder. The surfeit of parallel investigations was ludicrous."

Dabrowski found himself having to suppress a grin. How many other intelligence operatives in the world would use a word like *surfeit*? Well, maybe one or two in Britain's MI-6.

Booker continued. "Investigators were literally tripping over each other... Plainclothesmen and uniforms from the Mons police force,

Belgian National Police, NATO CID, Army C.I.[19], British C.I. (MI-5), FBI, Interpol, CIA Special Investigations… Oh yeah, and *me*.

"As you know Colonel, since Group's Cred Shed manufactured my credentials, my cover in Mons was that of a high-level Justice Department investigator, working directly under Attorney General Kennedy. I was able to carry off the ruse only at great personal sacrifice. I had to get a short haircut, put a high shine on my shoes, buy a new three-piece suit, plus two button-down white shirts and two sedate ties. It was all most disagreeable; but I digress."

Booker was sliding into full lecture mode now. "With a little ingenuity, I got first shot at Henry Fuchs. I told him I wanted full access to his files. He flat-out refused and couldn't be persuaded or intimidated into changing his mind. I was forced to drug him in his hotel room. By the time he woke up hours later I had gone through both folders, removed several documents, photographed them with my Minox, put them back and left."

"Two of them were of particular interest," Booker continued. "The first was a copy of a rambling intra-office memo from Chase to his staff, complaining that he was being frozen out of the efforts to catch the mole ensconced in NATO. Chase was of the opinion that his office deserved to receive the credit for catching Groundhog. Chase went on to state that he, Fuchs, and a secretary—Miss Deilia Le Grange—were headed to Mons to unearth the evidence necessary to identify Groundhog."

Booker raised an eyebrow. "I would add, parenthetically, that the memo reeked of alcohol."

"The second was a letter dated June 30, 1961 from Q to Chase," Booker said. "I can only describe it as a bitter diatribe against Q's competitors. While it didn't name names, it referred to certain upstart 'politicos' and 'military types' who were out to undermine the CIA's proud tradition in Western Europe, and 'hog all the prime assignments for themselves.' But the most interesting part of the letter was the last paragraph."

Booker pulled a sheet of paper from a folder, laid it on the table, and allowed the others to examine the closing paragraph.

---

[19] C.I. - Counterintelligence

My dear Llewellyn, if it is your wish to score
a major victory in Belgium, don't forget our
private motto from our days in Skull & Bones.
Think unconventionally, look for a conspiracy,
and act ruthlessly. Unlike the beasts of the
wild, when a man uncoils and strikes, he seldom
acts alone. The fact that one's target is
referred to in the singular is nothing more
than proof of most men's mental lassitude.

Fondly,

Q

The silence lasted for several seconds before Dabrowski broke it. "Do you have anything more to add about Chase?"

"Only my opinion," said Booker.

"Let's hear it," ordered Dabrowski brusquely.

"Very well," Booker said. "I do not believe that Chase could have been Jurist II. All the available evidence shows that Jurist II is extremely intelligent, sly, cautious, and resourceful. Chase, on the other hand, was a fool and a drunk. He could no more carry off the amazing things Jurist has done than Ed Norton or Ralph Cramden. Moreover, he wasn't part of any conspiracy. No self-respecting conspirator would have him. He got where he was strictly because of old-boy political connections, and the use of Q's brain. Although, why Q would have gone to the trouble to create and sustain Chase is anybody's guess. The answer to that little conundrum lies in the byzantine labyrinth of Q's mind."

Booker sipped from a glass of water, enjoying the tension he was creating in the room.

Again, there were several seconds of silence before Dabrowski spoke. "Alright, let's move on to Lieutenant Colonel Barton Spaniel. I want to hold Malachy O'Doherty until last. What can you tell us about Spaniel?"

Booker's voice carried a faint hint of impertinence. "If you would indulge me for a couple of minutes, Colonel, allow me to first offer a few observations on General Ames."

Dabrowski didn't object, so Booker continued. "The general does not always use the best judgment for an intelligence officer."

Now Mueller squirmed in his chair. Booker's outspokenness clearly made him uncomfortable.

"The rigid discipline of the chain of command is too ingrained in Ames," Booker said. "In other words, he is just too army, too open, and too much of a straight-arrow to be an effective intelligence professional. But is there any real possibility of his involvement with the Jurist II betrayals? Absolutely not. First, there isn't a shred of evidence of his involvement. To the contrary, he's done everything in his power to assist in Jurist II's apprehension. Second, as I've already pointed out, he's not a great intelligence man. I found the man to be almost totally guileless. He just doesn't have the kind of Machiavellian mind needed for the mental intricacies of intelligence work."

"I see," said Dabrowski. "Very well, let's move on."

"Fine, Colonel. What would you like to know about Spaniel?"

"Start off by telling us a little bit about the man."

Booker always liked an invitation to speak expansively and now he looked pleased with himself as he tilted his chair back slightly and put both hands behind his head.

"Bart Spaniel? Tough, smart, and courageous, with an impressive background in military law enforcement as a CID officer for twenty years, before moving over into G-2 investigations. I've known him since Korea where we worked together on some covert operations in Seoul, before Ridgway took it back from the North Koreans. His work is first-rate."

"Do I take it then, that you believe he is also in the clear?"

Booker moved forward and sat straight-up with both hands on the table. His demeanor instantly became more serious. "No, sir, I don't believe he's totally in the clear."

"Why not?"

"There are things about him which just don't add up. Individually, they may seem inconsequential. But taken together, they're troubling. For openers, during one of their dinners together, he mentioned to Mario Tonelli that he was investigating a former U.S. Marine who had emigrated to the Soviet Union. Lieutenant Colonel Spaniel strongly suspected this ex-Marine of being a courier between Soviet spies in the U.S. and the KGB in Minsk. He even went so far as to mention the American's name. I found that to be bizarre. Mario had absolutely no need to know any of that."

"What was the American's name?" asked Dabrowski.

Booker took a few seconds to search his memory. "It was... Lee. No wait, Lee was his *first* name. His last name was *Oswald*. Yeah, that was it... Lee Harvey Oswald."

The name sparked no glimmer of recognition among the other three men in the room.

"What else bothered you?" asked Dabrowski.

"Spaniel lied to Mario," Booker said "about a matter which Tonelli clearly had a need to know. He told Mario that *only* General Ames and his deputy, Colonel Stansfield, had unrestricted access and the combination to the Secure Room. That wasn't true. In fact, Ames and Stansfield kept Spaniel completely in the loop. He personally had the combination to the Secure Room, plus the combination to the safe."

"Equally disturbing was Spaniel's reaction when Mario told him about the odd behavior of Captain Jack Lurch at NATO Headquarters, in Brussels. For a security investigations guy and former cop, Spaniel responded far too casually, by immediately denying that any person with such a name was connected to NATO. Then, Spaniel told Mario that he would check on Lurch, and get back to him. He may have checked-out Lurch, but he never got back to Mario, despite the fact that he was fully aware of Mario's true mission at the G-2's offices."

The three officers listening to Booker's narration were riveted by his every word, as Mueller furiously scribbled notes in his pad.

"How were you able to come by such high-level information?" wondered Dabrowski.

"You would be amazed how many locked doors are quickly opened to an investigator working directly for the Attorney General of the United States."

Reitenhauser, who had been silent up to this point, took the opportunity to address Dabrowski and Mueller. "Gentlemen, Mr. Booker just finished his sixty page report of his Mons investigation yesterday."

Fred slid a copy of the report across the table to Colonel Dabrowski. "Each document to which Doug makes reference, and many others as well, are attached to the report as exhibits."

Dabrowski took about five minutes to leaf through the report and briefly examine the exhibits.

The heading toward the end of the report entitled, 'Peripheral Figures' caught Dabrowski's attention.

"What did you learn about Jack Lurch?"

"Absolutely nothing. After taking Mario by taxi to the hospital to be checked out, he evaporated into the mist and disappeared as silently and quickly as he had appeared. No one who I spoke to in Mons had ever heard of him. He just phoned in the report of the deaths at the Belfry to the local police, and was gone. I took the train to NATO headquarters in Brussels but there I was totally stonewalled. I couldn't get to speak to any of the higher-ups. General Norstad was said to be on an extended tour of all NATO bases, world-wide."

"Did you interview Colonel Spaniel?"

"Nope. He left, or *supposedly* left, Mons before I arrived, on an 'extra-jurisdictional investigation in Canada.' Canadian Intelligence professed to know nothing about it. I did, however, attach a log I prepared of Spaniel's comings and goings in the thirty-day period preceding the incidents at the Belfry. I think you might find it interesting."

With that, a break in the Q&A was taken. Gerda made a fresh pot of coffee, and the men helped themselves.

Dabrowski and Mueller spent a good half-hour perusing the log of Spaniel's activities. Reitenhauser, who had not yet found time to study the log, also reviewed it carefully.

Fred's eyes moved up and down the log, which was in chronological order and divided into four columns: 'Date, Time, Location, and Description of Event.'

Most of it was pretty boring stuff. Spaniel either knew how to camouflage his actions beneath a veneer of ordinariness, or he just led a dull life. Fred was almost certain that it was the former.

Reading about Spaniel's teaching a class at the NATO CID Academy in fingerprint detection, buying Belgian chocolates at a factory outlet for his staff, attending a soccer match and visiting his periodontist on Saturday mornings, was worse than tedious. It was mind-numbing. But as he read the final entries on page 5 of the log, something suddenly leapt off the page. It was a one sentence entry under 'Description of Event:'

```
Attended annual convention in Antwerp
of the Philatelists Society.
```

To one without special knowledge, the words would have seemed innocuous. There were hundreds of thousands of stamp collectors world-wide, and there would have been nothing unusual about Spaniel being one of them. What invested the sentence with ominous overtones was that the Philatelists Society was solely controlled by one man, Horst Berkenfeld,

Agent 14332. It was a fiction, a cover organization for 14332's espionage ring. Its original purpose, now greatly expanded, was to create an international vehicle for conducting covert communications between West Bloc agent-handlers and their East Bloc clandestine agents.

Founded in 1952, the Philatelists Society was the invention of Horst Berkenfeld, Uri Putyagin (Carlton), and Frederick Reitenhauser.

Thirty five minutes passed before Dabrowski looked up from the logs. Edwin Dabrowski, unlike Reitenhauser, was not a subtle man. From their long association, Fred had learned to read his demeanor quite well. His gestures, grunts, sighs and expressions clearly told Fred that Dabrowski also considered the detailed written memos and diaries from which the logs were prepared, to constitute an elaborate effort by Spaniel to camouflage activities he wished to keep secret. The fact that he kept diaries at all was highly unusual for an intelligence man and appeared to be an attempt at misdirection.

If anything in the logs had caught Dabrowski's attention, he made no comment. Pushing the report aside, he again turned to face Booker.

"Now tell me about O'Doherty."

"Okay, O'Doherty is a cipher, a really mysterious character and as elusive as quick silver. But unlike Spaniel and General Norstad, he didn't disappear after the incident at the Belfry. I know he had his eyes on me. Wherever I was—taking statements, examining the safe in the Secure Room, snapping photographs—he was lurking. A silent, ghostly presence. It was creepy. But what was frustrating was no one would talk about him. Not Ames, Stansfield, none of the other officers assigned to the G-2, nor their civilian and military staffs. The most loquacious of them would clam up as soon as I mentioned his name."

"I got really pissed off at some of the mid-level officers who headed up the various sections. I flatly demanded to know *why* they were afraid to talk about O'Doherty. To a man they all gave me the convenient dodge that although they knew who he was, their paths never crossed during the course of performing their duties."

"Finally, I grabbed an evasive section chief by the arm and said, 'look here, drop the bullshit about your paths not crossing. I want to know what the skinny is on O'Doherty. What are people saying about him, and don't tell me *nothing*, because every office everywhere has its gossips.'"

"This chap—his name is in the report—finally said 'take a walk with me in the town square.' As we walked, he told me that everyone was concerned about O'Doherty. Both General Ames and Colonel Stansfield had tried to get him to leave, but he refused. When they attempted to get General Norstad in Brussels to intervene, they ran into a stone wall."

"There were two camps among the speculators—one held that the president had sent O'Doherty to spy on everyone, because the White House did not trust the official effort to catch Groundhog. The other camp figured that O'Doherty had gone rogue, and had become part of the conspiracy."

"Finally, I got to speak to Colonel Stansfield about O'Doherty and he pretty much repeated what the section chief had told me. It was my last day in Mons and I think I finally got through to him about the urgency of the situation."

"Stansfield, and I am assuming Ames too, didn't seem to know much more than anyone else about O'Doherty. He did add that O'Doherty was so elusive and secretive that they had been unable to accuse him of anything. But Stansfield also revealed that General Ames had finally had enough of O'Doherty, and kicked him out of the G-2's offices that very morning; and told him not to come back."

"Well, what's your opinion of O'Doherty?" asked Dabrowski.

Booker again leaned back in his chair with his hands locked behind his head. "Colonel, I haven't a clue as to why O'Doherty was there, but to think that he was a co-conspirator would be to suspend belief in all of the basic principles of espionage. Whatever it is that he was up to, he's not an enemy spy."

"All right, thank you Doug. That's enough for one day. I need to sit down back in my office and read your entire report carefully. Fred, thank you for your hospitality."

"Let me just add, however, that I take issue with your opinion, Doug, that believing O'Doherty to be a spy would violate all of the basic principles of espionage. I would prefer to say all of the basic principles of espionage except for one big one: That in covert intelligence, things seldom are what they appear to be."

Part IV, Chapter 4

Behold a Pale Horse

One of Andre Catoiře's duties as City Coroner was to attempt to clear unidentified corpses lying in the morgue before they were buried in unmarked graves.

If the bodies weren't identified and claimed by family or friends within ninety days, they were moved out to a common burial ground beyond the city limits. There they could be identified by plot numbers.

Catoiře fancied himself as something of a detective and the adventure of matching a corpse with an identity was his favorite part of the job. Sometimes he had nothing more than a hunch to go on, and the rare occasions on which those hunches led to positive I.D.'s were among the proudest of his professional life.

He found the strange case of IU (Identity Unknown)—1193/61 to be especially intriguing. The man's face had been battered beyond recognition but the corpse was otherwise intact. He was found by a worker lying underneath a pile of debris at a construction site on the outskirts of the city.

Catoiře had examined the corpse of IU-1193/61 no less than a dozen times since it was brought in eight weeks before. Yet as he rolled it out of deep freeze once again, his enthusiasm for the challenge had not yet waned. Catoiře had written several books on criminology solely related to homicide—and his research had left him with more than a passing knowledge of known M.O.'s of the most notorious international murderers. In his early days as a self-styled sleuth, he was constantly back and forth between his home base and Regional Interpol Headquarters, where he scoured over the records of both solved and unsolved homicides. Now as his prominence was clearly on the ascendance, much of what he needed to know was stored in the archives of his brain.

Catoiře was motivated by interest, not ego, but was becoming famous almost in spite of himself. The condition of IU-1193/61's face had particularly piqued his interest from the beginning. The cause of death was extreme trauma to the brain inflicted by blows from a blunt instrument. Catoiře believed the weapon to be either a wooden club or a baseball bat.

For some odd reason, the coroner saw something slightly different about the mainly obliterated face than he had seen on prior viewings. What he must have previously taken as a random cut caused by the blunt instrument's impact upon the facial tissue, he now saw as a laceration that seemed to have a design to it. And the more he looked, the more he realized it had to have been made with a knife or razor blade, rather than the weapon which so pulverized the rest of the face. Using a ruler he measured the upward angle of the cut on the left cheek to be almost exactly one inch. It then extended horizontally across the bridge of the nose for very close to another inch and down the right cheek at about the same angle for precisely one inch.

Andre Catoiře stood straight up and allowed himself to enjoy the exhilarating rush of excitement mixed with a sense of triumph experienced only when he solved his most challenging cases. For he had indeed solved this one. He might not know the victim's identity yet, but he was confident that knowledge would follow within the next 72 hours. The reason was simple. He knew who had committed the crime. The length, location and angles of the distinct cut amidst the battered ruins of what had once been a human face, was the unique signature of one man only—the baneful Hateface Heidégger, the most infamous assassin of the Red Guards of Continental Europe. Heidégger committed political murders only, limiting his killings exclusively to Western Bloc officials and operatives.

Catoiře picked up the telephone and dialed the extension and number of the Belgian desk at NATO headquarters in Brussels, where he had many friends.

A receptionist answered. "Belgian Contingent, NATO."

"Henri Lavoissiér please."

"Just a minute, please."

While he waited, Catoiře worked hard at tamping down his elation. He didn't wish to come across as too excited. After all, what he was calling about was the murder of someone who could possibly be a colleague of his NATO friends.

"Henri Lavoissiér speaking."

"Henri, how are you, it's Andre?"

"I am fine, my good friend. To what do I owe the pleasure of this call?"

"This is an official call Henri in my capacity as Coroner and Chief Medical Examiner of Mons," said Catoiře evenly.

"I see. Go ahead Andre."

"Henri, would you be able to tell me if any NATO or other Western Bloc personnel have gone missing recently?"

"How recently?"

"I would estimate about eight weeks ago."

There was total silence on the other end for at least fifteen seconds. Finally, Lavoissiér responded. "Andre, are you at your office?"

"Yes."

"Please stay put while I call you back on a secure line."

September 30, 1961

British Prime Minister Harold McMillan, President John F. Kennedy, Paul Nitze, McGeorge Bundy, Tugwell Saylor, Edwin Dabrowski, Frederick Reitenhauser and Douglas Booker, among others, now knew that Llewellyn Chase was not now and probably never was, Jurist II. The reason they knew was that Llewellyn Chase was dead—his body lying in a mortuary in Mons, Belgium—positively identified through dental records and fingerprints. His family was en route to Belgium to claim the body and return it to the United States for burial.

Only five Western officials, however, knew the identity of the murderer. They were Harold McMillan, John F. Kennedy, McGeorge Bundy, Tugwell Saylor and Edwin Dabrowski. Until plans were in place to move in on the Red Guards, and in particular on Hateface Heidégger, it was simply too dangerous for anyone else to know.

Andre Catoiŕe was temporarily the guest of the U.S. government at a magnificent hill-top villa overlooking the Atlantic in the Azores, surrounded by a contingent of Marine guards, with two Coast Guard gun boats moored in the harbor. Catoiŕe was thrilled to be there in the lap of luxury and especially thankful for the time off to work on his new criminology textbook.

Fred Reitenhauser, on the other hand, was neither thrilled nor thankful. As he sat with Doug Booker over coffee at 0700 hours in the CO's office, the two chatted quietly about the new developments and the formidable challenges confronting them. Reluctantly, Fred had told Booker about the Spaniel-Philatelist Society connection. He could not solve the multiple puzzles now before him, alone. He needed Doug's first-rate mind, and his inner toughness as well. If Spaniel had gone rogue—been turned or doubled—the ominous portents for 14332 and his network were real. The other questions they discussed were, did Spaniel fit the profile for Jurist II? Did O'Doherty? Were Ames and Stansfield possible candidates? If Spaniel had gone off the reservation, might he have turned any of 14332's subagents; or almost unthinkably, 14332 himself? More hopefully, had Agent 14332 turned or doubled him?

On another plane, had Jurist II been instrumental in causing Hammarskjöld's death? How about Chase's death? And in still another theater of operations, what about Olney's agent number 18339? Had he fallen into Hostile's hands on the far side of the Berlin Wall; and, if so, what damaging information might he provide to the enemy under torture, or in the event he were turned? Olney now sat in his office only a short walk down the corridor from Fred and Doug as they spoke. For at least that fact they could be thankful.

The one overriding and most worrisome question of all—the one which always transcended their daily operations—was: How did all these developments impact Carlton? Did they place him in new jeopardy? If the answer was yes, the implications and possible consequences for Western Bloc intelligence and the Cold War were too staggering to measure.

Part IV, Chapter 5

Revenge Served Cold

October 5, 1961 London

Q's quite elegant apartment near Hyde Park and Marble Arch suited his purposes for the time-being. The theater district was close by and he made it a point to see three or four shows a week. At least one of them would be a Shakespeare Production—his favorites being Macbeth and Richard III—characters with whom he closely identified. This particular evening he would enjoy the rare privilege of seeing Sir Lawrence Olivier as Othello—performing in a limited engagement at the Royal National Theater.

Each morning, Q would walk to one of several dead-drops in or near the park to pick up his daily dispatches from his secretly-loyal CIA colleagues in Munich, Bonn, and Langley, Virginia. By prearrangement he would employ a different drop each day.

It was a source of great amusement to Q that intra-agency communiqués were uniformly hinting, without explicitly stating, that Q was persona non grata within The Company. Such implied ostracism was pure fiction—a mere contrivance to mollify Washington, NATO and Agency politicians mortified by Q's free-lancing attempt to preempt a NATO-sanctioned covert operation in Mons.

Q chuckled smugly to himself. "All these naïve people. Do they really think that with my network, with what I know and with what I have on certain people, my power and position could be weakened?" In point of fact, Q's so-called banishment from continental Europe had only increased his power—freed as he was from the niggling details of having to administer a CIA station. And besides, thought Q, anyone who controlled Antonin Slezak was untouchable. The consequences of the double agent reverting back to exclusive KGB control would be devastating to the West.

Such pleasant thoughts, combined with Q's excited anticipation over seeing the great Olivier in Othello in a couple of hours, put him in a good mood. He felt so upbeat that he even allowed his disciplined mind a rare flight of fancy. His mind's eye saw himself as the imposing Othello and Reitenhauser as the duplicitous Iago, against whom he would exact vengeance.

Actually, the revenge part of the reverie was no mere fancy. Q didn't really have anything personal against Reitenhauser but that was beside the point. Q worked hard at nurturing a taste for vengeance against his political enemies. So long as it was kept under control, the thirst for revenge was a very useful tool for an international power player. Its embers could be stoked whenever one wanted a hedge against waning enthusiasm or loss of interest.

All the knowing whispers about the ascent of Reitenhauser's star in Western intelligence circles were valid. But to credit him with having exposed Invictus was so overstated as to be ludicrous. Q took every opportunity in his high-level and very secret talks with the Director and Deputy Director, to scoff at the idea. He also made sure he debunked the notion of Reitenhauser's preeminence during each conversation he had with O'Doherty.

The simple truth was that he himself knew more about the full scope and details of Invictus than any man alive, save one: Alexander Shelepin, the dynamic and ambitious Chief of the KGB since 1958. There was a simple reason why Shelepin knew more about Invictus than any man on earth. He was its architect and author. The reason Q knew as much as he did was equally simple. Q had in his stable a prized thoroughbred of impeccable pedigree—the brilliant and ruthless Antonin Slezak, who held the position of Special Counsel to the Director of the KGB. In other words, Shelepin believed Slezak to be his loyal right-hand man.

Anyway, it was past time to bring Reitenhauser down. He was too much of a threat to Q's burning quest to become the top spy-master in the world. And what better way to eliminate Reitenhauser as a competitor than to liquidate the main source of his power and prestige—the opaque and mercurial spy who was known only as Carlton. To do this he had to dig deep to discover, if possible, the origins of the symbiotic relationship between Reitenhauser and Carlton. And where were most of the clandestine power-relationships of the present age born? In that mystifyingly complex and alluring island of intrigue called Berlin. Berlin was where Q would begin his search.

Part IV, Chapter 6

The Shelepin Deception

Paul Nitze likened KGB Chief Alexander Shelepin's campaign against the West to a 'brush fire' war. While a vast California-type forest fire raged, an arsonist could ride the fringes of the inferno starting brush fires wherever he chose, thereby diverting precious fire-fighting resources away from the main conflagration. Of course, this was all symbolism and metaphor; with Shelepin as the metaphorical arsonist.

Nitze analogized to Western Europe and the USSR's intention to sign a separate treaty with East Germany. This was the main conflagration, while the Soviets started "brush fires" in the Far East, Central America and Africa to distract and divert the U.S., and prevent it from devoting its full attention, arms and military personnel to the escalating crisis in Germany.

Alexander Shelepin had worked his way up the ladder of the Soviet Union's security system in the secret police run by the NKVD, the predecessor of the KGB. He was best known for his skills in counter-intelligence. Stalin had been obsessed with espionage and this opened the door for many bright young intelligence specialists. Khrushchev valued Shelepin's talents highly and when the latter provided him with a memorandum outlining a plan to force the dispersion of U.S. military forces throughout the world in order to bog them down in multiple hot spots, Khrushchev avidly embraced the plan.

The multifaceted plan of deception, said Shelepin, would preoccupy the U.S.A. and its allies while the Soviets resolved the "Berlin question" by entering into a separate treaty with East Germany, denying the Western powers access to Berlin.

The year 1961 started with Khrushchev's January pledge to assist movements of 'National Liberation.' Shelepin added particulars to the plan by advocating KGB-organized and armed uprisings against pro-Western governments.

The first target was Nicaragua where Shelepin proposed that the KGB partner with Castro's Cuba and the Nicaraguan Revolutionary Front to foment an armed mutiny. Next on his list were the instigations of armed uprisings in El Salvador and Guatemala.

Africa was one big fruit orchard for Shelepin, with colonial possessions of Great Britain, France, Belgium and Portugal ripe for the picking. And any illusions that the West held that South Korea and Taiwan were safe from communist armed aggression were dismissed by Shelepin out of hand. South Vietnam was already under attack and Shelepin hoped to add to that, joint military actions to "liberate" South Korea, Taiwan, Laos and Cambodia.

Of course, the CIA and Britain's MI-5 and MI-6 weren't exactly sitting on their hands when all this was going on. Q knew more about the details of the Shelepin plans and plots than just about any other intelligence official of the Western bloc. Slezak was a seemingly inexhaustible well of information, which Q could pump at will.

Counter-plots, insurrections and revolutions in all of Shelepin's targeted areas were being carried out by Western intelligence agencies with equal vigor. The battles raged all through the 1960's, 70's and 80's and it wasn't until the late 70's and 80's that the pro-communist Sandinistas began to secure a foothold in Nicaragua; and the leftist Contras began having success in El Salvador.

The American civilian population sat in their living rooms each night during the 60's and 70's, deploring scenes on television of both the horror of Vietnam and violent protesters at home. But once the news hour was over, they would quickly escape to Rowan and Martin's Laugh-in, the Dean Martin Show and All in the Family—essentially oblivious to the fact that while they laughed in front of their TV's, the Cold War was being fought in deadly earnest all across the globe—from Angola, Rhodesia and the Congo in Africa to Nicaragua, El Salvador and Guatemala in Central America; from the rice paddies of Southeast Asia to the 38th Parallel of the Koreas; from the Nile deltas of the U.A.R. to the back-alleys of Berlin, Warsaw and Prague.

The years 1946, 1950, 1962, 1968 and 1989 were all pivotal ones in the Cold War. But 1961 was unparalleled when it came to the day-by-day, hour-by-hour slug-fest between the communist and non-communist super-powers in most regions of the world. It was a grinding, tension-laden and often desperate struggle—beginning in the earliest days of January and continuing through the final days of December. Anguish and death were daily occurrences in the Congo, Angola, Cuba, East Germany, Laos and Vietnam. The pressure on NATO and Western heads of state was as unrelenting as the stakes were monumental.

From, however, the first glimmering light of 1961 to its last flickering flame, the fulcrum upon which all the tumult of the Cold War seemed to rotate was a place rather than an idea. That place was Berlin and it signified many things. To its four occupying powers it was a symbol of triumph and tragedy—of the pain Hitler and the Third Reich had inflicted upon their peoples, but also of their final victory and destruction of the 'Fuhrer' and his evil regime. To millions of Germans, Berlin was their spiritual capital—the historic center of their homeland. To the free nations of the world, Berlin symbolized an island of freedom in a sea of tyranny. To President Kennedy and Chairman Khrushchev, the Berlin of 1961 was the major battleground of the Cold War. It was their Gettysburg, Waterloo, and Stalingrad all wrapped up into one.

Part IV, Chapter 7

Perverted Patriotism

Q was not entirely without a sense of patriotism. He certainly did not want the Soviets to win the Cold War. He prided himself on the effective battle he waged against the Warsaw Pact powers on a daily basis. But that wasn't enough. His priorities were askew. As much as he did know, Q still had no idea who Jurist II was, whether Dag Hammarskjöld's death was intentional and, if so, whether Jurist II was behind it. But most disturbing in a high CIA official, he didn't really care. The fatal flaw in Q as an American and as a man, was that his real devotion was to himself and not to his country. Thus, it was that when Q wrote in his diary on the morning of October 17, 1961, "The offensive begins," he was not referring to an offensive against the enemies of the U.S., but rather against his own personal enemy, Fred Reitenhauser, whom ironically he didn't even dislike. But Reitenhauser stood in the way of Q's personal ambition and, therefore, had to go. And so megalomaniacal was Q that he deluded himself into actually believing that there was a perfect alignment between his personal ambitions and the interests of the country he served. His was a perverted patriotism.

Q had been building a documentary paper trail of Reitenhauser's military history for the past two months. His minions back in CONUS[20] had been scurrying all over the Armed Forces records depository in St. Louis, Missouri like a pack of rats over a cadaver. After several weeks of pestering and throwing the CIA's name around, Q's lackeys had managed to pull together a reasonable facsimile of Reitenhauser's 201 file, which they sent by official CIA courier to Q in London. The file was four inches thick.

Reitenhauser had enlisted in the Army at the age of 20 in 1938 and during his twenty-three years of consecutive service had been assigned to thirteen different duty stations on four continents.

---

[20] Continental United States

Q spent fourteen straight hours going through the several hundred pages of Fred's military records, line by line. Most of it was of no use to him, but there were two intriguing separate entries which stood out from the approximately one thousand others.

The first was dated August 23, 1945. The date of the second was September 7, 1945. They read as follows:

```
8/23/45 - Received the Four-Power Joint
Command Award for his dedicated and
unselfish action in risking his own life,
while saving the life of a Russian army
officer, a colleague of Second Lt.
Reitenhauser in the Inter-Allied War
Crimes Investigation Detachment.

9/7/45 - Was one of only two Inter-Allied
officers assigned as investigators to the
prosecution team at the Nuremberg War
Crimes trial of 1945-46. Reitenhauser and
a Russian officer served together as
co-chief deputies to Chief prosecutor,
Robert H. Jackson. The Russian officer
later became a Soviet government
official.
```

Q sat back, placed a Benson and Hedges cigarette in a plastic holder, and lit it with his gold Ronson lighter. As he puffed on his cigarette, he ruminated. By the time he finished it, he knew as surely as he knew that Nero liked big fires that the Russian officer had become Reitenhauser's mole.

This revelation, however, presented new questions and daunting challenges. In a bureaucracy as huge as that of the Kremlin, there were tens of thousands of government officials. And the entries in Reitenhauser's military records were fifteen years old. Was the mole still a government official? And, if so, how would one go about winnowing down a list of many thousands to arrive at a manageable number of suspects?

Then again, thought Q, maybe the job wasn't as difficult as he first thought. The mole was most likely a presently-serving official. Otherwise, his information would not have been as invaluable as it had turned out to be. Also, if he were anything other than a national defense or security official, he would not have access to the incredible strategic and tactical intelligence which he had produced.

The next morning, Q began stage 2 of his research over his second cup of coffee. With his feet up on the railing of the small patio outside of his tenth floor apartment, and his ample buttocks ensconced in a soft lounge chair, he gazed out at the stately Marble Arch and began his research with relish. On his lap was a copy of the CIA's latest biographical compendium of all known Soviet defense and internal security officials. The report was the work-product of the International Area Intelligence Desk back at Langley. There were three thousand names, photos, and brief biographical sketches in the bulky report. This wasn't going to be easy, mused Q, but then again what was?

The first thing Q discovered was that the overwhelming majority of Soviet defense officials had offices in five major cities: Moscow, Leningrad, Warsaw, Kiev and East Berlin. Even Shelepin himself had a major office in East Berlin. Q considered it highly unlikely that the mole was stationed in Moscow. The intense scrutiny from the secret police under which all government officials found themselves in Moscow greatly discouraged clandestine activities. The same was true to a lesser extent of Leningrad. Kiev was a little bit too much of a remote backwater in terms of international power politics and Q instinctively doubted that it was the mole's base of operations. But Warsaw and East Berlin were both strong possibilities. Of those two cities, Q asked himself which of them would allow the mole to operate the most effectively.

It wasn't even close. The answer was, far and away, East Berlin. Open borders between the East and West sectors of Berlin over the past sixteen years had made each of them a hot bed of espionage. Every major Western intelligence station in Europe had a thriving German Desk. East Berlin was swimming in Western Bloc spies, safe houses and dead-drops. The wall now standing between the two Berlins simply drove them further underground. Nowhere else on the Soviet side of the Iron Curtain would a Western Bloc spy have the contacts, facilities and communications systems that he enjoyed in East Berlin. He would put the question to Slezak when he arrived for their meeting later in the day, but Q doubted that the shrewd Czechoslovak would disagree.

Slezak did not disagree. What he did dispute, however, was that they could narrow the range of suspects while sitting on Q's patio. There were more than 850 Eastern Bloc defense officials in East Berlin. That list might be reduced to less than a hundred likely candidates. But one would need to go to East Berlin, talk to people in the know, do some detective work, sub-rosa; and even meet with the most likely suspects—employing some sort of deep cover.

Q asked Slezak if he would take on the job and leave for East Berlin the next morning.

"Sure, provided I get $5,000 in cash up front, plus expenses."

Q got up, walked into his bedroom and returned with a stack of newly-minted American bills—all twenties, fifties and hundreds. He peeled off $5,000 in spanking new bills and handed them to Slezak, plus another $500 for expenses.

Slezak's face was illuminated as he stuffed the money in his inside jacket pocket. Greed was his dominant character trait, and nothing perked up his spirits like cold cash.

Slezak and Q spent another hour discussing the details of the mission before Slezak called a cab to take him to Heathrow International Airport. He would fly first to Frankfurt where he would meet up with Hateface Heidégger, who then would accompany him to East Berlin. Slezak was not about to head into the boiling cauldron of East Berlin espionage without protection. Heidégger was expensive and Slezak would have to pay him his entire expense allotment of $500.00; plus a portion of his own fee; but it was well worth it.

October 21, 1961—West Berlin

Barton Spaniel had picked up Hateface Heidégger's trail in Bonn and had been following him ever since. Hateface's strength was not counter-surveillance. His tendency to track his prey with a single-minded relentlessness sometimes rendered him oblivious to the fact that he himself might be tracked. The fact that Hateface had been joined by Slezak in Frankfurt did complicate things somewhat, but not enough to cause Spaniel to scrap his mission. He still felt confident that he could bring Hateface back to Belgium in either handcuffs and leg irons or in a body bag.

Spaniel had dual-motivation for nailing Heidégger. First and foremost was his anger and embarrassment over the fact that Heidégger had murdered a U.S. emissary right under his nose in Mons. This was a blow to Spaniel's reputation and ego that he might never get over. The second was his bitterness over the fact that the higher-ups did not share with him the fact that Heidégger was the perpetrator. Spaniel took this as a direct slap in the face. Of course, he had felt bitter toward NATO for many reasons for a long time.

He didn't know what Slezak and Heidégger were up to but all his years as a cop told him they didn't plan on just sipping coffee in Brandenburg Platz. No, they were going to cross-over and he would be right on their heels. But what the fuck was O'Doherty doing in West Berlin? That slack-jawed weasel seemed to turn up everywhere at the most inconvenient times. Well, maybe he was there for the simple reason that Kennedy expected trouble with the Russians at the Wall. If that was the case, he was not likely to interfere with Spaniel's plans.

October 22, 1961—West Berlin

Under deep cover as U.N. agricultural consultants, Olney and Káz successfully crossed over to East Berlin at 0930 hours on 22 October at Checkpoint Charlie near the corner of Friederichstrasse and Zimmerstrasse. They had done a good job of affecting the appearance and manner of nerdy egg-heads, with their cheap gabardine suits, pocket protectors and thick-rimmed glasses—Olney's black; and Káz's tortoise shell. The border officials on the East Berlin side had orders to make them feel welcome. East Germany was having one of its worst wheat crops of the last twenty years. Walter Ulbricht was worried that if this kept up and he appeared not to be doing enough to improve the plight of the farmers, the Politburo of the Supreme Soviet might start scouting around for his successor. It was not that the Soviets gave a tinker's damn about the farmers. But they did want East Germany to remain economically strong. It was the single biggest contributor behind Russia itself to the arms production needed to keep the Warsaw Pact Armies the equal of NATO's forces.

Ulbricht had become obsessed with new methods of agro-technology and would accept the expertise of whomever was willing to offer it—even the hated United Nations.

Olney and Káz hailed a cab on the East Berlin side and gave instructions to the driver to take them to the East German Ministry of Agriculture. Once there, however, they simply blended in with the mid-day crowds and drifted away. Their real mission was to reach out to Agent 18339, set up a meet with him and give him an encoded message to place in a dead-drop for Carlton.

The CO was worried about Carlton. There were a lot of dangerous characters on the loose and some of them were leaving a trail of mayhem behind. It was no stretch of the imagination that Carlton might also be a target.

Most recently, there was the murder of Remington Pierce and then the attack on Tonelli which would have been fatal had not Jack Lurch been on the scene. Next came the assassination of Llewellyn Chase and, in all likelihood, of Dág Hammarskjöld. The list of individuals whom Reitenhauser did not trust was growing fast: Q, Antonin Slezak, Barton Spaniel, Malachy O'Doherty and of course, Jurist II—that is unless Jurist II was one or more of the preceding four—which was quite possible.

Paul Nitze had called Fred just two days previous to warn that the president expected a major international incident to be instigated by the Reds at the border between the two Berlins. What better time for Hostile to attempt the elimination of Carlton—to remove him as a threat to the success of whatever plans of aggression they had cooked up.

Fred had decided to again break his general rule against personal contact with Carlton. Carlton had to be fully informed as to everything that had happened since their meeting at Montmártre. And he had to be warned and offered help. This could not possibly be done by written message. The exigent circumstances demanded a personal meeting. The message placed by 18339 in the dead-drop would tell Carlton when and where he was to meet Olney and Penchak. Carlton would be in deep disguise.

Forty-five minutes after Olney and Káz crossed the border into East Berlin, Slezak and Heidégger also crossed over. Slezak was well-known to the crossing guards at Checkpoint Charlie and neither man was asked to show a permit.

Spaniel, wearing a Belgian-cut suit and a fedora, showed his visa, obtained through normal channels shortly after the wall went up. He timed his entry so as to keep Slezak and Heidégger in view at all times; and followed them into East Berlin.

O'Doherty did not cross into the Eastern zone. He sat at a nearby sidewalk café with a good view of the checkpoint and a pay phone only a few feet away. He ordered breakfast there at 0900 hours, lunch at 1300 hours and dinner at 2100 hours. He also ordered one glass of wine at about 1600 hours. Other than to visit the men's room and make multiple phone calls, he didn't leave his strategically located table until 2300 hours. By then a chain of events of historical magnitude had begun.

Part IV, Chapter 8

Countdown to Crisis

The combination of the erection of the Berlin Wall in August of '61 and the Soviets' exit from the nuclear disarmament talks in late June ushered in a stunning build-up by the U.S. of its military strength. After the Soviet Union broke its promise and resumed nuclear testing, President Kennedy expressed privately to a few close aides that Khrushchev was a liar, and that nothing the Soviets said could be believed. They were intentionally provoking a crisis over Berlin, said Kennedy, by their ultimatum demanding the withdrawal of NATO armed forces from West Berlin, followed by the building of the Berlin Wall.

Kennedy was already pushing hard in Congress for an additional $3.25 billion for military spending, when he decided in August to dramatically fortify West Berlin. He would do it in a way that would seem an unequivocal message to the communist powers and to the rest of the world. The message would be that the U.S. was not only rejecting Khrushchev's ultimatum but was throwing it back in his face like a duelsman challenging his opponent by slapping him with a white glove.

Kennedy did not believe however, that the Wall, built slightly on the East Berlin side of the border and legal under international law, should be removed by military force. In other words, he was not willing to start World War III over it. His position was consistent with the foreign policy of the U.S. during the two previous administrations of Truman and Eisenhower. But the U.S.'s rights to unimpeded access to West Berlin, guaranteed by the Potsdam Conference agreements of 1945—to which the Soviet Union was a signatory—were sacrosanct. Kennedy's mindset was that they were vital United States' interests which must be protected at all costs, including war, if necessary.

Kennedy fully bought into Dean Rusk's opinion that the Soviets were determined to win the Cold War. The Secretary of State saw "unity, preparedness and firmness of purpose as essential" to blunting threats to West Germany and Berlin. Kennedy agreed wholeheartedly but he was also a politician. He wanted some serious lobbying done at the United Nations to explain the United States' position to the community of nations and to gain as much support as possible within the world body. He called Adlai Stevenson, United States Ambassador to the U.N., to the White House to satisfy himself that Stevenson was fully engaged and on-board. He knew Stevenson was upset that the U.S. had resumed nuclear testing. Kennedy didn't care about Stevenson's personal point of view so long as he struck no discordant notes in implementing U.S. foreign policy.

At a meeting between the two of them with no aides present, shortly after the Berlin Wall went up, Kennedy addressed Stevenson's concerns, as well as his own.

"Adlai, the Russians want to communize the whole world, to push the communist system outward onto country after country. If we don't stop them, nobody will. By their actions they have created a grave threat to world peace."

"I understand, Mr. President, and I agree. But I fear that the resumption of nuclear testing will only start the cycle of reaction and escalation all over again until one side or the other goes too far, resulting in a nuclear show-down."

A certain tension now seeped into the president's voice. "Adlai, what choice did we have? They had spit in our eye three times. We couldn't possibly sit back and do nothing. All this makes Khrushchev look pretty tough. He has had a succession of apparent victories—space, Cuba, the Wall. He's working hard to create the impression that he's got us on the run."

"I see your point, Mr. President."

"Well, I need you to do more than just see my point! We need you fully on board. The impression that Khrushchev has us on the run stops now. Before you know it, he'll be trying to convert Cuba into a nuclear missile base. We can't have that. Go back up to New York and explain our position at the U.N."

The president shook his head. "No, that's not enough. I need you to do *more* than that. You're a great lawyer, so advocate for our position. Right now, your country needs you to be more of a fighter than a diplomat. The Soviets have converted every major locale and institution into Cold War battlegrounds. I intend to accept their challenge, and give them the fight of their lives. Unless we do this, there will never be any chance of world peace."

After the wall went up, Kennedy moved quickly. On August 19th he dispatched Vice President Lyndon B. Johnson and retired general Lucius D. Clay to Berlin. Johnson delivered a personal letter from the president to

West Berlin's combative major, Willie Brandt, in which Kennedy wrote that the troop reinforcement of West Berlin, to begin the next day, underscored the U.S. rejection of Soviet demands for "the removal of allied protection from West Berlin."

Vice President Johnson was ordered to greet the American troops traveling through the Eastern Zone to West Berlin. The president delayed his vacation in Hyannisport and remained in Washington to monitor the progress of the convoy.

On the morning of August 20th, upon Kennedy's orders, the 1st Battle Group, 189th infantry crossed the border from West to East Germany bound for West Berlin. The column consisted of 491 vehicles and trailers carrying 1600 men in full battle gear. East German police watched them all the way to Berlin from beside trees along the Autobahn. The distance from the border to West Berlin was 110 miles.

Prior to the August 20, 1961 reinforcements, West Berlin had been defended by three allied brigades—one from each of the United Kingdom, United States and France. Including the 20 August additions, the three Western allies had 4224 men in West Berlin serving under the command of General Frederick O. Hartel.

The front of the American convoy was met in East German territory by Vice President Johnson and Ambassador Clay just before noon on 20 August. The possibility of a military confrontation was factored into the equation but the very public greeting went off without incident. The vice president had fully expected shooting to start with him right in the middle of it.

Retired general Lucius D. Clay had been the general in charge of the Berlin Garrison during the first Berlin crisis of 1948. He had stoutly commanded American forces on the ground during the Berlin Airlift, which rescued West Berlin and ended the crisis.

Now on 20 August 1961 he held the position of Special Advisor to the President of the United States—with ambassadorial rank. Kennedy was sending a unambiguous message to Khrushchev by his appointment of Clay—an architect of the airlift that had broken the back of a Soviet blockade that Kennedy had no intention of compromising the status of West Berlin.

After Johnson and Clay greeted the U.S. convoy at the Helmstedt entrance to West Berlin the column paraded through the streets of West Berlin amidst a large and enthusiastic crowd.

When Vice President Johnson was greeted by Chancellor Konrad Adenauer at the Bonn airport the previous day, the West German head of state assured Johnson that his presence and the beefed-up Western military garrison in West Berlin would constitute an eloquent rebuttal to the sentiment expressed by a sign held by an elderly woman in the airport crowd. "Action, Not Words."

The real action, however, was yet to come.

Part IV, Chapter 9

Sliding Toward Armageddon

On August 30, 1961 President Kennedy ordered 148,000 national guardsman and reservists to active duty. On 1 November, the Air Force mobilized three more A.N.G.[21] units to add to those previously mobilized in October, which were comprised by 18 tactical fighter squadrons, 4 tactical reconnaissance squadrons and 6 air transport squadrons.

Following the U.S. military build-up in West Berlin, the Soviet Union redeployed sizeable numbers of combat troops and tanks to positions close to the Berlin Wall.

Kennedy believed that the United States had neglected its conventional forces in placing such a heavy emphasis on mutually assured destruction and nuclear superiority over the Soviet Union. If war broke out over Berlin, it was more likely to be conventional rather than nuclear. And, anyway, the United States already had enough ICBM missiles pointed toward the USSR and nuclear bombs on board S.A.C. manned bombers to destroy the USSR ten times over.

With that in mind, the president had tripled the draft, adding six new Army Divisions and two new Marine Divisions to America's military forces.

The temperature of the Cold War was clearly on the rise—symptomatic of a slow but inexorable slide toward an armed confrontation.

The presence of Lucius D. Clay in West Berlin had an impact on the city's population. With a grizzled old soldier like Clay on the scene, the West Germans became bolder, more confident and more defiant of the Eastern Bloc's power. Demonstrations, rallies and attempts to bring more Germans over the Wall to the West clearly spiked after Clay's arrival on 20 August 1961.

The denizens of West Berlin were not the only ones who became more aggressive. By the 1945 accords reached at the Potsdam Conference,

---

[21] Air National Guard

personnel of the four occupying powers were to be permitted free access at all times to the entire City of Berlin. But now British, French and American officials were being stopped at the checkpoints to East Berlin and often denied entry. Clay was not about to let this go unchallenged.

On 22 October 1961, the Chief of the U.S. Mission in West Berlin, E. Allen Lightner, was stopped in his car—bearing an Occupying Forces license plate—at Checkpoint Charlie, while attempting to drive into East Berlin to go to a theater. He was turned back by the border guards—raising Clay's ire to an all-time high.

23 October 1961—East Berlin—Final Countdown to Crisis Begins

An angry Lucius D. Clay resolved to probe the border between the two Berlins. His memory of the Soviet's total blockade of Berlin in 1948 spurred him on. An American diplomat, Albert Hemsing, known for his mental toughness, was designated as point man. After probing the border in a diplomatic vehicle, Hemsing was stopped by East German transport police who demanded to see his passport.

Three blocks away, Warren Olney and Uri Putyagin (Carlton) sat facing each other over a concrete chess table and board in Bismarckplatz, a lively East Berlin park. In the midst of other chess players, children jumping rope and old men playing cards, the two intelligence pros moved their pieces on the board while they engaged in a conversation far removed from the pleasurable game of chess. After each man opened conventionally with their pawns, Olney considered moving his bishop into action.

Seated between the two players was Káz Penchak, who held a time-clock and gave the appearance of tinkering with it to adjust some minor malfunction. All three men were dressed in the Bohemian style of the late 50's and early 60's—tight black pants, leather jackets, black berets and wire-framed eyeglasses. Uri wore a fake mustache, Penchak a faux goatee, and Olney longish side-burns. Olney sported a German cigarette hanging from the corner of his lip. Penchak chewed on a plastic holder containing an unlit cigarette.

On the table was a transistor radio from which the strains of Bach's Brandenburg Concerto could be heard in all its majestic glory.

As Olney captured one of Putyagin's pawns with his bishop, he spoke softly with his eyes fixed on the board. "The CO is very concerned. He believes there are those who are out to get you."

Before Uri could respond, the high-pitched sirens of U.S. Military Police jeeps shattered the morning calm.

Hateface Heidégger sat in a self-made cubicle of cardboard boxes in front of a third floor window of the warehouse across the street from Bismarckplatz. Adjusting the sight of his deer rifle to account for windage and distance, he pointed it at the back of the head of Uri Putyagin seated below him in the park. He could barely contain his excitement over what would occur in a few seconds—the explosion of Putyagin's head with bone fragments and soft tissue flying in every direction.

But he was a professional and would take the extra couple of seconds to make sure the target was perfectly sighted. As soon as he shot Putyagin, he would—a split second later—shoot Olney in the heart and then shoot Penchak in the side of the head. But, before he could squeeze the trigger even once, the wail of American M.P. sirens in the distance broke his concentration. This was all the time Barton Spaniel needed to tear aside the cardboard barrier, point his Smith and Wesson .44 Magnum at Heidégger's head and shout his command, "Drop your weapon and raise your hands in the air."

As was predictable, Heidégger disobeyed the command by swinging his rifle away from the window and toward Spaniel. His disobedience was punished by the administration of two gun shots to the center of the forehead from Spaniel's .44 Magnum.

The second shot almost blew the top of his head off.

Antonin Slezak sat in a rented Mercedes on the opposite side of the park with a clear view through his binoculars of the three Western Bloc operatives posing as chess players. When the military police sirens started blaring, Slezak figured that they might temporarily break Heidégger's concentration; but now it was fifteen minutes past the appointed time of the assassination and ten minutes past the time when Heidégger was to have joined him in the Mercedes. The three targets still sat there undisturbed, seemingly impervious to the sirens which were getting louder and closer.

Obviously, something was very wrong. Before they left their hotel room that morning, Slezak had tried to reach Q by phone five times with no success. He had no way of knowing that Q himself had also left for Berlin. If he could just get through to Q to let him know that the U.S. mole was Uri Putyagin, then at least one other person on their team would know the mole's identity. If Heidégger was still alive there would be two others, but Slezak was beginning to doubt that he was. Heidégger was now fifteen minutes late. If he was dead, then Slezak needed to reach Q, so they could regroup and plan their next offensive against Putyagin. However, it was too soon for him to abandon the rendezvous location. Heidégger may have just gotten into a jamb. Slezak needed to give him at least another fifteen minutes to get out of it.

While he waited, Slezak reviewed the events of the past 48 hours in his head. Up until now things had gone well. Armed with bios and photographs provided by Q of about 90 Soviet defense officials in East Berlin, he and Heidégger had spent hours committing the names and places to memory. They knew Agent 18339 was a U.S. spy before they even got to East Berlin. The U.S. agent had gotten careless. Without doing enough background research, he had travelled the previous month to Minsk, Russia, on a tip from his cousin there that her best friend, Marina, was keeping company with an American ex-patriot named Lee Harvey Oswald, an ex-Marine who was close to being flat broke. The rumor was that he was a CIA contract mule, but had gotten no work since moving from Moscow to Minsk.

Agent 18339 travelled to Minsk after his cousin arranged a meeting with Oswald. U.S. Army Intelligence paid reasonably well and he was optimistic that Oswald would accept his pitch to come to work for the American side. When Agent 18339 got one look at the girlfriend, Marina, and saw how stunning she was, he was confident that Oswald would need as much money as he could get his hands on to keep her happy. 18339 wasn't entirely wrong but what he didn't know was that Oswald was under surveillance by the KGB as well as the CIA. Oswald was painfully aware of that fact. When 18339 pitched him, Oswald said he would think about it and let 18339 know by mail the following week. What Oswald did instead was have Marina get a picture of 18339 from her friend under some pretext, and go straight to the KGB to report the pitch. By providing this valuable info to the KGB, Oswald who was on the brink of being arrested by them, probably did himself some real good. The following year, 1962,

Oswald was allowed to marry Marina and emigrate back to America with his new bride.

The photo of Agent 18339 was sent to KGB headquarters in East Berlin. Given his high station with the KGB, Slezak got 18339's name, address and a print of his photo on October 20th. Upon arriving in East Berlin, he and Heidégger went straight to 18339's address, picked up his trail and kept him under surveillance. They tailed him to the dead-drop where they saw him leave a message. They waited at the dead-drop to see who would pick it up. When Putyagin/Carlton picked it up, Slezak recognized him immediately from his picture. They kept Putyagin under constant surveillance until he showed up with two others in Bismarckplatz on 22 October, carrying a chess set.

The East Berlin police backed away from Hemsing's vehicle once six jeeps full of American MP's armed to the teeth pulled up and surrounded it—with sirens screaming. The Military Police escorted the diplomatic vehicle in the direction of Bismarckplatz. The shocked GDR police got out of the way. They were civilian officers and had no intention of interfering with armed military personnel of an enemy nation. That was a job for the Soviet and East German armies. But by the time the East Germans could deploy troops to engage the motorcade, it was safely back in West Berlin. Clay had, to use John Kennedy's expression, "spit in their eye."

October 24, 1961—West Berlin

Q wanted to speak to Slezak as much as Slezak wanted to talk to him. But it was just too damn risky for him to cross-over into the Eastern sector, assuming he was even able to pull that off. He wasn't just any American. He was a CIA station chief for God's sake—and wouldn't the Commies just love to get their hands on him? It was also too dangerous for him to leave word on the other side for Slezak to come back to meet him in West Berlin. They must not be seen together anywhere in Berlin. "I'm even taking a big chance being in West Berlin at all," Q said silently to himself. Q was, at his core, a monumental coward. But he was an even bigger power addict, self-promoter and egomaniac. Once U.S. troops had marched through East Germany to West Berlin, Q decided to go there. The line he most often spoke to himself was, "I'll be bloody-well-damned if I'm going to be caught sitting on the sidelines in fucking London when the balloon goes up for WWIII."

★ ★ ★ ☭ ★ ★ ★

Clay might have been content for a while letting things simmer down. After all, he had made fools of the East Germans and the Soviets with the Hemsing incident. More importantly, he had demonstrated that the U.S. could breach the border at will. He was, therefore, smugly pleased until another incident occurred. A British diplomat, attempting to drive into East Berlin, was stopped by East German Police who demanded to see identification. When the police told him they were confiscating his passport, he turned around and meekly drove back to West Berlin without protest.

When the incident was reported to Clay, he was furious. "This incident has reversed everything that we gained with Hemsing. There's always some dope who doesn't get the word."

But Clay's recriminations didn't last long. He soon recovered, and began formulating his next course of action. It was time to ratchet up the pressure...

★ ★ ★ ☭ ★ ★ ★

October 26, 1961—West Berlin

Spaniel wasn't the only one to spy O'Doherty, seemingly camped-out at the sidewalk café adjacent to Checkpoint Charlie. Q couldn't help but notice the broad-shouldered American with the high frontal hair-line. Rising from his forehead was a vertical peak of stiff black hair, roughly three inches high. It was O'Doherty's trademark—quite reminiscent of the peak for which John F. Kennedy was known before he began his quest for the presidency in 1958. Kennedy's political advisors then prevailed upon him to sharply trim back the promontory rising from his forehead, lest it became a target for cartoonists bent on drawing unflattering caricatures of the Boston Irishman. It was almost as if Kennedy's now defunct crest of hair had been reincarnated on O'Doherty's head.

Unlike Spaniel who didn't care one way or the other, Q did not want to be seen by O'Doherty. Quickly backing into a narrow alley next to the café, from which he could still keep O'Doherty in his sights, Q observed the latter get up from his table and walk the short distance to the nearby payphone. But something was out of kilter. Q's practiced eye was registering a negative visual. There was an unfamiliarity in O'Doherty's posture and gait which could only be picked up when he stood and walked. True, the width of his shoulders and his height were about right but they could easily have been enhanced by padding and lifts, respectively. Q would keep the man in view for a while from his present vantage point until he could find an opportunity to get closer and take a better look at his face.

October 26, 1961—East Berlin

Despite the growing tension in Berlin in the areas near the Wall, and in particular at Checkpoint Charlie, Olney managed on his fifth try to get a phone call through to Fred Reitenhauser.

Their conversation was brief but significant. "How are you making out Warren?"

"Fine, sir. Mission accomplished."

"Good job. Listen, I want you and Káz to stay put for a while. Things are starting to get hot there and no matter what happens, I want the two of you on the scene. Who knows, it might even be necessary for you to do some extractions. Understood?"

"Copy that."

"Okay, keep a low profile and try to reach me again before you make any major move. But if you can't, you're on your own. Incidentally, I am keeping Mitch Blake fully briefed on what's going on."

"Roger that."

"Be careful Warren."

"Yes sir."

When Uri had returned to his office on the 23rd, the phone was ringing off the hook and call-back messages were piled high on his desk. The whole place was a maelstrom gathering force. Nervous aides and secretaries scurried about while supervisors shouted at subordinates. The Kremlin P.R. people and propagandists were in a state of panic over the fact that the Americans had made them look so foolish and weak in the Hemsing incident. Looking for a scapegoat, they tried to cast the blame on the East Berlin office of the Department of Defense Preparedness for the Western Soviet Republics.

Uri could hardly keep himself from laughing out loud at the accusatory nature of the panicky communiqués his office was receiving from Moscow, and the exaggerated effect it was having upon his personnel.

Everyone in the Soviet defense hierarchy with even the most minute amount of influence and savvy knew that Uri's department had no real power to either cause or prevent anything important. Despite its fancy name, his department was strictly administrative—a good day was when they were successful in making sure the troops on the western front had enough fur-lined boots when winter set-in in the Baltics, Poland and Prussia. The USSR was a power-centric nation with all-important decisions coming from Moscow.

Uri's real problem had nothing to do with the chaos which had befallen his office during the short time he had been away meeting with Olney and Penchak. His real concern was the chilling warning they had brought him from Fred about Uri's new enemies: the unprincipled spy master called Q, the ruthless Antonin Slezak, the murderous Hateface Heidégger; and, perhaps, even O'Doherty and Spaniel. And to make things even more complicated, Fred believed it possible that either O'Doherty or Spaniel was Jurist II.

Under ordinary circumstances, this would have been a good time for him to take a prolonged vacation back in Moscow with his family. But with things heating up at the Berlin Wall, Uri knew that he had no choice other than to stay put and see what developed.

Antonin Slezak lay on his hotel room bed with his feet elevated to relieve the pressure on his spinal column. He considered his chronic back pain to be a badge of honor earned when he suffered three herniated disks in 1948 from being knocked to the ground by demonstrators during a Prague confrontation.

Armed with clubs—some embedded with metal studs—he had led a group of Red Guards into the midst of thousands of demonstrators protesting the Soviet coup in progress. He had broken the heads of many Social Democrats that day—a fond reminiscence analogous to that of a Comanche warrior proudly counting the number of scalps taken at Little Big Horn. That was the day Slezak had earned the nickname, "The Butcher of Prague."

Slezak quickly pushed those happy memories aside. He had too many present challenges to deal with, to spend time on memory lane. His inquiry at the city morgue on the 25th revealed that they did, indeed, have Heidégger's body. Apparently workmen in the building heard the shots and discovered the corpse after a search of the warehouse. The East German police were investigating but had found no clues at the crime scene pointing to possible suspects.

Slezak still hadn't been able to reach Q.

"Where is that fat bastard?" he spit out in anger. After venting his rage for a minute or two, Slezak imposed upon himself the icy calm which had served him so well throughout his career. Despite his present frustration, he now knew the identity of the Western bloc mole and exactly where he could be found. It was time for a new plan for liquidating Putyagin.

Barton Spaniel decided to stay in East Berlin for the time being. He was being put up comfortably by one of his many sources in the Eastern sector and felt under no compulsion to return to the West just yet. His instincts, finely honed by thirty years as a cop and an investigator, told him all hell was about to break loose. And when it did, there was no way he was going to miss it.

Part IV, Chapter 10

Staring into the Abyss

October 27, 1961—Berlin—0800 hours

Still fuming over the capitulation by the British diplomat to the East German police, Clay met Hemsing for breakfast at 0800.

"What do you say Al, are you up for tweaking the nose of the Russian bear again."

"You bet Lucius, just tell me what you want me to do."

"Same thing as last time. Just drive across the border at Checkpoint Charlie in a diplomatic vehicle with U.S. plates. But this time I expect a stronger response from the Soviets. I don't want us to be caught with our pants down if the worst happens; so I'm sending thirty two tanks and a battalion of infantry to Templehof Airport. I'll have them standing by just in case. If we have to deploy them, they can get to Checkpoint Charlie and the Brandenburg Gate in about a half-hour. They'll arrive at Templehof at 1030 hours and as soon as I get confirmation that they are there, you'll cross over.

In any event, regardless of what happens, I want the tanks to stay near the border. My ultimate goal is to have bulldozer mounts installed on the tanks and to use them to knock down parts of the Berlin Wall."

With this announcement, Hemsing uttered a low, "Wow."

Clay smiled broadly, clearly enjoying Hemsing's surprised reaction.

"Lucius, you realize if you do that you will be ordering an armed incursion by U.S. military forces across the Eastern Sector border—technically an act of war."

"Yes, I know. To take a step like that, I'll want more than just the agreement of the commander of the U.S. Military Mission, West Berlin. I'll need to get approval from General Clark, C.I.N.C.[22], U.S. Army, Europe; and Allied Commander for Germany, General Hartel.

---

[22] Commander in Chief

"At least," replied Hemsing, with sardonic understatement. Privately, Hemsing believed that the top generals in Europe would never approve such an offensive without the approval of the Joint Chiefs of Staff, who, in turn would not act without the approval of the president.

★ ★ ★ ☭ ★ ★ ★

Checkpoint Charlie 1025 hours

The broad-shouldered man with the vertical hairline strutted confidently toward the U.S. guard booth and the diplomatic car parked next to it. Behind the automobile were six U.S. Army military police jeeps parked in a column. He wasted no time in walking to the driver's window and giving it a tap. Hemsing lowered the window.

"Mr. Hemsing, how are ya? I'm Malachy O'Doherty," said the newly-arrived, as he flashed a plastic covered District of Columbia driver's license. "I'll be tagging along with you this morning."

A stunned Hemsing was momentarily speechless. Finally he managed an "I'll have to get approval from my supervisor."

"Fine, I'll just wait in the car" said the man as he walked around the vehicle, opened the front passenger door and climbed in. "The arrogance of power," thought Hemsing as he entered the guard booth to use the phone. Nobody in his right mind (himself included) had the cojones to tell the president's top enforcer that he couldn't wait in the car.

★ ★ ★ ☭ ★ ★ ★

"Hello, chief, it's Al—we've got a bit of a problem. Malachy O'Doherty just showed up at the checkpoint and announced he's going along with me for the ride."

"I'll be damned," said Clay. I don't want to throw off the timing of this thing but I'll have to try to get through to the president. Don't get back in the vehicle until I call you back."

"Okay, Lucius, I'll stay here next to the phone."

★ ★ ★ ☭ ★ ★ ★

"I'm sorry General, but the president is not scheduled to return to the White House until much later," said the White House operator.

"Well, is there some way I can reach him?"

"I wouldn't know that," replied the operator with a courteous but crisp tone.

"Well, is O'Donnell there?"

"No sir, I see here that he is with the president."

"Alright, thank you very much. I'll call later."

"You have a nice day, sir."

"Shit on a stick!" said Clay as he placed the phone back in its cradle. Seconds later the phone rang. Could it be the president calling back?

"Mr. Clay, this is Colonel Atwood calling from Templehof. Our contingent is fully deployed and at the ready."

"Thank you Colonel. Stand by."

Checkpoint Charlie 1035 hours

Albert, did O'Doherty show you I.D.?"

"Yes, a District of Columbia Driver's license with a photo that was definitely him."

Almost inaudibly, Clay spoke into the phone. "Nobody I know has a good enough retirement pension to give a flat 'No' to O'Doherty."

"Come again Chief?"

Loudly now and with a tone of crisp command, Clay issued his order to Hemsing. "Move out Mr. Hemsing, and tell O'Doherty to keep his head down just in case."

Burning Tree Golf Club, suburban Virginia, 4:35 P.M. E.S.T. (1035 hours, Berlin time)

"We only have time for five holes this afternoon before it gets dark. C'mon Kenny tee-up." The president was speaking to his top aide, Kenneth O'Donnell.

Succumbing to the presidential pressure and distracted by the Secret Service agents along the fairway, O'Donnell sliced his first drive badly.

"Nice one," said Kennedy teasingly. The next one to tee off was the president who used a two-wood instead of a driver to drive the ball straight down the fairway. Next came Harvard buddy, Bob Cassidy, who hooked his drive but not as severely as O'Donnell had sliced his.

"Okay, Mal, you're up. Stop cleaning your balls. They're clean enough," zinged the president.

The last member of the foursome, the real Malachy O'Doherty, used his driver to smash the ball 300 yards straight down the fairway.

Berlin, 1045 hours

Hemsing drove the black 1960 Lincoln across the border into East Berlin. Although no one interfered with his journey, East German police and KGB plainclothes men lined the route at intervals, making notes and snapping photographs.

When the motorcade reached Bismarckplatz, the alleged O'Doherty turned toward Hemsing. "I'll be getting out right here, Mr. Hemsing; please stop the car."

Hemsing obeyed and the entire motorcade stopped behind him.

As he disembarked, the faux-O'Doherty offered a cheerful farewell. "Ah... Mr. Hemsing, it was good to meet you... heard good things about you. I'll grab a ride back later."

With that, the broad-shouldered man with the high frontal tuft of hair, disappeared into the crowd.

Hemsing and his MP entourage drove back to West Berlin without incident.

Part IV, Chapter 11

Stand-Off at the Gate

Some men are just born for intelligence work. Warren Olney was one of them—a natural. As he sat on a park bench in the Middle of Bismarckplatz on this mild autumn day, October 27, 1961, every fiber of his being was alive with electricity. He saw the U.S. motorcade go by and then stop. He saw a man get out of the Lincoln embassy car and then disappear. His senses immediately went on alert when the motorcade left without the man. As soon as the motorcade departed, Olney felt, more than saw, heightened activity all around the park—the quickened pace of official—looking pedestrians—voices raised and tense.

Káz Penchak, a photography buff, was busy snapping pictures of ducks swimming serenely on a small pond, when he looked over to see a definite change in his partner's body language. Walking quickly to where Olney sat on the other side of the pond, he too began to pick-up on a growing frenetic atmosphere surrounding the park.

"What's the matter Oln?"

The taciturn man of few words gave Káz his answer with a meaningful stare.

Both men sat for a couple of minutes just looking and listening. Olney felt the rumble first—not so much sound as vibration—like a distant subway train approaching a station.

"You feel that?"

"Yes," replied Káz. "Let's get the hell out of here."

They walked at a normal pace, so as not to attract attention, back toward their hotel. Káz stayed a good ten paces behind Olney. Suddenly he stopped when he saw Olney's open-palmed signal to halt. The rumble had grown louder. Olney walked back to where Káz stood frozen.

"We can't go in the front entrance of the hotel. It's staked out by SMERSH[23] types—probably waiting for us."

---

[23] Soviet Secret Police

201

"Do you have anything important in our room?"

"Not a thing," said Olney. "I'm wearing my change of clothes under these. How about you?"

"Mine were in a brown paper bag which I threw into a dumpster first thing this morning."

The rumble was now loud enough for the two operatives to tell that it was coming from Friederichstrasse, a main thoroughfare which led to the Brandenburg Gate.

"Screw the hotel! It's time for us to join the parade, Káz."

The two men turned and headed toward Friederichstrasse.

East Berlin, 1400 hours

Olney and Káz chose vantage points on Friederichstrasse at opposite sides of the street, but each remaining visible to the other.

The rumble had now graduated to an incessant roar—a blend of engine noise, elevated crowd noise and tank tracks hitting pavement.

Káz was first to see the front end of a tank—gun's long barrel and turret perched atop a massive Russian T-64 tank. As the mighty behemoth of war reached Káz's position, he was merely one of scores of onlookers snapping photographs.

Olney, always the numbers man, began his count. How many tanks would roll past them? Looking eastward down the wide avenue, he could see at least a half-dozen spaced about twenty feet apart. Olney was mildly surprised when his count reached ten. After twenty had passed by his position he was astounded. "Is this the vanguard of an invasion?" he silently asked himself. When the parade of tanks topped-out at 33—all headed toward West Berlin and no more than a mile away from the border, Olney emphatically signaled Káz to join him. Standing together they counted two full battalions of infantry marching behind the last tanks.

The two Americans moved along with the crowd—mostly Germans but with some Russians, Poles and Slavs mixed in—like camp followers bringing up the rear of an army on the march. Of course, Olney and Káz were primarily concerned with reconnaissance, but they couldn't help being caught up in the possibilities. Were they about to become witnesses to history like the Union officials and their wives sitting in grand stands in their finery with binoculars in hand, hoping to watch the Army of the Potomac whip Lee's Army of Northern Virginia? If so, Olney hoped the result would be different. He had read enough Civil War books to know that on that day in 1861—100 years earlier Lee not only soundly trounced the Union forces at the Battle of Bull Run but routed the Army of the Potomac—turning it into a fleeing rabble—dropping their weapons on the ground and running for their lives. He prayed that the U.S. forces of 1961 would show more spine and skill.

East Berlin, 1500 hours

The Soviet tank column came to a halt at the Brandenburg Gate. Then ten of the tanks pealed off and drove to Checkpoint Charlie where they stopped about 75 meters from the checkpoint on the Soviet side of the sector boundary. The next fifteen minutes were spent getting the tanks into position so that all their big guns pointed directly at the boundary crossing and into West Berlin.

While Káz kept watch from an elevation in the road between the gate and the checkpoint, Olney found a pay phone and called Munich. Gerda put him right through to the CO."

"What's up Warren?"

"Thirty-three hostile T-64's near sector boundary at "The Gate" and at "Charlie," backed by two battalions of infantry."

"Any overt signs of aggression?"

"Big guns pointed across the border Sir."

"Are you and Penchak together?"

"Yes sir."

"Okay, stay put and report in as necessary, but at least every fifteen minutes."

"Will do, Sir."

"Warren, what uniforms are the troops wearing?"

"USSR."

"Copy that."

Reitenhauser hung up the phone just long enough to get a dial tone and then immediately called Dabrowski at Group.

West Berlin 1530 hours

Colonel Jim Atwood got his orders over the phone directly from Ambassador Clay. Clay was assuming unusual authority in bypassing the chain of command and going straight to the ground commander. But he was faced with an emergency and there was no time for rigid adherence to protocol. Besides, President Kennedy had made it clear that Clay was his man on the scene, implying strongly that Clay had been granted extraordinary powers.

Clay had known both Ed Dabrowski and Fred Reitenhauser, since the two daredevils had risked getting shot out of the sky over East Germany by Russian MiGs. It was 1948 at the very beginning of the Berlin Blockade and they had landed at Templehof in a light plane to personally give then-General Clay an up-to-the-hour intelligence briefing. So, when Dabrowski called five minutes before to say that two of Reitenhauser's agents in the Eastern sector had reported 33 Soviet tanks and two infantry battalions near the border, Clay did not doubt the report for even a second. As far as he was concerned, the two intelligence officers had the highest credibility.

"Colonel Atwood, I need you to get somebody over to "Charlie" and to "the Gate" ASAP. I just got a reliable intelligence report of 33 Soviet T-64s near the border, backed by heavy infantry."

"Will do, General," said Atwood, using the ambassador's former rank as a sign of respect. "One of my guys, Lieutenant Norm Sikes, spotted the tanks just a few minutes ago. I'll send him over to verify."

"Good. Call me as soon as you get any information."

"Roger that."

Berlin, 1545 hours

Lieutenant Norm Sikes chose tank driver, Sgt. Van McCarty, to accompany him on the drive from Templehof to the site of the Soviet tanks.

"I'll go get us a jeep, sir, said McCarty—with excitement in his voice."

"No, get a staff car. It'll attract less attention, and maybe give us better protection from gun fire. Tell them you have orders from the colonel.

As the two U.S. soldiers drove east past Checkpoint Charlie, they slowed a bit so they could take a good look around. They had no trouble locating the tanks at their two positions close to Checkpoint Charlie and the nearby Brandenburg Gate.

"Those are Russian T-64's alright, Sir."

"Yeah, but that's not good enough. The colonel needs proof for General Clay that they are actually being operated by the Soviets."

"With all due respect sir, who else would be operating Soviet tanks backed up by a shitload of Russian troops?"

"For Chrissakes... How should *I* know? East Germans, some other Warsaw Pact assholes... Maybe even fucking Martians. All I know, is we have our orders."

"Copy that, Lieutenant. Sorry I riled you up."

"Don't worry about it. This is one dicey situation. I hope we live long enough to tell our grandchildren about it."

With McCarty behind the wheel, the Americans circled each of the two tank positions, keeping a safe distance away. Sikes kept his eyes peeled and tried to observe every little detail through a pair of binoculars. There was no talk in the staff car for a good ten minutes. Finally, Sikes broke the silence.

"Van, the troops near the Gate are in a different mode than those at Charlie. At Charlie, they're running around in a frenzy, loading shells into the tanks, making frequent position changes and with crews not roaming far from their tanks. But at the Gate I saw at least a dozen crews milling around, smoking and having coffee with the ground troops. Everybody appears to be much more relaxed. And you know what, there seems to be absolutely no activity around the tanks on the outer perimeter—about 150 meters from the lead tanks. They're even partially blocked from view by bulldozers and construction cranes left over from the building of the Berlin Wall. I'll bet you those outer tanks are vacant."

"Oh shit. Lieutenant, if you're thinking what I think you're thinking, look out!"

"Van, I need to get into one of those tanks—one partly blocked by the construction equipment. You need to lay on top of the one next to it with your binocs, and keep a look-out."

"Whatever you say, Sir."

McCarty lay prone on top of a T-64 with a carbine at his side while Sikes carefully opened the hatch of the adjoining tank. Then, with side-arm in hand, Sikes scanned the interior. As he suspected, it was vacant. Slowly he climbed into the tank while McCarty peered through the binoculars at the ground troops and tank crews off in the distance. With the hatch of the adjoining tank still open, McCarty could hear Sikes rummaging around inside. He said a silent prayer that Sikes would find what he was looking for so that they could get out of there fast. "Ah, oh," said McCarty as suddenly he caught sight of one of the Russian Soldiers looking directly at them through his own binoculars. Then everything disassembled at once as the conglomeration of troops broke apart and scattered in many directions like so many refracted waves of light, creating colorful patterns as seen through a kaleidoscope. Some troops were running toward them while others were hopping into jeeps and trucks. One or two of the tanks were turning to face the Americans and aiming the big guns in their direction.

"Don't panic!," McCarty admonished himself as he clamored down the side of his tank and then practically vaulted up the side of Sikes' T-64. "Lieutenant, they've spotted us and are on the way."

Sikes grabbed two objects and sprang up the hatch. Both men quickly jumped off the T-64 and sprinted to their car as the sounds of men shouting and engines roaring grew louder. Then a single shot was fired—perhaps into the air—as the shouting of the Russians grew louder.

"Give me your carbine," ordered Sikes as they climbed into their vehicle. McCarty handed him the weapon while inserting the key in the ignition. Sikes frantically rolled down the window and stuck the barrel of the weapon through it.

McCarty and Sikes left the sound and smell of burning rubber in their wake as they pealed out and sped away—with two pursuing Soviet jeeps no further than fifty feet behind them. The fleeing American soldiers fully expected to be shot at—but perhaps unwilling to provoke an international incident—the Russian guns were silent, so far.

But now, two or three East Berlin police cars had joined the chase with sirens wailing. The East Berlin cops didn't have the same compunction as the Soviet soldiers and a bullet whizzed past Sike's outstretched carbine.

"Faster!" yelled Sikes.

McCarty floored it in response, and the speedometer needle soon registered 80 miles per hour, as McCarty wove in and out of the moderate traffic.

The staff car barreled down Friederichstrasse as two new shots were fired. One hit and knocked off the side view mirror on the driver's side, while the second smashed the rear window. But now they could clearly see the contours of Checkpoint Charlie in the distance. The East Berlin police cars were slowly gaining on them but McCarty's stunt-driving had thus far kept the police from getting off another clean shot. But there was still enough time for the pursuers to catch them and cut them off before they reached the border.

McCarty, a card-carrying member of the Oklahoma Stock-Car Drivers Association, depressed the accelerator to the floor even as he cleanly executed an intricate weave from behind a Mercedes, past a group of cyclists and then sharply in front of a bus. By the time they reached the final approach to the checkpoint, their speedometer read 85 m.p.h. McCarty slowed at the checkpoint and passed safely into West Berlin. The pursuing police and military stopped well before the checkpoint, turned around and drove away.

West Berlin, 1600 hours

Lieutenant Sikes and Sergeant McCarty stood in front of Colonel Atwood's desk at attention.

"At ease men."

"Yes sir. We're here to report on the results of our patrol," said Sikes.

"Proceed."

"With your permission sir, I'll skip the preliminaries and get right to the critical part."

"Granted."

We managed to get inside a Russian T-64 near Lindenplatz and the Brandenburg Gate. The Soviets eventually spotted us and gave chase as we headed back to Checkpoint Charlie. East German police opened fire on us and hit our vehicle. But thanks to some fancy driving by McCarty we made it back without getting shot. We retrieved these two objects from inside the Russian tank."

As he spoke, Sikes handed Atwood a Russian Army newspaper and a book of matches from a night club in the heart of Leningrad's red light district.

Sike and McCarty tried not to show how pleased and proud they felt over what they had accomplished. They were, however, perplexed when a wan smile appeared on Atwood's face and the worry lines in his forehead seemed suddenly deeper.

Atwood closely examined the two objects, turning them over and over. The silence in the room was oppressive.

Finally, he spoke. "Congratulations Lieutenant Sikes and Sergeant McCarty, on successfully completing your mission. You have discharged your duties bravely and skillfully. I intend to put in a recommendation that you be decorated."

Atwood then sat back in his chair and dropped the military formality from his voice. "And by the way fellows, you may very well have found the physical evidence which will either *start*, or *prevent* World War III."

West Berlin, 1615 hours

Lucius Clay closed his office door after first commanding his secretary to carefully screen all calls before interrupting him. He had many of his own calls to make and needed to concentrate.

The first call he placed was to the president. The conversation between Clay and Kennedy took about 15 minutes, counting the last five during which Secretary of Defense McNamara and National Security advisor Bundy were patched in. Clay briefed everyone on the items extracted from the Russian tank.

By the close of the conference call, Clay's orders from the president were unequivocal. He picked up the receiver as soon as he got off the phone with the White House, and called Colonel Atwood. "Colonel, this is an order from C.I.N.C., the White House. Redeploy all tanks and troops from Templehof to Checkpoint Charlie *now*! With guns facing the Eastern sector. All tanks and other weapons are to be fully loaded. Unless attacked, take no further action until you hear from me, or some other appropriate higher authority. If attacked, defend your position with all appropriate force. You are to fire if fired upon. Your written orders are being prepared, and will be hand-delivered."

"Copy that, General."

Next, Clay called General Bruce C. Clarke, Commander-in-Chief, U.S. Army Europe, to convey the White House's orders. Clarke was justifiably miffed that Clay had first gone directly to Colonel Atwood. Clay understood, but succinctly stated that the order of the calls had been determined by the White House, in order to prevent even the slightest delay. The president had stated clearly that he did not know what Soviet intentions were, and considered it a matter of the greatest urgency that allied tanks and ground forces be placed in position immediately to confront any possible aggression against West Berlin.

The president advised Clay that he would simultaneously call General Norstad, British Prime Minister, Harold MacMillan, French President Charles De Gaulle, and German Chancellor Konrad Adenauer.

General Lyman Lemnitzer, upon the president's command, was told to notify the rest of the Joint Chiefs of Staff and convey the president's order that the Navy place all Polaris submarines world-wide, on alert. The Air Force was to simultaneously place the Strategic Air Command on full alert. General Norstad did the same to all NATO forces.

Clay wasn't finished yet with his phone calls. He quickly dialed Ed Dabrowski's private number in Frankfurt and was connected without delay. He summarized the intelligence gathered by Lieutenant Sikes and Sergeant McCarty.

Dabrowski in turn briefed Clay on the information provided to Reitenhauser by his two undercover agents.

When Clay finished describing the configuration of Soviet and U.S. tanks and ground troops in Berlin, the bombastic Dabrowski could no longer remain silent. "Mr. Ambassador, I have standing orders from General Saylor that as soon as it looks like the balloon might go up in Berlin, I am to get my backside up there on the double!"

"Fine Ed, we'll need all the help we can get."

"Great, I'll see you in about an hour and a half."

Dabrowski, already at his private phone, let the adrenalin flow subside for a minute or two before picking up the receiver again and calling Reitenhauser.

"Fred, I'm sending a plane to pick you up. We have an armed stand-off in Berlin. Be at your landing site in a half-hour. It'll be like '48 all over again. We're flying into the shit. And Fred, bring a body guard."

An hour later the plane carrying Fred Reitenhauser and Mario Tonelli landed at Group's private site outside Frankfurt to pick up Ed Dabrowski and Matt Mueller. All four men were armed. The plane this time was a DC-6 prop plane—quite an upgrade from their piper cub of 1948. Within minutes they were airborne and bound for Berlin.

East Berlin, 1640 hours

From their vantage point among the Linden trees on a hilltop overlooking the most distant Soviet tanks, Olney and Káz had, some time earlier, heard the single shot fired and immediately peered through their binoculars in the direction from which they believed it had come. They witnessed the frantic efforts of two GI's to get into their Army car and high-tail it out of the area—quickly pursued by Soviet jeeps containing armed troops.

"What do you make of that?" Káz had asked Olney at the time.

"I haven't the slightest idea," responded Olney, "but my gut tells me it will be only the first of a bunch of wild and crazy things that we'll see today."

Olney's prophetic words received their first confirmation at 1640 hours when below them they saw a black limousine bearing a red hammer and sickle flag moving into the midst of the Russian tanks.

"That's a KGB limo," observed Olney.

"How do you know?"

"From the license plate, 'S-123-1172.' The last four numbers 1172, are code. K is the eleventh letter of the alphabet, G is the seventh and B is the second."

"What do you know? A guy can learn a lot hanging around with someone like you, Oln."

"Thank you," said Olney politely.

The limousine slowed and stopped. Only the uniformed driver got out. He walked quickly to a small group of officers, spoke to them briefly and then got back into the automobile. Had the driver known the identity of his four passengers he might have been more nervous than he appeared. His supervisor had told him they were important but not how important. Seated on one seat facing forward was Comrade Uri Putyagin, the Minister of Defense Preparedness for the Western Soviet Republics; and Antonin Slezak, the Deputy Komisar of the KGB. On the seat facing them sat top KGB spy, Georgi Bolshakov, and an American known only to the others as *Jurist*.

The four occupants of the limo chatted amiably, especially after a Soviet Army private brought them each a mug of hot coffee. They joked and guffawed among themselves in Russian. Of course, one of the occupants, Komisar Putyagin, had no idea that one of his three colleagues had independent plans to murder him as soon as darkness descended upon the East-West border.

Bonn, West Germany, 1645 hours

The last two telephone calls John F. Kennedy made to Europe on October 27, 1961 were to West German Chancellor, Konrad Adenauer, and West Berlin Mayor, Willie Brandt.

When the telephone rang inside Adenauer's official quarters in Bonn at 1645 hours, he didn't have to be told who was calling. He had been monitoring events in Berlin all day and his instincts as a life-long politician/statesman told him it was Kennedy. If their situations were reversed, this was the time he too would be placing a similar call.

During their ten minute conversation, Kennedy informed Adenauer that even as they spoke, over thirty U.S. Army M-60 Patton tanks carrying live munitions, with accompanying troops and vehicles, were headed in the direction of the Berlin Wall and would soon face-down a similar number of Soviet tanks.

"What can I do to help, Mr. President?" inquired Adenauer.

"Mr. Chancellor, all I can offer is a suggestion and I do so with the utmost respect for you as head-of-state of the Sovereign Republic of West Germany. I think it best that West Germany refrain from all military activity until we can get an idea of what shape this crisis is going to take. The last thing we want right now is to give Khrushchev a pretext for invading your country."

"I am fully in accord, Mr. President. And as soon as we hang up, I will take steps to ensure that our republic remains in stand-down mode. I will also beseech the Lord, our God, for his guidance in this moment of world crisis, and pray that he will keep the people of our two great nations—and all the peoples of the world—safe from the ravages of war."

"Ah... yes... ah, Mr. Chancellor, I ah... shall do likewise."

In his call to West Berlin Mayor, Willie Brandt, Kennedy praised the courage and tenacity of the citizens of West Berlin and called on both the Mayor and all West Berliners to stay strong and determined during this crisis, "a crisis created by a force-not for good, but bent upon depriving freedom-loving people of their fundamental rights."

East Berlin, 1655 hours

Barton Spaniel had picked up Slezak's trail the moment the latter emerged from East Berlin KGB headquarters an hour earlier. He had seen him conversing with the driver of a black Soviet limousine parked in front.

Spaniel was no more than fifteen feet away and his recently-acquired uniform of an East German motorcycle patrolman fit him well. The erstwhile occupant of the uniform was hitch-hiking in his underwear ten miles outside of the city. Spaniel was now grateful for all the time spent in the gym warding off middle-age flabbiness. He now was waiting along with three other motorcycle patrolmen who would escort the limousine to its destination.

Slezak kept looking at his watch and pacing back and forth in front of the KGB building. He appeared to be waiting for the arrival of other passengers. The next to arrive upon the scene were two thirtyish-looking men who also emerged from the front entrance of the KGB building. One was tall and graceful, dressed in an elegant gray tailored suit. The other was short and wore an ill-fitting brown polyester suit. Spaniel recognized the shorter man immediately. "I don't believe it," Spaniel muttered to himself. He also recognized the taller of the two—but only from his photograph in the book of known hostile agents, back at G-2 headquarters. A fourth passenger soon joined the group. Spaniel did not recognize him.

At last all four passengers took seats inside the limo and with its police escort, drove to the location of the Soviet tanks facing the border—standing with gun turrets manned and at the ready about 75 meters east of Checkpoint Charlie.

Unlike the other patrolmen who apparently had orders to depart from the tank-site as soon as the limousine safely arrived, Spaniel alone lingered behind.

Feigning a conversation with someone on his walky-talky, he remained at the site for an additional ten minutes—all the while keeping the limos and its occupants under close surveillance. After departing the scene he drove to a service station about one eighth of a mile away, removed his clothes from the bike's carry bag, and changed into his civvies in the lavatory. He threw the uniform in the trash can, abandoned the motorcycle and headed back to the Soviet tank site on foot.

He arrived back at the site at 1655 hours—about the same time that Olney and Káz abandoned their hill-top position and headed toward the same place.

By a combination of fate and coincidence, by 1700 hours on 27 October 1961, Uri Putyagin, Antonin Slezak, Barton Spaniel, Warren Olney, Kázimir Penchak and Jurist II were all within 100 meters of each other.

West Berlin, 1700 hours

The U.S. tanks and support troops arrived at the border on the West Berlin side at 1700 hours sharp and took up positions with guns pointed at the Eastern sector, approximately 75 meters west of Checkpoint Charlie. Like the Soviet T-64's, the U.S. Patton tanks were loaded with live munitions.

Thus did the stand-off begin. Altogether, 65 tanks of the two super-powers combined stood with the others' guns trained on them and with their guns in turn pointed at the others. Each of perhaps the combined 130 crew members stared straight ahead with rigid concentration—fixed on one thing only—each's equally deadly counterparts on the opposite side of the boundary.

Beginning at 1700 hours and at all times thereafter, the tank crews were locked in a choking tension which never eased but only grew more suffocating. Each man's stress was a tether which could be neither untied nor loosened. And so they stood—caught in a hellish stasis. An hour went by, and then two, and three and four. There seemed no escape from the unbearably oppressive stillness. They could neither shoot, move forward or move backwards. They could not exit the tank or move from their claustrophobic individual spaces within.

What were the odds against a single gunner among 65, getting spooked, cracking under the pressure and delivering a deadly salvo into the enemy position, a mere 150 meters distant? Probably no more than fifty-fifty. And then what would the odds be in favor of other tanks on one side or both sides unleashing the fury of their 100 mm guns? 60—40? 75-25? 90-10? And if that happened, would a major tank battle commence? Almost certainly. And would the battle escalate into war; and war into massive conflagration and conflagration into Nuclear Armageddon? Did anyone possess the decree of certitude necessary to unequivocally declare that it would not?

After four consecutive hours of the wrenching physical and psychological stand-off, the uniforms of most crew members were soaked through with perspiration. The cramped compartments within the T-64's and the M-60 Pattons were now dank and fetid. Still, the men were held in a type of suspension—impotent to affect their fate—their decision-making function usurped not by superiors in the chain of command but by civilian statesmen, diplomats and politicians. Men and machines with the capacity to demolish and annihilate had been transformed into mere pawns on a global chess board.

West Berlin, 2100 hours

Olney and Penchak had explicit orders from the CO that if they were unable to reach him by phone at the 409th, they were to try to reach him or leave a message for him at the guard station at Checkpoint Charlie. But there were no messages there, which meant that they had been out of contact for almost five hours. Fred's concern now grew by the minute. Clay had given orders that a table and two phones were to be set aside at the Checkpoint station for Dabrowski and Reitenhauser; and there they now sat—Dabrowski chain-smoking Lucky Strikes and Reitenhauser stroking the bald spot on the back of his head.

In a state of restlessness, Clay had his driver taxi him back and forth repeatedly between the checkpoint, where he would consult with his two intelligence advisors, and the site of the U.S. tanks. He stayed in constant touch with the White House on the telephone installed in a private room for him at the checkpoint station.

Colonel Atwood had established his command post at the tank-site rather than the checkpoint, wanting to be as close as possible to his men at all times. He had placed several urgent phone calls to U.S. Army Europe for replacement tank crews so that eventually the fatigued two-man crews could be given some relief. Clay had also given him assurances that General Norstad at NATO headquarters was hard at work trying to get the British to commit six tanks of their own to augment NATO's Berlin position, currently composed of U.S. forces only.

Q, comfortably ensconced in a triple-A rated hotel and occupying a full suite on the top floor, had a perfect view of the U.S. tank position from his balcony. It was dark now but the U.S. site and checkpoint were well-lighted. Dressed in a smoking jacket, Q sipped slowly from a brandy snifter and pondered his next move.

East Berlin, 2130 hours

Olney caught a quick glimpse of Spaniel. Both of them were well-removed from the perimeter of the Soviet command post. Spaniel had just darted into a small copse of trees. Olney hid behind an abandoned wreck that had once been an Opel Kadet sedan. It was too dark for him to see the man's face but Olney's superb powers of observation told him immediately that the man was an American. The clothes, hairstyle, posture, movement and tan bucks on his feet were tell-tale signs.

For Olney the evening had been full of surprises. While there was still daylight he had been able to identify two of the limousine's passengers as Antonin Slezak and Carlton. Slezak was notorious and Olney had been shown many photographs of him during and after advanced surveillance training at Group. He recognized Carlton from one grainy photograph Reitenhauser had removed from his office safe and exhibited to Olney, just one time; as well as from their meeting in Bismarckplatz.

He and Káz had decided to split up but then meet behind the wrecked auto at 2200 hours. Two men together made a better target for Hostile and narrowed their own surveillance capacity as well.

Combining their takes on the limo passengers, they made them to be Antonin Slezak; top KGB Agent Georgi Bolshakov; Carlton; and a diminutive unknown American. The last time it was light enough to see, they noticed that the locations of the four passengers had changed since their arrival. Bolshakov had entered the CP tent at about 1900 hours. That was the last time they had seen him. Slezak roamed the perimeter, stopping every now and then to talk with small groups of what appeared to be Russian Commandos. The short American sat alone in the rear-most seat of the limousine—in perfect isolation. Carlton had moved to the front seat where he and the limo driver appeared to be engaged in light-hearted small talk.

Uri Putyagin—always the most sociable of men—was acting consistent with his nature. The contrast between him and the strange, introverted, Jurist II was striking.

Olney's antennae were picking up the vibes of excessive movement in front of him. Then he saw shapes. He couldn't tell how many. But as they came closer, the shapes solidified into contours and finally into the clear outlines of figures—of men—menacing and threatening men, all moving softly toward the copse of trees—eight armed commandos in all. He wished there were some way he could warn the American hiding in the trees, but it would have been impossible without imperiling himself and probably getting both of them killed.

Oddly, however, the commandos did not attack. Instead they encircled the group of trees, trapping Spaniel within.

Olney at once recognized the maneuver for what it was. The American was being isolated and neutralized. There could be only one plausible reason for taking such action—to mount an aggressive move elsewhere.

But where? Against Káz? Highly unlikely. Knowing Káz, he wouldn't let himself get discovered.

Olney's question was soon answered. Out of the corner of his right eye he caught a glint of something, produced by the light cast from the full moon. The glint was metallic but amorphous. Its formlessness presaged violence. Olney closed his eyes and opened them again, trying to adjust his eyes to the shining object and bring it into focus. Then it began to acquire definition and slowly reveal itself. Now he knew what it was and that knowledge produced in him a split second of horror. The glint came from a silencer attached to a Walther PPK—in turn attached to the right hand of Antonin Slezak. With the stealth of a cougar, Slezak inched slowly toward the front passenger window of the limousine. In a few seconds he would assassinate Uri Putyagin, America's top spy of the Cold War—still known to Olney only as Carlton. Olney was a good forty feet away and not sure he could take down the crouching Slezak, with his Colt .45, in the dark and at that distance. But he had to try. Olney raised his .45 with both hands, resting his elbows on the frame of the wrecked car to steady his aim. He pointed his long-barreled gun at Slezak who was only a few feet from the limo window and who held his Walther PPK straight out at shoulder level and in position to shoot Uri in the head, through the glass.

Olney blinked and took aim. He hoped for a clean shot through Slezak's torso. A mere non-demobilizing wound would not stop a professional assassin like Slezak from killing Carlton. He began to squeeze the trigger, eyes locked on his target. But suddenly the target moved!

Slezak's body jerked violently and spasmodically. His mouth emitted a single choking gasp, his death knell as Káz tightened the garrote around his neck from behind and squeezed the life from his body.

Slezak's body crumpled to the ground. Uri and the limo driver were oblivious to what had just happened—so preoccupied were they with their conversation. But, Jurist II saw everything and now slumped down in his seat to hide his head from view. Olney quietly intoned a single and emphatic "yes" to himself and punched the soft earth with joy. Káz disappeared as suddenly as he had emerged—a silent but deadly apparition.

But as he had garroted Slezak to death he had placed his lips to the bastard's right ear and whispered ferociously, "This is for my grandfather, my uncle, and my cousin. Let the revenge of the Penchaks escort you to hell-you evil prick!"

Spaniel decided to make his move. He would rather die than allow Jurist II escape his clutches without a fight. Crouching low between two fallen trees, he let loose a violent barrage of gun fire around the entire perimeter of the trees.

He only managed to wound one of the Russian commandos, but his objective was merely to create chaos so that he could make good his escape from the enemy's encirclement. He readied himself to spring and dash out of the trees. He needed to keep at least one bullet in the chamber of his semi-automatic Beretta to fire into Jurist II's temple as the traitor cowered in fear in the limousine.

Then, Spaniel would make a dash for the border. At his age, no one would mistake him for a track star and the commandos would probably catch him and bring him down before he could reach Checkpoint Charlie. Any prospect of his scaling the wall and crawling through the barbed wire was out of the question. The border crossing would be his only chance, and a slim one at that.

Olney changed the direction of his weapon as soon as the flurry of gunshots from the group of trees began. He saw one commando drop his Kalashnikov AK-47 and clutch his right arm.

"Okay!" Olney exclaimed to himself as he began firing at the shapes of the commandos approximately 75 feet away. He hadn't engaged in a good fire fight since Korea and in this one the stakes were even higher. Spaniel, realizing he had picked up unexpected help, felt his spirits soar. Instead of bolting from his position immediately he would stay and do his part in trapping the commandos in a cross-fire. Two signs of real trouble suddenly appeared. Shouts coming from the vicinity of the command post told him the commandos would soon be receiving reinforcements. Also he caught from the corner of his right eye movement away from the trees. He suspected that one or two of the commandos had pealed off to the right to flank his unknown ally's position.

Olney caught the attempted flanking movement too. That plus the noise coming from the Command area meant real trouble. He had all he could do to hold his own against the enemy commandos at the tree line. But suddenly a flurry of shots from a position fifteen feet to his left took out the two commandos who were attempting the flanking movement. Káz had anticipated the Russians would try to flank Olney's position and now was firing two pistols with the fury of Apollo hurling lightning bolts to earth. In his left hand he held Slezak's Walther PPK with silencer removed and in his right hand he held his own Luger. The commandos, caught in a withering three way cross-fire, were soon eliminated. The reinforcements, running straight into the teeth of a tsunami of gunfire were similarly mowed down. A few stragglers limped back to the command post where they would regroup with a fresh infusion of new troops. Soon a reconstituted force drawn from two infantry battalions would descend upon the Americans' position. It was time to get the hell out.

Káz and Olney ran to the copse of trees but the other American was already gone. As fast as the two young men could run they began their sprint to their predesignated fall-back position on top of the hill east of the outer reaches of the Soviet tank site. They avoided detection and collapsed at their hilltop redoubt—their legs like putty and their lungs on fire.

In the general bedlam caused by shock, violence and death, the lead Russian tank had fired off a single warning shot from its 105 millimeter gun into the air. The entire Soviet position had been cast into the throes of chaos. Spaniel exploited the confusion of the enemy by running a zigzag route toward the limousine. When he got there Putyagin and the driver had already left the vehicle and taken cover at the command post.

Only Jurist II remained in the limo, frozen in his seated position in the rear. The sole difference from before the fire fight was that Jurist II now held a .38 revolver in his right hand. When he saw Spaniel staring and pointing his Beretta at him through the limo's back right window, he raised his .38.

Spaniel ducked below the window, anticipating Jurist II's shot, which followed a second later. But Jurist II did not fire his weapon at Spaniel. Instead, he, Henry Fuchs, inserted his .38 into his own mouth and blew off the back of his head.

West Berlin, 2215 hours

"Lt. Sikes," shouted Atwood, "move down the line fast and see if that tank blast hit anything."

With McCarty again at the wheel of the jeep and Sikes his passenger, they zipped from tank to tank—all 32 of them—without finding any evidence that the tank shell fired by the Soviets had landed anywhere near the U.S. position. Sikes and McCarty then reported their findings to Colonel Atwood and Ambassador Clay, who had just arrived back at the C.P. Atwood next urgently communicated by radio transmission to all tank commanders that they had not been fired upon and were not to return fire except upon orders from him personally.

"What do you make of all that gun fire coming from the East sector?" asked Clay.

"Beats me," replied Atwood. "I was about to ask you the same question, General."

Clay wore a quizzical expression on his face but said nothing. What he really suspected was that Dabrowski's boys on the other side of the Wall had been up to some mischief. But Atwood had no need to know about any of that stuff so Clay simply replied, "I don't know but I'm going back to the checkpoint to do some investigating."

Back at Checkpoint Charlie, Clay ordered everyone out of the station except Dabrowski and Reitenhauser.

Fred was greatly concerned about the extent of the gun fire everyone had heard only fifteen minutes earlier, but was maintaining an even strain as always. It was hard for him to imagine, based on the vast number of rounds fired—that if Olney and Penchak were involved—they could have come out on top. But then again, with men like that, you never knew.

Clay poured himself a cup of black coffee, pulled over a chair and sat down at the table with Dabrowski and Reitenhauser.

"Okay, boys, I need to know what's going on over there. I know you have two agents on the other side and I want you to tell me straight-out what they're up to. But before you start, I'm going to tell you fellows something that even you don't know. We have a third man over there— Major Barton Spaniel, Chief Investigator for G-2, NATO. And I know you have your suspicions about him but you can forget it. Bart and I go back a long way—longer than with you two guys. You can take it from me that he is a great soldier and a great American. And I can't help but think that his presence there may have had something to do with all the gun play. So now tell me, what's going on with your boys."

Dabrowski deferred to Fred Reitenhauser; but before Fred could explain Olney and Penchak's mission in the eastern sector, they were interrupted by a guard who announced that a man in civilian clothes was demanding to see the officer in charge. He had identified himself as Major Spaniel.

"Let him in," ordered Clay. A few seconds later a tattered-looking Bart Spaniel entered the room. Dabrowski had met Spaniel on several occasions so no introduction was necessary. Fred and Spaniel were quickly introduced, shook hands and exchanged perfunctory pleasantries. Fred politely thanked Spaniel for taking good care of his undercover agent (Tonelli) during the agent's time in Mons.

After Dabrowski got Spaniel a cup of coffee and a roll, the latter wasted no time in getting down to business.

"I have a lot to cover Mr. Ambassador so I better not waste any time."

"We're all ears, Major," replied Clay. For the next half-hour, Clay and his two intelligence advisors, sat mesmerized and spellbound as Spaniel related a story which sounded like it came straight from the pages of a Graham Greene novel.

But Spaniel told the tale in a succinct, matter of fact style which rang true. A little more than a week ago, he had picked up Hateface Heidégger's trail in Frankfurt and then followed him and Antonin Slezak into East Berlin. When Heidégger attempted to assassinate someone in Bismarckplatz, from an upper story warehouse window, Spaniel intervened and killed Heidégger. Spaniel again picked up Slezak's trail earlier this day, followed him and three others in a limousine to the Soviet tank-site and took up surveillance. When Slezak attempted to assassinate a high Russian official, Uri Putyagin, through the front passenger window of the limo, an unknown figure materialized out of nowhere and garroted Slezak to death. When this happened, Spaniels' position was already surrounded by Soviet commandos. He began shooting in an attempt to escape and get to the limo in order to kill Jurist II, who it turns out was Henry Fuchs, top aide to the now-deceased Llewellyn Chase. The reason Spaniel pursued Heidégger in the first place was that strong evidence had come into his possession that Heidégger had murdered Chase and may have also played a role in the death of Dag Hammarskjöld. Spaniel admitted he had no intention of bringing back Heidégger alive because no prison could hold him and it was best to simply rid the world of a virulent pestilence. However, he would have very much preferred to capture Jurist II and bring him back for interrogation and then justice; but Soviet troops were after Spaniel and he knew there would be no time. So he decided to put a bullet in Jurist II's head instead. As it turned out, Jurist II/Henry Fuchs saved him the trouble by taking his own life. By using an excellent disguise as Malachy O'Doherty, Fuchs had gotten through Checkpoint Charlie and into East Germany handily. He had abandoned the disguise by the time he resurfaced and entered the limousine earlier in the day. In addition to Putyagin, Slezak and Fuchs, the fourth passenger in the limo, top Soviet agent, Georgi Bolshakov, was not in the limo at any time after 1900 hours and Spaniel had no idea where he had gone. He felt certain, however, that Bolshakov would surface again before the U.S.—Soviet stand-off reached its culmination—whenever that turned out to be.

Spaniel felt deeply gratified that within one week's time the world had been purged of the pernicious trio of Heidégger, Slezak and Jurist II. Spaniel was justifiably proud of the role he had played in it but also hoped he would have the opportunity to personally congratulate the young lieutenant for his fine work in Mons and the mysterious stranger who rid humanity of the blight known as Antonin Slezak.

"Well, meeting the young lieutenant is no problem," said Dabrowski as he picked up his walky-talky and spoke to the first sergeant of the guards. "First Sergeant Quinn, please escort Tonelli into the station. Soon the mutually-surprised Mario Tonelli and Bart Spaniel were warmly shaking hands—genuinely pleased to be reunited. When Mario was informed of the death of Jurist II he was overwhelmed with happiness and relief. Jurist II's identity, however, would not be released to anyone except the appropriate personnel at the White House, with a need to know. As far as Clay was concerned, those persons were the president, McGeorge Bundy, and Paul Nitze only. It was the White House's call as to how the identity of Jurist II was handled thereafter.

West Berlin, 2400 hours

At the U.S. tank position, Colonel Atwood was growing increasingly concerned. The tank commanders and gunners had, with the exception of short latrine breaks, been virtually glued to their stations in high alert status for seven straight hours.

Stress and fatigue were beginning to take their toll. The gunners in particular were getting antsy. A fist fight had broken out between a gunner and his commander when the gunner heard a truck on Friederichstrasse back-fire and began insisting that they had been fired upon.

Another tank commander's stress was expressing itself in a rampant case of paranoia. Despite the fact that Atwood had established a tight perimeter of crack infantry all around the tanks' position and had numerous patrols out simultaneously searching for enemy bazooka crews or other demolition personnel, the spooked tank commander kept tying up the radio air waves to the C.P. with reports of saboteur-sightings all around him.

What worried Atwood the most were the reports he was receiving of several tank crews becoming dysfunctional. The most serious were those who were trigger-happy. Sikes was bringing back reports of tank commanders speaking in a zoned-out and disassociated manner of the need for pre-emptive strikes against the Russians. These crews appeared to be more lethargic than rebellious and Sikes felt that they were beginning to lose touch with reality. Atwood would have replaced them in an instant if he had any relief crews. "Where were the replacements from USAR Europe and what was taking the British tanks so god-damned long to get here?" Well soon he would have no choice. He would be forced to pull some of the worst cases out of their tanks, rendering those units non-operational. Otherwise he ran the risk of having a few acutely stressed out commanders or gunners firing their 100 mm. guns all over creation.

At 0100 hours, 28 October 1961, eight hours after the stand-off began, Atwood ordered two tank crews to stand-down and sent them to meet with the Battalion psychiatrist. At 0115 hours, a tank gunner began vomiting non-stop and had to be pulled off the line and sent to the medical tent. At 0130 a tank commander lapsed into a catatonic state and also had to be pulled. Atwood lost only one tank, as he was able to team up the healthy commander from the one crew with the functioning gunner of the other. But then another gunner was immobilized by acute back spasms and had to be pulled out of his unit. Atwood was now four operational tanks down and counting.

The problem was not with the fiber of the men. These were good soldiers. But, they were part of a peacetime army. Most of them had never seen action and lacked combat-toughening. What was being asked of them was enough to tax the endurance of the most combat-seasoned veterans. These raw and previously untested tankers were simply not ready for the grueling ordeal in which they had found themselves.

East Berlin, 0200 hours

The problem with the morale and effectiveness of the Soviet forces was not the tankers. Most of them were seasoned veterans of the 1956 Hungarian Revolt, and were holding up well. The big problem was the supporting infantry. With the exception of the commandos, whose ranks were decimated in the firefight of a few hours before, most of the other infantrymen were inexperienced conscripts from the Ukraine, which itself boasted of a million-man army. The Soviet Union, however, had an unprecedented need for infantry. The sheer enormity of the borders it had to patrol and defend gave it an insatiable need for more and more ground troops.

From Vladivostok on the Pacific Coast to the Chinese border, then north west to the Baltics and along the borders of Finland, Latvia, Estonia, Lithuania, Poland, East Germany, Czechoslovakia, Austria, Rumania,

Bulgaria, the Balkans, Greece, Turkey, Albania, Iran and Afghanistan, the manpower demands of protecting and defending the borders of the USSR were prodigious.

The regular Soviet Army troops at the Russian tank site were straight out of advanced infantry training and totally uninitiated in combat. The firefight had led to widespread confusion and panic among the ranks. The officers were just as green as the troops they commanded. Without the cadre—the NCOs of the two battalions—the Russian ground troops might have disintegrated into a rabble.

The Soviet Command at the tank site had been shocked by both the presence of apparent U.S. infiltrators within their ranks and the poor performance of their troops in response. As the ninth hour of the potentially explosive stand-off came to a close, a debate raged among the senior officers at the Soviet command post as to whether an initiative should be made to the Americans to open negotiations for a withdrawal by both sides. The decision was soon taken out of their hands.

The White House, 28 October 1961, 0100 hours

A bleary-eyed Paul Nitze sat outside the Oval Office waiting for the president to see him. Secretary of State Dean Rusk was also reportedly on his way to the White House. Nitze had not been surprised to receive a telephone call from Georgi Bolshakov in East Berlin. The unofficial back-channel between Nitze and Bolshakov had been in place since the first week of the Kennedy Administration. It had been used four previous times: after the Bay of Pigs incident, during the erection of the Berlin Wall, after hostilities in the Congo involving Soviet troops and following the death of Dag Hammarskjöld.

It was now 0700 hours in Berlin. Ambassador Clay had reported U.S. tank crews suffering from "optimum stress conditions" after fourteen consecutive hours in full combat mode. Bolshakov didn't say so in so many words, but reading between the lines, the ever-astute Nitze gathered that the Soviet tank crews were being similarly affected.

The Pentagon had just raised the possibility of an unplanned discharge of tank fire from one side or the other, to Code Red, reflecting the maximum likelihood of such an incident. Also, for reasons unknown to Nitze, the promised relief from USAR Europe and British forces never arrived. Unconfirmed rumors held that they were running into great

difficulty getting across the border from West Germany into East
Germany. NATO reconnaissance aircraft had reported that there were also
no signs of any relief for the Soviet tank position.

Nitze carried in his pocket a two-sentence telegram from Bolshakov,
containing the Soviet's proposal to end the confrontation.

```
BOTH SIDES ARE TO STAND-DOWN SIMULTANEOUSLY
AND WITHDRAW TO PREVIOUS DEPLOYMENT STATIONS.
STOP.

RESTORE UNCONDITIONAL STATUS QUO ANTE BELLUM.
STOP.

BOLSHAKOV, G.
```

The meeting in the Oval Office didn't take long. Upon Rusk's arrival,
Nitze and the Secretary of State were escorted into the president's office to
find Kennedy already conferring with McGeorge Bundy, General Maxwell
Taylor and the ubiquitous Kenneth O'Donnell.

0130 hours Washington, D.C. time—0730 hours Berlin time.

"Simultaneous withdrawal is not acceptable Mr. Bolshakov. The Soviet
Union moved its tanks in first and must withdraw them first."

"I am disappointed to hear that Mr. Nitze. My government was anxious
to avoid bloodshed."

"Well, Sir. The means to avoid bloodshed rests firmly in the hands of
the Soviet Union. Let me be blunt Mr. Bolshakov. Had your tanks rolled
into West Berlin fifteen hours ago, they would have had a distinct
advantage. But it would be sheer folly for your leaders not to consider the
steps that NATO has taken over that period of time to maximize its air-
strike capacity. You are aware of the various locations in West Berlin from
which devastating air strikes may be launched. U.S. B-52's and fighter-
bombers can be over your tank position in minutes. It is unlikely that a
single Soviet tank will cross the border before they are all reduced to scrap

metal. The fifteen hour stalemate has permitted NATO to exploit its vast air superiority."

This statement by Nitze was met by stony silence on the other end of the telephone.

It was a full thirty seconds before Bolshakov offered his rejoinder. "Forgive me for saying so, Paul, but your words are both cavalier and reckless."

"They are not my words, Georgi. They are the words of the President of the United States."

The last conversation that Paul Nitze and Georgi Bolshakov would ever have ended with Bolshakov's succinct, "I will convey the message."

The back-channel was now closed permanently.

In the ensuing hours, official negotiations would take place between Secretary of State Dean Rusk and Foreign Minister Andre Gromyko.

At 1100 hours on October 28, 1961, the Soviet Union was first to withdraw its tanks from the West Berlin border. The gravest cold war crisis since the Korean War was over. No separate treaty between the Soviet Union and East Germany sealing off West Berlin was ever signed. Open access to West Berlin was preserved for the remaining twenty-nine years of the Cold War.

Part IV, Chapter 12

Afterwards

Checkpoint Charlie, 28 October 1300 hours

Olney and Káz walked quietly into the checkpoint station. They were bedraggled, filthy, smelly, exhausted and famished. They were each also happier than they had ever been.

Escorted by a guard into the room where Clay, Reitenhauser and Dabrowski were still working on the wind-down of the Berlin incident and preliminary postmortems, they stood silently in front of their commanding officer.

Fred felt waves of anxiety and worry instantly recede from his body. He tried hard not to show this flow of emotion.

"For God's sake men," boomed Dabrowski, "take a load off. Sit down and relax."

"Corporal," said Dabrowski, addressing the guard, "go find Tonelli and bring him in here."

Mario was stunned to see his two comrades, and could not contain his elation. Giving both of them a hug, all he could say was, "You guys had us worried."

Sandwiches were distributed to everyone and they all helped themselves to coffee. After the quick lunch filled with masculine ribbing and the high spirits normally accompanying a sudden release of tension, Tonelli was dismissed so that Olney and Káz could be debriefed by Clay and the two intelligence officers.

The agents' recitation of the events which occurred after they entered East Berlin filled in key gaps in Spaniel's narration. When they were done, the debriefers were amazed by how the seemingly disconnected actions of the two agents on the one hand and Spaniel on the other, had blended together seamlessly to form a perfect mosaic of skill, bravery and an intelligent brand of patriotism. Olney and Káz had known nothing of Spaniel's mission—or even his existence; and he had no knowledge of them. Yet some potent brew of random accident, D.N.A., training and shared mission caused the three men to take separate and independent actions at critical moments, which by some quirk of fate became integrated; and meshed like the smooth gears of a Rolls Royce.

Had they not taken those actions at pivotal moments, Putyagin, Olney and Káz would be dead; Heidégger alive; Slezak still a force for evil; Jurist II as effective a foe as always with identity still unknown; and Spaniel dead or captured as a spy. Moreover, the case could be made that without the cumulative decisions and actions of the three men, the Berlin stand-off might have erupted into a deadly exchange of fire, placing the entire world at grave risk.

"Though we can't give you many details, we will tell you that Jurist II is dead," volunteered Dabrowski. Neither Olney nor Káz seemed particularly surprised by the news, which told Reitenhauser immediately that they had figured out on their own that Jurist II was the American in the limousine.

"Of course," continued the voluble Dabrowski, "there are still two questions—one that you probably want to ask and one that we would like to ask. Both questions shall remain unasked. I believe yours would be "what was the true identity of Jurist II?" Ours would be, "how did the two of you manage to get back across the border without attracting attention— especially given your exceedingly disheveled appearances?" Since the answer to both questions is, "you have no need to know," they shall remain unasked."

"Well," said Káz, "can you at least tell us who the American was that we fought side by side with at the Soviet encampment?"

"I'm afraid we can't, Penchak," responded Dabrowski. "We think there will be a bounty on his head and a lot of KGB and GRU assassins trying to track him down. In fact, we've already put him in cold storage for a while. Somehow, however, I believe the three of you will ultimately meet. I know he would like to thank you for saving his life."

Later as the three senior men sat alone, putting the final touches on their "top secret" after-action report, Dabrowski allowed himself a bit of retrospection. "Henry Fuchs was an unlikely master spy. He didn't fit the profile."

"Well, I guess you intelligence guys better make some adjustments to the profile," interjected Lucius Clay.

Dabrowski took the criticism in stride. "General, when you're right, you're right. As it turns out, it was the fact that he didn't fit the profile which we allowed to get in the way of our catching him."

Fred had said little so far but now weighed in. "Fuchs hid in plain sight, in Chase's big shadow. He totally sublimated his own identity beneath Chase's dominating aura. I'm sure FBI and CIA will be interested in finding out whether he was a sleeper agent—perhaps in place for decades. Fuchs was, by all outward appearances, a non-entity—an obsequious lackey. In reality, however, he was calling the shots with Chase as his unwitting dupe. Maybe Fuchs represented a distinct species of covert operative, the *parasite* spy. He fed completely off the body of opportunities which only someone like Chase could provide. First among those opportunities was Chase's massive ego and persona. It provided close to perfect cover for Fuchs and allowed him to remain virtually invisible. Second was Chase's unlimited access. As a presidential envoy Chase was privy to almost all of NATO's most sensitive information. But he was so lazy and consumed by his own image that he delegated that special access to Fuchs by default. Finally, Chase was a totally dependent individual. He wasn't lacking in intellect, but essentially he had gotten where he was because of political and family contacts. He had the right pedigree which he was able to parlay into great power through political adroitness. But, this is key—Chase would never have succeeded without Fuchs. He was totally dependent upon him. At first Fuchs was Chase's alter ego but through a process of slow evolution, Chase ultimately became the alter ego of Fuchs."

"A most perceptive analysis," said Clay.

"Fred," said Dabrowski with clear admiration in his voice, "no one at Group has your way with words or your keen insights. I want you to write the final intelligence report for dissemination to all the main Western intelligence agencies, and somehow I would like you to work into the title, 'Profile of a Parasite Spy'."

West Berlin, 28 October 1961, 1130 hours

Q morosely boarded a CIA charter plane at Templehof Airport for his flight to London. No one had to tell him Slezak was dead. He just knew. And the mission was a total disaster—he had lost his top asset in Slezak, failed to eliminate Reitenhauser's mole and still didn't know the man's identity.

Nevertheless, he himself was still alive and plenty of intrigue, deception and mischief lay ahead, mused Q as he sipped his first Bloody Mary of the day with a sigh of satisfaction.

Munich, December 2, 1961

Although Doug Booker's case of insomnia was far worse than Fred Reitenhauser's, the latter's was still bad enough that he often found himself in the office at 5:30 A.M.

It was then during the quiet prelude to another day of potential drama that the two intellectuals, the only persons in the office, save for the duty officer, would linger over their first cup of coffee and review world developments which might impact their mission. Gradually these informal chats in the coffee room evolved into a ritual during which Booker would provide the CO with a briefing on important current events.

Leaning against the coffee supplies cabinet, Booker was now holding forth. "Khrushchev has retreated quite a distance from those heady days in Vienna. The cockiness and open contempt he displayed toward Kennedy at the summit are a distant memory. He even told reporters last month that at least for the time being it was not good for Russia and the U.S. to push each other too hard. When I read that in the *International Trib*, I about split a gut. It was the best laugh I had all week."

"So I take it Doug that a separate treaty between K, and Walter Ulbricht is a dead issue."

"Well, at least for now, but you never know what Khrushchev has up his sleeve. In his latest open letter to Kennedy he stressed Soviet dedication to 'the principles of peaceful co-existence?'"

"Oh really. I wasn't aware that Mr. K *had* any principles."

Doug warmed to the irony of the contrast between Khrushchev's words and actions. "Right, next he'll be pressuring one of his stooges like Nasser to nominate him in for a Nobel Peace Prize."

"Stranger things have happened," Fred said. "But seriously Doug, what did you take away from the statements made at the recent Soviet Party Congress?"

"Good question. I read the new foreign policy mission statement which came out of the Congress. I was struck by how the Soviets hedged their more bellicose statements of the past with all kinds of self-serving crap about the duty of the super-powers to make new commitments to avoiding nuclear war. Yet at the same time the statement was full of renewed pledges to help developing nations throw off the oppressive yoke of colonialism and establish successful socialist governments. Time and again, Communist Cuba was cited as a beacon of enlightenment."

"Doug, I'd like your take on the article Dean Rusk wrote for this month's *Foreign Affairs Magazine*. It seemed to be a warning to our allies not to be seduced by recent moderate words coming out of communist mouths. Rusk stated forcefully that as far as he's concerned, the USSR is as determined as ever to win the Cold War, even at the risk of Armageddon. I thought Rusk even hinted that in the coming year the Soviet Union might try to arm Cuba with nuclear missiles."

"Well, Fred, as you pointed out a few minutes ago... Stranger things have happened!"